75
FSG

THE ART OF LOSING

FARRAR, STRAUS AND GIROUX

New York

THE ART OF LOSING

ALICE ZENITER

Translated from the French by Frank Wynne

Farrar, Straus and Giroux
120 Broadway, New York 10271

Copyright © 2017 by Flammarion / Albin Michel
Translation copyright © 2021 by Frank Wynne
All rights reserved
Printed in the United States of America
Originally published in French in 2017 by Flammarion, France, as *L'Art de perdre*
English translation published in the United States by Farrar, Straus and Giroux
First American edition, 2021

Library of Congress Cataloging-in-Publication Data
Names: Zeniter, Alice, author. | Wynne, Frank, translator.
Title: The art of losing / Alice Zeniter ; translated from the French by Frank Wynne.
Other titles: Art de perdre. English
Description: First American edition. | New York : Farrar, Straus and Giroux, 2021. |
Translated into English from French.
Identifiers: LCCN 2020046597 | ISBN 9780374182304 (hardcover)
Classification: LCC PQ2726.E55 A7713 2017 | DDC 843/.92—dc23
LC record available at https://lccn.loc.gov/2020046597

Our books may be purchased in bulk for promotional, educational, or business use.
Please contact your local bookseller or the Macmillan Corporate and
Premium Sales Department at 1-800-221-7945, extension 5442, or
by email at MacmillanSpecialMarkets@macmillan.com.

www.fsgbooks.com
www.twitter.com/fsgbooks · www.facebook.com/fsgbooks

1 3 5 7 9 10 8 6 4 2

Contents

THE ART OF LOSING

Prologue

For some years now, Naïma has been feeling a new kind of pain: one that arrives like clockwork with her hangovers. It is not just the splitting headache, the furred tongue, the churning, malfunctioning stomach. These days, when she opens her eyes after a night's drinking (she has to space them out a little; she could not bear this torment to be weekly, let alone twice-weekly), the first words that come to her are:

I can't do this.

For a while, she wondered about the precise nature of this unequivocal surrender. "This" might be her inability to deal with the shame she feels about her behavior the previous night (you talk too loudly, you make shit up, you always have to be the center of attention, you act like a slut), or her remorse at having drunk too much, at not knowing when to stop (you're the one who was shouting, "Hey, come on, guys, we can't go home yet!"). It might even refer to the physical pain she feels crushing her . . . And then she realized.

The days she is hungover lay bare the overwhelming challenge of simply being alive, one that she usually succeeds in ignoring through sheer force of will.

I can't do this.

Any of this. Getting up every morning. Eating three meals a day.

Falling in love. Falling out of love. Brushing my teeth. Thinking. Moving. Breathing. Laughing.

There are times when she can't hide it, and the words slip out while she's working at the gallery.

"How are you feeling?"

"I can't do this."

Kamel and Élise laugh or shrug. They don't understand. Naïma watches them move around the exhibition space, their actions barely slowed by last night's excesses, exempt from this revelation crushing her: everyday life is a high-level discipline from which she has been disqualified.

Because she can do nothing, it's vital that hangover days be completely empty. Empty of the good things that would inevitably be ruined, and of the bad things that, meeting no resistance, would destroy everything within.

The only thing she can tolerate on days when she's hungover are plates of pasta with butter and salt, in comforting quantities: a taste that is bland, almost nonexistent. And box sets.

Critics have been raving lately that we have witnessed an extraordinary transformation. That television dramas have been raised to the level of art. That they are glorious.

Maybe. But Naïma can't shake the idea that the real reason for the invention of box sets lies in hangover Sundays that need to be filled without leaving the house.

The day after that is always a miracle. When the courage to live returns. The feeling that she can do something. It's like being reborn. It's probably because such days exist that she continues to drink.

There is the day after a bender—despair.

And the day after the day after—bliss.

The alternation between the two creates a fragile dissonance in which Naïma's life is mired.

*   *   *

This particular morning, she has been holding out for the morning that follows, like the old tale about Monsieur Seguin's Goat holding out for sunrise:

Occasionally, Monsieur Seguin's kid goat looked up at the twinkling stars in the clear sky and said to herself:

"Oh dear, I hope I can last till morning . . ."

Then, as her vacant eyes are staring into the blackness of her coffee, which reflects the ceiling light, a second thought slips in after the brutal, parasitic, habitual first ("I can't do this"). It is a deflection more or less perpendicular to the first.

At first, the thought flits by so quickly that Naïma cannot quite perceive it. But later, she begins to make out the words more clearly:

". . . know what your daughters get up to in the cities . . ."

Where does it come from, this fragment that runs back and forth inside her head?

She sets off for work. Through the day, other words cluster around this initial fragment.

"wearing trousers"

"drinking alcohol"

"behaving like whores"

"What do you think they get up to when they say they're studying?"

And while Naïma is desperately trying to work out what connects her to this scene (was she present when the words were said? is it something she heard on television?), the only image she can bring to the surface of her febrile brain is the furious face of her father, Hamid, brows knitted, lips tightly pursed to stop himself from roaring.

"Your daughters who go around wearing trousers"

"behaving like whores"

"they've forgotten where they come from"

Hamid's face, twisted into a rictus of fury, is superimposed over the prints by a Swedish photographer that hang on the gallery walls all around Naïma, and every time she turns her head, she sees him, floating halfway up the wall, in the antireflective glass that protects the photographs.

*   *   *

"It was Mohamed who said it, at Fatiha's wedding," her sister tells her that night. "Don't you remember?"

"Was he talking about us?"

"Not you. You were too young; you were probably still at high school. He was talking about me and our cousins. But the funniest thing . . ."

Myriem starts to laugh, and the sound of her giggling merges with the strange, static crackles of the long-distance call.

"What?"

"The funniest thing is that he was completely shit-faced, and there he was trying to give us a lecture about Islamic morality. You really don't remember?"

When she patiently, fiercely racks her brain, Naïma unearths fragmentary images: Fatiha's pink-and-white dress of shiny synthetic material, the large tent in the municipal gardens for the reception, the portrait of President Mitterrand hanging in the registry office (He's too old for that, she had thought), the lyrics of Michel Delpech's "Le Loir-et-Cher," her mother's flushed face (Clarisse blushes from the eyebrows down, something that has always amused her children), her father's pained expression, and Mohamed's remarks—she can picture him now, staggering through the crowd of guests in the middle of the afternoon, wearing a beige suit that made him look old.

What do you think your daughters get up to in the cities? They claim they're going there to study. But just look at them: They're wearing trousers, they're smoking, drinking, behaving like whores. They've forgotten where they come from.

It's been years since she saw Mohamed at a family dinner. She never made the connection between her uncle's absence and this scene now resurfacing in her memory. She simply assumed that he had finally embarked on adult life. For a long time, he had gone on living in his parents' apartment, an overgrown teenager with his headphones, his Day-Glo tracksuits, and his cynical lack of employment. The death of his father, Ali, gave Mohamed an excellent excuse to hang around for a little longer.

His mother and sisters addressed him by the first syllable of his name, drawing it out endlessly, shouting it from room to room, or through the kitchen window if he was loitering on the benches by the playground.

"Moooooooooooh!"

Naïma remembers that when she was little, Mohamed would sometimes come and spend weekends with them.

"His heart's been broken," Clarisse used to tell her daughters with the quasi-clinical compassion of those who have lived a love story so long and so untroubled it seems to have blotted out even the memory of what it means to be brokenhearted.

With his garish clothes and his Converse high-tops, Mo had always seemed faintly ridiculous to Naïma and her sisters as he traipsed through their parents' huge garden or sat beneath the arbor with his older brother. As she thinks back on him—and with no way of knowing what she's making up now to compensate for the memories that have faded and what she made up back then out of spite at being excluded from grown-up conversations—Mohamed was miserable for a lot of reasons that had nothing to do with a broken heart. She thinks she remembers hearing him talking about a misspent youth, marked by cans of beer in stairwells and small-time dope dealing. She thinks she remembers him saying he should never have dropped out of school— unless that was Hamid or Clarisse speaking with the benefit of hindsight. He also told his brother that living in a *cité* in the 1980s was completely different from what Hamid had experienced, how it wasn't fair to blame him for not seeing any way out. She thinks she saw him crying under the dark flowers of the clematis while Hamid and Clarisse murmured reassuring words, but she can't be certain about any of it. It's been years since she thought about Mohamed. (Sometimes she silently runs through the list of her uncles and aunts just to make sure she hasn't forgotten anyone, and sometimes she does forget, and that upsets her.) From what Naïma remembers, Mohamed was always sad. At what point did he decide that his sadness was as vast as a vanished country and a lost religion?

Her Day-Glo uncle's words go around and around inside her head like the grating music of a merry-go-round set up just under her window.

Has she *forgotten where she comes from?*

When Mohamed says these words, he's talking about Algeria. He is angry with Naïma's sisters and their cousins for forgetting a country they have never known. Not that he ever knew it, either, having been born in a cité in Pont-Féron. What was there for him to forget?

If I were writing Naïma's story, it wouldn't begin with Algeria. Naïma's birth in Normandy. That's where I would begin. With Hamid and Clarisse's four daughters playing in the garden. With the streets of Alençon. With vacations in Cotentin.

And yet, if Naïma is to be believed, Algeria was always present somewhere in the background. It was the sum of different parts: her first name, her dark complexion, her black hair, the Sundays spent with Yema. This is an Algeria she has never forgotten, since she has carried it within her, and on her face. If someone were to tell her that what she is talking about has nothing to do with Algeria, that these are simply distinguishing factors of North African immigration in France, of which she represents the second generation (as though immigration were a never-ending process, as though she herself were still migrating), and that Algeria, meanwhile, is a country that physically exists on the far side of the Mediterranean, Naïma might pause for a moment before acknowledging that, yes, it is true that, for her, the *other* Algeria, the country, did not exist until much later, not until the year she turned twenty-nine.

The journey was a necessary part of that. She would have to watch from the deck of a ferry for Algiers to appear, for the country to reemerge from the silence that cloaked it more completely than the thickest fog.

It takes a long time for a country to reemerge from silence, especially a country like Algeria. Its surface area is 919,595 square miles, making it the tenth-largest country in the world, and the largest country in Africa and the Arab world. Eighty percent of that area is taken up by the Sahara. This is something Naïma found out from Wikipedia, not from family stories, not from setting foot in the country. When you're reduced to searching Wikipedia for information on the country you supposedly come from, maybe there is a problem. Maybe Mohamed was right. But this story does not begin with Algeria.

Or rather, it does, but it does not begin with Naïma.

Part I

PAPA'S ALGERIA

What resulted was a complete disruption in which the only possible survival of the old order was fragmented, extenuated, and anachronistic.

—Abdelmalek Sayad, *The Suffering of the Immigrant*

Papa's Algeria is dead.

—Charles de Gaulle, 1959

On the pretext that, in a moment of anger, the dey of Algiers had struck the French consul with a fan—though it might have been a fly whisk; accounts of the incident differ—the French army began its conquest of Algeria in the first days of the summer of 1830, during a sweltering heat wave that would only get worse. If we believe that it was a fly whisk, then, in imagining the scene, we have to add to the blazing sun the drone of blue-black insects buzzing around the faces of the soldiers. If we opt for the fan, we have to acknowledge that this cruel, effeminate, Orientalist depiction of the dey was no more than a flimsy excuse for a vast military undertaking—as was the blow to the consul's head, regardless of the weapon. Of the many pretexts used to justify a declaration of war, I have to admit that this one has a certain poetry I find charming—especially the version with the fan.

The conquest was conducted in several stages, since it meant waging war against a number of Algerias: first and foremost, the Regency of Algiers, ruled by the Emir Abd El-Kader; then Kabylia; and, half a century later, the Sahara—the Territoires du Sud, as they are called in metropolitan France, a name at once mysterious and banal. From these multiple Algerias, the French create *départements*. They annex the territories. Incorporate them. In doing so, they know that they are fashioning a National History, an Official History, by which I mean a great bulging belly capable of ingesting vast tracts of land on the condition that they consent to being assigned a date of birth. When the newcomers become restless inside this great belly, the History of France pays them no more attention than might a man who hears his stomach rumbling. He knows that digestion can be a slow process. The History of France marches shoulder to shoulder with the Army of France. They move as one. History is Don Quixote with his dreams of greatness; the army is Sancho Panza, trotting alongside him, taking care of the dirty work.

The Algeria of the summer of 1830 is one of clans. It has *multiple* histories. But, when history becomes plural, it begins to flirt with myth and legend. Seen from metropolitan France, Algeria sounds like a tale from the *Thousand and One Nights*: the resistance of Abd El-Kader and his *smala*, the little village that appears to float above the desert, the battles with sabers, horses, and men dressed in burnooses. It has a certain exotic charm, some Parisians cannot help but mutter as they fold their newspapers. They use the word "charm"; they mean it is not *serious*. The plural histories of Algeria do not have the heft of the Official History, the one that unites. And so French writers pen books that absorb Algeria and its histories, transforming them into a few brief pages in *their* history, one crafted such that it appears to proceed in an orderly fashion, punctuated by dates to be learned by rote, a history in which progress is made flesh, takes shape, and shines forth. Then in 1930 comes the centenary anniversary of colonization, a ceremony of assimilation in which Arabs have only walk-on parts; they are a decorative backdrop like the colonnades of a bygone age, like Roman ruins or a forest of ancient, exotic trees.

And yet, already on both sides of the Mediterranean voices are protesting that Algeria should not be a chapter in a book it has had no hand in writing. For the time being, it seems, these voices go unheard. Some happily accept the official version of events; they vie with each other in their praise of the civilizing mission running its course. Others remain silent because they imagine that History unfolds in a universe parallel to their own, a universe of kings and knights in which they have no place, no role to play.

For his part, Ali believes History has already been written and, as it advances, is simply unfurled and revealed. All the actions he performs are opportunities not for change, but for revelation. *Mektoub*: "it is written." He does not know quite where: in the clouds, perhaps, in the lines on his hand, in minuscule characters inside his body, perhaps in the eye of God. Ali is happy to believe in mektoub, because he finds it easier not to have to make decisions about everything. He also believes in mektoub because, just before his thirtieth birthday, riches were bestowed upon him almost by accident, and believing "it was written" means that he doesn't have to feel guilty about his good fortune.

Ali's misfortune, perhaps (or so Naïma will later think when she tries to imagine her grandfather's life), was that he had played no part in this reversal of fortune; he had seen his dreams fulfilled without needing to lift a finger. Magic had entered his life, and this kind of magic, along with the habits it brings with it, is difficult to shrug off. Up in the mountains they say that fortune can split stones. This is what it did for Ali.

In the 1930s, Ali is a poor adolescent boy from Kabylia. Like most boys in his village, he is hesitating between breaking his back in small family fields dry as sand, tilling the lands of a colonist or some farmer richer than he is, or going down to the city, to Palestro, to work as a laborer. He has already tried the Bou-Medran mines: They don't want him. The elderly Frenchman who interviews him lost his father in the 1871 Mokrani Revolt and doesn't want natives working for him.

Having no profession, Ali does a little of everything. He is a sort of itinerant farmhand, a traveling laborer, and the money he brings in, together with what his father earns, is enough to feed the family. Ali even manages to save the small dowry he needs in order to marry. At nineteen, he marries one of his cousins, a young girl with a beautiful, melancholic face. This union brings him two daughters—a terrible disappointment, the family mutters by the bedside of the mother, who promptly dies of shame. A house without a mother is dark even when a lamp is lit, according to the Kabyle proverb. Young Ali endures this darkness as he does his poverty, telling himself that it is written, and that to God, who sees all, his existence has greater meaning than the splinters of grief it brings.

In the early 1940s, the family's precarious financial situation crumbles further when Ali's father dies in a rockslide while chasing a runaway goat. And so Ali enlists in the French army, which is rising, phoenixlike,

from the ashes, and joins the Allied battalions embarking on a recon-
quest of Europe. He is twenty-two. He leaves his mother to care for his
brothers and sisters and his two young daughters.

When he comes home (this ellipsis in my story is the one that appears
in Ali's story, the one that Hamid and Naïma will encounter when they
try to retrace his memories: no one will ever say anything but two words,
"the war," to account for these two years), Ali is faced with the same crippling poverty, which his military pension alleviates only a little.

The following spring, he takes his little brothers, Djamel and Hamza,
to wash in the wadi swollen with the waters of the melting snow. The
current is so strong they have to cling to rocks and tufts of grass on
the riverbank to avoid being swept away. Djamel, the scrawniest of the
three, is terrified. His brothers laugh, they mock his fears, playfully tug
at his legs, while Djamel sobs and prays, thinking that the current is
pulling him under. And then:

"Watch out!"

A dark mass is hurtling toward them. The sound of roaring water
and clattering stones is joined by the creak of a strange craft jolting
against the rocks as it plunges downstream. Djamel and Hamza scrab-
ble out of the river; Ali does not move, but simply crouches behind the
rock he is gripping. The object crashes into his chance barricade, shudders to a halt, then once again begins to pitch. It rolls onto one side and
seems about to be borne away by the current when Ali clambers onto
his fortuitous bulwark and, crouching on the boulder, attempts to catch
hold of this device being swept along by the current: a machine of baf-
fling simplicity, a large, dark, wooden screw set into a heavy frame that
the floodwaters have not yet pulled asunder.

"Help me!" Ali calls to his brothers.

In the family, what follows is always told like a fairy tale. In simple,
spare phrases. A fluent, graceful account that demands a lyric simplicity: *And so they took the oil press from the floodwaters, mended it, and set it
in their garden. No matter that their meager lands were barren; there were
others to bring olives to make into oil. Soon they were wealthy enough to buy
olive groves of their own. Ali was able to remarry, and to marry off his brothers. His aging mother died some years later, happy and at peace.*

Ali does not have the arrogance to believe that his good fortune was merited, nor that he created the conditions for his wealth. He still believes that it was mektoub, fate, that brought the oil press on the raging waters and, with it, everything that followed: the olive groves, the little shop on the hill, the regional wholesale business, and—especially—the car and the apartment in the city, indisputable symbols of success. Similarly, Ali believes that when misfortune strikes, no one is to blame. Any more than they would be if the roiling floodwaters rose so high that they swept the oil press from his yard. And so, when, in the cafés of Palestro or Algiers, he hears men (some, not many) argue that employers are responsible for the poverty in which their workers and laborers are forced to live, that a different economic system is possible—one in which workers would have a right to share in the profits in almost equal proportions to the owner of the land or the machine—he simply smiles and says, "You have to be mad to defy the floodwaters." Mektoub. Life is made up of unchangeable acts of fate, not mutable historical actions.

Ali's future (which, as I write, is already the distant past for Naïma) will never succeed in changing his worldview. He will never be able to see his life story in terms of historical, political, sociological, or even economic factors that might afford a glimpse of something bigger, the history of a colonized country, or even—not to ask too much—that of a peasant farmer in a colonial regime.

This is the reason why—to Naïma and to me—this part of the story seems like a series of quaint photographs (the oil press, the donkey, the mountain ridge, the burnooses, the olive groves, the floodwaters, the white houses clinging like ticks to steep slopes dotted with rocks and cedar trees) punctuated by proverbs; like picture postcards of Algeria that the old man might have slipped, here and there, into his infrequent accounts, which his children then retold, changing a few words here and there, and which his grandchildren's imaginations later embroidered, extrapolated, and redrew, so they could create a country and a history for their family.

This is one more reason why fiction and research are equally necessary: they are all that remains to fill the silences handed on with the vignettes from one generation to the next.

The expansion of the business run by Ali and his brothers is made easier by the fact that the neighboring families on the mountain ridge do not know what to do with the tiny, fragmented plots of land left to them after years of colonial expropriations and seizures. The land has been parceled out, broken up until there is nothing left. Into this land that once belonged to all, or was passed from one generation to the next without need for documents or words, the colonial authorities have driven wooden and metal stakes, their tops painted in bright colors, whose positions are determined by the metric system rather than by the requirements of subsistence. It is difficult to farm these tiny plots, but to sell them to the French is unthinkable: to allow property to pass out of the family is a dishonor from which no one can recover. Hard times force these peasant farmers to expand the notion of family, first to distant cousins, then to the neighboring villagers, to all those on the mountain ridge, and even to those on the ridges opposite. To everyone, in short, except the French. Many of the farmers not only agree to sell their parcels of land to Ali, they thank him for sparing them a more shameful sale, one that would see them definitively excluded from the community. *Bless you, my son.* Ali buys and consolidates. He amalgamates. He expands. By the early 1950s, he is a mapmaker who can draw the boundaries of his own land at will.

Ali and his brothers construct two new houses, flanking the old white cob-walled building. They move among the houses, the children sleep where they please, and in the evenings, when the families gather in the main room of the old house, they sometimes seem to forget the extensions they have built. They grow without growing apart. In the village, people greet them like dignitaries. Ali and his brothers can be spotted from quite a distance; they are tall and fat now, even Djamel, whom the villagers used to compare to a scraggy goat. They look like giants of the mountain. Ali's face, in particular, is an almost perfect circle. A moon.

"If you've got money, flaunt it."

This is something people say in the mountains and also down in the valley. It is a strange injunction because it means spending money in order to show that you have it: to prove you're rich, you have to become a little poorer. It would never occur to Ali or his brothers to put money aside, to "make it bear fruit" for future generations, or even for a rainy day. Money is spent as soon as it is earned. Gradually they acquire glistening jowls, potbellies, costly fabrics, the substantial heavy pieces of jewelry that fascinate Europeans, who keep them in cabinets and never wear them. Money *in itself* is nothing. When transformed into an accumulation of objects, it is everything.

Ali's family tells a centuries-old story that demonstrates the wisdom of their approach and the folly of the "saving" urged on them by the French. They tell it as though it happened only yesterday, because in Ali's house, as in those around it, people believe that the country of legend begins the moment you set foot outside the door, the moment you snuff out a lamp. It is the tale of Krim, a poor *fellah*, who dies stranded in the desert next to a sheepskin bloated with gold coins that he has just discovered. Money cannot be eaten. It cannot be drunk. It cannot be used to clothe the body, to protect against the bitter cold or the blazing sun. What manner of thing is money? What kind of master?

According to ancient Kabyle tradition, you should never quantify God's generosity. You should never count the men at a meeting, the eggs in a clutch, the grains in an earthenware jar. In some parts of the mountains, it is even forbidden to say numbers aloud. On the day the French came to take a census of those living in the village, their questions were met with dumb mouths. "How many children do you have? How many still live with you? How many people sleep in this room? How many, how many, how many . . ." The roumis do not understand that to count is to circumscribe the future, to spit in the face of God.

The wealth of Ali and his brothers is a blessing that rains down upon a wider circle of cousins and friends, binding them into a larger, concentric community. It takes in many of the villagers, who are grateful. But it does not make everyone happy. It overthrows the erstwhile supremacy of another family, the Amrouches, who, it is said, were rich back when lions still roamed. The Amrouches live farther down the slopes, in what the French misleadingly refer to as the "center" of the seven *mechtas*, the series of hamlets strung along the rocky ridge like pearls on a necklace that is too long. In fact, there is no "center," no "middle" around which these clusters of houses sprang up. Even the narrow road connecting them is an illusion. Within the shade of its trees and its walls, each mechta is its own little world, but in an administrative sleight of hand the French government has fused these little worlds into a douar that exists only in their eyes. At first the Amrouche family mocked the efforts of Ali, Djamel, and Hamza. Nothing would come of it, they predicted; a poor peasant farmer could never make a competent businessman, he simply does not have the tenacity. The fortunes and misfortunes of every man, they said, are written on his brow at birth. Later, they sneered to see Ali's efforts rewarded with success. Finally, they accepted it (or pretended to accept it), sighing about the benevolence of God.

It is for them, too, that Ali spends and flaunts his money. Their successes, like their farms, exist in opposition to each other. If one extends his barn, the other adds a floor. If one buys a new oil press, the other acquires a new mill. The necessity and the efficacy of these new machines, these enlarged spaces, are debatable, but Ali and the Amrouche family do not care: They well know that their purchases are a response not to the land, but to the other family. What wealth is not proportionate to one's neighbors'?

The rivalry between the two families opens a rift between them and among the villagers, each siding with his own clan. The rift brings no hatred, no anger. In the early days, it is simply a matter of pride, a matter of honor. In the mountains, *nif* is almost everything.

*   *   *

Looking back over the years, Ali feels it was written in the heavens that he would have a destiny rivaled by few others, and he smiles as he folds his arms across his paunch. Yes, everything is like a fairy tale.

In fact, as so often in fairy tales, the happiness of his little kingdom is marred only by the one thing it lacks: The king has no heir. After a year of marriage, the woman Ali took as his second wife still has not borne him a son. Every day, the two daughters from his previous marriage grow, and every day, their high-pitched voices remind him that they are not boys. He can no longer endure the taunts of his brothers, both of them now fathers of sons, who mock his virility. Truth be told, he can no longer endure even his wife—when he enters her, he thinks he feels a strange dryness; he thinks of her womb as a desolate garden scorched by the sun. Eventually he divorces her, repudiates her, since this is his right. She weeps and pleads with him. Her parents come, and they, too, weep and plead. Her mother promises to make her daughter eat herbs that can work miracles, to take her on a pilgrimage to the shrine of a marabout someone has recommended. She tells him of this woman or that woman who, after years of barrenness, was rewarded with a life in her womb. Ali cannot know, she says, perhaps there may already be a child sleeping in her daughter's belly that will waken later, at harvesttime, or perhaps years later, such things have been known to happen. But Ali refuses to be swayed. He cannot bear the fact that Hamza has had a son before him.

The young woman returns to her parents' house. There she will remain for the rest of her life. Tradition dictates that it is Ali, now, rather than her father, who decides on the dowry required to marry her. Ali fixes no dowry. He does not want money for her. He would gladly give her away for a measure of barley flour. But the opportunity does not arise. No man would marry a barren womb.

Her dark, worried eyes flit between the faces of her parents and this man she has never seen, who introduces himself as a messenger from her future husband. In his features, she tries to discern those of this other man, the one to whom she has been given (often people bluntly say "sold," and no one is offended) by her father.

Laid out on a rug between her father and this man are gifts from her husband-to-be, a representation of the life as a woman, as a wife, that awaits her.

For her beauty: henna; alum; oak gall; the pink stone known as *el habala* because it has the power to provoke madness, which is used in the preparation of cosmetics and love-potions; the indigo that is used as a dye but is also used in tattooing; trinkets of silver for their value; and others of copper for their luster.

For her scent: musk, oil of jasmine, attar of roses, cherry stones and cloves that she will chew to create a perfumed paste, dried lavender, civet.

For her health: benzoin, black-walnut root for healing gums, staves-acre to repel lice, licorice root, sulfur to be used as a remedy for scabies, rock salt and mercury chloride for treating ulcers.

For her sex life: camphor, believed to prevent women from conceiving; sarsaparilla, drunk in a tisane as a prophylactic against syphilis; and cantharidin powder, an aphrodisiac that produces an erection by irritating the lining of the urethra.

For her taste buds: cumin, ginger, black pepper, nutmeg, fennel, and saffron.

For warding off spells: clays of yellow, ocher, and red; styrax, to protect against djinns; cedarwood and small bundles of herbs carefully knotted with woolen thread to be burned during incantations.

At the sight of this charming assortment of objects of every shape and color, this miniature bazaar laid out in her home, spilled out across the rug, she might clap her hands, might allow herself to be intoxicated by the potent perfumes, were she not so nervous. She is fourteen years old and she is marrying Ali, a stranger twenty years her senior. When told of the decision, she did not protest, but she still wishes she knew what he looks like. Has she already seen him by chance, one day when she was sent to fetch water? As she drifts off to sleep, she finds it difficult—almost unendurable—to think about this man without being able to put a face to the name.

As she is lifted onto the mule, motionless in her jewels and rich fabrics, she is afraid for a moment that she might faint. She almost hopes that she will. But then the procession departs to the sound of reed flutes, ululations, and tambourines. She catches her mother's eye and sees mingled pride and fear. (Her mother has never looked at her children any other way.) And so, determined not to disappoint, she sits up straight and sets off from her father's house without showing a flicker of fear.

She does not know whether she finds the route along the mountain ridge too long or too short. The farmers and shepherds who see the procession pass briefly join in the revelry before going back to their work. She thinks—perhaps—that she would have liked to be like them, would have liked to be a man, or even an animal.

As she arrives at Ali's house, she finally sees him, standing on the threshold, flanked by his two brothers. Her relief is immediate: she finds him handsome. Of course, he is considerably older than she is—and much taller; in her mind she subconsciously connects the two, as though people never stop growing and, twenty years from now, she, too, will be almost six feet tall tall—but he stands upright, his moonlike face is frank, his jaw is powerful, his teeth are not rotten. She could not reasonably have hoped for more. The men begin the *lab el baroud*, firing a first salvo into the air to welcome the new bride—despite the prohibition imposed by the French, most of the men have kept their hunting rifles. Dazed by the acrid, joyous smell of gunpowder, she smiles and thinks herself lucky, and she is still smiling as she dons the *khalkhal*, the heavy silver anklet that symbolizes her bonds.

From now on, she is part of her husband's house. She has new brothers, new sisters, and, even before her wedding night, new children. She is almost the same age as one of her stepdaughters, the girls born to Ali's first wife, and yet she must behave as a mother to them, must ensure that she is respected and obeyed. Fatima and Rachida, the wives of Ali's brothers, do nothing to help her. From the moment she crosses the threshold, they mistreat her because (or so she will later claim in the cramped kitchen of her apartment) they think the young bride is too pretty. Fatima already has three children, and Rachida two. Their bodies are heavy and sagging, bear the marks of childbirth. They do not want this young girl's shapely, curved, bronzed body accentuating their decline. They do not want to stand next to her in the kitchen. They respect Ali as head of the family, but they are constantly looking for ways to snub his wife without failing in their duty to him. They walk a tightrope, now and then venturing a cutting remark, a petty theft, a favor denied.

At fourteen, the bride is still a child. At fifteen, she becomes *Yema*, the mother. In this, too, she considers herself lucky: her firstborn is a son. The women gathered around her when she gives birth immediately pop their heads around the door and cry: "Ali has a son!" The news will compel her sisters-in-law to treat her with greater respect. She has given Ali an heir at her first attempt. Standing by her bedside, Rachida and Fatima choke back their disappointment and, as a gesture of goodwill, mop sweat from the new mother's brow, wash the baby, and wrap him in swaddling clothes.

After long hours of labor and a birth that feels as though it might cleave her young body in two, the young mother must welcome the various members of the family at her bedside so they can congratulate her and shower her with gifts, a whirlwind of faces and offerings distorted by her exhaustion, and suddenly from the haze appears a *tabzimt*, a silver *fibule* set with red coral and richly decorated with blue and green enamel, the traditional gift to a woman who has borne a son. The one offered to Yema is so heavy that she cannot wear it without getting a headache, yet she delightedly sets it on her brow.

The boy who is born in the *saison des fèves* (this is to say, the spring of 1953, although he will not be assigned a solemn French date of birth until they have to secure the papers for his escape) is named Hamid. Yema loves her first son with a passion, and that love spills over onto Ali. This is all she needs for their marriage to work.

"I love him for the children he gave me," Yema will tell Naïma much later.

Ali loves her for the same reasons. He feels as though he kept his affection for her in check until his son was born, but, like a river, the arrival of Hamid lifts his heart, and he showers his wife with pet names, with grateful glances, and with gifts. This is enough for both of them.

Despite the resentments, despite the arguments, the family functions as a united group that has no other goal than to endure. The family does not strive for happiness, merely for a common rhythm, and they find one. It is governed by the cadence of seasons, by the pregnancies of the women and of the animals, by harvests and village feasts. The group inhabits a cyclical time, endlessly repeated, and the various members complete these temporal cycles together. They are like clothes spinning in the drum of a machine until they form a single mass of fabric as it whirls and whirls.

Sitting in the shade on one of the benches in the *tajmaat*, Ali watches the village boys, with their disparate ages, heights, and hair colors. The Amrouche children have coppery manes, the little Belkadi boy a frizz of blond hair, others have jet-black curls, like Hamza's son, Omar, whom Ali does not like because the boy had the temerity to be born two years before Hamid.

They are gathered in a circle around Youcef Tadjer, the eldest, an adolescent boy kept in childhood by poverty. He has never taken on the responsibilities of a man. Although he is related, through his grandmother, to the Amrouche family, they refuse to help him or give him a job because of a debt that his father failed to honor. The mountain people say that debts are like guard dogs: they lie outside the door and prevent wealth from sneaking in. Although Youcef's father is long since dead, the boy has inherited his shame and, at the age of fourteen, must fend for himself. He has become a street hawker in Palestro. "No one knows what he sells and no one knows what he earns," Ali often says with amused contempt. "Probably nothing, but it takes up all his time." Youcef is forever trekking up and down the mountain, from the village to the town, forever asking whether there is a bus or a cart going to this place or that, forever insisting that it is urgent, that it is "for work," but for all his hustle and bustle, Youcef never has a sou.

"If I was paid by the hour," he often says, "I'd be a millionaire."

Since the men mock his futile efforts, Youcef prefers the company of younger boys who idolize him. On this particular day, their heads pressed close to protect the circle, the boys are both the theater in which Youcef is performing and his audience. Ali wonders what they are hiding behind their scrawny bodies. Maybe they are smoking cigarettes. From time to time Youcef gives them some. Once, Hamza beat Omar with a stick when the boy came home stinking of tobacco. Ali steps forward to check. Instantly the boys step aside, but they do not run away—they like Ali and his pockets full of jingling coins. They step aside because an adult presence instantly breaks the circle, which is held together by the magic of childhood and shatters the moment a grown-up approaches. It saddens Ali, just as in time it will sadden Hamid, that this boundary can be crossed only once and in only one direction.

"What are you looking at?" he asks.

Omar, his nephew, shows him the little photograph they have been passing from hand to hand. It depicts a man with a long beard wearing a European suit covered by a burnoose. His fez is probably red, but in the black-and-white photograph, it looks darker than his brows. Omar cradles the photograph in the palm of his hand as though it were a relic or a wounded bird. Youcef watches, smiling. There is a gap between his front teeth through which he blows cigarette smoke. When the boy looks up, Ali sees thinly veiled defiance.

"Do you know who this is?" Omar asks.

Ali nods. "It's Messali Hadj."

"Youcef says he's the father of our nation," one of the boys announces proudly.

"Oh really? And what else does Youcef have to say?"

The lad does not respond but allows the younger boys to answer.

"He says that if he could, he'd go and train in Egypt so he could join the Algerian revolution," one of the Amrouche boys says, his voice filled with awe.

"Do any of you even know where Egypt is?"

Instantly a dozen arms shoot out, all pointing in different directions.

"Stupid asses," Ali says tenderly.

He hands the photograph back and walks away without another word. From behind, Youcef calls:

"Uncle!"

It is the respectful honorific for elders in this society in which family represents the noblest bond, on which the vertical hierarchy of the colonists (marked by the constant calls of, *Sidi*, "My master") has not yet been imposed. Ali turns.

"Independence isn't just a kid's dream, you know," Youcef calls. "Even the Americans say that all people have the right to be free!"

"America is a long way away," Ali says after a moment's thought. "You have to cadge a ride from me just to get to Palestro."

"That's true, uncle, that's true. Actually . . . I don't suppose you could take me there tomorrow?"

Ali smiles at him. He cannot help himself: he is fond of the boy— perhaps simply because the Amrouches do not like him. Perhaps because Youcef possesses a sort of joyful bravura that even his hardships as a widow's son have never managed to crush. This autumn, come harvest, Ali thinks, he will ask the boy to help with the picking or to manage one of the oil presses. He only needs to make sure that Youcef does not get too close to the women. The boy's quick tongue has a tendency to offend husbands, fathers, and brothers. If he has managed to get off lightly so far, it is because people feel sorry for his mother. Every time her name is mentioned, someone adds: *Poor thing*. It has all but become the usual manner of referring to her in the village: "Poor Fatima."

That evening, when the families of Ali, Hamza, and Djamel are gathered for a dinner of couscous, Omar asks the men whether they like Messali Hadj. (He says "like"; he does not say "support," or even "agree with." He does not yet realize that the man is a political leader. He sees him simply as a father figure.)

"No," Ali says curtly.

Omar feels a pang of sadness because his uncle's response opens up a rift between him and Youcef that might affect his place in the gang. Youcef is the eldest of the group, Omar the youngest, meaning that he is *tolerated*. If Youcef were to change his mind, Omar would have to stay at home with Hamid, who is still a baby, trying to teach the toddler games he constantly messes up. Omar is sad because, moments earlier, Youcef had given him the photograph and he had tucked it into his belt. But now he knows that he will never again be able to look at the portrait of Messali Hadj without thinking of his uncle's response; the photograph will be forever tarnished by that "No," as though the word were carved onto the brow of the old man with the eyes of a wrathful prophet.

"Why?" he asks timidly.

"Because Messali Hadj doesn't like the Kabyle people." (Ali, too, says "like"; he does not say "support the cause," "encourage regionalism," "acknowledge the claims.") "As far as he's concerned, independence for Algeria would mean us all becoming Arabs."

Omar nods and pretends he understands, although since the family is largely Arabic-speaking (only the women ever speak Kabyle), and Ali has just made this pronouncement in Arabic, he can see no reason to share his uncle's indignation. He watches, bewildered, as all the adults nod in agreement, even the women, who are on their feet, serving. The little boy counts out long seconds before daring to ask:

"And . . . what have we got against the Arabs?"

Better to be sure.

"They don't understand us," Ali says before turning to his brother to talk about the coming harvest.

Omar, who does not understand his people, either, goes to bed with the gnawing fear that this may mean that he is an Arab.

> To stand aloof from the struggle is a crime.
>
> —First proclamation by the Front de Libération Nationale,
> November 1, 1954

Since 1949, Ali has been vice president of the Palestro branch of the Association des Anciens Combattants. The role does not mean much, and very little happens at its headquarters. First and foremost, the Palestro War Veterans' Association is a space: a hall that the French administration has put at their disposal. Sometimes it is empty. Sometimes a few men gather there. They play cards or dominoes, chat. Sometimes they come wearing their medals. In this space, such things have meaning. In the mountains, they might impress children who adore anything that glitters, but no one knows what each metal decoration, each ribbon, signifies.

For Ali, it is a good reason not to go straight back up to the mountains when he finishes work in the valley. (He works as a sales representative, a noble task.) He has never brought his brothers or his nephews here, nor has he brought his son. The association belongs to him alone and to the others who fought in the army. It is not something to be shared with one's family.

In this peaceful space, they drink anisette. It is a habit many men brought back from the army. Before 1943, Ali had never tasted alcohol. He started in Italy, after the battle-he-never-speaks-of (and that is what he likes about this place: he doesn't need to speak of the battle for it to exist). It began as a slightly absurd form of protest: the army insisted that soldiers recruited from North Africa eat the pork in the rations supplied by the Americans, so, they argued, the army should give them the rations of wine they had been denied. Ali remembers joining the ringleaders who launched this crusade because they were young men he liked, and, when the campaign succeeded, he found himself sitting like a fool in front of a glass of wine. So he drained it with a grimace, thinking it was less about alcohol than about equality. Later, when they arrived in eastern France, there were the bottles hidden away by those who had fled the deserted farms where the soldiers set up camp, and the insidious cold made drinking them necessary. Ali carried on drinking. Even his return to the land of sun and Islam did not take away his taste for alcohol. He knows Yema does not approve, so he drinks only when he visits the association, once a week, in small, guilty, delicious sips. Those more badly injured than he resort to methylated spirits when the anisette runs out. They see no problem in this: it is cheaper and gets them just as drunk. Only a roumi would think of alcohol as a sophisticated pleasure.

Some people suggest the racist slur *bougnoule* comes from the expression *Bou gnôle*: Father Moonshine, Father Bottle, a contemptuous term for alcoholics. Another explanation links it to the imperative: *Abou gnôle!* ("Bring the booze!"), a phrase used by soldiers from the Maghreb during the First World War, hence its adoption by the French as a nickname. If this etymology is accurate, then here in the hall lent to them Ali and his comrades are joyfully—if discreetly—behaving like bougnoules. But in behaving like bougnoules, they are actually mimicking the French.

At the association two generations meet but never mingle: those who fought in the First World War and those who fought in the Second. The old men of 1914–18 fought a war of *entrenched positions*, the younger men a war of *movement*. They moved so quickly that between 1943 and 1945 they crisscrossed Europe: France, Italy, Germany. They were everywhere. Those in the Great War spent long months buried in one trench before being moved to another. No two things are more alike than two trenches. The old veterans wish that the younger men would acknowledge that their war was worse (by which they mean better). The young men are not interested in stories of mud and Flanders. They prefer stories of tanks and airplanes. And besides, the Germans were not really Germans until they became Nazis. Kaiser Wilhelm was hardly Hitler. Between the two groups a certain distance has developed based on rivalry and mutual incomprehension. Although they are friendly toward each other, they rarely converse. From time to time a WWI and a WWII veteran will find themselves alone in the hall, and there will be an awkward silence—fleeting but undeniable—as though one or the other has come to the wrong place.

The president of the association is Akli, a veteran of the First World War. So that both generations feel equally honored and represented, it seemed obvious that the vice president needed to be a man who had fought in the Second. Ali was the one elected. Akli and Ali, it sounded good. More often than not they address each other as "son" and "uncle," but when they are joking around in public, they call each other "Monsieur le Président" and "Monsieur le Vice Président." They find it funny. They respect army ranks just as they do a soldier's scars. But civilian titles are meaningless. Tiny jewels on an ugly woman, old Akli jokes.

For Ali, one of the other advantages of the association is that the hall is always humming with news that never reaches the village. Up in the mountains, there are no radio sets other than his, and most mountain folk are illiterate, as he is. Down in the valley, news circulates. At the association, there are men who know how to read and write, who bring in newspapers and comment on them. Here Ali has access to a source of news the village could never provide.

At the association he hears of the guerrilla attacks of November 1, 1954, and, for the first time, of the FLN. On that day, even the numerous antennas of the association members are not sufficient to gather reliable information. No one knows where exactly these men have come from, nor what means they have at their disposal. No one really knows where they are hiding. Any links they have to known nationalist figures, such as Messali Hadj or Ferhat Abbas, are unclear to the veterans. They seem to belong to a third group, though what differentiates them from the other two is not clear to anyone.

Be that as it may, one thing is certain: The balloon has gone up. The better-informed speak of dozens of attacks with bombs and machine guns, against barracks, police stations, a radio station, the Pétroles Mory depot. There are rumors that farms owned by colonists have been razed, along with the cork and tobacco warehouses in Bordj Menaïel.

"They killed the forest ranger in Draâ El Mizan."

"No bad thing, in his case," Mohamed says.

No one defends the forest rangers; theirs is a shameful profession. Before the French reclassified the forests as public land, as they are in France, they provided a source of timber, and pasture for livestock. In theory, felling trees and grazing animals there is now forbidden; in reality, the practice continues, but at the risk of penalties. No one wants to run into the rangers who patrol the forests, issue fines, and keep a portion of the money for themselves. No one understands why the French would wish to set themselves up as masters of the pines and the cedars, beyond an overweening pride they find incomprehensible.

Kamel says that he has heard—and this detail momentarily stops every man in his tracks, hits him in a place he cannot precisely identify, but may be located somewhere near the liver, the chief organ of the Kabyle language; this piece of news is an attack on their sense of honor, their honor both as men and as soldiers, two things that are frequently confused—that those behind the attacks killed a young woman, the wife of a French primary school teacher, who died alongside her husband in the hail of bullets.

"Are you sure about this?" Ali asks.

"I'm not sure about anything," Kamel says.

They once again fall silent, thoughtfully stroking their beards. To kill a woman is a grave offense. According to an ancestral code, war should be waged only to protect one's home—and therefore the woman who lives there, as the house is her domain, her sanctuary—from the outside world. A man's honor is measured by his ability to protect his home and his wife from outsiders. War, in other words, is fought only to prevent war from crossing one's threshold. War is fought by the strong, the active, by Subjects of Law: by men, only by men. How many times have they bitterly complained about the insult—often unintentional—of the French soldiers who dare enter Kabyle homes uninvited, speak to their wives, and give them messages to relay concerning business, politics, or military matters, topics that can only sully a woman and pull her away from the home? Why would the FLN commit this same insult? Of course, the men realize that when acting in haste, mistakes are sometimes made, but to publicly introduce themselves with a series of attacks that have claimed the lives of the weak does not augur well.

"If this was a choice on their part, I'd like them to explain it to me," old Akli says. "And if it was a mistake, then I fear these men are fools."

The others nod. They are all more or less in agreement that day: they would like a little more explanation.

"What do you think is going to happen now?" Kamel asks.

What will happen is what has been written, Ali thinks, even if nothing good comes of it. No one here is unaware of what can happen when the French are roused to anger. The colonial authority made sure that its power to punish left a lasting impression. In May 1945, when demonstrations in the town of Sétif resulted in a massacre, General Duval— aware of the long-term impact it could have on the populace—warned the French government: "I have secured you peace for ten years." Even as the region of Constantine was sinking into chaos and cries, several members of the association were parading down the Champs-Élysées to the clash of cymbals, marching in step down that broad Parisian thoroughfare, and hailed as heroes of France. In Paris, women were waving handkerchiefs, while along the roads of Sétif, bullet-riddled bodies were being laid out. The fatalities were counted by the French army, who always refused to give a precise death toll. This has not been forgotten. Sétif is the name of a fearsome monster that is forever prowling, always too close, wrapped in a cloak spattered with blood and reeking of gunpowder.

Today, the only evidence of the massacre is a single segment of film (used by Barbet Schroeder in *Terror's Advocate*, his documentary about Jacques Vergès). The images are almost abstract, black-and-white smudges shifting and engulfing each other from which, now and then, a human face appears, the white-on-white of placards against immaculately whitewashed walls, a man standing stock-still, the triangle formed on his chest by his burnoose. But mostly there are the sounds:

the voices, the thud of footsteps, chanted slogans and ululations, and then the gunfire; there is no one left, yet still the din carries on, the clatter of a machine gun that never stops and even—but what do I know?—the distant roar of mortar fire.

Ali leaves the association and heads toward Claude's shop. Down in the valley, Ali has French customers—not many, but a few. They are men who frequent the association because they, too, are veterans. Most French veterans have their own organizations; they do not mingle with those they call natives, Muslims, Arabs, or sometimes *bicots*. But some of them venture into the association because they are looking for someone, a soldier who fought alongside them, under their command, or simply because they want to chat for a while. Claude is one of them: he served in the Army of Africa, the Armée B as it was called when they disembarked in Provence. He likes to recount how he saw France for the first time during Operation Dragoon. It is a small lie, but one that allows him to make clear that he considers himself Algerian.

Claude runs a grocer's shop in Palestro. When he discovered that Ali was in the business of selling olive oil, he asked to sample it. He is one of the few Frenchmen Ali knows who does not, on principle, insist on buying only from colonists. There is still something childlike about Claude, something that makes him immediately likable: he is short, quick-witted, voluble. When he feels hurt by something, he drags his feet and bows his head; when he is happy, his face stretches into a broad smile, as though kneaded by some giant hand.

Ali's French is rudimentary, and Claude, though willing, has never managed to master either Arabic or Kabyle. His clumsy lips mangle a few words from time to time, and Ali hides his amusement, nodding thoughtfully. The two men do not really talk to each other. At first this created an awkwardness: Claude did not know what to make of the strapping Kabyle standing in the middle of his shop who visibly could not understand his questions, nor the answers that, in his embarrassment, Claude felt he had to supply himself, carrying on a frantic monologue that relied heavily on gestures, winks, and smiles. On the day that Ali first brought Hamid, Claude completely forgot his discomfort.

In the huge arms of the mountain man, the child looked tiny. Claude thought he saw in Ali a paternal tenderness at odds with traditional masculinity—with the code that dictates how a man should behave in the mountain villages, this set of rules that is published nowhere Claude might read it, but he finds the man's behavior both fascinating and fearsome. He recognizes himself in Ali, for he, too, is a besotted father. Claude has been a widower for four years—his wife died giving birth to their only child. Her portrait takes pride of place on one of the walls of the shop. The fixed sternness of her expression contrasts with the emotion that wells in Claude's eyes whenever he looks at it.

Annie, the grocer's daughter, is a little older than Hamid. When they are together, the two children babble in a language that does not exist and, in those moments, Claude dreams of what his home might have been like if his wife had not died so soon and if, together, they had filled the house with children who looked like them. Sometimes, when Ali goes to the association, he leaves his son with Claude, who sets him on the counter, and there Hamid sits, smiling like a Buddha, until Annie demands he come and play with her. Ali has never been able to talk to the grocer about his situation, but he pities the man for having only a daughter, and so, as a gesture of kindness that Claude perhaps does not understand, he lends the man his son.

In the blazing mouth of the clay oven, Yema bakes the *kesra*, the un-leavened flatbread, for the whole family. Hamid claps his hands, as he always does when the house is filled with this rich, warm aroma. Since he stopped being fed at his mother's breast, he eats greedily, smearing himself with olive oil and laughing gleefully whenever food is present. Over and over, his mother tells him that he is handsome, that he is her sun, her light, her little partridge. He laughs louder. Ali smokes a cigarette as he watches his wife and son out of the corner of his eye. He wishes he could look inside her body and catch a glimpse of the soon-to-be-born child that swells Yema's belly, stretches the fabric of her dress taut, and means she has to tie her patterned *fouta* so low that from time to time she trips over it, sighing as though the fouta were a child constantly playing the same trick, one she no longer finds funny. Ali hopes that it will be another son. One is not enough: he could turn out bad, or worse—they are so fragile. The man who has only one son hobbles on one leg. His brothers' wives assure him that, from the shape of Yema's belly, they can tell it will be a girl. It will soon be known, in any case; Yema's belly is so heavy that she rests it against the table whenever she can.

Little Omar runs into the house.

"Hurry, uncle, hurry! The whole village has to gather on the square to listen to the qaid."

Startled, Ali quickly stubs out his cigarette. The qaid does not often visit the villages, preferring to stay in his big house down in the valley and send others in his stead. Like most of his kind, he controls the douar from a distance, relying on reports from administrators and rangers to take the pulse of the area entrusted to him (or, rather, rented, since it is rumored that the qaid paid dearly for the role of *commissaire rural*) by some French civil servant. A 1954 governmental memorandum outlined his responsibilities as "to inform, to supervise, and to anticipate." From the villagers' point of view, his role seems to be to punish and to steal, though always through intermediaries. Though he is little seen, he is liked even less. People say he does not care for people, only for gold and honey. Ali does not like the man, either, but he is indebted to him: he could never have developed his business if the qaid had opposed it. And the qaid would not have given his consent but for the fact that his wife is a distant cousin of Ali's. It was the qaid who allowed Ali to buy up plots of land in the mountains—an area of no interest to him. Encouraging the rising fortunes of this man who is—vaguely, very vaguely—related to his family also meant that he could thwart the ambitions of the Amrouche family, who, for too long, have had no rivals in the forgotten peaks. Ever since then, the qaid has maintained a precarious equilibrium by allocating favors and exacting tributes from the two families without even having to make the difficult climb— only the French army jeeps can scale the mountain without panting for breath. In return, whenever the harvest allows, Ali gives him a little more than is required, while Yema makes him honeyed pastries for every formal occasion.

In the doorway, Omar is impatiently stamping his feet. He has already notified his father and Djamel (not the elder brother first, Ali notes; the boy has clearly been badly brought up), who are already outside waiting, so that they can walk down to the village square together, slowly, majestically, as their status deserves, as their corpulence requires.

Ali takes his ivory-handled cane; he does not need it, but it gives him a certain presence. He considers putting on his military uniform to remind the qaid that he is not just a rich farmer, but lately he has had trouble buttoning the jacket over his belly, and his heroic stature would be undermined if one of the buttons were to pop.

As the three brothers arrive at the square, the villagers step aside to allow them through. They take up their positions on the opposite side of the circle to the Amrouches, whom they greet with solemn nods. From the far side, the Amrouches do likewise.

The qaid does not get out of his vehicle until everyone has gathered, just as an actor on a film set might hole up in his trailer until everyone else is on set. His wealth can be seen, entirely localized, in the huge, fat belly that looks like a prosthesis on a body shriveled by old age and forces him to stand with his back arched so the weight of his paunch does not pitch him flat on his face. The qaid has countless servants and retainers, but nothing and no one can prevent his every step from being a grueling battle between him and his potbelly, something that always puts him in a foul mood.

"As qaid of this village," he begins, bringing a wave of angry, mocking whispers from the crowd, "it is my duty to warn you of recent incidents in the region about which you may have heard rumors. My role in the administration means that I am particularly well-informed, so I am asking you to trust me and what I am about to tell you. Farms have been looted and burned. Bridges have been destroyed. These farms provided work for the fellahin. Those bridges made it possible for them to travel to work. Now many families are in dire poverty and do not understand why, families that others think can be fed with declarations. The men who committed these acts are bandits, known criminals already being hunted by the police. In a few weeks, a few months at most, they will be arrested and thrown in jail, where they will spend the rest of their days. If you encounter any of them, you should not help them, feed them, or shelter them. They are dangerous men who could cause you serious harm. These dishonorable men have killed women and children. Some will tell you that they're mujahideen, that they're fighting for our country's independence. Don't believe them. They know nothing of Algeria. They are being manipulated by Egyptian revolutionaries and Russian Communists. They are traitors prepared to allow strangers to invade this country on the pretext of fighting the French. What is it that they want? The Communists would be worse than the French. They would take what little the roumis have left you because they don't believe in private property. They don't believe in religion. They would try to take Islam from you. In Russia, they have demolished the churches. Here, they would do the same with the mosques. And mark my words, if you help these outlaws, no one will be able to protect you from reprisals by the French army. This village will be another Sétif . . ."

The qaid knows that in naming Sétif, he is invoking a fearsome monster. Yet he does not hesitate to use it. Almost imperceptibly, the villagers hunch their shoulders, bend their backs, shrinking from the ghosts that follow on the heels of those two syllables.

"France will punish you," the qaid roars, stamping his foot. "And the terrorists who brought the thunderbolt down upon you will quietly slink away to the scrubland, to the mountains, to the maquis, where they hide like the criminals they are, leaving you to pay the price. As your qaid, I have spoken to the French administration on your behalf. I have promised them that there will be no trouble here, that we are men of law and honor, not criminals. I've persuaded the army not to come up and search your houses." (In this, of course, the qaid is lying: the French army has never considered coming to the village, which is hundreds of miles from Draâ El Mizan or Bordj Menaïel, where the attacks took place. But since History has offered him the opportunity, for once, he is enjoying playing the hero, pretending that he is defending the people who, for years, have been paying fines and taxes to him.) "But I won't always be able to protect you. So, listen to me: Don't listen to the propaganda of these outlaws. Protect yourselves."

With these words, and flanked by his henchmen, he pushes his way through the crowd and climbs into the car the local boys have been inspecting, clambering over, and stroking ever since he began his speech.

No sooner does he leave than the circle breaks into two groups: those loyal or beholden to the Amrouche family and those loyal or beholden to Ali and his brothers. Standing between the two groups are those whose allegiances are not pledged, either because—a rare thing—they get along with both families, or because they have quarreled with both. The villagers discuss what was said by the qaid—that arrogant, mercenary dog. Since the Amrouche family are aware of Ali's (vague, tenuous) connection to him, they start from the principle that the entire speech was a lie. Since Ali knows that the Amrouches will attack the speech, he feels obliged to defend it. (Years later, Naïma will wonder whether Ali understood the disastrous, incalculable consequences of this knee-jerk rivalry, whether he ever replayed the scene in his mind, taking a different stance, or whether he was caught forever in the concepts of mektoub and nif as in an indestructible spiderweb.)

What Ali wants in that moment is to protect what he has acquired. The future interests him only as an extension of the present. Ali carries his family, his business, with infinite care, holding his breath to ensure that nothing topples, nothing changes. He has managed to turn a humble house into a prosperous home, one he wishes might last eternally. The world beyond the boundaries of his lands is a concept too vague for him to invest his hopes in. He has sometimes dreamed of his prosperous home existing in an independent country (and, although he cannot know it, the way he pictures this happening is very like the magical journey taken by Dorothy, in which the twister sweeps her and the family farmhouse to the land of Oz), by which he means a country where he no longer has to stand and salute every passing roumi, that is to say not so much a free country as one in which he, personally, is free, once more illustrating how Ali's dreams do not stray beyond the limits of his universe. What happens on his mountain is more important than anything else, and it must be protected. It is imperative that French soldiers do not come and take from them what little they possess, the good fortune brought to them by the flood. In other words, it is *because* the French are vile and terrifying that it is so important to appease them.

"Do you really think they'll catch the maquisards?" someone asks.

"Of course they will," Ali says without a moment's hesitation.

He has fought alongside the French army, has seen it win impossible battles. It is not about to be defeated by a handful of agitators. As happens every time he thinks about what happened *over there*, in Europe, a shadow flickers across his face, making him seem gaunt, sketching a dozen fleeting expressions that do not linger. He jerks his head to shake off the memories welling inside and says, simply:

"They can't lose."

Old Rafik, who spent many years laboring in the steelworks of Haute-Marne, agrees:

"They've got machines we can't even possibly imagine that produce metals we can't possibly imagine. What exactly does the glorious independent army of Algeria plan to do? In this country, we've never produced so much as a box of matches."

The conversation carries on for a long time. To counter the qaid's bluff self-assurance, they bring up the names of those who took refuge in the mountains in the past, the men the French authorities had so much trouble catching, never managed to lay their hands on. The old men talk about Arezki, the honorable outlaw from the forests of Yakouren, the chief of Sebaou who was dubbed the Kabyle Robin Hood by the French newspapers. They laugh as they recall how, even after being on the run for many years, he managed to organize a celebration of more than a thousand guests in honor of his son's circumcision, and how the French gendarmes, belatedly informed of the feast, arrived to find the village utterly deserted.

"So what?" Ali says. "They guillotined him in the end."

Evening draws in, bringing the sudden chill of nights in the mountains. It bites into the skin like a tiny, invisible creature. And yet Ali wants to stay here. He would like to be told that he's right. For the first time in a long time, he feels uncertain about what he is saying, in his opinions. But he carries on. He does what he is supposed to do. He expounds. He pontificates. He performs.

During the night, after hours of screaming, Yema gives birth to a little girl. The child is named Dalila. Her mother loves her a little less than she does Hamid. Her father accepts her.

Some years after the death of Claude's wife, his sister, Michelle, comes to Palestro to help him run the shop. People say there were scandals she wanted to leave behind in France and her departure was not so much selfless as it was necessary. She is a magnificent woman, and her beauty has given her such self-confidence that Michelle is incapable of seeing that her confidence stems from her physical beauty and its effect on others. She believes that she was born confident and, as proof, cites leaving the family home at an early age, her determination to get a degree, the romantic affairs in which she has always had the upper hand. In Palestro's French community, she is a scandalous and fascinating figure. Men cannot find the words to describe her, adjectives simply do not seem to apply. They say: Her breasts are . . . her legs are . . . her lips are . . . and the silence that follows the naming of a body part is filled with their more or less secret fantasies, with their admiration and their contempt. When Ali goes into the shop and she is serving behind the counter, he instantly loses the power of speech. Unlike other European women, Michelle does not wear stockings to cover her bronzed legs. She does not frustrate men's eyes with this garment as sheer as an onion skin or a film of sweat. She claims it is much too hot, and when she climbs onto the first or second rung of the stepladder to tear open one of the boxes hidden above the shelves, she reveals almost two feet of bare leg, both left and right, or a good three feet of bare flesh if they were laid end to end, which is more than enough to prevent Ali from being able to speak. Hamid, on the other hand, is not daunted by Michelle. He clings to her calves, tugs at her skirts, slips his chubby hands into her curly hair. Michelle adores the little boy, she kisses and hugs him, and when Ali sees her do so, he cannot help but dream that it is on his body that the woman is pressing her lips, her hands. Since knowing there is a chance that he will run into her, he has been coming to the grocer's shop more and more often, not daring to admit to himself why he is there. He attributes it to Hamid's growing friendship with Annie and its benefits to the boy. While the village boys are grazing their skin on thorny shrubs and jagged rocks in the mountains, Hamid is calmly playing with a little French girl who treats him like an equal. Ali simply thinks—in bad faith—that in bringing him to the grocer's to play with the little girl, he is just doing what is best for his son.

Claude never complains about their visits; on the contrary, he is always delighted to see them and always offers to look after the little boy for a few hours. When Michelle, Annie, and Hamid are with him in the shop, Claude feels happy. Together they make for a curious little tribe, he tells himself, a repudiation of his loneliness and his widowerhood. When talking to friends, he refers to Hamid as "the little Arab boy we've more or less adopted." Yema would claw at her face if she heard him say such things, but Claude, who has never been up to the mountains, imagines that the little boy needs the new family he has decided to give him.

The shopkeeper's fondness for Hamid is not sufficient to break one of the tacit rules of colonial society: the separation of public and private domains. He always receives the boy and his father in the shop, never in the apartment upstairs, or only for the time it takes Annie to go up and fetch a toy. It is a scene that is played out in various ways all over the country: although the various communities intersect, converse, socialize, it is always on a street corner, in front of a shopwindow, or on the terraces of certain cafés; it is never—or very rarely—in the domestic sphere, the private sanctum of the home, which remains strictly segregated. Claude may well love the boy like a son, as he claims, but his love is expressed only on the ground floor.

Here, in the shop, he teaches Hamid a few words of French so that he can greet the customers as they come in.

"*Bonjou!*" the child chirrups, like the cry of some fantastical animal, every time someone comes through the door.

Reactions are varied.

"Aren't you afraid?" a customer asks one day, seeing Hamid play with Annie.

"Afraid of what?" Claude asks.

"Well, there's the issue of hygiene, for a start," stammers the customer. "And besides . . . he might abduct her."

"He's three years old."

Claude chuckles. The lady does not laugh. In her eyes, Arabs are like animals; they mature more quickly than the French. By the age of three, a cat can hunt, can feed itself, can reproduce. Not that she would argue that the Arabs do likewise, but all the same . . .

"Old bag," Michelle says when the lady leaves.

"*Au'voi!*" Hamid calls.

"*Au revoir,*" Claude corrects him with the firmness of a schoolmaster. The grocer dreams that the boy will go to school when he is old enough. Annie has just started; Claude has enrolled her in the public school rather than one of the Catholic institutions most of the French favor. He wanted his daughter to attend a school that reflects the country— not necessarily the one he lives in, but the one he would like to live in: integrated. When school started, he realized that almost all the pupils were Europeans, the sons and daughters of those who could not afford to send their children to private schools. As for the rare Muslims (Claude never knows what to call them, he shifts from one euphemism to another, but finds none of them satisfactory), they are the children of local dignitaries—all boys, whose parents are already Frenchified. There is no mingling, no mixing, no easy fraternity on the school benches. And yet, it seems obvious to Claude that Algeria can be built only if all children have an equal education. It also seems obvious to him that, if Hamid is to be able to make choices in life, he must have an education. He is convinced that it is the only weapon available to a farmer's son.

When he speaks to Ali about Hamid's future, the man shrugs. They teach nothing at school, or at least nothing about the land with which Hamid's future is intimately connected. Why raise other possibilities?

But working the land is so arduous, even when it brings wealth, that it is better to allow children to run and play as they choose until the day they have to start work. Forcing children to sit at a desk during the only years when they can enjoy their freedom is no kind of life. Hamid is still at an age when participation in the group (family, clan, village) does not necessarily take place through work. It is accepted that a child should do nothing but play. For an adult, on the other hand, idleness is despised. An idle shepherd must whittle his own crook, as they say in the village.

The boundary between the two phases is unclear. Right now Hamid believes that his childhood will last forever, that adults are a different species. This is why they bustle about, go into the city, slam car doors, walk the fields, visit the *sous-préfet*, the local governor. He doesn't know that one day he, too, will have to join this perpetual motion. And so he plays as though he has nothing else to do, which is true—for the moment. He hunts insects. He talks to the goats. He eats whatever is given to him. He laughs. He is happy.

He is happy because he doesn't know that he lives in a country where there is no adolescence. Here, the sudden shift from childhood to adulthood is brutal and harsh.

Choosing one's camp is not the result of a single moment, a solitary, specific decision. It may well be that one never actually chooses, or less often than one might wish. Choosing a side involves many small decisions, trivial things. One might not realize that one is committing oneself, but that is what happens. Language plays an important role. The members of the FLN, for example, are alternately called "fellagas" and "mujahideen". A "fellag" is a bandit, a man on the wrong side of the law, a tough guy. A "mujahid," on the other hand, is a soldier waging a holy war. To refer to men as "fellagas," "fellouzes," or "fels," is—in a roundabout fashion—to present them as a threat and to justify one's right to defend oneself against them. To refer to them as "mujahideen" is to make them heroes.

In Ali's house, for the most part, they are simply referred to as the FLN, as though he and his brothers feel that even to choose between "fellag" and "mujahid" is a step too far. The FLN did this. The FLN did that. One might even think that the front is not made up of men at all, that the FLN is a strange miasma, a political ideology that has solidified into a body with numerous tentacles capable of wielding guns or stealing sheep. But when they need a word on the tip of their tongue to refer to a handful of specific men, rather than to the octopus, the eagle, or the great lion as a whole, Ali and his brothers use the term "fellagas," without anger or contempt: it is simply the first word that comes to them. But who can say whether the choice of term stems from a preexisting political position, or whether, on the contrary, the word will gradually cement that position? Settling in their minds as an irrefutable truth: the fighters in the FLN are bandits.

At the association today, the veterans are more numerous than usual, and more nervous. There are no packs of cards on the tables. No dominoes. This is an unplanned *djema'a*, a spontaneous meeting to discuss recent events that they find worrying.

Since its formation, the FLN has decreed that Algerians should have no dealings with the French colonial administration: they should not vote or take part in the electoral process, and, most importantly for the men gathered here today, they should not draw a military pension. There is nothing surprising in this, nothing new: it has been the position of various nationalist movements for more than a decade. But on this occasion the FLN has reinforced its public proclamation, distributing posters and pamphlets in a village where two members of the association live. According to the poster, anyone who violates the policy decree is guilty of apostasy and will be sentenced to death. So on this particular evening, the association throngs with a boisterous, bustling crowd. The men want to discuss the position they should adopt with regard to these restrictions. A pamphlet is passed around. Even the illiterate among them study it carefully, knitting their brows, weighing it in their hands. They peer at the letters lined up like insects pinned to the page, hoping—perhaps—that they might suddenly start to move or speak to them as they seem to speak to others.

"They've even banned smoking cigarettes," one man sighs.

Ali cannot help but laugh. The man speaking glares at him, then, gradually, regains his composure, repeats what he has said, and smiles, too. It is ridiculous. Cigarettes? Is that really the key to the battle for Algerian independence? Boycotting the cigarettes that they all smoke?

"How would that help us get rid of the French?" Ali asks. "We're the ones who'd suffer . . ."

"It's like chopping off my hand and expecting the roumis to feel the pain." This from a veteran of the First World War.

His remark is greeted with much nodding.

"If we're to win independence, there have to be sacrifices," protests Mohand (Second World War). "You can't just sit here on your fat backsides and expect to get independence with a click of your fingers. Here . . ."

He drops his cigarette onto the tiled floor and grinds it under his heel.

". . . I'm giving them up. If that's what it takes. It's no big deal."

"And our pensions, I suppose that's no big deal, either?" asks Kamel. "If I stop drawing my pension, do you think the FLN are going to provide for my family?"

"And where do you get off talking about independence? You with your big ideas . . . You won't see independence in your lifetime, take my word for it."

"The French are not about to leave this place," Guellid says. "Have you seen all the new buildings going up? Do you really think they are going to leave them to us?"

"So we shouldn't even bother trying?" Mohand sneers.

"The only thing the FLN will do is create bloody havoc. And who'll bear the brunt of the chaos? Them? Like hell they will. We'll have to bear the brunt, as usual."

Someone is bound to say it, to utter the name of the ogre. And they do:

"Did you see what happened in Sétif?"

"Thousands of dead! Thousands! All that just for hoisting an Algerian flag. We have a right to our own flag, don't we?"

"I've never even seen it . . ."

"And whose flag is it, exactly? You think it's our flag, the flag of the Kabyles? You think the Arabs are going to go easier on us than the French?"

"Krim Belkacem is a Kabyle."

"Krim Belkacem wants you to hand over your cigarettes to him!"

There is another burst of laughter, briefer and more bitter this time. Mohand roars:

"But the French want us to hand over the whole country!"

"Country," "flag," "nation," "clan," these are words they rarely use. Words that, back in 1955, could still hold a different meaning for each man: the meaning they chose, the one they hoped for, or the meaning they feared the word secretly conveyed. But to every man in the association, one thing is concrete, tangible, a thing that may seem pettyminded when measured against the sweep of history, but one that gleams brightly in this white hall, which is that following the orders of the FLN would mean giving up their pensions.

"But, that . . ." Akli mutters, "that would mean we fought for nothing?"

He almost has tears in his eyes. It is not simply the money that would disappear, but their status, their memories, the very reason for the existence of the association: to give meaning to the grotesque carnage in which they took part. And for Akli, if his pension is a sign that he has sold himself to the French, he sees the transaction as proof of his dignity rather than the contrary. His pension is proof that the French cannot simply raid their colonies for cannon fodder, his pension means that Akli's body belongs to him, and if he chooses to hire it out, he is entitled to compensation. Without that compensation, who owns the body?

It doesn't belong to the FLN, surely?

Ali is uncomfortable. He knows that in his case, he cannot argue necessity. Unlike most of the men here, he could give up his pension and still feed his family. But even if he is not threatened with starvation, must he really slash his income drastically? In order to assuage his embarrassment, he transforms it into altruism:

"What about the war widows?" he asks. "Are they supposed to give up their pensions, too? They've got nothing. They've lost their husbands. The children have lost their fathers. What is the FLN planning to do, marry them and tend their gardens?"

"After spending several months out in the maquis, I'm sure there are a lot of them who would be only too happy to tend their gardens," Guellid says with a little smile.

The joke is met with sniggers and scowls.

"'Give me your fig and your well of sweet waters,'" Guellid sings softly. "'Open the gate of your garden to me . . .'"

It is an old tune, one that they all know, but that evening none of the men take up the song and Guellid allows it to die on his lips as though this were his plan all along. He lights another cigarette.

"All the same, after the bloody attacks on All Saints' Day, they've proved themselves to be pretty clever," Mohand says. "The roumis, the qaids, they all said they'd wipe the FLN off the face of the earth. And what happened? The FLN are still here, and now they're the ones laying down the law in the villages."

"I'll believe it when I see them," Ali mutters.

"Well, I'd rather not see them," says Guellid.

The discussion carries on late into the night, but goes around in circles.

What Ali does not mention are the personal reasons prompting him to defy the FLN. Ali is thirty-seven now and is rankled by the youth of the rebel leaders whose names have begun to crop up, some in the newspapers, others only by word of mouth. He is also rankled by their lack of education. He thinks of them as a gang of angry young peasants and doesn't see why he should be led by men who have done nothing to earn the ranks and titles they have awarded themselves. Most are not even married, nor head of their household. And yet they claim to be in command of a *katiba* or a whole region, and some claim to lead the country itself. If he is to obey anyone, Ali would prefer if it were someone he admires, by which he means—though he does not quite admit it to himself—someone unlike himself. Someone whose superiority is so palpable that he cannot be jealous. They say that before launching the 1871 revolt, El Mokrani—who had until then obeyed and even anticipated the orders of the French—declared: "I am prepared to follow the orders of a soldier, but not those of a shopkeeper." Ali feels much the same.

As he leaves the association, he reminds those present that Hamid's circumcision takes place next month. He has planned a huge banquet. He reels off the list of meats and dishes. And despite the solemnity of the evening, despite the tensions, he issues an invitation to everyone present, even the old men from the First World War whose stories are all alike, even Mohand, who believes in the revolution the way a child believes he can find the roots of the fog. On this joyful note, they go their separate ways with the impression that life is here, urgent, and that the gunshots are too distant to influence its course.

It is an inky, impenetrable darkness, one of those nights when it is impossible to tell whether the vast expanse of blackness just above is the dark sky or the unseen slopes of the mountain. It is a deep, still night.

Suddenly light burns its way through the dark fabric, slashing the night with flames, yellow, orange, and red, puncturing it with sparks. The first person to see the blaze wakes the neighboring houses with a shout:

"Fire! There's a fire up on the mountain!"

A second bonfire begins to blaze on the rocky ridge opposite the first.

"Over there! Another fire!"

A third, a fourth flare in turn. The slopes above the village are ringed with fires, they can smell the smoke, hear the crackle. Nothing else is carried on the night—the lights and sounds of the city are miles away—making the flames, which are too regularly spaced to be a brush fire, seem enormous against the tranquil emptiness of the mountains. And yet they do not spread, do not send tongues of flame darting in search of dry grass. They rise into the air, menacing, controlled by invisible hands.

Men rush from their houses. Those who own hunting rifles are clutching them. Children woken from their slumbers begin to scream and sob. Soon a donkey joins the chorus—the wild intensity of its braying echoes around the rocks.

Three shadowy figures move toward the village. As they approach, it is possible to see that they are wearing military uniforms and appear to be heavily armed. They grab the villagers who are already outdoors and order them to gather on the main square, then knock on the doors of the public figures, the Amrouche family and Ali and his brothers.

"Round up all the men," they say in a tone that is calm but brooks no objection. "We need to talk."

The thin cotton trousers Djamel hurriedly pulled on before opening the door do little to hide his erection.

"Sorry to disturb you, brother," one of the men says with a knowing smile.

"Make yourself presentable," Ali brusquely orders his youngest brother.

He has heard that the men of the FLN are brutes. He is surprised by their good manners, their neat appearance. By comparison, Djamel looks like an animal in his unseemly pajamas, his eyes puffy with sleep.

As they walk toward the square, Ali looks at the fires surrounding the village, gauges how far away they are. Faded reflexes he thought he had long since forgotten reemerge; with them, fear also returns, a shudder running the length of his spine he does his utmost to stop, or at least to hide. He sees the silhouettes of several men moving in front of the flames in a shadow play; the straight line of the rifles slung over their shoulders makes it look as though each man has a single antenna. How many are there? Twenty? Fifty? A hundred? The constant movement makes it impossible to estimate. The man who seems to be the leader of the FLN detachment watches Ali watching.

"Yes," he says. "We are many."

And with such solemnity that Ali cannot but wonder whether it is tinged with irony:

"We are the nation."

He is the only man carrying a submachine gun, a Sten gun—Ali recognizes it immediately. (Even to Naïma it would look familiar: it is the weapon used by resistance fighters in every war film she has ever seen.) He has the gaunt face of a maquisard, the prominent nose, the slightly sunken eyes. He is close-shaven, something he has not been in a long time, since the skin that has reappeared is pale and delicate. This soft pallor accentuates the thick brown mustache that perfectly frames his upper lip. This man has made an effort to be presentable before coming here, and this fact reassures Ali: if he is trying to make a good impression, then he has not come to kill them.

The other two inspire less confidence. One has eyes caked with sleep, the other a scar running across his brow that deflects his gaze. Only the man with the mustache, the one the others address as "Lieutenant," fits Ali's image of a warrior. At best, the others look like chicken thieves. Ali senses that the lieutenant thinks as he does and the proximity of his acolytes makes him nervous: he never takes his eyes off them.

When the villagers are all gathered, the lieutenant has the crowd sit down and he himself sits cross-legged. Ali notices his lithe movements and realizes that his body, though scrawny as a starving man's, is far from having lost all its muscle. There is something of a wild beast about the man. Ali doesn't know that, in private, the army and the French police refer to him as the "Wolf of Tablat." The name suits him. Before long, the newspapers will pick it up. When he sets about haranguing the crowd, he does not trouble to introduce himself. He gets straight to the point.

"We have taken to the maquis to fight in the name of our country. We are here to stand up to France because the time has come for us to win our independence or die in battle. Yesterday, there were barely a handful of us; we worked in secret. The French exploited this to lie about us, slander us. They are simply trying to mislead you. We are not thieves; we are not bandits. We are mujahideen—we are warriors. It is the French who steal from you, the French who kill you. How much innocent blood is on their hands? For a long time, the French have been hunting us. They have never found us. Today, we show our faces. See: We are not outlaws! We are like you, we are Kabyles, Muslims, and most importantly we wish to be free men. This mountain belongs to us. This land"—here he picks up a handful of sand and gravel and smiles at its coarseness—"this soil is hard, it is meager, but it is ours! Surely the olive trees, the springs, the goats, the fields of grain, the vines in the valley, the cork trees, the ore they mine from the plundered earth in Bou-Medran are ours, too?"

The villagers waver between exaltation and fear. Exaltation because everyone here believes that the French have no right to what the mountain lands offer to the Kabyles. Fear because of the word "we," used so casually by this man who no one here has ever seen.

"We are a rich country. The French have made us forget this, because they keep everything for themselves. But when they leave, it will be a paradise. That time has come. You have no need to fear. We are powerful, we have weapons, and we are not alone. Tunisia, Morocco, and Egypt will help us. Believe me: the French will leave soon, whether they like it or not. This is not a riot, it is the revolution."

Whoops of excitement echo around the square, and though they cannot see what is happening, the women in the houses respond with whoops that pass through the cob walls and rise into the dark night, up to the fires, to the stars.

"We are a proud people," the lieutenant goes on, "a people united in struggle. The revolution is everyone's business. You, too, will help to drive out the invader."

"How?" Ali asks.

The lieutenant turns, sizes him up (is it worth acknowledging his interruption?), then tilts his head to one side.

"The FLN is not asking you to fight, not today. But you can keep us informed of the movements of the French army, the comings and goings up here in the mountains, the places where they set up roadblocks. You . . ."

He points to Walis, Farid Belkadi's young son, who puffs out his chest.

"You will be the lookout."

Walis improvises a military salute. There is something about the scene that Ali finds disturbing. Walis's display of pride is not enough to hide the fact that he has been expecting this, perhaps he already knows the lieutenant. Ali discreetly looks around. How many here are in the same situation? Did someone invite the FLN to the village? Who? And in exchange for what?

"You," the lieutenant says.

He is pointing at one of the Amrouche boys. Ali feels his heart freeze, as though his blood has suddenly become thick and cold.

"You will collect the tax. From now on, you will no longer pay the qaid—that dog who has sold out to the French. We will arrange for the revolutionary tax to be collected in the village. I promise it will be fair, but it is necessary. If our men need to rest here before going back up into the maquis, *you* will provide them with food and shelter. It is for you that they are fighting. For Algeria. Long live Algeria!"

At these words, the whoops ring out again. An able speaker, Ali thinks, one who manages to inflate the chests of the crowd just enough so that they do not have time to worry about what has been asked of them. Ali knew men like this ten years ago, on the other side of the Mediterranean. Men capable of leading their troops, singing, to certain death without giving them the time to think.

"Long live Algerian Algeria!" the village roars.

"Long live Kabylia!" shouts an old man.

"Long live Algerian Algeria!" the lieutenant's two acolytes roar more loudly still.

The old man is not to be so easily silenced; he begins to sing:

> *I swore that from Tizi Ouzou*
> *All the way to Akfadou*
> *None would make me heed his law.*
> *We may break*
> *But never bend.*

The poem by Si M'hand is taken up in chorus. During the jubilant commotion, the mujahid takes a Qur'an from his pouch and a dagger from his belt.

"Now," he says, "swear on the Qur'an that we are all brothers, all united in the struggle for our country, and that you will tell no one we have been here."

And the entire village swears, in an unaccustomed show of unity, Ali and the eldest of the Amrouche boys, Walis the lookout, young Youcef with a loud yell, little Omar with a newfound solemnity.

"Good," the lieutenant says. "The Qur'an is good. A vow made is a noble thing. But you should also remember this . . ."

And he tosses the dagger from hand to hand, not in a way that seems brutal or aggressive, but with a blithe nonchalance. He smiles, for the first time baring all his teeth, and Ali catches another glimpse of the savage beast he saw earlier, magnificent and terrible.

"We won't waste bullets on traitors," he says simply.

With this, he gets to his feet, signaling that the meeting is over. The men of the village, still worked up, look at him in surprise. It is as though the music has stopped in the middle of the dance. The revolution has just been announced, they have been made to swear allegiance to the struggle, but all the details remain vague. They do not want the three men to leave. They have a thousand questions to ask. For example: What is the plan for the revolution? What is the next stage? The men from the FLN reply that they cannot tell them.

"It's better for you, my brother. This way you have nothing to tell the French if they interrogate you."

Someone else wants to know what will happen if the army should get wind of this visit, of the village's pledge, and decide to take revenge. How can they get in touch with the FLN?

"You can't," says the mustached mujahid.

"You won't protect us?"

The man hesitates.

"You are not at any risk," he says after a moment.

"Can we join you up in the maquis if we're threatened?"

The lieutenant adjusts the shoulder strap of the Sten gun and signals to his men. They leave the village, moving quickly, and are soon engulfed by the darkness. Almost simultaneously, up on the ridge, the fires gutter out and the silhouettes disappear. It is as though the village had dreamed this moment.

Ali does not go back to bed next to Yema. He walks in the olive groves, breathing in deep lungfuls of the night air. He wishes he had an anisette. Air does nothing to calm him. In the recovered darkness, leaves brush against his face, his feet stumble over roots and broken branches. What has just happened is going around and around in his head. He cannot deny that he cheered, that he pledged with all the others. It was more than the speech; he liked the man. This is a man he would not be ashamed to follow. But unlike most of the villagers, who were so impressed by the scene that they are now expecting independence to arrive within days, Ali was not convinced by what the lieutenant said about the power of the FLN. He finds it difficult to believe that neighboring countries can send rifles all the way to the mountains. And surely if Egypt was sending arms, these men would have better weapons? Ali saw the one Sten gun slung over the leader's chest and the simple hunting rifles of those flanking him. He considers, calculates, reasons that in coming here the rebels did everything to present themselves in the best possible light, as demonstrated by their pristine military uniforms, their freshly shaved faces, which means that they also showed up with their best weapons. So those farther up the slopes must have rusty old muskets at best. And then there is the matter of ammunition. Ali knows how difficult it is to get: he has not had any in a long time. The French have imposed rationing. Even owners of registered rifles are entitled to buy cartridges only once a year. The only way to get any more is to buy black-market gunpowder and make the cartridges by hand. Ali has already tried this. Half the time, they blow up in the gunman's face. The other half, they break up inside the breech the moment the trigger hits home.

He goes and sits under the arbor that protects the new oil press, a much more sophisticated machine than the one brought by the flood. Close by, he hears a donkey grazing. He lights a cigarette and, in the glow of the flame, he is surprised by how old his hands look, the fingers that have grown chubby and feeble with time. Could he still fight?

Ten years ago, he was promised that war would make a hero of him. Now, he cannot even think of it without trembling from head to foot. He knows that such promises are all the more enticing because they obscure the risks and shroud the prospect of death. He is afraid. He did not think that he would live to see war come knocking at his door again. Naively, he had thought: Each generation has one.

But does he even believe the lieutenant with the wolflike gestures when he announces that the time has come, that war is here? If the FLN had the means to arm the villages, they would surely do so: they would launch a general uprising. But tonight the lieutenant seemed more eager to dissuade those men who wanted to go up to the maquis. Why? Ali is convinced that they lack weapons and the means to train the new recruits.

"Did you see how many men there were up there?" Hamza asks the following morning.

The ballet of bonfires on the mountain ridges took his breath away. Unlike his brother, he did not realize that it was an elaborate stage set created to produce a specific effect, designed to be seen from a distance, since close up it would lose its magic, reveal its secrets.

"If it were dark and you were to walk back and forth three times, you would look like three men, too," Ali says, and shrugs.

That night, he comes to a decision. He needs proof if he is to believe in the struggle. If he cannot be certain of being on the winning side, he will not fight. He has already been there.

Yema is pregnant with her third child and is finding the preparations for the banquet exhausting. Sweat trickles in the folds of her neck, dark with the henna she uses to tint her hair, tracing dark rivulets over her golden skin. Leaning over the basin, she washes herself quickly so that she can get back and be with her son before the ceremony starts. Her back is aching. She has carefully made the couscous from scratch, helped by her sisters-in-law and her stepdaughters. She is not yet twenty, but already she feels old. Besides, she does not know her age. She knows only the number of her children and, when the third comes, she will be old.

She just has time to anxiously embrace Hamid before she is sent away. The boy stays behind in the house with his father and his uncles, mountain men who gather around him wearing traditional dress like preposterous caricatures, like Kabyles dressing up as Kabyles for the occasion. First the barber comes to cut the hair. He snips only a single black curl, but in doing this, he sets in motion the process from which the boy will ultimately emerge a man. Then, in deep bass tones, the men speak of manly virtues to one who is not yet a man. Bravery, they say, decency, pride, strength, power. And these words sting Hamid like gadflies.

At school, Annie is taught that the Mediterranean divides France just as the Seine divides Paris.

* * *

Once the men have left the room, the women are once more permitted to enter. They shower Hamid with kisses and compliments. They give him a basket filled with pastries, tiny sweetmeats that melt under the tongue, leaving fingers sticky with honey, and Hamid plunges his hand in with evident delight. Yema watches him, her heart heavy. She realizes that her son knows nothing of the pain that is to come. He is happy about the ceremony because he has been told that it will change his status, but all he knows of scars and bruises are grazes and scratches from stones and thornbushes. This is probably what he imagines will happen to him tomorrow: a little scratch. But Yema is mostly sad because after the ceremony Hamid will no longer be a child—that is to say, a being of undefined gender—but a man, or at least a boy. Which means he will no longer remain with her, tied to her apron strings, within easy reach of her loving arms. Henceforth he will be Ali's son, his partner, his future. Tomorrow, she will lose him, this boy who is only five years old.

"Eat, my son, *ya ibni*," she whispers.

At school, Annie learns that René Coty is the president of the republic. The teacher shows the children a portrait. Annie thinks he looks a little too old for that.

Once he is full, Hamid holds out his right hand so they can apply the henna. The women sing:

> *Your hands will take on the color of henna,*
> *Will become those of a man, of a sage.*
> *Oh, dear little brother, how you sleep*
> *In the bed of a prince, of a king!*

Claude sets up a table outside the grocer's and sits on the pavement, enjoying the last rays of sunshine.

Hamid is put to bed the moment he shows signs of tiredness. His half sisters, his aunts, his female cousins all gather around him in a rustle of fabric, a tinkle of jewels. Into his ear they whisper stories in which men are brave warriors and women paragons of purity, tales in which war knows no treason and love no disappointment. As Hamid, smiling, drifts off to sleep on this, the last night of his childhood, downstairs the banquet carries on, extending through the house and out beneath the olive and the fig trees. In the glow of torches and cast-iron lamps, the shadows of trees mingle with those of dancers. Despite her tiredness, despite the ache in her back that almost makes her weep, Yema, too, dances to honor her firstborn, the sun at the center of her universe, who is slipping away from her. A pale dawn rises over the exhausted celebrations.

Having finished her morning routine of setting up shop, Michelle opens the new issue of *Paris Match* on the counter of the grocer's. She reads: "Bigeard Strikes Like a Thunderbolt."

The women gather to welcome the guests, who have already begun to arrive. The celebrations the night before were reserved for close family and friends, but now the doors are open to all those who wish to accept Ali's generosity. Pallid with exhaustion beneath the rouge, the kohl, and the henna tattoos, Yema and her sisters-in-law valiantly remain standing and find a friendly word for every guest.

By late morning, every bench, every cushion, and every rug in the house is occupied by men: those from Ali's family, those from Yema's family, the villagers, members of the association, some of whom have come up from the valley—an exhausting trek whose undertaking reflects glory on Ali. Together they share the *asseksou*, the traditional meal. The platters of meat and of couscous are so enormous it takes several people to carry them, and, despite enthusiastic hands and hungry mouths, the food seems inexhaustible.

This vignette sounds like something from the *Odyssey*, reminiscent of the canto in which the companions of Odysseus, profiting from their captain's slumber, fed on the sacred cattle of Helios:

Once they'd prayed, slaughtered and skinned the cattle, they
cut the thighbones out, they wrapped them round in fat, a

double fold sliced clean and topped with strips of flesh. And since they had no wine to anoint the glowing victims, they made libations with water, broiling all the innards, and once they'd burned the bones and tasted the organs—hacked the rest into pieces, piercing them with spits.

Meanwhile, in the midst of this jubilant scene, where no one stops eating except to laugh, Ali's joy is spoiled by a gnawing fear that half blocks his throat, preventing him from swallowing his food: the Amrouches are not here. They have not come to join in the meal. The antipathy between the two families is genuine, it is well-known, but it is on occasions such as this that the village rises above its divisions and shows that it can function as a whole. It is during such celebrations that one realizes that these rivalries are not an angry wound inflicted on the flesh but a simple line of honor traced between clans.

The Amrouches are not here. Ali cannot help but think that the arrival of the men from the FLN in the village is to blame for their absence. Ever since one of their family was appointed tax collector, the Amrouches have decided that they now belong to a new camp, one that does not live according to the precepts of the village. They have external imperatives. They have adopted the logic of war.

To a customer who notices the open article in *Paris Match*, Michelle smiles and whispers:

"I've known men who strike like thunderbolts. Honestly, it's nothing to boast about."

"I mean, really," the customer says in the same mocking tone, "all these men falling from the skies, and so far not one has thought to land in my garden!"

The meats give way to pastries, and lips glossy with fat are now silken with powdered sugar and honey, with crisp golden crumbs.

The ritual plays out like a piece of theater, like an opera, with trapdoors from which a deus ex machina might suddenly appear. No sooner has the last cake been eaten than, from outside, come the high-pitched wails announcing the arrival of the *hadjem*, the circumciser. This is the signal for Messaoud, Yema's brother, to go and fetch the child from the group of women. He gets to his feet as lightly as he can since the banquet has left his stomach heavy and his legs numb.

When she sees Messaoud, Yema hugs Hamid more tightly against her chest. She no longer knows whether she is playing the role allotted to her in the ceremony, or whether her refusal to let her son go is real. Hamid, confused, frightened by his mother's wails, begins to sob, too. He loses the self-assurance of prince and king. He forgets the words his father recited to him yesterday. He forgets bravery, forgets decency, forgets strength. Messaoud grabs the little boy under the arms. Yema holds on to his feet, she pins to his costume a silver brooch, to protect him; she kisses him. With each of these gestures, she is following the ritual, and although she wishes it would stop, she sings, or, rather, sobs a melody:

> *Do your work, circumciser,*
> *May God guide your hands,*
> *Harm not my son,*
> *Lest I should hate you,*
> *Do your work . . .*

Now that Messaoud has a firm grip on his nephew, Yema lets go. All around her, women take up the song:

> *Do your work, circumciser,*
> *Let not the blade grow cold.*

The hadjem is an old man from the ridge whose date of birth is lost in the mists of time. He is accustomed to the tears of the children and those of their mothers. In a corner of the room where the ceremony will take place, he calmly unties the bundle in which he keeps his materials: a piece of wood with a hole, a knife, a length of string with a wooden ball at each end, juniper berries. At this point, Ali leaves the room. When the knife cuts the flesh, neither parent may be present. Alone, or at least without their help, the boy must endure the first pains of manhood.

Hamid is passed between his uncles: his mother's brother, Messaoud, gives him to his father's brother Hamza, who sits him on his knee. The hadjem spreads the boy's legs, and on the ground he sets a plate filled with earth, which will collect the blood and the foreskin.

As the hadjem grips the tip of the foreskin, sliding in the juniper berry to protect the glans, Hamid starts to scream at the top of his lungs. He calls to his father and his mother for help. Suddenly it seems as though everything has been a trap: the beautiful clothes he is wearing, the food, the laughter, and the songs. All this was just a ruse to cut off his penis. Despite what he has been told, he now *knows* that it is the whole organ, slipped through the hole in the board, that is going to be cut off by the old man with the blade. (Twenty years later, Naïma will sob just as fiercely the first time her father tricks her into thinking he has stolen her nose, showing her the tip of the thumb he has slipped between his index and middle fingers. And seeing his daughter cry, Hamid will vaguely remember the anguish of his circumcision.)

He is five years old, and he is convinced that he is going to die horribly mutilated. He needs to get out of here. He struggles on the lap of Hamza, who cannot keep him still, and, in a clumsy attempt to calm the boy, whispers:

"If you wriggle too much, he'll cut off the wrong part."

This serves only to make Hamid sob more loudly. Outside, Yema is tempted to rush into the house to save her son. The other women hold her back. Don't you want your son to become a man? Not yet, Yema wants to say, not yet. He has his whole life to do that. I just want them to stop making him cry. Can't you hear that he is terrified? That he still needs his mother?

Indoors, the old hadjem looks into Hamid's eyes with patient gentleness.

"I'm only going to take a tiny piece," he explains. "It is stopping your penis from growing. Once I remove it, you'll be able to grow into a man."

Hamid, his face smeared with snot and tears, becomes a little calmer.

"Snip," says the hadjem with a smile, as though it is a joke.

He matches the word to the action. The earth in the dish immediately absorbs the blood that spurts, and the flap of foreskin lies on the dark surface, like a piece of food dropped during the feast.

Hamid's reaction is twofold: At first, he is relieved to realize that most of his penis is still attached to his body. A moment later, pain hits like the lash of a whip. He wants to howl again, but already his uncles are congratulating him: *You were very brave. You're a brave little man. We're all proud of you.* And Hamid does not want to make liars of them. Before the circumcision, he could still allow himself to cry, but now? On this day, without knowing it, he sets out on a life of clenched teeth and fists, a life without tears, his life as a man. (Later, by a kind of cultural reflex, he will sometimes say, "I was moved to tears," to indicate that he feels overcome, but in truth his eyes ran dry when he was five years old.)

The old man carefully cleans his hands, then prepares a poultice of pine resin and butter, which he applies to the boy's glans. Hamid bites his lower lip to stifle a whimper. Lastly, with the deft movements of a magician, the hadjem pierces a hole in the shell of a raw egg and inserts the child's penis. All of the men get to their feet and, one by one, drop banknotes into the hands of the freshly circumcised boy. Outside, the voices of the women and the music of flutes and drums start up again. Hamid has become a man.

"'From Flanders to the Congo,'" Annie diligently recites to her father over dinner, "'there is but one law, and that law is the law of France.'"

"What did you say, darling?"

"It's a poem by François Mitterrand."

When, finally, they lie down next to each other after three days of celebrations, Ali pretends not to hear Yema's sobs. Her head buried under the blankets, she weeps for a long time, unable to sleep. The little dovelike coos she makes as she tries to choke back tears are filled with such youth, such innocence, that Ali, too, abandons sleep, and takes her in his arms and listens as she whispers, "My little boy, my little boy . . . I've lost him."

"Nothing is going to change," Ali reassures her. "Everything will be fine."

He, too, wishes that arms bigger and stronger than his own—the arms of God? of History?—would enfold him and lull him to sleep, would make him forget the dreadful worry that the absence of the Amrouche family has planted in his heart.

The rock face of the gorge rises vertically and cascades down as scree, punctured here and there with limestone tracery, widening to accommodate a river that summer drinks and dries up. But when the river flows, the gorge is softened by waterfalls, by rivulets, by little waves. It is verdant with festoons of greenery and mossy cushions. Delicate early poppies spatter the slopes blood-red with their petals. Fishes and eels glide, flashing silver in the current. Over two miles of rocky gorges border the meanders of the River Isser and the narrow road that runs between the water and the sheer rock face. In the early twentieth century, the gorges to the north of Palestro attracted many tourists and contributed to the development of the town: inns and cafés flourished, catering to hikers who wore soft leather boots and pastel hats. The gorges of Palestro are among the wonders of nature few would think to visit these days, now that Palestro is no longer called Palestro and foreign tourists have fled Algeria after the Black Decade.

On May 18, 1956, a section commanded by Hervé Artur sets out on a reconnaissance mission. It is principally made up of young soldiers who have just arrived in Algeria. So far, they have barely had time to settle into the section house, to marvel at the sweltering heat, and to take a few meals together, sitting at the long tables in the refectory, shoulder to shoulder, chewing in unison. They have strung up a net to play volleyball. In the magnificent surroundings, they forget their uniforms and offer their pale skin to the sun, already imagining heading home, tanned and muscular, and swaggering through the streets of their villages. They strike up those instant friendships that make it possible to share every moment of the day. They take photographs for those not fortunate enough to glimpse this dazzling landscape. "It would be lovely to come here on vacation!" one of the boys writes to his parents. But on May 18, as they are moving through the Palestro gorges toward Ouled Djerrah, the sheer rock face closes in and crushes them. Artur's section has walked into an ambush set by the FLN. The young soldiers, their corporals, and their officer cadet—caught in the sights of the combatants perched high on the slopes—fall one after another. From the rocky overhangs, it is almost too easy to pick them off, trapped as they are in the narrow gorge. The reconnaissance mission ends barely hours after it began.

Is it because they are young that the army forgets that its mission, like that of the FLN, is to fight, to kill, perhaps to die? Is it because in metropolitan France people still refuse to use the word "war"? Is it because the ambush lasted less than twenty minutes, a skirmish so brief it was an insult? Is it because the bodies were found with their throats cut, riddled with stab wounds, their eyes gouged out? Whatever the reason, in France this day in May will be spoken of as a massacre that no one could have expected. The newspapers will report that the men of the Artur section had their guts ripped out and their bodies filled with stones. The press will say that their genitals were cut off and stuffed into their mouths. It will emphasize sickeningly sophisticated barbarism. It will show readers in France that in Algeria people *die* and, at the same time, imply that they die more when they die young, and even more when they are mutilated.

The soldiers who remained behind in the section house, like many of those posted in the region of Kabylia, are driven mad with grief and rage when they discover the fate of the Artur section. The news bulletins— whether true or false—sting them like hornets. Tiny blood vessels in their eyes burst. They scream.

In May 1956, the French army begins a series of reprisals that radiate from Palestro; columns of soldiers launch assaults on the mountains. To take revenge. To kill. They have been told by the authorities that they have complete freedom. Some of the reprisal squads take the path that seems right, or, if not right, a path that seems justified: they march on Ouled Djerrah, they head into the gorges to wound shoot kill, they overrun Toulmout and El Guerrah. Other units are happy to simply kill beat slash, whoever, wherever. There is no logic to it. They advance on Bouderbala, almost reach Zbarbar.

The columns setting off to seek revenge encounter columns of villagers simply leaving, fleeing, with no goal, no purpose beyond sheer panic. From a vantage point high above the peaks, the slopes appear crisscrossed in every direction, moving lines, an anthill run amok.

In 2010, Naïma spends a night drinking beer in the deserted gallery of an Irish artist who is exhibiting photographs of a devastated Dublin. Warning her that it is a mediocre film, he insists on showing her a scene from *Michael Collins*, saying:

"This is what a war of independence looks like."

On the small computer screen, the armored cars, angular as praying mantises, bristling with machine guns, enter Croke Park stadium during a Gaelic football match. The crowd watching the match are families, all wearing green and white, smiling and cheering. It is obviously a Sunday. She watches as the tanks roll onto the pitch. They stop. One of the players completes a play beneath the turrets of these strange beasts. The crowd cheers. The British open fire, randomly shooting into the fifteen thousand spectators.

This is what a war of independence looks like: in response to the violence committed by a handful of freedom fighters who, for the most part, were trained in a cellar, a cave, in some dark corner of a forest, a professional army, shimmering with cannons, marches out to crush civilians going about their business.

For the first time, Ali's village is visited by a convoy of jeeps filled with French soldiers, their faces masks of fury. With kicks and blows from rifle butts, they force the villagers from their homes and order them to lie facedown, hands on their heads. They search the houses, turning everything upside down, smashing earthenware jars, ripping apart beds. Their brutality is so random it is clear they do not know what they are looking for.

Above all, they want to make it clear they have understood: The mountains mean death. The natives mean death. This is not a summer vacation anymore. This is war, no matter what those back in France say.

Ali immediately lies down, and his brothers do likewise. Lying there, side by side, the three giants of the mountain look like sea creatures washed up on a beach. Old mother Tassadit, a woman so ancient she is almost a living mummy, a widow who can eat only because of Ali's generosity, does not react when she is ordered from her house. The soldiers drag her from her home, spewing insults. They interpret her confused gestures as provocation.

"She's deaf!" Ali says, half sitting up.

He puts his hands to his ears, miming the inability to hear.

"She's deaf! You understand?"

"Shut the fuck up," one of the soldiers roars, and kicks him in the stomach.

Ali falls back heavily, his jaw slamming against a stone. He feels a wave of heat, tastes the blood in his mouth. Having dragged her from her house, the soldiers snatch away old mother Tassadit's walking stick, and one of them—the youngest, hardly more than a boy—beats her with it. Sitting on the step of his jeep, the sergeant does not intervene. As the motionless villagers watch, the old woman's skin turns red, then blue, then black. Only when the cane snaps in his hand does the soldier finally stop.

"Shit!" he yells.

"You okay?" another soldier asks with a concern that, in these circumstances, has a surreal ring.

Ali's eyes are at a level with the boots, the well-oiled gun barrels, the whirling dust, the inert bodies. He hears a volley of gunshots and forces himself to believe that they are being fired into the air. He dares to lift his head a few centimeters, hoping he will see the wolf-lieutenant from the FLN appear from nowhere. If he genuinely has lookouts in every mechta, he will have been informed of the column of jeeps before the villagers even heard the engines ... And if he should suddenly show up now, Ali vows that he will never leave the man's side, that he will follow him like a shadow, kill for him if necessary. Another volley rings out and is followed by whimpers and prayers muttered between clenched teeth. Ali closes his eyes and he waits.

As he lies motionless, his body racked with cramps, he thinks: It's amazing that not moving can be so painful. He lies there for so long that time ceases to elapse. Up in the sky, the sun has halted its sweltering, oppressive course, the hours do not pass. Ali is frozen, time itself is frozen and it is agonizing.

"Let's go, we're done here!" the sergeant suddenly barks.

The soldiers gather around the jeeps. They are about to climb in when, at the last moment, two of the soldiers have a whispered discussion with their commander. Ali cannot hear what they are saying, but by painfully contorting himself, he can see the three soldiers nod their heads before turning back to the villagers still sprawled on the ground. They take a few quick steps, grab the two men nearest to the jeeps. The soldier who kicked Ali earlier is now staring in his direction, he glances at him briefly, then at those around him. Ali knows that the solider is looking for him—*Where's the brave bougnoule who saw fit to open his mouth?*—but he does not recognize him. To him, the villagers all look the same. The Frenchman takes a few steps toward Ali, hesitates, then grabs Hamza. Ali moves to stand up.

"Stop, you idiot," Djamel hisses, grabbing his belt, "or we're all dead."

Ali wavers, he does not know whom to protect. His little brother is being hauled away by the Frenchman. But this is also his little brother lying next to him, pleading with him to do nothing. Later, outside the house, Yema, Rachida, and Fatima are three pairs of wide eyes, three ragged breaths tremulous with tears. Yema is lying on her side, her huge belly so round that it no longer seems part of her, but looks like something that has been placed next to her. This time, his sisters-in-law have assured Ali that it will be a son. Ali slumps to the ground with all his weight, wishing that the earth would take him, would embrace him.

Hamza is too tall and too fat to be dragged to the jeep single-handed. The soldier can only push him, jabbing him in the back with his rifle. Ashamed that he cannot make a show of force, he takes his revenge by raining insults on Hamza. "Son of a bitch," he shouts. "Filthy bougnoule. Raghead bastard. Goat-fucker. Your mother is a goat." The jeeps drive off, raising a cloud of dust that settles over the faces of the prostrate villagers. It tastes of chalk and gas fumes.

As they get to their feet, each of them glances around to make sure their families are still alive. Two women rush over to old mother Tassadit. The old woman is still breathing, but feebly. They carry her into her house. Hamza's son, Omar, has a gash in his cheek: a stray bullet shattered a branch, and a sliver of wood hit him in the face. Ahmed the redhead has a broken arm. Bodies creak. But no one was killed.

"They know . . ." old Rafik says.

He slowly dusts himself down.

"They know the FLN have been here."

"No," Ali says, loudly enough for everyone to hear, "it's just a reprisal for what happened down in the gorge."

If the French army suspected them of being separatists, he does not believe they would have been let off so lightly. If they had been informed of what happened that night, the night of the dagger and the Qur'an, they would hardly have spared Walis, the lookout, who is struggling to his feet, his eyes rolling wildly, his hair tousled and white with dust, as though he has disguised himself as an old lunatic.

"They know, I'm telling you," old Rafik says stubbornly.

Ali shoots him an irritated glance. He is convinced that the ones who know what just happened, the ones who did not lift a finger, are the maquisards. They are not protecting anyone. They are not protecting Ali. They did not protect Hamza.

"What will happen to him?" Rachida sobs.

Yema and Fatima are trying to calm her with hugs and whispers, but she refuses to be consoled by her sisters-in-law, who have not lost their husbands. She wails louder still.

"If they hurt him, I'll kill them," says little Omar, the gash on his cheek like a smear of war paint.

Without thinking, Ali slaps the boy.

"I'll go down to the valley tomorrow," he says to reassure Rachida. "I'll put on my uniform and my medals. They'll see we're not terrorists. They'll let him go."

*   *   *

In the early hours of the morning, Hamza comes back by himself, dazed but unscathed. He has suffered no bruises, no wounds. He spent the night in a cell, and after twelve hours the door was opened without a word of explanation.

"I don't understand," he says.

The families of the two other prisoners wait all day for their men to return. But the mountain road unspools, empty and silent, between the pines. No one else comes back from Palestro. Faced with the pleas and the threats of the villagers, the *amin* heads down to the barracks to find out what has happened. Along the way, he mutters to himself. Having been appointed by the qaid, who was appointed by a civil servant, who in turn was appointed by the sous-préfet, the amin is the last bastion of a colonial authority divided between the various ranks, of which his is the lowest. He has never asked the French army to explain itself, and his insides are churning with panicked diarrhea as he asks to speak to an officer. The sergeant who led the column of jeeps receives him courteously, assures him that the two villagers were released at dawn, as Hamza was, indeed almost at the same time. "I don't understand," the sergeant mutters. "Where can they have gone?" The amin cannot decide whether the man is mocking him. He says that he has no idea.

"If you hear from them," the sergeant says as the amin is leaving, "please, do let me know. I'm worried about them."

He smiles ruefully. He gives a little wave.

Back in the village, the amin recounts the interview over and over, slowly, meticulously, as though the tale might suddenly reveal some answer, a clue. Hamza insists that when he was released from the barracks, he was alone, he did not see the others. At first people congratulate him, tell him he was lucky. But as the days pass, as the absence of the two men is felt more deeply, people begin to eye him with suspicion, to mutter that if he was released, it can only be because he talked. But talked about what?

"They know more than you and me about what's happening in the maquis," he says to Ali. "I don't know what I could have told them."

Even so, the rumor spreads throughout the village and, in the Amrouche household, finds a sounding board only too eager to amplify it: Hamza has betrayed the oath he swore on the Qur'an, the dagger will soon come. For some time, Ali and his brothers sleep with guns by their beds. But the dagger does not come, just as help did not come, and Ali sees in this the proof that he was looking for: the FLN is not powerful enough to wage its war of independence.

The deaths up in the mountains have shaken the foundations of daily life for the Europeans in Palestro. The gorges are devoid of ramblers, anglers, artists, and those who gather wildflowers. The singsong French of butterfly hunters no longer echoes around the rocky walls. Customers increasingly shoot black looks at Hamid when they see the boy playing in Claude's grocery.

Some cease to shop there, transferring their loyalties to those they consider more worthy. It is rumored that the owner of the large Café du Centre has offered to buy a round of drinks for any soldier who brings him the ear of a fellouze. What might a man not do to knock back a glass of Fernet-Branca bathed in the aura of a hero? At nightfall, a few recruits set a bloody hunk of cartilage on the zinc counter. *Vive la France, les gars!* You've earned it.

Claude's family no longer goes for Sunday walks in the country. Annie stamps her feet. She wants to see the eels wriggling in the River Isser. She feels too hot here in town. Her father tells her that the sun is so strong it has scared away the fish. He tells her to be patient.

"Still," he says to Hamid, "it's a shame they picked the most beautiful spot in the area for a massacre . . . It's pretty selfish."

"Se'fish," Hamid echoes.

French words make him laugh. They sound like farts.

In late summer, when heat has paralyzed the mountain and only the flies are active, Yema gives birth to Kader. The baby's first cry is unusually restrained.

"He knows that there's a war on," Fatima jokes.

In September 1956, Ali goes to Algiers on business. He is looking to buy an apartment. Officially, he wants to take the last step that separates him from success, to have a presence in the largest city in the country. Among farming folk, success is—paradoxically—measured by one's distance from the land. It means having the land tilled by others, then by machines, no longer having to toil in the fields. Later, it means not having to personally check that the work has been done, no longer having to set foot in the fields. Ultimately, it means leaving even the sale of produce to others, no longer having to do anything. The ability to be everywhere. Or nowhere.

This last point is the unofficial reason for Ali's trip to Algiers: he believes that the situation in the village could deteriorate. The visits by the qaid, the FLN militants, and, now, the army have sullied what was once a refuge. Unhealthy tensions have sprung up. The village is under pressure from conflicting forces, and it is possible that the unhurried, communal life that has been a bulwark against the outside world will eventually crumble, triggering bitter animosities that Ali knows may be aimed at him. Algiers, with its labyrinthine streets, its tens of thousands of faces, can offer him some necessary anonymity for a while. Here, his hulking frame can disappear. In a move contrary to that of the freedom fighters who are holed up in the mountains, he has found his maquis at the heart of the largest city in the country.

He does not like the Algiers local who shows him around the

apartment in Bab El Oued. The man asks too many questions, talks too much of money, calculates as the French do, as though life itself can be divided into drops that can be counted. Ali will find another place. In the meantime, he wanders through the center of the city, savoring the cool breeze of sea air that rises all the way to the boulevards, losing himself among the tall buildings. He encounters sunburned men and women in light summer dresses, floral patterns spreading like corollas around their legs. Algiers is filled with their elegance, their laughter, their long hair, the shocking red of their painted lips. He walks past the tailors and tanners, passes a fishmonger whose marine tang stings like a whip, the stone slab writhing with scaly monsters. Could he really live here, this man of the mountains? What about Yema? And the children?

He strolls around, trying to imagine what life would be like if none of this were alien to him. He almost smiles, stares at a café across the street, clean, bright, vaguely Parisian. In fact, it is not even a café—a Moorish tradition that Europeans and Arabs share—it's an AIR-CONDITIONED TEAROOM, according to the sign painted on the window. Ali has never set foot in such a place. Not because it is forbidden, nor even because he would not dare—it simply would not occur to him to go in and mingle with the gilded youths he can see, linen trousers, knee-length skirts, striped sweatshirts, hatless heads. Perhaps if Ali's family lived here, Hamid would casually step through the door on his way to meet his friends . . . Ali dreams of all the things his son might be. Suddenly a white-hot blast filled with shards of glass sends him sprawling.

The plate-glass windows of the Milk Bar are shattered by a spectacular explosion. The terrace tables skitter or take off and land in the middle of the street as if they were weightless. Smoke rises in thick plumes. Then, through the door, through the jagged holes that once were windows, the screaming, howling customers flee. First the able-bodied. Then the wounded, some of them crawling. Children. Many children. A little boy spattered with vanilla ice cream and blood, one foot missing. His eyes meet Ali's.

I had sworn not to plant any more bombs, Saadi Yacef, the man responsible for the bombings of the Milk Bar and La Cafétéria, will say in 2007, *not because of the deaths, I didn't give a damn about the dead, we all die sometime, but because of the mutilated, the severed arms, the severed legs, it made me sick, so I said to myself, no more bombs, no more bombs. And then you get caught up . . . I would forget and start again.*

Inside, there are bodies strewn everywhere. There could be fifty, though from where he is standing, Ali cannot be sure. All that his eyes can tell him is that there are too many. Groans begin to reach him through the pall of smoke, eventually he feels the ground shaking. He is aware of the surreal nature of the scene: on the tables, some of the glasses are intact, sporting paper umbrellas. They rise like absurd details above this mass of flesh, glass, and dust. *Here's to the FLN,* they seem to say. *Have a nice Sunday!*

Ali gets to his feet, dazed. Without a second thought, he flees. He runs away before the police or the army arrive. He does not want to be the bougnoule darky in the wrong place at the wrong time. He runs as fast as he can. He cannot remember where he parked his car. He is lost. He races past groups of children playing, dancing barefoot around a tin can spinning on the ground. He sees the worried looks of women, their backs bowed by the weight of sacks of dirty laundry, who anxiously peer past him, looking for the policemen who invariably follow a running Arab. He scares away the crowds of mangy cats that depend on trash cans and the pity of old women for their food. He does not recognize where he is, he zigzags through the streets at random. The maze of alleyways and flights of steps that make up Algiers are like a trap closing in on him, forcing him to run aimlessly.

His lungs are burning, he feels as though they are shriveling inside his rib cage. Still he does not stop. He will hold out. Twelve years ago, when it was snowing in Alsace, he held out. He got away. Suddenly it is as though he can hear German voices shouting all around. To dispel the ghosts, he screams. Then, from nowhere, his car appears, an island of tranquility, parked next to the curb. He jumps inside and almost collides with a milk truck as he pulls away.

"See what happens when you give an Arab a car?" the driver says laconically to the delivery boy next to him.

Ali drives. He tries to focus simply on keeping the car in a straight line. As he leaves Algiers, roadblocks and checkpoints spring up in his wake like flesh-eating plants soundlessly blossoming. The city snaps shut like a deadly snare. A few days later, the Battle of Algiers begins. Ali will never buy his apartment.

"Baba! Stop, Baba!"

Hamid drops the fruit jellies Claude has given him onto the car seat and suddenly starts shouting and pointing at a figure by the side of the road.

"Look, Baba, it's Youcef!"

The boy is holding a newspaper over his head with one hand, trying to protect himself from the fine autumn drizzle, while with the other he is trying to hitch a lift. He is wearing only a gray short-sleeved shirt and baggy trousers; his bare feet are caked in damp dust. Water trickles from his black curls over his forehead and down his neck. Camus would say he looks like a shepherd from ancient Greece, but Hamid simply thinks that he must be cold. Ali brakes and opens the door, without stopping completely. Youcef leaps in and gives him a broad smile. No sooner has he sat down than Ali punches him in the shoulder, eliciting a cry of pain.

"I just wanted to make sure you're not a ghost."

Youcef has not been home for three weeks. The amin went down to the barracks ("This is starting to feel familiar . . ." he grumbled), where he learned nothing (which, for the village, is also starting to feel familiar). Ali consulted the unofficial sources at the association, but in vain. Nobody knew the whereabouts of the young man whose straw mattress, night after night, lay empty. The village was bent by the blow of this new disappearance. His mother began to wonder whether she should be wearing mourning dress, and her constant keening became thick with sobs. Youcef does not seem concerned. He settles his puny body into the car seat. His feet trail mud over the floor of the car, making Ali frown. The boy laughs at Ali's irritation, and Hamid, almost automatically, laughs with him.

"Give me a fruit jelly," Youcef says, turning to the boy.

He places the jelly on his tongue with an expression of rapturous delight, exaggerating for the little boy, rolling his eyes, pretending to die of pleasure, thrusting the pink tip of his tongue through the gap between his front teeth. Hamid laughs louder, ever a captive audience for Youcef's antics, or simply for Youcef even when he is doing nothing.

"Where have you been, you little bum?" Ali interrupts.

"Oh, somewhere that will not please you, uncle . . ." On Youcef's lips, the respectful title sounds more ironic than ever. He curls up on his seat and nods to Hamid in the rearview mirror.

"What have you been up to?"

"Making choices," the boy says vaguely. "Everyone has to make choices these days."

Ali shrugs. "You call it making choices? When the other side has a gun to your head?"

"I was tired of waiting. I went to join the FLN," Youcef says, pretending he has not heard.

Ali says nothing, but from the back seat of the car a wriggling Hamid gleefully screams:

"Messali Hadj!"

The two men flinch. A few months after his cousin's circumcision, Omar took a photograph of the leader of the Algerian National Movement from its hiding place and showed it to Hamid. He was old enough to understand politics, Omar said, Egypt, the revolution, the right of peoples to "self-tedermination," et cetera. Hamid has only a vague memory of the speech, but the name comes back to him when he hears their grave tones. He repeats the name as though it is an incantation that will grant him entry to the world of grown-ups.

"Ouechkoun?" Youcef snaps. "Messali Hadj is washed-up. He's old. He's scared of the French."

Exit the prophet with the coal-black eyes. These days Youcef's heroes are thirty and have a taste for weaponry. They no longer say: Negotiate. They say: Step 1: undermine the colonists' sense of security, foment fear; Step 2: we'll work that out when we get there.

"So what are you doing back home, then, O warrior of the revolution?" Ali asks.

Youcef sighs, screws up his face and takes another fruit jelly. His mouth full, he begins to explain:

"When I moved out of my mother's house, I tried to join the maquis. I met a guy here in Palestro who told me his cousin was a maquisard. You'll see, he told me, he'll take you up there. So we hang around waiting for this guy two nights, three nights, but he doesn't come. Finally he shows up and gives me this look like I don't make the grade. What is it? I ask him. I don't like the look of you, he says straight out. So what? I say. Are you looking for someone to fight or someone to marry? This makes him laugh. I'm not the one who makes the decisions, he says. I'll take you to see one of the leaders, but don't get your hopes up, they're pretty tough. I say to him, I'm not here to meet weaklings. So, I go with him and he sets up an appointment with an officer. I say to the cousin, So what are they going to ask me? Will they ask if I know how to use a gun? Because I've used a rifle, but that's it. I'm a quick learner, though. 'Speedy' is my middle name. The cousin, he just shrugs and says: I don't know. Bullshit! He knew exactly what they'd ask. But up in the maquis they all look out for their own. So the leader shows up, he has a face like a dog's backside. I tell him I want to join up. I'm straight with him, I tell him I'm fed up, that I want to fight, that I love Algeria. I tell him my father's dead. That it was the French who took him from me. So I lay it on a bit thick, but there's no harm done. He says, Who do you know up in the maquis? I say I don't know anyone. Then there's nothing I can do for you, the guy says. When I insist, he says, What are you prepared to do? I say: I'll do anything. All right, he says, take that gun and go down to Palestro tonight. Go to this street, to this number. There's a big green gate and, behind it, a white three-story house. Go inside and fire at everyone you see. Whose house is it? I ask. That, he tells me, is none of my business. It is my business, I say—I wasn't scared of this guy—because

I'm pretty sure it's the sous-préfet's house, and I know it's pretty heavily guarded. I'll get gunned down. You'll be dying for your country, he says. So, tell me something, brother—it really pissed him off, me calling him 'brother'—tell me something: What use am I to Algeria if I'm dead? I'm not doing Algeria any favors. I'm young, I'm strong, I love my country. I want to be around to rebuild it. If all the guys like me get killed, who exactly is going to create this independent Algeria? Women and old men? You don't understand, he says, I'm not letting you join us unless you kill a colonist or a traitor, those are Krim Belkacem's orders. And who exactly has this guy killed? I say, pointing to the cousin who brought me. Someone, he says. Well, no one that I've heard about, I say. So everyone else gets to join if they've killed some old man or a donkey, but I'm expected to take on the whole French army? You think that's fair? You make the FLN sound like one of those private clubs that only the French are allowed to join, but no one tells us why. Why would you want to go into one of those clubs, he says, do you love the French? It's just an example, I say, a figure of speech. He says: I don't give a shit about poets. I tell him he doesn't have a clue. He punches me and I head back down to Palestro with the cousin, who called me every name under the sun becaused I'd damaged his honor and reputation. Can you believe that, Hamid?"

Youcef turns to the little boy with a big smile.

"Even if you want to fight for the revolution you have to have the right connections—"

"Leave him out of this," Ali growls.

In the back seat, Hamid has stopped listening to the grown-ups and is collecting, with the wet tip of his finger, the specks of sugar that have fallen on his shirt. Ali adds:

"You'll end up worrying your mother to death, do you realize that?"

"Yeah, and if I stay at home, she'll end up nagging me to death. Do you realize that?"

Ali laughs as he thinks of Poor Fatima. Youcef leans back against the headrest and closes his eyes. Without turning around, he reaches his left hand toward the back seat and Hamid, generously, gives him the last fruit jelly.

A morning in January 1957. It is colder than Naïma dreams Algeria could be; until she finally "goes back," she thinks of the country as a vast desert, scourged by the sweltering sun. The air is glacial, and in spite of his thick coat and his sheepskin cap, Ali can feel it trying to claw at his skin. He turns up his collar and hurries toward the association. He is nearly there, he tells himself, a few more steps and he will turn the corner by the Café des Sports, pass the electrician's workshop. If there is a boy hanging around, he will send him to buy oranges, which he will patiently peel for his breakfast in the vast, bright hall. The street is surprisingly quiet, he thinks, as he notices the closed shutters.

Propped against the daubed wall of the association, Akli's corpse seems to be waiting for him. The veteran's gray eyes are open, staring. The body has been stripped naked. Instinctively, Ali looks away so as not to see the man's penis, but too late, he has already noticed that it looks ridiculously small, wizened, pathetic. A dark, glistening military medal hangs from Akli's mouth, like the tongue of a grotesque puppet. Someone has carved the letters FLN onto his chest. Behind him, on the wall, the same letters are daubed in blood and, next to the old man, is a sign that reads: ALL THE DOGS WHO HAVE SOLD OUT TO THE FRENCH WILL SUFFER THE SAME FATE. Ali remembers the impromptu gathering at the special djema'a of 1955, remembers Akli talking about "selling" himself to the French army. Who owns the body, he said, if the French do not pay for the efforts that this body provided? The French do. He believed that in drawing his pension, he was emancipating himself from slavery. The FLN thought differently. But Ali feels certain that the men who killed Akli never spoke to him: they have called him a dog and a sellout simply because he was president of the association, one of those tiny jewels on an ugly woman that Akli was the first to mock.

Akli's throat has been cut from ear to ear. The French call it the "Kabyle smile," as though it is something that happens routinely, perhaps even daily, up in the mountains—like growing olives or making jewelry. But this is the first time that Ali has seen a body mutilated in this way. The slashed throat does look like a second mouth, gaping in a fearsome scream that no one heard. Ali finds it disturbing, the intimacy the death required between killer and victim: a man stood, pressed up against Akli, wrapped his arms around the old man in order to slit his throat with a blade. Akli was forced to endure this last embrace, to feel the warmth of another's skin, to smell his sweat, his breath. Ali wishes the old man had been gunned down.

Once, talking to Ali abut Flanders, about the war he fought, Akli told him: "A horse is three times bigger than a man, so when it dies, it is three times more shocking." Akli's body looks tiny, propped against the blood-smeared wall. A bomb silently explodes, a bomb that does not burst beyond the bounds of Ali's body. Shards of grief and rage ricochet inside his skin, careering off in different directions, surging through his veins, moving faster than his pulsing blood. The shrapnel of hatred. Kill. Avenge. Fragments embedded in his flesh throb at the slightest movement.

When a small detachment of soldiers arrives on the scene, their captain immediately notices this hulking figure who is watching, apparently oblivious to the cold. There is a steely rage in his eyes—a rage the officer knows, that he knows he can put to good use. He may even have received a manual such as *A Practical Guide to Pacification*, or a memo instructing him how to use the anger of the natives to his advantage. He has the man brought back to the barracks and rushed into his office.

In one corner, an oil stove gives off a stultifying heat. Wintry light filters through the metal slats of the blinds. The little office, with its

gray-green furniture, cluttered with maps and dossiers, is comfortable,
but it makes Ali nervous. He does not know why he is here. He is afraid
he will be accused of murder. Wrapped up in his coat, he is stifled and
pouring with sweat. When the captain comes in with a young interpreter, Ali relaxes a little. He knows the boy, his father sells chickens
in the market. He had not realized the boy had put on the uniform (the
phrase used by the villagers for those who join the army). Although "put
on the costume" might be better in this case, since the uniform looks
comically big on him. Ali nods at the boy.

"You know each other?" the captain asks.

With the exaggerated solemnity of a liveried herald-at-arms announcing guests in a Viennese palace (Naïma has seen many in the film
Sissi), the interpreter explains who Ali is. He talks about the village up
on the mountain ridge, about the olive groves. Ali thinks he sees the be-
ginnings of a smile flicker over the captain's face, but he turns and looks
out the window. By the time he turns back, the man's expression is once
more grave. The captain's lustrous thick black hair is slicked back with
pomade, reminding Ali of the actors on the movie posters at the Palestro
cinema. His every emotion is magnified by his broad features, and, in
particular, an abnormally expressive nose. Like a mask that is slightly
out of sync with what he is saying, it is as if, independent of the officer's
words and of his will, the face is moving to a rhythm all its own, led by
the supple, quivering tip of his nose. The captain asks:

"Did you know the deceased?"

"Yes," Ali says.

"Do you know why he was murdered?"

The nose twitches with an autonomy that is faintly obscene. As he
stares at it, Ali has trouble focusing on what the interpreter is saying.

"He kept drawing his war pension," he says, forcing himself to turn
away. "After the FLN forbade it."

"Was he the only one who did so?"

"No," Ali says. "We all did."

He sits up straight in the uncomfortable metal chair and says in a
firm voice:

"That money belongs to us."

"I agree." The officer nods. "But you realize what this means? You know they're not going to stop at this."

Ali shrugs. He almost wishes that they would come now, that they would come in the light of day so that he could fight, so he could pound their faces with his fists.

"The army can protect you," the captain says. "You, and the association, and your family. That's why we're here."

"What do you want in return?" Ali asks. "I'm too old to be back in uniform."

The captain says nothing for a moment, tilts his chair back, and studies Ali.

"Is it true what he said?" the captain asks, nodding at the interpreter. "That you come from Seven Peaks?"

Ali hesitates. He has never heard the place called this. He finds it disturbing, this French obsession with tallying everything—especially since no one can come from the *seven* peaks, he has to choose *one*. Even so, he nods. The smile Ali glimpsed early in the conversation reappears. This time it is broad, beaming. The smile completely fills the captain's face, distending his jaw, lifting the cheekbones, screwing up the nose. The officer lowers his chair so all four legs are on the floor, then, almost tenderly, he says:

"I want the Wolf of Tablat."

"Who?"

"The FLN lieutenant up in the maquis. I'm sure you've met him. And even if you haven't, you probably know someone in the village who has. Just give me a name."

The words cause Ali to flinch more surely than any slap or insult would have. This is the sort of thing one might ask a child, a beggar, a black sheep, someone whose loyalties do not lie with the group. It is not something you can ask a man, the head of a family, one of the leaders of the village. He looks at the officer with contempt and says curtly:

"I can't help you."

"In that case, I can't help you, either."

The captain's smile abruptly fades.

In the gray-green office, all three are stock-still. Even the tip of the captain's nose is motionless. The only sounds are the asthmatic wheezing of the oil stove and the uncomfortable swallowing of the interpreter.

"The dead man . . . ?" the officer says after a moment.

In Ali's mind, the image of the corpse immediately reappears. It is focused on two points: the tiny penis and the gigantic wound. He blinks rapidly, hoping to dispel the image, but it persists.

"Was he a friend of yours?"

Ali nods slowly. The image is now so vivid that he wonders whether the others can see it, too. The thick reddish-brown spots. The pallid gray of the wrinkled skin.

"I'm sorry for your loss," the captain murmurs.

He pushes his chair back with a shriek of metal. The interpreter instantly runs to the door and opens it. A blast of cold air rushes into the room, causing the three men to shudder. Ali's vision fades. He gets to his feet as quickly as he can.

"Do you smoke?" the captain asks as he is leaving. "Wait for me outside, I'll fetch you a couple of cartons of cigarettes."

Shivering, Ali paces up and down the yard. A number of French soldiers emerge from their barracks and, seeing the mountain man waiting, get an idea.

"Psst! Hey, Mohamed!"

Ali turns, a little irritated. The soldiers hold out gaudy magazines and flick through the pages covered with images of naked women with golden hair, jet-black hair, jutting breasts, pert, rounded buttocks. They snigger:

"What do you think, Mohamed? You like 'em?"

Long legs swathed in black stockings with intricate garters, feet misshapen by the extraordinary curve of shiny high-heeled shoes. Ali does not understand what they are saying. He looks away, but the soldiers giggle and flutter the photographs close to his face, pestering him with tits, asses, pussies, whichever way he turns.

Why are they doing this? What on earth are they thinking? Ali has been married three times, he has probably seen more naked women than these boys, who have been dragged from their farms and thrown into barrack rooms where they feel obliged to play at being men, to compete in seeming manly.

The captain reappears and shoos them away, as if they were a pack of noisy but friendly puppies. The soldiers casually go their separate ways, and a few pages from the magazines litter the courtyard. A crimson mouth, lips parted. Breasts that seem about to burst from a lace bodice. The officer hands the cigarettes to Ali, who walks away without even saying thank you—walks away in what he hopes is a dignified silence.

As he leaves the barracks, the interpreter, seemingly disappointed, says:

"You didn't press him very hard . . ."

The captain looks at him with a mocking gentleness.

"Why would I need to press him? People saw him come in here. He talked to me. Pretty soon he will realize that that alone is enough to compromise him. And when he does, he'll help us."

The children are chasing the chickens among the three houses. They let out wild cries and the hens respond with outraged cackles. Ali and Djamel watch them play, talking in low voices.

The two brothers are sitting in front of the cob-walled shack. Ali's hands are still trembling as he describes the pitiful corpse that death has hurled against the white walls of the association.

"I didn't know that Akli was a traitor," Djamel says.

"He wasn't a traitor."

"Then why did they kill him? He must have done something wrong."

Ali feels the urge to slap his brother, who does not understand anything. He forces himself to remain calm. (He refuses to let war divide his family.)

"He didn't do anything wrong," Ali says, "except to die."

In life, nothing is certain, everything is still to be played for, but once a person dies, his story is set in stone, and it is the killer who decides. Those killed by the FLN are traitors to Algeria, and those killed by the army are traitors to France. What they did while they were alive no longer matters: death resolves all things. As he is talking to Djamel, Ali realizes that it no longer matters how he acts, that his decision to remain silent when he met with the captain this morning was meaningless, since it is the FLN who will decide whether he is a traitor, whether they should slit his throat from ear to ear. With the flick of a blade, all the honor and integrity Ali has demonstrated in life will vanish, and in death he will be recast as a traitor.

The following week, he goes back to the barracks.

"Ask the Amrouche family," he tells the captain. "Ask them, they'll know where to find your man."

Now he is a traitor in his lifetime. And he was right: it makes no difference.

"You drink too much," Claude says as he hands Ali the bottle of anisette.

"I know."

The real problem is that he drinks alone. Since Akli's death, no one has been coming to the association. Mohand and Guellid announce that they will immediately stop drawing their war pensions—Guellid because he is afraid, Mohand because he has intended to ever since the first FLN pamphlet. The others probably still collect their pensions, but they no longer come to the association. It is too incriminating. In accordance with the captain's promises, soldiers now regularly patrol the street outside the door that Ali keeps shut on his solitude and his glasses of anisette.

Since he last visited the barracks, the French have arrested two of the Amrouche boys, the one who was collecting taxes and one of his younger brothers. Ali tries not to think about it. They are the ones who started all this. There is nothing he can do. He had to protect himself.

He refills his glass and sets the bottle on a tottering pile of booklets. He has not opened the shutters, but he turns to the window and stares at his reflection. His eyes are yellow, glassy.

A few days earlier, the soldiers patrolling the area came in and asked him to share among the members of the association what Robert Lacoste referred to in a statement as "lavishly illustrated booklets." Ali was sent hundreds of copies, which are now piled up around the room. He could see no reason to refuse them. He takes one from the pile and leafs through it as he sips his drink. It is entitled *The True Face of the Algerian Rebellion*—not that he can read it, but one of the soldiers told him so— and it concerns the Melouza Massacre. In the high plains to the north of M'Sila, the FLN slaughtered almost four hundred villagers accused of supporting the MNA (Messali Hadj's Algerian National Movement), the FLN's rival in the struggle for independence. In the photographs, the lines of corpses look no bigger than twigs. Ali takes a drag of his cigarette, exhales a plume of smoke, and, in the deserted association, he reels off the list of questions: Why them? What did they do? Were they traitors? They were freedom fighters before you came along! How could they betray you before you even existed? I suppose you have an argument to justify killing them, too? A rousing speech? He enunciates the questions in his deep, tremulous voice. Ali has never been to the theater, has never understood why the French line up to see plays, and yet, as one glass of anisette follows another, his voice—in its rage and in its grief—begins to take on the inflections of Madeleine Renaud, of Robert Hirsch, or of André Falcon when they play the great tragic kings and queens.

More often than not, after he has spent two or three hours holed up in the association, shame catches up with him and forces him back to reality. He checks the level in the anisette bottle, always hoping he has drunk less than it reveals. When he gets to his feet, the world pitches and reels a little, but it is nothing he cannot handle. He splashes water on his face, rinses his mouth. He once more catches a glimpse of his reflection in the window and is stunned to see a moon whose age is hidden beneath layers of fat. He restacks the pamphlets that have fallen over and prepares to leave.

He knows the pamphlets are nothing but propaganda, the French attempting to drum up support, especially among the village leaders. Slowly and deliberately, the French unfold these leaflets to reveal the sickening photographs; they claim to have recovered an FLN hit list from a captured fellag, a list that they say includes the name of the village leader they happen to be talking to. "Doesn't look too good for you," they say. "You'd better put your village under our protection or what happened in Melouza could happen here." Often, it works. After all, everyone knows that the French have ways—that they are prepared to use any means necessary—to extract information from the fellagas they arrest. So it must be true. Later, of course, the village leader discovers that this protection has to be *paid for* and, as in every gangster movie, the price just keeps rising.

Yes, Ali knows that what he is looking at is a piece of propaganda circulated by a colonial regime, he is not stupid, he was not born yesterday; but it so happens that he and France now have a common enemy, and propaganda makes an effective weapon.

In the back of the shop, Hamid and Annie are building a castle with cans of tomatoes. Annie wants it to be Versailles, Hamid wants it to be the castle of an ogre. The game quickly degenerates into a quarrel. Annie can be formidable when she does not get what she wants.

"Quiet, children!" Claude calls in a nervous tone the children do not recognize. "We can't hear ourselves talk."

Faced with the prospect of giving in, Annie knocks down the castle. Hamid sulks, staring down at the black-and-white-tiled floor. She takes him in her arms and kisses him.

"I love you," he says.

"You're only a little baby," she says.

That evening, Hamid asks his father what he thinks about love. Under normal circumstances, Ali would tell him he has no time for such childish notions, but, softened by the anisette, he ponders for a while.

Marriage is order, structure. Love is chaos—even when it is joyful. It is hardly surprising that the two do not go together. It is hardly surprising that people choose to build a family, a home, on the foundations of an enduring institution, on a straightforward contract rather than on the quicksand of emotions.

"Love is a good thing," Ali tells his son. "It's good for your heart, lets you know it's still there. But it's like summer, it passes. And afterward, the world is cold."

And yet he cannot help but imagine what it would be like to live with a woman he loved with the passion of an adolescent. Someone whose smile transfixed him every time. Whose eyes would leave him lost for words. Michelle, for example. It is pleasant to daydream for a moment. He does not know that, for his children, and even more so for his grandchildren, this fleeting daydream he indulges will be the standard against which they measure their own love lives. They will want love to be the heart, the foundation of marriage, the reason that compels them to start a family; they will struggle to describe how everyday routine can coexist with passion without the one stifling and destroying the other. It will be a constant battle, often lost but endlessly refought.

Late in 1957, Yema gives birth to a little boy whom his father decides to name Akli. He has large blue-black eyes that are constantly open. From the moment he is born, his faltering health worries his parents. He is sickly, has difficulty breathing, and often has a fever.

"It's because of the name you gave him," Yema rebukes her husband. "You might as well have put a curse on him."

Ali does not believe such old wives' tales. When spring comes, he says, the boy will feel better, like everyone else. It is the cold that is making him ill, and the snow that has begun to fall, slowing everything. Hamid is anxious for his little brother to get better, because he wants to show him to Annie. This is an *amazing* toy, he will say, it's a *living* toy.

One night, when the silence of the ridge is still thick with a snow that has blanketed every surface and lulled even the mountains to sleep, Akli, in his crib, lets out a howl and does not stop. The whole family gathers around the tiny body convulsed by screams. The little boy's forehead is burning up and his chest is covered by a red rash. Yema tries to breastfeed her son, but again and again he turns his face away. She massages him, pushes a finger dipped in honey into his mouth, but still Akli is feverish, crying incessantly.

"Maybe we should send for a doctor," his father says.

He says the words only to hear them out loud, to hear a rational voice among this commotion. He knows it is out of the question: the roads are blocked with snow; it is as impossible to drive down to Palestro as it would be to drive up. While his parents bustle about, the baby cries as though unaware that he is crying, as though this sound coming from him is alien.

"Go get the *cheikh*," Yema says to Ali.

"So that he can recite some nonsense about djinns and wave his hands around?"

"So that he can save your son."

As soon as the dawn casts its pale light over the ridge, Ali sets off on a donkey (the donkey cart is unaccustomed to snow, it seems to rear and balk like a skittish animal) and makes his way to the healer's home. The cheikh lives some distance from the mechtas, in a house with a domed roof that reminds Ali of the tombs of marabouts to which his mother took him to pray as a child. Even now, he is overawed by this house that looks like a *kouba*, and he enters the building with the same fearful respect with which he might enter a cemetery. There is no wife, no children, no servant to greet him. The cheikh lives alone—because he is an ascetic, according to his devotees, because he is a pervert or an alcoholic, according to his enemies. He watches the visitor enter without a word.

"My son is sick," Ali says timidly, removing his snow-covered hat.

"I am not a doctor," the cheikh says gently. "I know no medicine."

"He's screaming and . . . he screams all the time . . . and my wife . . ." Ali tries to explain. "She . . . she thinks there is a demon in his body. Because I gave him the name of a dead man."

The cheikh hesitates, then nods.

"I will come with you."

He collects some things into a large leather bag and mutters, as much to himself as to Ali:

"To listen to women, the world is full of djinns who roam about everywhere. As though demons had nothing better to do . . . It's rare, indeed very rare, for encounters between them and us to occur. Often people come for me and there is no demon. All they need is to take an aspirin, or stop drinking alcohol, or something. But they are disappointed when I tell them this. They desperately want to be possessed by demons."

The ride home is long. Under the weight of the two men, the animal struggles to go on, its back begins to sag. Ali can feel the other man's body against him with every jolt, each time the donkey's worn-out shoe stumbles on a sharp stone. By the time they arrive at the house, the sun is a perfect circle in the sky and, in the light, the snow shimmers like a wedding dress. Akli's wails have grown more feeble, hoarse, and pained, yet still the little boy wrenches them from his thin chest, his mouth quivers, his eyes bulge. Examining the child, the cheikh seems satisfied.

"You were wise to send for me," he tells the parents.

Behind the healer's back, Yema cannot help but shoot a triumphant look at Ali. The healer first rolls an egg slowly over the boy's body, focusing on his underarms, his groin, and his throat. Then he asks Hamid to bury the egg in the garden. From his bag, he takes strips of paper inscribed with Qur'anic verses. Rocking back and forth, he intones the verses over the child, who continues to wail. After several long minutes, he hands them to Yema.

"Sew them into the lining of his diapers," he says.

Finally, since the baby has still not stopped crying, the healer burns a bundle of herbs, filling the room with smoke and with a heady scent. He takes the sharp edge of a flat stone and, having held it in the flame, uses it to makes a number of fine incisions on the child's forehead, his arms, and his chest. Finally, Akli falls silent, his great dark eyes focused on the healer, two ink-black lakes lost in his wrinkled, sweaty little face.

"There, there," the cheikh murmurs. "All is well . . ."

Ali carries the man back on his donkey. Now that the panic is over, they sleep for much of the journey, their bodies slumped against each other, until they arrive back at the small circular house.

"You didn't believe, did you?" the cheikh says, stoking the embers of the *kanoun.*

Ali shrugs, embarrassed.

"Don't worry. I would not have believed, either, I suppose," the healer says gently, "if it weren't for the fact that I was born with the ability to see."

As he pokes the embers, sparks fly up and soon a few crackling flames appear along the charred wood. With a sigh of relief, the two men hold out their cold, numb hands.

"I do not claim to have powers, you know," the cheikh says. "In fact, I have only the word of Allah, and that is something I have learned, it is not a gift. But I know that djinns move among us and I know that a powerful sura can send them back to the desert."

"Is there a sura for everything?"

"Two years ago, an old woman came to see me, her son had been tortured by the army. She asked me for a sura she could put above her house that would keep the French at bay . . ."

The two men smile at each other.

"Not that I have anything against the FLN," the cheikh says, "but I'm starting to think that I might have use for such a thing."

Perhaps it is the exhaustion that creates an intimacy between the two men, perhaps it is the heat after the two long journeys through the snow, or the relief of hearing Akli's screaming stop. In the white-and-green house shaped like a kouba, they speak simply, candidly.

"Have you been threatened?" Ali asks.

"Their scholars, their *ulama*, do not approve of us. They say we have corrupted Islam with what they call our idolatry. They speak in the name of *pure* Islam. But what does that mean? To me, the religion that I practice is pure. I spend my days meditating about Allah; I place each second of my life in his hands. No one could ask for more. So clearly they want less . . . And I cannot give them that."

When he returns home, Ali finds Yema cradling the sleepy newborn. Her eyes are ringed with gray circles, but she smiles up at her husband.

"See how quiet he is."

In her arms, Akli is dreaming, and a bubble of drool forms on his lower lip. Curled up on the bench, Hamid has also fallen asleep. He makes a slight purring sound, like a contented animal. As the sun quickly rises in the sky, Ali's household ignores the daylight and embarks upon the night of which it has just been deprived.

"When you sleep, you forget your troubles," Ali has always told his sons to cajole them into going to bed. "It is a wonderful opportunity, and it lasts only a few hours, so make the most of it."

When they wake in midafternoon, haggard and disoriented by the rhythms imposed by exhaustion, they find that Akli has stopped breathing. The child is cold, motionless, his lips and fingertips a purplish blue. His eyes are closed and stiff, as though stones have been placed over them. When Naïma thinks of this scene, a line from a poem she learned long ago comes to mind: *No one, tonight, will wake the sleeper.*

Snow melts, there comes a faint sound of little waterfalls, inviting one to bend and watch as the flakes on the glittering branches become ghostly, protean water. But Ali walks, stiffly upright, beneath olive trees white with hoarfrost. Hamid and Kader trot behind him. He asked them to come with him. The two boys breathe plumes of vapor into cold, crisp winter air that seems to make every detail of the landscape sharper than ever.

"Why are we here, Baba?" Hamid asks.

"Why, Baba?" Kader echoes.

"So we can be together," replies Ali. "All men together. To face our misfortune as men."

The three continue to walk in silence across the winter fields. From time to time, Ali turns back to his two eldest sons and, though he dare not say it, he thinks and hopes they will understand him. "Look carefully at everything around you, commit each branch to memory, each plot of land, because we can never know what will be ours. I wanted to give you everything, but now I am not sure of anything. Perhaps we will all be dead tomorrow. Perhaps these trees will burn before I work out what is happening. What is written is unknown to us, happiness may embrace or shun us, and we do not know how or why, we will never know, we might as well search for the roots of the fog."

From this point there will be no more vignettes, no more brightly colored images that have faded over time to the sepia of nostalgia. From here on, they have been replaced by the twisted shards that have resurfaced in Hamid's memory, refashioned by years of silence and turbulent dreams, by snippets of information Ali has let slip only to contradict, when asked, what he has said, by snatches of stories that no one can have witnessed and that sound like images from war movies. And between these slivers—like caulk, like plaster oozing between the cracks, like the silver coins melted in the mountains to create settings for coral trinkets, some as large as a palm—there is Naïma's research, begun more than sixty years after they have left Algeria, which attempts to give some shape, some structure, to something that has none, that perhaps never had.

In June 1958, General de Gaulle comes to power. The mood in the barracks in Palestro is triumphant. De Gaulle is the savior of France, the father of the army; de Gaulle is de Gaulle, for fuck's sake. He'll know what to do, and what's more, on the world stage he has influence. On the café terraces, soldiers raise their glasses and toast: *To the General! To French Algeria!*

Behind the counter of the grocer's, his ear pressed to the radio, Claude is more uncertain:

"He says that he has understood us . . . Fine, but who exactly is 'us'?"

Since the death of their son, Yema has refused to allow Ali to touch her. More often than not, he sleeps alone in the Palestro apartment. For years, the apartment has served no purposes beyond being mentioned in conversation as evidence of Ali's success. It smells mildewed and dusty. Some nights Ali simply sits in a chair at the association and waits for daybreak.

Daubed on the boulders lining a dirt road that leads to Zbarbar:

THE FRENCH ARMY WILL STAY AND WILL PROTECT YOU ALWAYS

"Why are you so late coming home?" Annie asks Michelle.

"I'm seeing someone . . . A soldier. I never thought I'd be into men in uniform."

*   *   *

On the stalls in the covered market, the scent given off by fruits, flowers, and vegetables pounded and caressed by the rising morning heat is so heady it is difficult to say whether it is delicious or nauseating. Just picking up a tomato, you could accidentally poke a finger to the heart of it. In the Café des Halles, a man is reading an article about the Constantine Plan announced by General de Gaulle on October 3. It is a long list of numbers and promises: housing construction, land redistribution, industrialization, the creation of tens of thousands of jobs, exploitation of the oil and gas fields discovered in the Sahara.

"They wouldn't be investing all this money if they were planning to leave," the man says. "They're in this for the long haul."

Youcef once again disappears from the village. He is no longer seen on the square. He is not down at the river, the meeting point for all the boys' games. He is no longer wasting his life wandering the roads.

Omar takes advantage of his absence to move up in the gang. Hamid simply waits for him to come back.

In accordance with the Challe Plan, a rain of precious stones falls across the country that autumn: Operation Ruby, Operation Topaz, Operation Sapphire, Operation Turquoise, Operation Emerald. Death, as it rains down on the region of Constantinois, has rarely borne such beautiful names.

Villages are forcibly evacuated and summarily rebuilt elsewhere, ringed by fences and ditches. There are processions of snail-people, like the ones in the nursery rhyme, who seem to carry whole houses on their backs—in kit form. The French authorities simply describe such people as "resettled."

Bombs—and sometimes napalm—are dropped on the ghost towns that have been forcibly cleared. Naïma will not believe her eyes when she reads this, having always believed that another, later war held exclusive rights to this noxious liquid. Among themselves, the military officers talk about "special canisters."

War marches on under cover of euphemism.

*   *   *

The snow returns prematurely. It lays a thick blanket over little Akli's tomb that no one dares remove. Next to it, the bowed shadow of Yema is barely visible.

Jumbled memories of Hamid and Ali, vaguely situated in late 1959. French soldiers finally reach the mountain ridge, an endless fleet of small green trucks as ugly as toads.

"Do you know Youcef Tadjer?"

A rough hand grabbing a collar, or even a fistful of hair.

"Youcef Tadjer, does that name ring a bell?"

A thumb digging beneath the collarbone, a fist crushing the wrist.

"Where is he?"

Every "I don't know" is followed by a blow from a rifle butt or a vicious kick. They are particularly ruthless when it comes to Poor Fatima, Youcef's mother. Between ragged sobs and missing teeth she tells them she has no idea where her son might be, that he is a bad son, worse, he is an absent son. She almost forgets that the men standing in front of her are soldiers and reels off a litany of grievances in Kabyle. How he never behaved like a man after his father's death, how he was her only son, and still he has left her alone and destitute.

"Well, then, you won't be missed by anyone," the sergeant says.

He puts a bullet in her head. Hamid is standing close by, gripping the hand of his cousin Omar. He watches Poor Fatima's body crumple. A sagging doll cut down while singing her old refrain. Blood sprays against the wall in a fine mist. Collects in a large pool beneath her crumpled body. When old Rafik rushes toward her, the sergeant guns him down, too. The children run away.

Down below, in distant groves, farmers have noticed an infestation of olive flies. Busy checking the fruits for punctures in which female flies have laid their eggs, the men have heard nothing. They are alerted by the screams of the children. Instantly they run toward the screaming. When they find them, the men do not ask, "What is it?," they ask, "Who is it?"

"It's the *francaoui*," Omar sobs. "They were looking for Youcef. They killed Poor Fatima!"

"Stay here," Ali tells the children, nodding to a deep ditch. "Lie down at the bottom and don't move, all right?"

Meek and trembling, the two boys obey. They huddle in the ditch, amid the smell of grass and earth, faces pressed into the blades of grass, which tickle the inside of their nostrils, exposed to the quick, capricious movements of insects. They are children, nothing has ever happened to them—even four years of war have gone straight over their heads like airplanes flying so high that the passengers cannot be seen through the windows. And, being children, they have been dreaming that something might happen to them ever since they were old enough to dream, but surely not this, not this face-to-face meeting with death, this smack in the face that death has dealt them, not this time spent lying in the ditch so that death takes on the form of weeds, of tubular flowers, death like a beetle whose back is divided into two black shields.

Along the road, overripe figs have dropped from the trees and become a dark, viscous slime. Ali slips, falls, grazes his hands and his knees, gets up, walks on.

The captain's interpreter, the son of the chicken farmer, is with the detachment that has overrun the village. It is to him that Ali runs, keeping his hands in the air as though surrendering while attacking, or attacking while surrendering. He gives his word of honor that Youcef has disappeared, that no one is hiding him. Tell them, tell them that. He's been gone for weeks, we haven't seen him, he often does this. Tell them that, please, tell them. Ali repeats the captain's name, points to the soldiers who saw him at the barracks. They know me, tell them that, they know they can trust me.

The sergeant watches as he gesticulates and pleads with the interpreter. At length, he gestures for his men to regroup. Two of them lower the rear panel of one of the trucks. They unload a rigid body caked in dirt and dried blood and toss it on the ground. It is the FLN lieutenant, the Wolf of Tablat. The French soldiers lash the body to a stake.

"The body will stay here so that none of you forget!" the sergeant barks. "Death spares no one, is that clear? There are no heroes, is that *clear?*"

The French depart in a cloud of dust. The corpse hangs there. With a mustache caked with dust, rigid in death, the mujahid looks like a pitiful puppet, an Algerian warrior in a bad Punch and Judy show.

"Thank you, my son," old mother Tassadit says to Ali.

She hobbles over and kisses his hands. Other villagers also come to thank him. When Ali later remembers the scene, what always comes back to him is this moment, since made inexplicable by History: nobody spits in his face, nobody criticizes his links to the army. The villagers truly believe that he saved their lives.

Imprisoned in his vertical position, the Wolf of Tablat looks on through dusty eyes as people pass crying and wailing, carrying the remains of Poor Fatima and old Rafik to the steep cemetery. The corpse attracts animals, jackals, vultures, tabby cats, foxes, and, later, smaller animals that look like shrews, or rats, or field mice, a tiny swarming mass of sharp teeth. Does it really serve as an example? At this stage of the "events," the "troubles," the "war"—call it what you will—one would have to be a fool not to realize that death is looming over everyone, regardless of which side they are on. And besides, the villagers in the mountains probably find a corpse less frightening than all the disappeared whose absence has left memories with a wound that takes on their shape, their voice, a wound that smiles on clement days and is mournful when it rains.

There are disappeared waiting in the watery depths for someone to claim them, there are others in holes out in the desert, at the bottom of some mountain gorge. There are the disappeared whose bodies are found, but not the faces, which acid has obliterated.

At least the Wolf of Tablat had the good fortune not to be an anonymous corpse; in death he had a name, a body, a face. And his soul? What has become of his soul? Hamid and Omar, who come back to stare at the corpse in spite of their parents' warnings, find it hard to believe his soul is in paradise with Allah while his body is rotting, lashed to the wooden stake. His soul must still be here, somewhere, watching.

All men who are good / Have run off to the wood. The lines from the old poem by Si M'hand evoke a world peopled by women, children, and cowards, ringed by forests that hide so many freedom fighters, or are ringed by so many fighters that you cannot see the trees—I am not sure. And yet, as he walked to the river, and swam there, Hamid did not see a soul. Now he is climbing the slope overgrown with grass and oleanders. The current swept away one of his shoes and he is hopping. He knows that Yema will yell, blame him for having ventured too far, for losing his shoe. Every day she tells him that he cannot go out, and every day he negotiates, with tantrums, with smiles, with flattery, with all the weapons in the arsenal of childhood, to be allowed out for a little while. He cannot understand his mother's fear because he cannot imagine dying—it is an adult activity. Today he secretly crept out of the house, but he is not really afraid of the tongue-lashing that awaits him. Yema will pretend to be angry even as she trembles with joy at seeing him come home unscathed. He will pretend to be contrite, still filled with the exhilaration of his escape. It is a game they often play.

He hears a whistling from somewhere in the pines and recognizes the familiar melody, a smutty little song the village boys sing behind their parents' backs. He heads toward the whistle, in spite of what his father has told him: *Nothing good happens in the mountains now.* The tune leads him to a place he knows, where rocks form a massive throne with gentle curves. This is where the children used to come to dry off and lounge in the sun after a swim, back when they were free to spend their days outdoors. When he sees a lanky figure lying on the gray stone, Hamid's heart bounds in his chest. Can it be true?

The whistler opens his eyes and smiles, and Hamid recognizes the gap teeth—the villagers used to say he stored food in the gaps between these teeth of hardship and cunning.

"Youcef!"

The little boy's cry of joy sets a few birds to flight, and the young man's response is a mocking echo:

"Hamid!"

They shake hands, they press their foreheads together, and they clasp each other around the neck. Hamid has never quite known how much of this greeting is affection and how much aggression, but it is theirs, it is the greeting used by all the mountain boys. Youcef has to stoop to press his face against that of eight-year-old Hamid. After a few seconds of this silent, smiling face-to-face, they separate.

Youcef is painfully thin, his skin clings to his bones like a damp white cloth or a cigarette paper, so thin that it looks as though it might rip if he were to move his jaw. He has been missing for months, nobody in the village has seen him since the death of Poor Fatima. They later learned that Youcef went up to the maquis. The boys, even those too young to remember, often talk about him. When he was there, he was their missing leader; once he had gone, he became their idol, the only one among them who was old enough to choose.

Sometimes Ali says that no one can be sure what has happened, that Youcef may have "disappeared" like so many others, that he may be languishing in a Palestro jail. But Omar, Hamid, and the other boys believe the heroic stories they invent in which Youcef is a warlord, a new Arezki, a Kabyle version of Robin Hood. And here, today, Youcef—alive and free, as Hamid always imagined—is standing in front of him, and the boy is as happy as if it were a divine apparition.

"Tell me, tell me," he pleads. "What was it like up there?"

"It was tough at first . . . I nearly died of starvation and a bunch of other things, but the hunger was the worst. Sometimes I thought I'd come back down to the village, I was so desperate to eat. It gives you stomach cramps, far worse than I imagined. I even started dreaming about food I used to hate, galettes made with mutton fat, or sheep's tail—sheep's tail used to make me vomit. At night, I'd see my mother's ghost beside my bed holding a dish of sheep's tails and I'd weep for joy, I would kiss her feet and beg her to forgive me for everything I said about her when she was alive . . ."

Youcef grimaces, completely distorting his handsome bony face.

"They promised us everything would be fine. They swore that Nasser's army was going to come and help. Yeah, right. We never saw signs of any Egyptians. There we were, hiding out . . . Sometimes I'd think to myself, I'm twenty years old and I'm hiding in a cave like an animal, it made me furious."

"Why did you stay, then?"

"You tell me. Do you support an economic system based on oppression and inequality?" Youcef asks Hamid.

"Huh?"

They laugh, both of them aware that the phrase is meaningless to an eight-year-old. Youcef is not entirely sure that he understands it himself, but he has learned to parrot it. Sometimes it seems crystal clear. Sometimes it's just a string of words, like pebbles lined up along the roadside.

"I spent the first fifteen years of my life being treated like a dog," he says when the laughter dies away. "I didn't want things to go on that way. The FLN promise that the suffering will stop if we can just kick the French out of Algeria. The French promise the suffering will stop if I go to school, learn to read and write, if I get a technical diploma, if I get a job with a good company, if I buy an apartment in the city, if I renounce Allah, if I stop wearing sandals and start wearing a roumi hat, if I lose my accent, if I have only one or two children, if I put my money in a bank instead of stashing it under my bed . . ."

Wide-eyed, openmouthed, Hamid looks at him with the rapt attention of a child watching a magician.

"That's a lot of ifs, don't you think?" Youcef asks softly.

Hamid nods vehemently. The two are silent for a moment, perhaps they are counting ifs as they stare up at the treetops swaying in the breeze.

"We'll drive the French out," said Youcef. "At this stage, it's only a matter of days . . ."

"What about Annie?" Hamid asks worriedly.

"Well, what about her?"

"I want to marry Annie," Hamid says with great solemnity. It is the first time he has voiced this hope aloud, and the moment has the air of a delicate ceremony.

"That's never going to happen," Youcef says with a laugh.

"Are you going to send her back to France?"

Youcef shrugs. "She'll leave of her own accord. Do you really think the French are here because they like the scenery? Take my word for it, the day we tell them they can't grow fat at our expense, they'll pack their suitcases faster than you can say 'République Française.'"

"Not Annie," Hamid insists.

"You little idiot." Youcef laughs and pats Hamid's head.

He pulls on his vest, his military jacket, his lace-up boots. Hamid thinks that he looks imposing in his outfit, it lends him a certain manliness, and out of the corner of his eye he studies Youcef's every gesture so he can imitate him.

"Can I come?" he asks shyly.

"You?" Youcef bursts out laughing. "You? You poor bastard—your father would have a heart attack if you went up to the maquis."

Hamid does not see why: he feels that it is Yema who would be the real problem. She would be too sad. He waves as Youcef begins to walk away. Perhaps to foster a sense of mystery, a throwback to the spy games they used to play, or perhaps out of genuine concern, Youcef turns and tells the boy not to watch which way he is headed. Hamid immediately claps his hands over his eyes.

"Listen," Youcef says as he walks away, "listen to me carefully . . . The people who have sided with the French are idiots, they're fools. But it's not too late. They can still join us. If they come to the maquis with a gun, having killed a French officer, they'll be forgiven. Algeria does not devour her own children. Spread the word."

Ali often goes to the barracks now, to exchange information with the captain. He does not say much (Nothing at all, he imagines himself saying later, during the tribunals held in the camp, not a word, any names I gave were of men who were already dead), just enough to maintain the tenuous link with the army that protects the village.

Later, as she reads witness statements that could be (but are not) by her grandfather, Naïma will tell herself: He chose to seek protection from murderers he despised with other murderers he despised.

In June 1960, French representatives meet in Melun with a delegation from the Provisional Government of the Algerian Republic.

"De Gaulle is abandoning us," the soldiers grumble.

The failure of these preliminary negotiations does little to persuade them that their erstwhile hero is still on their side.

In the streets of Palestro, a few European businesses begin to close their doors. They are not many. It is barely noticeable. An empty shopwindow, a missing sign, a light turned off.

On a visit to the captain, Ali sees Michelle walking quickly away from the barracks. As always, her mere presence robs him of all the words he thought he knew. But on this occasion, Michelle, too, is silent. Two blazing red circles the size of coins appear on her cheeks, fading to a soft, pale pink as her face flushes all the way to the tips of her ears. He longs to touch that face with his fingertips. Abruptly she turns away, and, on the other side of the courtyard, Ali sees the captain, with his large, expressive nose, staring at them. The three stand, frozen, no one knowing what to say, as each realizes that it is impossible to watch two people at once.

In the barracks, the soldiers are sullen, they look daggers at Ali as he steps into the captain's office.

"De Gaulle has announced a referendum on Algerian self-determination," the interpreter explains. "They don't know what to think anymore."

In the covered market, the town crier beats his enormous round drum and, in a hoarse voice, announces that the Président du Conseil, General de Gaulle, will visit in December. A number of Europeans spit on the ground or shrug. Yeah, sure. They no longer believe.

"It's just a ruse by de Gaulle," Ali tells his brothers. "They'll never give up Algeria: they've defeated the maquis, and from a military point of view they control everything. The FLN are deluding themselves."

"But what happens if people vote for independence anyway, *rhouya*?"

"Don't you think we should . . . ?"

All three are remembering Youcef's implicit warning.

At night, in hushed barracks across the country, rifles are being stolen, men are deserting at an increasing rate. The atmosphere between French soldiers and their indigenous auxiliaries has soured. They no longer play dice together around the jeeps. They no longer teach each other to swear in their different languages. Men who, after long years of service, have been thrown out by the army trudge back up to the mountains.

"The captain told me to go home," they say with a shrug.

Many disappear moments after they set foot in their villages, or sometimes even before they reach them, at a bend in the road, near a dark oak grove. No one asks what has become of them. The FLN has issued a decree: Anyone who donned a uniform cannot simply take off that uniform and go back to his former life. He must first wash himself in the blood of a French officer.

When he hears this news, Ali cannot help but compare his role liaising with the captain to that of the men who have left the French army. He probably finds it easy to persuade himself that they have nothing in common. People say that Fattah, a scrawny youth from Tablat, took part in "special interrogations," wielding the whip. They say Boussad, the Giant of Mihoub, dug the graves. These men left a trail of destruction so terrible that, even if the FLN had not come for them, the families of the dead would have taken up arms against them. They were doomed; they could no longer find peace in their villages. But Ali is asking only for protection for himself and his family—the same protection those around him have enjoyed. He has paid for this protection, as is right and proper for an honorable man who does not allow a debt to lie on his doorstep. He cannot be blamed. The position he holds on the mountain means that he is safe from rash acts of retribution—that, at least, is what he believes, what he wants to believe, what he will later say that he believed.

Ever since the discovery of the olive press in the swollen waters of the river, he has played the role of the beneficent landowner too assiduously for the villagers to forget the favors he has done them. He offered work to those who needed it: to the sons of the poor, the sons of widows. He treated them as friends, offered them the chance to be men rather than losers. Surely they will remember that. He believes that people will say that perhaps he made a political error of judgment, but within the mountain community he was always a good son, a good brother, a good father, a good cousin, a good leader, a good husband, in short, a good Algerian.

That year, surrounded by his clan, he harvests the olives, not knowing that he will never again see these trees heavy with fruit.

How is a country born? And who brings it into the world?

In certain parts of Kabylia, there is a folk tradition some call "the sleeping child." It explains how a woman can give birth even though her husband has been gone for years: according to tradition, having been fathered by the husband, the child then dozes off in the womb and does not emerge until much later.

Algeria is like that sleeping child: it was conceived long ago, so long that no one can agree on a date, and for years it slept, until the spring of 1962. At the time of the Évian Accords, the FLN insist on the fact that Algeria is *regaining* its independence.

Almost half a century after the accords were signed, Naïma writes up the following account of the agreements, a Word document with lots of edits and italics.

Agreements Relating to Algerian Independence

Declarations Drawn Up in Common Agreement at Evian, March 18, 1962, by the Delegations of the Government of the French Republic and the Algerian National Liberation Front

I. CEASE-FIRE AGREEMENT IN ALGERIA

ARTICLE 1
Military operations and all armed action throughout the Algerian territory will be brought to an end on March 29, 1962, at 12 o'clock noon.

ARTICLE 2
The two parties pledge themselves *to prohibit any recourse to acts of collective or individual violence.*

Any action of a clandestine nature and in violation of public order must cease.

II. GOVERNMENT DECLARATIONS OF
MARCH 19, 1961, RELATING TO ALGERIA

GENERAL DECLARATION
The French people, by the referendum of January 8, 1961, recognized the right of the Algerians to choose by means of a consultation of direct and universal suffrage their political destiny in relation to the French Republic.

The formation, after self-determination, of an independent and sovereign state appearing to conform to the realities of the Algerian situation, and in these conditions, cooperation between France and Algeria corresponding to the interests of the two countries, the French Government considers, together with the FLN, that *the solution of the independence of Algeria in cooperation with France is the one which corresponds to this situation.*

CHAPTER I

Organization of Public Powers During the Transition Period and Self-Determination Guarantees

a) The self-determination consultation will permit the electors to make known whether they want Algeria to be independent and in that case whether they want France and Algeria to cooperate in the conditions defined by the present declarations.

c) The freedom and the *genuineness* of the consultation will be guaranteed in conformity with the regulations fixing the conditions for the self-determination consultation.

h) The full exercise of individual and public liberties will be re-established within the shortest possible time.

i) The FLN will be considered a legal political body.

l) Persons in refuge abroad will be able to return to Algeria. Persons who have been relocated will be able to return to their regular place of residence.

CHAPTER II

Independence and Cooperation

A) Independence of Algeria

I. The Algerian State will exercise its full and complete sovereignty both internally and externally. This sovereignty will be exercised in all spheres, in particular in defense and foreign affairs.

The Algerian State will freely establish its own institutions and will choose the political and social regime which it deems to be most in conformity with its interests. On the international level, it will define and implement in full sovereignty the policy of its choice.

The Algerian State will subscribe unreservedly to the Universal Declaration of Human Rights and will base its institutions on democratic principles and on *equality of political rights between all citizens without discrimination of race, origin or religion.*

II. Individual Rights and Liberties and Their Guarantees

1. Common provisions

(As she is typing the lines below into her keyboard, Naïma is struck by their remarkable clarity and brevity. They were written to protect her grandfather. These few lines below—Naïma thinks as she types them out—also proved to be remarkably ineffective.)

No one shall be subject to police or legal measures, to disciplinary sanctions or to any discrimination on account of:
—*opinions expressed at the time of events that occurred in Algeria* before the day of the self-determination vote;
—*acts committed at the time of these same events* before the day of the cease-fire proclamation;
No Algerian shall be forced to leave Algerian territory or be prevented from leaving it.

2. Provisions concerning French citizens of ordinary civil status

(For Naïma, the articles that follow, those most cluttered with figures and legal periods, are the least easy to read. In fact, she has simply copied-and-pasted them in imposing blocks, finding them impossible to paraphrase. These are the articles intended to protect those who would later be called *pieds noirs*. Naïma finds it funny—or tragic—to think that, in spite of the precision of the arrangements put in place, most of those to whom Article A guaranteed a place had left the country long before the time limit set out.)

a) For a period of three years from the day of self-determination, French citizens of ordinary civil status,

—born in Algeria and giving proof of ten years of permanent and regular residence on Algerian territory on the day of self-determination;

—or giving proof of ten years of permanent and regular residence on Algerian territory on the day of self-determination and whose father or mother was born in Algeria and fulfills or could have fulfilled the conditions for exercising civil rights;

—or giving proof of twenty years of permanent and regular residence on Algerian territory on the day of self-determination, *will enjoy, by right, Algerian civil rights and will be considered therefore as French nationals exercising Algerian civil rights.*

At the end of the above-mentioned three-year period, they shall acquire Algerian nationality by an application for registration or confirmation of their registration on the voters' lists.

b) In order to assure to Algerians of French civil status *the protection of their person and their property* and their normal participation in Algerian life, the following measures are provided for:

—They will have a just and genuine part in public affairs;

(How, Naïma wonders, can anyone ensure a *just* and *genuine* participation? In fact, what do the two adjectives mean in the previous sentence?)

—In the assemblies, their representation shall correspond to their actual numbers. In the various branches of the civil service, they will be assured of fair participation;

—Their property rights will be respected. *No dispossession measures will be taken against them without their being granted fair compensation agreed upon in advance;*

—They will receive guarantees appropriate to their cultural, linguistic and religious particularities. They will retain their personal status, which will be respected and enforced by Algerian courts comprised of magistrates of the same status. They will use the French language within the assemblies and in their relations with the public authorities.

(Chapter 2 included a capital "B" section, but it is one she never rereads. It deals with mining rights for hydrocarbons that France refuses to cede to the newly independent state. It is not news to Naïma that colonialism was pursued via multiple means, many of them devious. She has seen the word "Françafrique" in newspapers since she was old enough to read. Even so, she notices that subsection B and its articles take up more space in the Évian Accords than the measures intended to protect her grandfather. She notes the fact, nothing more, with the feigned casualness that strains to say so much while saying nothing.)

CHAPTER III

Settlement of Military Questions

The French forces, *whose numbers will gradually be reduced as of the cease-fire*, will be withdrawn from the frontiers of Algeria when self-determination is realized. Their total force will be reduced to 80,000 men *within a period of twelve months from the time of self-determination. The repatriation of these forces will have to be completed by the end of a second twenty-four-month period.*

—Algeria shall lease to France the use of the Mers-el-Kébir base for a fifteen-year period, which may be renewed by agreement between the two countries;

—Algeria shall also grant France the use of a number of military airfields, the terrains, sites and installations necessary to her.

CHAPTER IV

Settlement of Litigation

France and Algeria will resolve differences that may arise between them by means of peaceful settlement.

Hamid runs along the road, streaming with sweat, his knees aching so much it feels they might dislocate.

"You go to the shop, you give the money to Hamza, and you come straight back," Ali made him promise. "You're not to dawdle along the way, and you definitely don't stop."

Hamid promised, and, despite the blazing sun, he runs as fast as he can. He is intoxicated by the sense of his own speed. Suddenly a man appears in the middle of the road, arms outstretched to catch the boy. When Hamid slows, he smells the stench of his own sweat.

The man in the middle of the road smiles. His fine white teeth glitter in the midst of the black-and-red thatch of his beard. They look as though they are resting there, in a nest of hair.

"You're Ali's little boy, aren't you?"

He looks happy to have run into him. Hamid nods.

"Are you running errands for your father?"

Another nod. The smile broadens.

"Can you do one for me, too?"

Hamid nods, skipping from one foot to another. He hopes it will not take too long. He wants to set off again, to run so fast he can outrun the smell of his own body.

"Tell your father . . ." the man says, slowly running a finger across his throat, "that any day now, we're going to cut his throat."

He says it with a smile, as though trying not to scare the boy, as though it is a settled and pleasant prospect. Years later, Hamid will still wonder whether the man was trying to help them, to warn them so they could escape the knife he mentioned, or whether he was simply sharing a shimmering fragment of the radiant future the FLN had planned for everyone. *This is how things are going to be, all right, thank you.*

Part of him still likes to think that it was Youcef who sent him this last messenger, in memory of the old days down by the river.

Hamid repeats the smiling man's words to his father, studying his face for the slightest flicker. He longs for Ali to dismiss the threat with a wave of the hand and go on drinking *lebn*—buttermilk—stately, imperturbable. But Ali turns pale and sets his glass down on the table with a clack.

"Who was he?"

Without realizing, he has grabbed Hamid by the collar and is shaking him. Little Dalila covers her eyes.

"One of Farid's sons, I think," Hamid stammers.

Ali curls his lips into a sneer.

"He said that to you? He is planning to avenge the country? The guy's a Martian! He didn't start believing in independence until after the accords were signed! And now he's swaggering around saying he's going to kill the French. That guy would have sold his father and mother to France, if France had had any use for them!"

It is a phrase Hamid will hear many times in the years that follow: *He's a Martian.* Eventually he will come to understand that it refers to those who joined the FLN in March 1962, when the Évian Accords were signed. But right now it signifies nothing, it doesn't even evoke the fluorescent-green aliens he will later discover in the murky pages of comic books. It is an insult that hangs in the air, devoid of meaning.

Over the remains of dinner, the sibilant whispers of Djamel, Hamza, and Ali drift through the walls and reach the sleepless children.

"It's your fault, Ali. It's your fault, my brother. Why did you have to go around telling everyone you sided with the French? Now the FLN are going to come and kill us all."

"You're out of your mind," Ali says. "I never said I sided with the French and I've never so much as touched a gun. No one has any reason to hold a grudge against us. People asked me about the families up on the ridge, and I answered. I told them so-and-so is so-and-so's cousin. But it was common knowledge. They asked me to tell them about such-and-such a place, and I told them, where the river ran, where the rocks were. But that's all. I'm no traitor."

"Even if you'd done only half of that, they'd say it was too much. Do you really think the Amrouches need proof to come and take our farm from us? Don't you realize that this is exactly what they've been waiting for? They've been salivating at the prospect for years. And now Farid's sons are getting involved!"

"They'll take everything! They're bound to take everything. And it's all your fault, Ali."

"So you're saying you were a mujahid?" Ali says spitefully. "You're saying that's why they released you without so much as plucking a single hair?"

"I don't know why they released me!" Hamza roars.

They fall silent, shattered, exhausted, three hulking bodies crushed beneath the weight of what is to come.

"They're going to set the dogs of independence on us . . ."

A warm spring turns into a sweltering summer, the mocking songs that follow Ali wherever he goes turn into insults. He cannot say when the change occurred, it seems it evolved naturally, gradually, the way the buds are slowly transformed into flowers and then fruits. Men standing by the roadside with hoes over their shoulders whistle between their teeth when he passes. One by one, the laborers who till his land stop coming to work. Ali and his brothers have no choice but to once again pick up their tools. Every night, hands made soft by years of idleness blister and bleed.

One morning, Ali notices that children are throwing stones at him. It is something that could be terrifying, but they do it as children do everything: with a mixture of cruelty and beaming delight, babbling all the while.

Around the deserted stall and around the barns, strange men prowl, their heads bowed, their eyes shining. When asked why they are there, they say they have come to buy olives, but when Ali holds out a bucket or a jar, they wave their arms wildly.

"No, no, we don't want them now. We'll be back later. Do you understand? *We'll be back . . .*"

And they stalk off, laughing, rolling their eyes in disbelief.

Yema has decided not to leave the house, since a man at the village well insulted her and ripped off her yellow headscarf fringed with black. At night, as she falls asleep, she huddles tightly against Ali so that her arms, her legs, are screened by his body.

Slipping silently out of the house before his parents wake up, Hamid discovers that someone has shat on their doorstep. Curiously, he does not find the smell offensive. It smells like rotting flowers.

The following day, he finds an ear. This time he goes in search of his father.

The growing tensions can be measured by the mounting stacks of sandbags against the barrack walls. The soldiers often asked Ali to help unload trucks, and the weight of these natural bulwarks made his back creak. That June morning, the entire barracks has an inner lining of sacking and sand that muffles every sound in the shriveled courtyard.

As usual, Ali asks to speak to the captain. Scarcely looking up from his magazine, the soldier on sentry duty tells him the captain is out.

"Well, who can I talk to?"

"Sergeant Daumasse is here."

Daumasse has the face of a rat, or a cuckoo, with his jutting Adam's apple. This is the officer who watched his men beat old mother Tassadit without intervening, the man who gunned down Poor Fatima and Rafik in cold blood. Ali hates the man and the feeling is mutual: Daumasse cannot help it, he hates all natives. He thinks every last one of them should have been gassed, the way Americans gassed mosquitoes with

DDT when they landed on the Pacific Islands. It was the only way to make the place inhabitable.

"What d'you want?" the sergeant asks.

He asks only as a matter of form.

"I need you to protect my house," Ali says.

"That's impossible."

"Then give us guns."

"Impossible."

"Then move us somewhere else, to one of the French bases."

"That's not possible."

"Well, throw us in jail, then! At least we'll be safe there."

The sergeant shrugs.

"The FLN has promised not to seek revenge on the *harkis*."

Ali lets out a bitter, dissonant laugh that echoes through his nose.

"And you believe them?"

Daumasse is well aware of what has been going on around the country in recent months: the kangaroo courts set up in villages, the scores settled in the dead of night, the roadside ambushes. News that the accords had been signed had not yet reached those in remote rural areas before the "widows of the liberation" began to blossom.

Ali shifts his weight from one foot to the other, his hulking frame swaying like the needle of a metronome as he stares into the eyes of the increasingly impatient sergeant. It's always the same with fucking bougnoules: give them a hand and they want the whole arm. Daumasse cannot help but wonder which shit-for-brains son of a bitch came up with the bright idea of enlisting them.

"Listen, pal," he says in a last effort, "all you had to do was choose the right side."

"So you're saying you chose the wrong side?"

"No, but that's because I'm French."

"So am I."

Days from now, when the French are making preparations to leave the barracks, and Daumasse is collecting army-issue weapons from the harki soldiers the army is about to abandon after long years of service, he will jerk his thumb at them and say: "If they try to climb on the trucks, stomp on their fingers." He will even give them a demonstration, black boot sole against knuckles white with strain. "Go on, fuck off, don't even think about trying!"

On an old poster announcing the referendum, next to the Palestro train station:

GENERAL DE GAULLE TRUSTS YOU. TRUST HIM. VOTE YES.

The journey from the mountain to the valley has become too risky now that every tangled corner of the forest, every thicket of velvet-leaved rockrose, seems to harbor maquisards. Ali resolves to leave the mountain ridge and take his family to live in the small downtown apartment, far from the areas controlled by the Amrouche family and the sons of Farid. In the broad streets of Palestro, it is still possible to believe that law and order are being upheld by the police and the French army.

Yema and the children are not allowed to go out, or to answer the doorbell. Ali double-locks the door whenever he leaves, and then only after peering through the kitchen curtain to check that no one is waiting for him in the street.

On their first day in the apartment, Hamid, assuming he can flout his parents' rules, as he did up in the mountains, tries to sneak out behind his father. For his pains he gets a beating unlike any he has experienced. Before they fade, the bruises shift through every color ever seen in the market that is no longer held on the Grand Place: eggplant, overripe apple, banana, lemon . . .

Every morning, Ali goes back to the barracks to try to speak with the captain. Every morning, he is told the captain is not there.

The flow of Europeans is a hemorrhage that has left pockets of silence around the heart of the city. The Café du Centre is closed, as is the electrical shop, and the record shop. Boards have been nailed in an X over the coal merchant's window.

"It could just be a ruse by de Gaulle," Ali says to himself. "To flush the last of the maquisards out of the woods, and make the rebels hiding abroad show themselves."

He cannot believe that this is the end. He has never seen a country change hands. He does not recognize the signs.

When he finally bumps into the captain, it is by sheer coincidence (or at least they pretend that it is a coincidence that the officer is emerging from Claude's grocer's shop—in other words from Michelle's house). For want of an interpreter, they have to speak in short phrases, disjointed sentences quickly exchanged with no certainty that they can be understood.

"I've been to see you a number of times," Ali says.

The captain sighs. "I'm sorry."

"You have to help me," Ali says. "I've lost the mountain. I don't want to lose my life."

They stand in front of the little grocer's, its window empty, revealing the bare shelves inside.

"They're going to transfer me," the captain says, his hands miming the brutal and yet effortless motion of a transfer. "I'll be gone in a few days. There's nothing I can do."

"Why are you leaving?"

The captain sighs again.

"Look," he says, "I may as well be honest: they don't want me to see what happens next. They're afraid I'll take it badly. Apparently the top brass think I'm a little too sensitive . . ."

Between the dried tomatoes and bags of couscous, the usual crate of peppers is missing. The counter is bare and already covered in dust.

Claude, Michelle, and Annie are leaving, too. They have no faith in the clauses of the Évian Accords that assure them full protection of persons and property. They are not sure exactly what they believe, but there will be time to work that out when they are safe. Claude has organized their departure. Within two weeks they will leave Palestro.

"Some men came to see me, told me not to go," he says to Ali. "Shady types. They say it's up to us to set an example now that de Gaulle has turned tail. Telling me that this is our home, that we should stay here, and all that nonsense . . . Do they really think I want to leave Algeria? That I'm doing this for the hell of it?"

He falls silent.

"I'd like to go, too," said Ali. "To France."

"Well, then, come!" Claude says almost cheerfully. "I won't feel so alone."

"I don't have any papers. I'm scared. I'm scared for my children. For Hamid . . ."

At the mention of the boy's name, Claude flinches. His elbow bangs against the metal cash register that still sits on the counter. With a melodious tinkle, the empty drawer shoots out.

It's tactical, Ali thinks, his face pressed to the kitchen window. Once they've evacuated all the French and the Algerians who stayed loyal to them, they'll come back and bomb the country. That's one more reason we have to leave . . .

Claude's guilty conscience crystallizes around a phrase: "the little Arab boy we've more or less adopted." These nine words are enough to make him lose sleep. Despite the huge wooden fan that hangs from the ceiling, his bedroom in the upstairs apartment is stifling, and the words constantly come back to haunt him.

He cannot have said this, said it over and over, only to abandon Hamid now that he is leaving, without worrying what will happen to his family. And so amid the hurried preparations, he begs Michelle to talk to the captain. Everyone in the city knows that he still has powerful contacts. People say he has managed to get papers for some of the Palestro harkis.

Claude piles up furniture, folds clothes, dusts and dismantles the large wooden frames, muttering without conviction:

"Maybe we should postpone our departure."

*   *   *

In the captain's quarters, little remains except a large mattress on the floor. During the gentle doze that follows lovemaking, the captain promises Michelle that he will do everything in his power. Michelle runs her fingertips over his taut white stomach, toys with his pubic hair, gently circles his navel.

There is something absurd, obscene, or poignant in the fact that a family's survival can depend on Michelle's curvaceous body, her heavy breasts, her full buttocks, her face in the half-light of the bedroom, the fringe of hair that falls over her eyes.

"If you manage to get as far as Téfeschoun, you'll be able to get passage to France," the captain tells Ali. "There's a camp there that takes in harkis and puts them on boats. I've called them and given your name. They think you're one of my men."

"See you in France," Claude says, pretending that he believes the words.

The sound of a metal shutter falling. A last glimpse of Annie's blue-and-white skirt as she climbs into a big black car. Claude's movements, jerky and birdlike. Michelle's lips. Her golden skin. The boxes, the trunks, the legs of a table sticking up from the roof of the car.

In the late 2000s, Naïma is finishing work on a catalogue for a Thomas Mailaender exhibition. Next month, the gallery is exhibiting his photographs of "cathedral cars," vehicles stuffed to the bursting point (trunks open) with brightly colored bundles, their roofs piled with pyramids of suitcases in precarious equilibrium. Mailaender photographed the vehicles in 2004 on the docks in Marseilles. There are no licence plates. They could hail from any country; they could be going anywhere or nowhere. Perhaps they were genuinely stopped here, in this ghostly parking lot. Perhaps one of them contains a tattered teddy bear like the one that Annie had. According to Thomas Mailaender: "These rolling containers are an obvious embodiment of the concept of borders and cultural tensions that result from them."

*   *   *

In the back of the car, wedged between a suitcase and a child's desk, Annie struggles to turn around and wave.

List of priorities probably drawn up by Ali (more or less consciously):

1. Save Hamid
2. Save himself
3. Save Yema, Kader, and Dalila
4. Everything else

Staring at the shadows that streak the ceiling, he mentally pictures the route that separates them from the camp in Téfeschoun.

Memorandum from Brigadier General Le Ray, dated August 24, 1962:

> Respect for the independence of the newly formed state of Algeria and a desire to relieve France of a needless burden make it necessary that we afford protection only to people of genuine interest who are in real danger for their role fighting alongside us, to the exclusion of any others . . . Such protection can only be afforded to those who come to our camps and solicit it. Going into villages to look for people so that families may be saved is forbidden.

In the chaos of the sweltering summer, Ali's younger brother Djamel disappears. The two farm laborers working alongside him had their throats cut.

"I'm staying," Hamza decides, in spite of everything.

Ali's daughters by his first wife, now married, also decide not to leave. The family bound together by the changing seasons disintegrates: war finally cleaves it like a plowshare splitting a mound of earth, scattering it in little divots of farewell.

*   *   *

Téfeschoun (modern-day Khemisti) is situated on the coast between Tipaza and Algiers, just over a hundred miles from Ali's village. A two-and-a-half-hour drive, Naïma learns from Google Maps. But that is the optimal travel time that makes no allowances for slowing at every bend in the road, for the numerous checkpoints that existed in 1962, some manned by the French, some by the FLN. At the point when Ali sets out, it is a journey time that can tip over into the eternity of death.

Ali's car, unlike Claude's, contains no suitcases, no furniture. It does not even contain the whole family. There is only the father and his eldest son. Nothing that would suggest that they are trying to leave Algeria. It is just a routine journey, a brief business trip. Yema will join them later, bringing the other two children. Her brother, Messaoud, will drive them to the camp.

"What will happen if they stop us, Baba?" Hamid asks as his father starts the car.

"Don't worry."

Fifteen years earlier, the officers who gave orders to Ali on the battle-fields of Europe made no mention of the danger of sending their men into battle. They could probably see no reason to do something so point-less: even if they had given the estimated percentage of casualties, each man would have assumed that this figure referred to others, not to himself. Soldiers may *theoretically* understand that, for them, death is a likely outcome in battle, but their understanding remains purely mathematical—or, at least, that is what I imagine. They do not inter-nalize the information. The self, the "I," cannot die. Ali perhaps feels protected by his inability to imagine his own death. This might explain how he had the nerve to make this trip. If he does not think about it too much, this inability resembles immortality.

Between 1954 and 1962, many experienced such magical thinking. Until the endlessly postponed last moment, those who were dragged into the murderous villas of Algiers, into the ravenous jaws of remote farms, into the gaping maw of the protection squads, those who were dangled over the abyss, those who had their heads pushed underwater, those whose glandes split from the electric shocks administered directly to their penises, those whose bodies were dismembered, limb by limb, continued to believe that something would spirit death away and that they, though wounded, battered, even torn to shreds, might still live. Death was standing next to them in the room, giving them the unmistakable signal of its inexorability, and still they dismissed it with frantic gestures and grimaces, with blood-flecked foam on their lips, with groans and howls of terror, urine pooling beneath them, fingers clutching their brothers' arms. Until the very last minute, they continued to believe that their feeble twitchings might keep death at bay.

Naïma does not know how, by what stroke of luck, reproducing itself with each mile, her grandfather and her father, followed by her grandmother, her uncle, and her aunt, managed to pass through the roadblocks and reach Téfeschoun unscathed.

She pictures watchtowers rising over the desert and a huge iron gate, like some prehistoric creature, against which distraught survivors pounded with their fists.

From the camp, the family is divided up, hidden in trucks, and quickly transported to the docks in Algiers.

Glimpsed through a rip in the truck's tarpaulin, daubed on the walls of the capital:

VIVE SALAN

YOU WILL UNDERSTAND US

THE OAS IS WATCHING

FRANCE WILL REMAIN

The ships are enormous and, on the sea, their flanks are like a wall of metal. The ships are enormous, as is the throng of people milling on the waterfront, desperate to get aboard. The ships are enormous, but seen against the flood of people demanding or begging for a place aboard, they look small.

Who decided who or what would be granted refuge?

Animals are brought aboard, chickens, sheep, donkeys, and horses. The horses look ridiculous dangling above the waves, girth straps tight around their bellies, their legs bound, harnessed and winched aboard like crates, whinnying frantically, their wild eyes rolling in the bony capsules of their skulls.

The pitch and swell of the ship maddens the horses. Some break a front leg. Others topple overboard. They look as though they are jumping.

They load the horses.

They load French furniture, potted plants with tumbling blossoms, sideboards as big as cars. As it happens, they are also loading cars. French cars.

Later, they even repatriate statues, unscrewed from their Algerian plinths and given refuge in villages throughout France, where officers of the French army of 1830, forever immortalized in bronze, may peer through their telescope, or command their invisible soldiers.

They load statues aboard.

Then, perhaps while attempting to hide behind their backs the horses, the cars, the sideboards, and the statues, they tell the thousands of dark-skinned men:

There's no room.

They mark time on deck while waiting to go down into the hold in single file. In the queue of men and hunched women, Ali is conspicuous because of his height. He has lost his hat in the stampede of jostling bodies. His high forehead, made even higher at the temples by the widow's peaks gradually encroaching on his hairline, gleams in the pale sunlight. With a nervous hand, he grips his eldest son's shoulder but remains upright. From the railings of the upper deck, a handful of pieds noirs, some in tears, others incensed, hurl hoarse insults at Ali, singling him out as a scapegoat, as a representative of those who will soon be Algerian citizens of the newly independent Algeria, something he will never be.

"It's just a bluff. You'll see," he says to Yema. "Six months from now we'll be back in the village."

"Insh'Allah," she says.

For the first time, he feels that in saying this she is disparaging him, reminding him that God is above him and his geopolitical analyses, just as He is above his futile attempts at action (a credo Ali firmly believed back in the village, one that made him happy). Today, he needs the reverse; he needs his wife and his children to believe in his power, in his strength.

"Six months from now . . ."

"*Azka d azqa*," Yema says, this time in Kabyle.

She has no desire to play his little game of trust and confidence. She has no need of promises. *Azka d azqa*: "Tomorrow is the grave."

*   *   *

As the ship shudders and the engines roar to life, churning the sea into foam, Ali tries to fix this landscape in his mind—in case he is wrong, in case France really does abandon Algeria (impossible)—so that he can take a precise memory with him to the far side of the Mediterranean.

But what is this landscape? It is not his. This is not Kabylia. It is Algiers, a series of streets and houses that hold no memories for him. He tries to fix the scene in his mind, but nothing sticks, nothing makes sense. One section of wall is followed by another section of wall, each of them part of a building inhabited by people he does not know, people who are nothing to him, he does not know the names of the streets, and it feels as though, even as he looks at them, the images immediately fade, he remembers nothing, retains nothing of the landscape he is seeing. He even starts to think that the intensity of his gaze is erasing other memories. As though the energy he is expending on this last glimpse (surely not the last—six months from now . . .) is drawn from the same source as the energy needed to preserve old memories. As though images of his mother, perhaps images of the fig tree, images of his time in Italy, or images from one of his marriages are being replaced, not by images of Algiers, but by nothing. The blinding sun. A landscape that seems to shatter and crumble into pieces.

Slowly, the ship lurches backward, moving astern through the waters of the harbor. Ali suddenly has the curious notion that a rope connects the stern of the huge ship to the coastline, so that, as the ship moves away, the country is being slowly but inexorably towed into the sea: the cathedral and the Casbah, the Grande Poste, the botanical gardens, and behind them the interior of the country is disappearing beneath the waves. Médéa. Bouïra. The ship pitches sharply, giving the rope a sharp jerk: Biskra and Ghardaïa sink into the sea, followed by Timimoun and the desert sands that flow from the wound made by the departing ferry. Grain by grain, the vast Sahara slips into the Mediterranean.

For Hamid, it will be different. It is something they will never speak about. But in the mind of the little boy, this vision will endure. Algiers the White. Dazzling. An image that resurfaces the moment the country is mentioned. At once detailed and distant, like a model city in a museum display cabinet. The streets that carve the houses into blocks, the peeling buildings that cling to the steep hill. The villas. The cathedral of Notre Dame d'Afrique that makes Algiers look like Marseilles.

This is the image that is burned onto Hamid's retinas, the one that reappears whenever someone says the word "Algeria." And, to him, it is a strange sensation, because he saw the city for the first time as the ship sailed away. It is not Algiers that should represent the lost country. This city cannot be lost since it was never owned (in the sense that human beings can come to "own" a city by hours of walking, by the ability to mentally replace every street sign with an incident that took place there). And yet it is Algiers that he takes with him, without meaning to. Algiers creeps into his suitcase.

For Naïma, it will be different again. Because for her, the ship will be traveling the other way. It is Marseilles that she will watch recede and Algiers she will see heave into view. She will think of her father, her grandfather. She will think that Algiers does not seem very white. She will think, I'm going to cry, but the tears will not come, and she will even try to force them, telling herself, I need something to happen, even if it is something upsetting or something feigned, because I am arriving in Algeria and I can't just stand here leaning against the gunwale.

She will think that it was a mistake to make the journey alone, because this is something she would have wished to share with someone.

She will think of Christophe. Not for the first time, she will think that she should stop seeing him. Because she cannot imagine him on this ship with her. Not that she would not want him here. Perhaps she would. But it is so blindingly obvious that he would never do such a thing, even her imagination cannot overcome this obstacle and conjure a scene to enchant her for a few seconds. Even in her imagination, Christophe-on-the-deck-of-the-ship has a sardonic smile that says: For God's sake, Naïma . . . Stop being such a child and get me off this ship. We both know this isn't happening.

Part II

COLD FRANCE

Trapped between the Sahara and socialism, they may
have been tempted to come to France.

—Jean-Marie Le Pen

The young will no longer accept what their parents once
accepted.

—Report on the "Logis d'Anne" resettlement camp, 1976

(INA online archives)

Every family is the site of a clash of civilizations.

—Pierre Bourdieu, *Algeria 1960*

I can't remember how the *Aeneid* begins, the first adventures of Aeneas and his companions after they leave Troy—or rather leave the place where Troy once stood, now reduced to rubble, to the stench of blood and smoke. I remember only the first verse I translated in Latin class more than a decade ago: *Arma virumque cano . . .* "I sing of arms and the man"—followed, I assume, by a relative clause, "the man who . . ." from which the whole story unfolded, but in my memory, I have retained only those three words. Although, in my memory, this epic poem filled with incident is all but reduced to silence, one thing remains clear: at the end of his painful wanderings, Aeneas arrives back in Latium, where his descendants will found Rome.

What story is played out between the moment Ali first sets foot in France in September 1962 and the moment Naïma realizes she knows no more about her family's story than I remember of the *Aeneid*? A story without a hero, perhaps. Certainly, an epic that was never sung. It begins in a sheet of tattered canvas and a barbed-wire fence.

The "Joffre camp," also known as Rivesaltes camp, where Ali, Yema, and their three children arrive after a long, sleepless journey, is a pen filled with ghosts: those of Spanish Republicans who fled Franco only to end up here, those of the Jews and the Gypsies that the Vichy regime rounded up in the *zone libre*, those of a few prisoners of war of various origins, felled far from the front lines by dysentery or typhus. Since its creation thirty years earlier, the camp has been a place where those whom no one knows what to do with are incarcerated while—officially—a solution is sought, and—unofficially—they can be forgotten until they disappear of their own accord. It is a place for people who have no History; none of the nations that might offer them one is prepared to take them in. Or a place for those whose twofold Histories confer on them a paradoxical status, as is the case for the thousands of men, women, and children who flock there from the summer of 1962.

Algeria will speak of them as rats. Traitors. Dogs. Terrorists. Infidels. Bandits. Unclean. France will not speak of them at all, or will say little. Just as it stitches the borders of the resettlement camps with barbed wire, so France sews up its lips. Perhaps it is better not to name them. The various labels suggested all seem incongruous. They do not stick, do not seem to say anything meaningful. *The repatriated?* Many of these people have never before seen the country where they disembarked, so how can one say they are returning, coming home? Besides, the term would make them indistinguishable from the pieds noirs, who demand that they be seen as distinct from this dark-skinned, frizzy-haired mass. French Muslims? That would be to deny that there are atheists and even a few Christians among them, and it says nothing about their history. *Harkis . . . ?* This is the only name left to them, even though the actual harkis—those who served as auxiliaries in the French army units known as *harkas*, working on renewable fixed-term paramilitary contracts, from what Naïma later understands—comprise only a small percentage of the thousands of people living in the camp. They rub shoulders with *moghaznis* who worked for the SAS (Special Administrative Section) and the SAU (Urban Administrative Section), with members of the GMS (Mobile Security Groups), veterans of the GMPR (Mobile Rural Police Groups), colloquially referred to as "Jean-Pierres," members of the GAD (self-defense groups to whom the French army gave guns and grenades to protect their villages), the "Muslim auxiliaries" of the French administrations (qaids, qadis, amins, and rural police officers), elected local officials, minor civil servants, professional soldiers, the PIMs (military prisoners, members of the FLN under high surveillance who were forced to take part in attacks), marabouts, *zaouïa* chiefs . . . And to that disparate band of men must be added the families who came with them, wives, children, elderly relatives. All of these people are lumped together by the term "harki."

Is a baker's son a baker?

Is a hairdresser who changes professions still a hairdresser?

Is someone who sells clothes a tailor, simply because the two professions are similar?

The camp is a makeshift city, hastily erected over the ruins of the previous one. Hardly have the new barracks been built than they are inadequate. Every day—or rather every night, since the shipments are done in secret—the camp grows still bigger, fed by the continual flow of covered trucks arriving straight from Marseilles, or coming from the Larzac camp, where numbers are being reduced to avoid a humanitarian disaster. By autumn, the inhabitants of this fragile emergency city, peopled by the lost, number almost ten thousand inhabitants, making it the second largest in the département, just behind Perpignan.

Hamid and his family walk along a narrow lane lined with tents with flaps that twitch to reveal curious, weary faces. The eyes peer, linger, assessing their features, gauging the size of the packages Ali is carrying under his arm. Irritated by this wall of peering eyes, Hamid and Dalila stick out their tongues. A frightened Kader whimpers and clings to Yema's skirts. Before long, they will be no different: they, too, will watch the stream of new arrivals, expecting to see a familiar figure or hoping that someone's luggage contains one of the many commodities lacking here.

When a soldier shows them the tent where they can "settle in" (his voice falters and cracks as he says these words), Ali replies:

"*Merci, monsieur.*"

At Rivesaltes, it is impossible to forget the war they have fled. Everything here is a reminder. The formalities of the camp, the bleakness, the partitions, all suggest army life. While, officially, the families are "in transit," they are deprived of their freedom of movement. "All comings and goings are subject to a certain degree of scrutiny, and permission to leave the camp can be authorized only for the most serious purposes," Pompidou remarked in a memorandum. But nothing that Ali manages to stammer in his halting French to an officer is considered "serious." The miming he uses to fill the gaps in his grasp of the language undermines his efforts. And so he is forced to stay at the Rivesaltes camp, attempting to adjust to the new life imposed on him, attempting to give his family the impression of a strong man when in fact he is no longer in control of anything, not even the smallest details of their day-to-day routine.

Every morning, as the flag is raised to the accompaniment of a wheezy, badly played bugle, they stand in the cold and watch as the Tricolour inches up the metal pole. Mealtimes are announced by a siren blasted through loudspeakers mounted on poles. Clutching billycans, hordes of people with nothing else to do immediately emerge from tents, from shacks of cardboard and corrugated iron that afford little protection (especially against the wind, the unrelenting wind that gets inside their heads, the *tramontane*—whose name fascinates Hamid as much as the wind irritates him). Clothes are regularly distributed, tons of rags tipped out onto a tarpaulin on the ground in order to clothe the thousands of shivering souls surprised by the cold and the mud.

The children band together into gangs in the alleyways and measure themselves against the barbed-wire fence that encircles the camp. Hamid comes to just above the fourth wire. Kader barely reaches the third. During the day, they can sometimes be heard laughing, or seen darting between the shacks like a flock of wild birds, but as the light fades and the sky gutters out, the sounds of Rivesaltes abruptly change.

Nights in the camp are a theater of screams and shadows. It is as though invisible ogres are prowling the alleyways, creeping into tents, squeezing throats with huge hands blackened with blood and gunpowder, crushing chests and rib cages with their enormous palms, kissing the children's faces with their gaping mouths filled with rotting teeth and the stench of death. The time has long since passed when there was but a single, common ogre called Sétif. Now every child has a personal ogre, a compact ogre that boarded the ship with them and comes out at night. Shrill wails go up along the line of tents, then come the mothers' voices crooning lullabies, the neighbors carping and calling for silence, the whispers muffled by the thick canvas.

Although the nocturnal ogres are born of memory, they feed the fears of the present and of the future. When those called harkis, for want of a better name, ask why they are held here, when they might see the rest of France, they are told it is for their own good, that they are still being hunted by the FLN and need protection. They spend their nights trembling at the thought of their throats cut soundlessly, one by one, to finish the job. Every morning they instinctively bring their hands up to their necks.

To keep the steadily increasing crowd of men and women occupied, they are offered lessons in Initiation into Metropolitan Life, during which the men are taught to abridge a message so they might send a telegram and the women are shown how to operate an electric sewing machine or an iron. As for the children, they are immediately taught traditional French songs—as though their lives depend on it. The purpose of these lessons, although the pupils do not yet realize it, has little to do with imparting knowledge but everything to do with a carefully orchestrated publicity campaign. The lessons are a means of showing the French that newcomers with their mysterious ways are being taken in hand so that they, in turn, will become good French citizens, capable of reading, writing, keeping house, and singing. And it is true that in the early days there are cameras trained on the camp. Television news bulletins chart the journeys of those who have come in their thousands. The cameramen like to take close-ups of their unusual faces: the blackness of their coarse hair, the tilt of their heads, the depth of their eyes, the gesture of the women as they tighten a white *haik* or colored kerchief around their heads, the gap-toothed children, the babes in arms, the bodies wearing clothes that are baggy or too tight since the Red Cross does not stock the correct size. Above all, the silence. The news cameras film the absence of a language with which to communicate. The silence of those who wait.

The website of the National Archives has reels of such footage, shot in Rivesaltes, in the Larzac camp, or in the forest settlements where the harkis were first sent to work. In one of the archive videos, which was reused in the documentary *Muslims of France; 1904 to the Present Day*, it is possible to make out Hamid—tiny, but immediately recognizable by the slight droop of his left eyelid—in a crowd of other children in a prefab hut, singing at the top of his lungs:

> *Sur le pont d'Avignon, on y danse, on y danse*
> *Sur le pont d'Avignon, on y danse tous en rond!*

Not one of the children is smiling, and the song has never seemed so sinister.

"Which do you like better?" a journalist asks the children he manages to stop. (Some refuse to talk, they are clearly afraid of him.) "France or Algeria?"

When a child answers, "France," he says: "You must be really happy, then." When they answer, "Algeria," he seems surprised. "Really, why?" And, seeing their uneasiness, he suggests:

"Because the weather is warmer?"

He asks adults the same questions, with only slightly less condescension. And the adults, with only slightly less fear and unease than the children, respond: "France." One man, his bushy black eyebrows knitted into a frown, bites his lip as though trying not to scream and says:

"Not Algeria. Never again. We need to forget Algeria."

Simply saying the words clearly requires a great effort on his part. His whole face is tensed. For these people to forget an entire country, they would have had to be offered a new one. But the doors to France were not thrown open for them, only the gates of a camp.

"I didn't imagine it would be like this."

It is a phrase that recurs often in the alleyways, though there is no camera to capture it. Men mournfully chew and spit the words; women exchange them with a sigh. Most of them, though they have never set foot outside the *bled*, had some notion, some image of what France would be like. And it was nothing like the Rivesaltes camp.

Seen from the village up on their mountain ridge, France was neither frightening nor alien. No one thought of it as a foreign country, still less *el ghorba*—exile. During the years of fighting, French government ministers had repeatedly insisted, *Algeria is France*, but, to most villagers, the phrase meant the reverse. *France is Algeria*, or at least an extension of Algeria where men had been going for almost a century, first the farmers who spent several months working in the fields before coming back to the village, later the factory workers. For Yema, it was a large city that was farther away than Algiers, farther even than Constantine, a place where Algerians met and mingled. Ali had been to France during the war in 1944. It had not left a lasting impression. "France is like going to the market," old Rafik used to say back in the village. "You spend a little more time there, but you come back with the goods."

"I didn't imagine it would be like this."

Why does nothing here resemble the stories they have heard? Did the old folks lie?

Every Wednesday, there is a curious ritual known as the "process of acquisition of nationality by declaration." Before a judge and his clerk, the residents of the camp are called on to respond to a single question:

"Do you wish to retain French nationality?"

Men who were willingly or forcibly enlisted, many of whom were unwittingly complicit in a war by any other name, were assured that they were French. Since then, they have lost Algeria. Now they are being asked whether—by chance—they wish to abandon France. They cannot see what that would leave them. Everyone needs a country.

"Do you wish to retain French nationality?"

"Yes, sir," Ali says.

"And you, madame?"

The judge looks at Yema, a tiny figure standing in front of the desk, but it is once again Ali who answers.

"In that case, sign here," the clerk says coldly.

Ali nervously wrings his hands. From the gloomy corridor where he was told to behave himself, Hamid sees his father bow his head in shame. He is watching him from behind, so it looks as though his head is slowly retracting into his broad shoulders, being swallowed up by quicksand.

"What's the matter?" the clerk asks.

"I don't know how to write, monsieur."

The clerk gestures for him to dip his finger in the inkwell and affix his fingerprint at the bottom of the document. From where he is standing, Hamid cannot hear what is said, but he can see lips moving, or at least those of the clerk and the judge, he cannot see those of his parents, only their backs. He can see only two of the four pairs of lips, but it is enough for him to know that neither of the men sitting behind the desk is telling a story, asking how his parents are, or even explaining that the situation is a little more delicate than they might think—bear in mind that, well, how can I put this, democracy, you might say, or human rights, or the postwar boom, are like a delicious cake, and when you see a photograph it looks like a huge cake, in a magazine, for example, or in a cookbook where it is set against a white background and there is no frame of reference to show how big it really is, but when you see it on a table surrounded by all the people who are entitled to a piece, and all the people who are potentially entitled to a piece, or would like a piece, the same cake—you have to admit—does not look so big, far from it, and dividing it into crumbs is a long and difficult task that, in spite of the effort involved, will leave no one's hunger satisfied, which is why we have to—I'm sure you understand—we have to ask whether maybe you wouldn't prefer an apple for dessert, or even to skip dessert and have coffee, if you see what I'm getting at. No, when Hamid recalls the scene, he is certain that neither the judge nor the clerk takes the time to indulge in metaphors, culinary or otherwise. (France is a vegetable patch exhausted by overcultivation, France is an ocean depleted by overfishing.) They move their lips only to issue terse instructions, and each time his father complies, pressing his inky finger on the proffered document, nodding his head, slowly walking away when told to do so. The little boy gets a glimpse of a different Ali, deferential, eager to please, but incapable of doing one of the first things France expects of him—signing his name. In spite of himself, Hamid trusts the polite if slightly condescending smiles of the judge and his clerk and thinks that learning to write cannot really be so difficult. He watches as Ali and Yema leave the office, holding up the inky forefingers they do not know what to do with, and there is something foolish in their bearing and in their glassy eyes.

Rivesaltes is constantly changing. Arrivals and departures. Addition, subtraction. Some people appear to leave the camp almost before they have arrived—mostly soldiers enlisted in the French army who can quickly be given a new posting, or civilians who have family already settled in France and have somewhere to go. For everyone else, the future is uncertain. The constant arrivals and departures are bewildering. As the weeks and months pass, the men and their families are organized, distributed, and redistributed, resulting in the separation of neighbors, friends, and relatives who happened upon each other here and whose chance grouping afforded considerable solace. They blame this new separation on their misfortune, on a cruel twist of fate or the working of a world about which they know little. Nobody tells them that the Department of French Muslims, attached to the newly established Ministry of Repatriation, has issued recommendations that "families from the same area should not be relocated to the same villages" since "in times of difficulty this invariably leads members of such families to join forces, and, in doing so, to present a greater resistance when it is necessary to implement disciplinary measures." Using a principle some trace back to ancient Greece and others to the Roman Senate, a principle made so popular by Machiavelli that it has become proverbial, the French authorities practice divide and rule. Some leave for the north, where the gaping mouths of the mines await them. For the most part these are strapping, broad-shouldered young men, muscle without the power of speech. Others are scattered like a galaxy of stars around the hundreds of settlement villages that the National Forestry Office has built to generate employment. Still others head west, to the département of Landes, where what awaits is not employment, but a camp outside Bias, where they will replace the French from Indochina, who are being relocated to a different camp in a game of musical chairs for those who lost the colonial wars. As they look at those climbing aboard the trucks, those still left behind in Rivesaltes quickly realize that they are destined to be sent to a place for the aged and the infirm, a place to die.

For many months, Ali and his family are not sent anywhere. Hamid feels ashamed that no one seems to want his father's brawn; those powerful arms that he has always seen as the epitome of brute strength dangle limp and useless by his sides. The family decides to rearrange the space they have been allocated in Rivesaltes while they wait for some semblance of order to return to their lives.

Using plastic bags stapled to wooden frames, they fashion a door that they place outside the opening of their tent. By the following day, other families have done the same. It becomes something of a trend in the camp—one day, there should be a study of how and why this is possible: that trends can appear even in conditions of abject poverty, that it is possible for a *particular* way of being poor to emerge that others strive to imitate. After the slightest gust of wind, families have to go and fetch their "door" a few alleys away. But still the families fashion doors, patiently, meticulously. The doors sustain the illusion that, within the tent, they can maintain a crowded privacy that is theirs alone, that they can choose whether to open or close their domain, that they are masters in their own homes.

Elsewhere in the camp is an area dubbed the "bachelors' district," into which Ali has forbidden his children to venture. It is a cruel name for the solitary men billeted there, since many are not, in fact, bachelors. Some are widowers, others were unable to bring their families with them. They were told: They can join you later, but right now you're the only one with papers. They were told: You go on ahead, once you're in France you can take care of the formalities. But afterward, chaos reigns on both sides of the Mediterranean: the French administration refuses to implement its policy of reuniting families, the Algerian government refuses to allow harki families to leave the country, revenge attacks see the houses of harkis in Algeria looted and hastily abandoned, letters are returned because no one now lives at the address—how can they find out where to write to, where their wives are hiding, whether some relative took her in . . . In this sector of the camp, there are constant brawls, fights that flare up for no reason other than to feel a fist slamming into another's face in the hope that it might dispel the tenuous but persistent feeling that this is a nightmare, fights that are not marked by anger or exultation. But Hamid likes to defy his father's orders, so he visits the area. He has taken a liking to one of the old men, whose face reminds him of the comic books brought by volunteers from Secours Catholique, or La Cimade, or the Red Cross—Hamid cannot tell the difference: with their gentle, teary smiles they all look alike. He leafs through the comics, his imagination providing the dialogue for the speech bubbles he cannot read. The Indian mystic who helps Mandrake the Magician in one of his adventures has the voice of the old man who lives in the bachelors' district. A voice whose sad, heavy tone keeps it in a lower register, a deep bass that is almost a growl. Even when the speech bubble is tiny, Hamid manages to squeeze in a whole story:

"One night," the old mystic says, "a group of mujahideen came knocking on my door. So I invited them in and I gave them food. And they asked me if I had a dog and I said yes. And they said: We must kill him. And at first I laughed: Why do you want to kill my dog? Do you think he's a spy for France? I can tell you he's not. They explained that every time their soldiers passed, the dogs barked and alerted the French. Not mine, I said, my dog is trained. Did you hear him bark when you came in? No, you didn't. We still have to kill him, the mujahid said. You can't, I said, I am a holy man, my religion and my brotherhood prohibit all forms of violence. And they said: Are you a marabout? And before I could answer, they dropped their plates and said they were sorry to have broken bread with me. I thought they were going to leave but they gave me a stick and said: Hit him. I said no. They got angry. They said: It's either you or the dog. I should have said: In that case, take me. I don't know what I was thinking. Maybe I thought we could work things out. If I'd known that what would come next was the camp, that tomorrow is the grave, I'd have said: Beat my own brains out; said: My brothers, let me die here, in my own country, among the members of my zaouïa, near my cheikh. I was afraid, I was a coward, I beat my dog. It's amazing how tough a dog is, it doesn't want to die, it clings to life. And when it's in pain, when it's dying, it howls like a completely different animal, it shrieks like an owl, and I could see in my dog's eyes that he couldn't understand why I was doing this to him. In the end, it was taking too long, so they cut his throat. They said: Next time, you obey orders or you'll be the one who gets it."

"I will avenge you," Mandrake promises with a swish of his silken cape, "and I will avenge your dog."

During one of the clothing handouts, Kader is given a bright red pair of pajamas that—for once—fit perfectly. The flannel one-piece buttons up the front from crotch to throat and has a woolly pom-pom at the back, over the coccyx. It is not so much a sleep suit as a fancy-dress costume for a rabbit or some imaginary animal.

From the moment he puts them on, the pajamas become Kader's favorite outfit, one that he refuses to take off. He wears the pajamas every day, and every night he hides them so that Yema does not toss them into the sad pile of clothes to be washed. Amid the drab military colors of the tents and the shacks, the crimson flash of Kader-the-red-rabbit is a burst of laughter. On his head he wears a hat so big it all but covers his eyes, but keeps his shaved head warm—all of the children were required to leave their hair at the gate of the camp out of concern for hygiene. On his feet, he wears rubber boots, a little too tight, that he cannot take off by himself. Thus attired, Kader runs around the camp. He leaps over puddles and mires, he turns sharply from one alleyway to the next, mimicking a screech of brakes (a rabbit with brakes?), his boots creak on the planks and timbers that offer the only dry walkways, which he pretends are bridges strung across a dizzying abyss. He kicks holes in cardboard boxes. Sometimes he stumbles, slips on one of the bridges, and plunges one boot into a puddle (watch out for the crocodile!), sending up a jet of brownish water that spatters his magical rabbit fur.

At the end of the day, he is a small red muddy ball that Yema struggles to wash using the basin. (There are no showers in the camp, but soon, soon, they are promised.) When she peels away his vermilion fur, the little boy struggles and squeals, he wants to be washed wearing it, he never takes it off.

"Kader, let Yema wash you," Hamid snaps.

He envies the boy the childish playfulness that war does not seem to have soured. A childhood full of magical rabbits and adventures filled with bridges. Dalila is not like that. She has just turned eight and is more like Hamid: war brought a darkness to their eyes that instantly chased childhood from their faces. Hamid dreams of going back—to him, the lost country is not Algeria but a carefree life. He tries to make the fantasy grow—he sees it as a pinkish soufflé—so that there will be no room left for the world outside. It is something he will almost succeed in doing when he meets Clarisse, but that is ten years away. For now, in the Rivesaltes camp, even comic book heroes like Mandrake the Magician and Tarzan cannot prevent the outside world from impinging on his fantasy.

In early November 1962, the trucks bring a new load of harkis, many of them wounded veterans. Among them is Yema's brother, Messaoud, his head swaddled in gray bandages. Hamid is the first to see beyond the wounds, to recognize the face he knew when they lived up in the mountains. He lets out a delighted whoop and jumps into his uncle's arms. Ali is next; he gives Messaoud a brief, manly hug. Yema takes all the time in the world. She gazes at him, caresses him, sobs into his shoulder, saying:

"You've grown so thin . . ."

"At least I'm in one piece," Messaoud says.

He briefly recounts how, in August, after leaving Yema and the children in Téfeschoun, he was captured by the FLN. Having spent two months in captivity, he managed to escape (like Mandrake the Magician! Hamid thinks excitedly).

"Actually, one of the guards let me escape," his uncle corrects himself.

"He said to me: You're to be executed tomorrow, but I'll be so tired by tonight that I think I might forget to lock the door . . . I ran away and I walked for two whole days. I was taken in by our cousins in Algiers."

What followed (boat, train, truck, camp) they know only too well. They do not even go over it, and this ellipsis in the journey that occurs in every conversation with a new arrival makes it seem as though Algiers and Rivesaltes are neighboring towns, as though the sea between them does not exist. Space is made for Messaoud in the already overcrowded tent so that he does not have to live in the bachelors' district, and the evening takes on a festive air. Ali and Yema are determined to share what little they have with him. They shower him with sweaters, with mismatched shoes, cans of sardines, sugar cubes . . . Messaoud laughs and pushes away each thing once, twice, before eventually accepting it. Even here, the unwritten laws of the village must be respected: a gift should not be refused. A recipient should simply consider what he may be able to give later. Gratitude creates a sense of obligation, which is a bond like any other, perhaps the only kind of bond that they can forge here.

"Tomorrow I'll tell you what you need to know to get by in the camp," Ali promises.

And with this simple statement, he recovers a little of the status of a patriarch, a public figure, a little of the confidence he had back in the bled. In Hamid's eyes, he seems to grow in the small space of the tent, to become once again a mountain man.

When the children have gone to bed, the adults drink the tea that Yema has made on the rickety stove, and their whispered conversations take on a mournful tone.

"I watched them burn the olive groves," Messaoud says.

He turns to check that the children are asleep (Hamid allows his eyelids to grow slack, to close in an imitation of sleep), then he shows them the scars on his wrists, scars from the crude barbed-wire handcuffs that dug into his flesh for weeks.

It is the newcomers, like Messaoud, who bring news of the bled, who put silent fears into words. They are like news bulletins to the camp inmates. The inhabitants of the alleys gather around a man as soon as they discover the name of the village or the town from which he hails.

"Do you know what happened to my brother Taleb?"

"What about Malika? You must know her, she had a small farm outside the village, just before the crossroads. Do you know what's become of her?"

"Is the house still standing?"

"Did they hurt my father?"

Sometimes there are healing answers:

"I saw him, he's fine."

Others elicit wails:

"They sent him to clear mines along the Tunisian border."

(This is one of the punishments the FLN reserved for traitors: clearing mines with their bare hands along borders booby-trapped by the French.)

Sometimes the questions only prompt further questions.

His body tensed from the tips of his toes to his fingers, Hamid tries to gain a few inches as he reaches for an apple, trying to grab his dessert before he is ousted from the line. If he creates a delay, someone will jostle past, elbow him out of the way, or simply lift him by the armpits and deposit him elsewhere, as though he were a child, which he is, but more especially as though his small size means that he cannot be starving, as though an empty stomach is not really empty in such a small body. He hates mealtimes, when he has to get not just enough food for himself, but enough to feed Kader and Dalila, since his mother has entrusted them to his care. He is the eldest, he is responsible for his siblings, he cannot fail. He stretches his hand half an inch, grazing the smooth skin of the apple with his fingertips. Unfortunately, rather than grasping the fruit, they merely push it farther away.

"Here, my son."

A dark-skinned man—practically a Negro, as Yema still says, since even half a century in France has not taught her to say the word *khel* (Black) without a disdainful pout—takes his hand, opens his fingers, and deposits the apple.

"Do you want another one?"

Behind the long distribution table, a young soldier objects: only one piece of fruit per person. The dark-skinned man shoots him a look that instantly reduces him to silence. The words catch in his throat before he even realizes he has stopped talking. The man picks up a second apple, and a third, without anyone objecting. He leads Hamid away a little, has him sit down on a patch of mangy grass.

"For as long as we let them think that what they are doing is charity, we won't get anywhere," he says to the boy, or to himself, or to some imaginary figure Hamid can only guess at. "They are just giving us our *due*. They need to understand that. And so do we, we need to realize that."

Hamid bites into the apple, nodding.

"How old are you, boy?"

"I was born in the season of the broad beans," Hamid says.

It is the last time he will give this answer. The French authorities refuse to accept this formulation. Soon he will give his age as a number, calculated from a date of birth for which there is no evidence, no proof that it was not simply made up when he needed papers in order to be able to escape. And yet, though the date may be false, the age it confers on him is more reassuring to roumis than the truthful answer that they cannot understand (the year of *what*?), one that Hamid quickly learns not to give.

He munches happily on one of the apples, although the flesh is soft and beginning to spoil. He quickly reaches the core, and rotates the central column of the fruit in his mouth to remove the smallest pieces of flesh, performing a painstaking dissection with teeth and tongue, spitting out only the seeds and the stringy casing. The man watches, smiling.

Hamid does not understand why Yema suddenly hurls herself at him, screaming, why she grabs him by the ear and drags him back into the tent, slaps him in a moment of anger and fear, apologizes, slaps him again, kisses him, shakes him. Stunned, he makes no protest while his head, his arms, his legs flail in every direction. Dalila lets out a series of long, piecing wails, a single note she struggles to hit, then holds for a long time—the shrill internal alarm of body-as-machine; when she screams like this, she is no longer a child, she is a creature intent on survival.

"Do you know who that man is?" Yema asks Hamid, still shaking him. "Do you?"

Hamid struggles, protests, all he knows is that the man gave him an apple; he realizes that the apples he took for his brother and sister have fallen out of his pocket. He wants to go and look for them, but he cannot break free of his mother's grip.

"You're never to go near that man again! Do you hear me? Never!"

"Why not?" the boy snivels.

"Because he's not a man. He's a panther. A demon."

"What did he do?"

"Everything. All the things that only exist in nightmares. He was a member of the Commando Georges."

Three years earlier, the man whom Yema called a demon was standing in line with his brothers-in-arms to receive a medal from the hands of Charles de Gaulle. It was on national television. He was told that he was a hero. He was told that France needed him, he was told that France would soon be victorious, all the things that are said in time of war, any war, to those at risk of being blown to pieces. Over time, the words should have come to seem hackneyed, but the demon still believed in them. He shook hands enthusiastically. He was tacitly thanked for having tortured and killed, because, despite its motto, "Eradicating poverty," the Commando Georges mostly eradicated humans, something at which it excelled.

Today, the man who was briefly a hero on the nightly news in 1959 is behind barbed wire. It goes without saying that Algeria despises him, it goes without saying that France has forgotten him—he has been expecting this ever since his unit was disbanded in March. What he finds surprising is that, even here, others fear him, shun him, scorn him. There is a hierarchy of criminality in Rivesaltes that excludes him from community life. Here in the camp, as in Algeria, the end of the war means that there are accounts to be rendered, scores to be settled, and the lack of anything to do in Rivesaltes means that the harkis have time to do just that. Most people in the camp deny having been traitors, having done anything wrong, they dream of a chance to explain themselves to Algeria, to present a defense. *I didn't kill anyone, I didn't torture anyone, what exactly am I being accused of?* Sometimes, among themselves, they play out these imaginary tribunals. If you were Ben Bella, someone says, I'd explain everything. And even if the person they are speaking to already knows the story, they tell it again, they risk condemnation and hope for a pardon—which almost always comes. For those who were members of Commando Georges, however, to speak would only expose them to condemnation, so they do not dare. The evil they have done is too public for them to defend it or to plead mitigating circumstances— the evil they have done has been seen on television; they have dug their own graves. Despite awarding members of Commando Georges thirty medals and almost four hundred mentions in dispatches, the French government refused to allow them to be repatriated. Those who did not manage to secretly make the crossing have paid dearly—even in the camp, everyone knows that. The FLN captured many of those who stayed. Lieutenant Georges Grillot, the leader of the unit, was boiled alive in the middle of summer by the people. It was like a scene from an old Tarzan movie, from *Tintin in the Congo* or the first *Star Wars* trilogy: a hog-tied man in a huge cauldron set atop a crackling fire while around him the natives howl with savage glee. Condemned as a traitor among traitors, a criminal among criminals, the lieutenant deserved the most painful death imaginable. The decision as to how to execute him was, I imagine, a difficult one, since none of the countless dead could come from the grave to offer a comparative study. I don't know who suggested that he be boiled—it is original.

"We don't talk to people like that," Yema snaps at Hamid and the other children. "We don't go near them. Is that clear?"

The French people who live around the camp do not understand why the men are constantly fighting. Some are quick to assume it is an Arab trait, others talk about the disruption caused by being uprooted. Still others blame the shortages in this makeshift town. They do not seem to understand that the people penned up together do not share a common cause. To Yema, a member of the Commando Georges is a monster. To Ali, a Messali Hadj supporter is a fascist proponent of Arabization. To the separatist rivals of the FLN and to the old French-speaking elites, Ali is nothing but a selfish peasant, and so on. Hostilities are exacerbated by the enforced proximity of life in the camp. Insults quickly fly, as do punches. Stabbings are rarer, although from time to time a glittering blade will suddenly appear—from who knows where—in a fist.

The administration find that the mass distribution of tranquilizers offers a fast and effective response to the angry outbreaks that flare up in the walkways. When drugs prove insufficient, they are reinforced by a stay in a psychiatric hospital. Hamid becomes accustomed to the presence of large white ambulances parked between the shacks. Sometimes he sees medics lead out strange creatures with vacant eyes, drooping faces, and bandaged heads that look (vaguely, only vaguely) like men. These are the men who screamed too loudly, who fought back when the doctors tried to treat them. For the sake of peace, law, and order, they are dispatched, using drugs or a lobotomy, to a land of mist and fog. They will never return.

Separated as they are from earth and sky by only a thin layer of canvas, families in the Rivesaltes camp find their lives controlled and ravaged by the weather. In late autumn, torrential rains lash the camp. Rain hammers against the canvas with a thunderous roar. On the night of the first downpour, Hamid does not recognize the sound; to his anxious ears the drumming rain sounds like machine gun fire.

"Let them empty their magazines," Mandrake the Magician reassures the boy as he drifts off to sleep. "They can never kill me."

The following day, he begins to distinguish between the different notes made by the rain. Against the various stacks of canvas sheets and corrugated iron, a whole symphony of raindrops hammers, echoes, bursts into semiquavers, becomes the rumbling roll of a bass drum. After long nights spent listening, he learns to recognize them, he can picture them as they clatter above his head. Almost unconsciously, the boy slides his hands from under the blankets and, with unseen gestures in the darkness, he becomes the impromptu conductor of the tempest.

One morning, he wakes to discover that it has rained so hard that a wave of mud has swept away four tents. He is sorry to have slept through the deluge. He would have liked to watch the wave engulf the fragile buildings, to see the drab Rivesaltes camp transformed by a catalycsm straight out of the pages of a comic book.

The winter of '62 is particularly cold. For the first time, many of the Algerians from the south and the plains witness snow. They are astonished to see the pale, opalescent sky shatter into snowflakes that drift over the camp. Some of the children sob fearfully when snow lands on their skin. Others laugh and open their mouths, gather snow in their tiny fists and compact it into balls of ice they suck for ages. Hours later, they suffer stomach cramps. Hamid is too familiar with snow to be surprised by its sudden appearance, and, besides, his mother needs him.

While the other children are running around, Hamid is helping place the family's billycans around the tent. When they are full, Yema melts the snow on a gas stove and stores the water in jerricans. The pipes in the communal toilets have frozen and there have been repeated water shortages in the camp.

Ali creates a makeshift coal-fired stove out of an old tin can. It smells of burning paint and makes the children cough. But it is better than the one next door; no one knows what chemicals were in the canisters Younes used to make a stove, but it stinks to high heaven whenever he tries to warm himself up. Men set up braziers outdoors, so they can carry on talking beyond the cramped, overcrowded confines of their homes.

Seen from above, the comings and goings in the alleyways are surprising. People move from one fire to another, short shivering hops they make while rubbing their hands, panting for breath, small gulps of icy air that barely make it into their throats. It is much too cold to move any distance from a fire. Movement is limited, punctuated by frequent stops. The inhabitants of the camp develop a social life based on necessity and discomfort: they do not look at who is standing around the fire. When the cold bites hard, they join the nearest circle and find themselves rubbing shoulders with strangers whom they greet only after sliding in next to them. To reach the shower block, which has finally been built on the far side of the camp, Hamid has to make at least three stops. Before he leaves the tent, he calculates the location of every brazier along his route: the one outside Ahmed's tent, the one outside the infirmary, the one next to the trash dump . . . He sets off at a run. The misty white clouds of his breath are so dense they seem to slow his breathing.

Before long, hurrying feet have turned the snow to an icy mud that clings to the soles of their shoes.

To protect them from cold, Yema lines the children's clothes and shoes with sheets of newspaper. She rips up everything she can lay her hands on, and it is possible that among the broadsheets she cannot understand there are some of the copies of *Le Travailleur Catalan* that Naïma will later read during her research, whose editorials urge the Rivesaltes council to get rid of "mercenaries" and the "scum" living in the camp. Words are of little interest to Yema; it is the paper that counts. When thickly layered, the local newspapers not only protect against the bitter cold, but provide the perfect armor to allow the children to jab each other in the stomach without doubling up in pain. Their battles resound with the dull thud of pummeled paper and raucous cries of vengeance. To ensure that his copies of Mandrake the Magician do not suffer the shameful fate of lining his disgusting rubber boots, Hamid carefully hides his comic books between several layers of tarpaulin in the roof of the tent. Although the magician becomes somewhat damp and warped, he survives the winter.

In spring, as the freezing temperatures subside, the space enjoyed by the inhabitants increases. Hamid can once more wander aimlessly without having to stop, Kader-the-magic-rabbit reappears, and suddenly there he is, bounding, leaping, hopping. One by one, people remove the layers of tarpaulins that accumulated over the winter and gave the impression of living inside an onion made entirely of skins.

In the tepid sun and the drying mud, the camp once more looks like a camp. By the time Hamid and his family are finally sent to Jouques, to a newly opened forest settlement, the boy is stunned to realize that they have spent eight months in Rivesaltes. But for the changes in the weather, it feels as though he has only lived a single day, endlessly repeated.

"You'll like it there," a gendarme tells him as they are about to set off, "it looks a bit like Kabylia."

The photocopies Naïma managed to find of letters written by the préfet of Bouches-du-Rhône refer to the Jouques camp as the "cité of Logis d'Anne," named in honor of a shepherdess turned Catholic saint about whom she can find no information. Built in 1948 near the banks of the Durance close to Road RD96 for the workers digging the Provence Canal, it was home to the harkis from 1963, and—although described as temporary accommodation—was not closed until 1988.

Nothing remains of it today. When she comes back from Algeria, Naïma will want to visit the place where her father spent almost two years of his life; she will drive along the A51, she will cross the Mirabeau Bridge, built in 1845 over medieval footings, that still stands next to the cliffs of Canteperdrix, flanked by twin-towered porticos that rise in a series of pale stone vaulted arches, as beautiful and strange as a set abandoned by Peter Jackson when he finished filming *Lord of the Rings*. Of the site where the village once stood, she will see only a dark green gate, locked with a chain, behind which—for reasons she does not understand—there is a huge boulder spattered with fluorescent pink paint. The whole site is surrounded by a chain-link fence. She tries to see what is behind the fence, but the road that winds away from the gate leads into the pines and the undergrowth. To the right of the gate, between the main road and the fence, is a memorial erected in 2012. Rising almost fifteen feet and faced with marble, it represents—I read somewhere—a Moorish doorway, or something like that. From a distance, Naïma thinks it looks like a giant keyhole flanked by a pair of horns.

Pulling herself up using the gatepost, she scales the fence. The metal clinks and sways under her clumsy attempts. Once on the other side, she sets off in a straight line, walking deeper and deeper into the pine forest. There is nothing. The road trails off. Naïma keeps going through the tall grasses, climbs a steep slope dotted with scrawny trees. If she leans down and pushes aside the brambles and the thorns, she finds vestiges of the settlement's former life: a doll's arm, gray with age, bottled gas regulators, drains that sink into the ground—signs of civilization in a place that nature has reclaimed.

At the top of the hill, she turns and gazes at the River Durance meandering slowly, shimmering glints of light that turn blue between the pale rocks. She hears the steady chirrup of the cicadas perched on trunks, invisible lutes the color of tree bark.

This view, these sounds, surely, despite the years, this is something she shares with Hamid, with Ali.

They live in cabins constructed fifteen years earlier of wood, fiber cement, and asbestos. Those housed nearest to the road are entitled to single-story yellow-and-white prefabs that look like something between a bungalow and a toolshed. Ten occupants is not uncommon. Ali and Yema are lucky: they live with their three children and with Uncle Messaoud. Six people is not so bad. Even so, every morning the place smells of children's farts and the sweat of sleep.

In the little overcrowded houses, before they realize that the liquid washes away colors, the women scrub every square inch with "bleach," something the social workers have told them is a *must* when it comes to hygiene. The woodwork, the enamel, the windows, the plasterwork, everything is scoured with bleach. Yema and her neighbors even discuss using this magical liquid to wash fruit and vegetables. The only thing that stops them is the fear that "bleach" may contain alcohol.

Yema wants her tiny home to be spotless, to be the cleanest of all the houses. It is her way of rejecting poverty, of replacing one pecking order with another where she might still find a place at the top. In her house, there will be no dust balls, no fly specks, no food hidden beneath a table leg, no dark smears on the smooth Formica surfaces. Each square inch she polishes becomes hers.

"She'll wear down the walls," Ali tells the neighbors.

But the rules of the village, laid down by the French authorities, and in the first line of the document that was read to them when they moved in, states that cleanliness is one of the preconditions of their stay, so Ali lets Yema scrub the house. The rules begin:

> *The inhabitants of the forest settlements have greatly benefited from the solicitude of the government.*
>
> *They benefit not only from a salary afforded by regular, guaranteed employment, but from free housing that many who live in substandard housing might envy them.*
>
> *In addition, qualified personnel are on hand to provide all necessary care, to facilitate the process, and to provide them with ongoing support.*
>
> *These benefits come with certain responsibilities and proscriptions.*

What follows is a relatively brief list that can be summarized even more briefly: they must be healthy, sober, and compliant. *Nonobservance of any of the aforementioned rules will result in the immediate eviction of the offender. The house thus vacated will be allocated to another returnee and his family.* There are warmer ways to phrase a welcome pack, as even the "qualified personnel" who read the text are aware.

It is decided that the children in Logis d'Anne will be divided up among the three neighboring primary schools, Jouques, Peyrolles, and Saint-Paul-lez-Durance—though only after they complete their fourth year of primary school. Within the camp, a nursery school and remedial school are set up, both requiring a unique teaching system: How can they teach anything to children who know nothing? There are doubts about their intellectual abilities. Doubts about their ability to adapt. Doubts about their honesty. The staff do not seem to be teaching so much as conducting a first contact with a hitherto unknown species of aliens. Classes begin haltingly.

"My name is Hamid, I'm from Kabylia."

"My name is Mokhtar, I'm from Kabylia."

"My name is Kader, I'm from French Algeria."

"No, Kader," the teacher nervously interrupts. "French Algeria doesn't exist anymore."

A moment of bewilderment leaves the children dumbstruck. The statement chimes with some of the things their parents have said: Don't think about Algeria, forget Algeria. And to them, it is as though their country has been physically erased. How can you make a country disappear? they wonder.

"When I was at school," Hamid will say much later, perhaps fifty years later, and some years after Naïma's journey, "I pinned a world map to my bedroom wall to help me study. One night, I came home and Algeria had been burned with a lit cigarette end. There was a round burn hole."

"Who did it?" Naïma will ask.

"Your grandfather, I assume . . ."

Very quickly, the teacher in charge of the remedial class gives up trying to teach the pupils to read and write. It is too complicated. There are significant age gaps between them all. Conversations take place in bleeding hunks of three broken languages: Arabic, Kabyle, French. What hope is there of getting results from ؈ people and ✗ people, using a method that was devised to teach French children who have been lulled by the language since infancy? He decides to get them to draw flowers. He decides to teach them rugby.

"You can't blame the man," Hamid will say to Naïma. "He kept us busy and cheerful, I think. And that was no easy task. Every time an airplane flew overhead, the little kids pissed themselves and big kids like me threw themselves on the ground. Every time we heard a footstep, we stopped listening and watched the door. To get us to smile, to teach us to play again, was really something. But it wasn't really school. Or, at least, not French school."

And this is what Hamid has been dreaming of ever since he arrived in the country: mingling with the French. At this point, he is not demanding equality or justice. He just wants to see Annie again, and he knows that will not happen on the benches of this third-rate school. He misses the little girl's laugh; he is convinced that if he could hear it again, he would return to his childhood. He reassures himself with the thought that, from what he has seen since he arrived, France is so small that he can cross it in no time.

On the far side of the Mediterranean, in Palestro, which has lost its name, the grocer's and the upstairs apartment that Claude's family hastily abandoned have been looted a number of times. The most recent looters even took the taps. After months of creaking boards and gathering dust, the shop is finally allocated to the young revolutionary fighter Youcef Tadjer. His smile as he steps through the door reveals his gapteeth, the teeth of a child born up on the mountain, of a street hawker that independence has transformed into a respectable shopkeeper. He kicks an empty can, sends it rolling under the counter, and, his arms in the air, his mouth wide, he silently roars: "GOAAAAAAAAAAAAL!"

Like all of the men in Logis d'Anne, Ali works for the National Forestry Office. The house and the job come together: Siamese twins. No one asked them to fashion or to dream what their life in France might be. They will live among the trees; they will work among the trees. Years later, when Ali thinks back to the village, close-up images of tree bark come to mind, brown and red islands separated by deep cracks and crevices teeming invisibly with bustling life, a microcosm of plate tectonics, if he knew the term. He chops the trunks whose bark peels like sunburned skin, he clears the pathways, cuts back the roadside hedgerows. The small groups of laborers rarely encounter locals when they venture out. It is the ideal occupation to ensure that the presence of the harkis does not rile the surrounding villages. Their job is to keep the forest clear and so prevent wildfires from spreading.

One day, Ali and three other men from the camp are caught in a shower of caterpillars as they are felling a tree. The silken nests of *Thaumetopoea*

pityocampa are ripped open by the tumbling branches, disgorging caterpillars, little furry monsters whose tiny barbed hairs sting the men's
skin and irritate their eyes. Hours later, their arms, necks, chests, stom-
achs, and faces are covered with red blotches. The prickly hairs move
along rivulets of sweat, covering every inch of their bodies. The four
men scratch and swear, their eyelids swell, and the narrow slit is blurred
with tears. When they get back to the Logis d'Anne, the women stare in
astonishment at the red, swollen men twitching frantically. Bashir, the
eldest, says grimly:

"We were ambushed. There was nothing we could do. We were
outnumbered."

They all burst out laughing and, though he laughs with them, Ali is
shocked that they find a joke about war amusing. He can sense he is not
the only one who is surprised: the men and women laugh louder and
longer than Bashir's feeble quip warrants. They are laughing because
they can laugh. They are laughing at the realization that, in their minds,
the war has retreated, like the waves at low tide, and on the rediscovered beach they can use the vocabulary of horror without giving in to
panic.

"Take your clothes off outside," Yema tells her husband. "I won't
have you bringing itchy clothes into the house."

All the men do likewise, crowding between the cabins to remove
their work clothes, revealing a rash that completely covers their bodies.
When the women bring them soap and basins of water, they wash like
children, letting out happy squeals, chasing and splashing each other.

Eventually the women persuade them to sit down on the ground
so they can brush their hair with big sweeping movements, and, with
the help of tape, remove the last barbed hairs. Others prefer to gently
scrape the skin using a knife. Bashir's wife gently pours milk over the
orange swelling on his skin. The place looks like an improvised open-air
beauty salon, and the women laugh as the men wince at the slightest
pain, sucking air and saliva through gritted teeth each time their wives
rip off a piece of tape.

After this ambush, the threat of caterpillars means that the men
have to be covered from head to foot. It is like being in a hammam;

they sweat inside their overalls, gloves, knee-length socks, and goggles. Seeing them in this garb, the children think they look like low-budget astronauts or grubby scientists stumbling toward some secret laboratory. Ali develops such a loathing for these caterpillars that he begins to imagine them slithering over the walls of the house, the edge of the bed, sometimes even his plate. The slightest rustle of leaves makes him start in a way that sets his children howling with laughter.

Hamid thinks he remembers that it was here, shortly after they moved in, that they celebrated their first Eid el-Kabir since leaving Algeria. He still has photographs from the camp, bleating sheep dragged along by men and women who are cursing the stubborn beasts. Overcome by fear, the sheep shit foul-smelling droppings all over the lanes in between the houses. Ali squandered a significant portion of his salary on his animal. He could not help himself: he wanted a bigger, fatter sheep than his neighbors'. He led the huge, noisy animal home, beaming as though it were a wild beast he had hunted and captured. Hamid hates the sounds of the sheep rubbing its body against the walls of the house, of its stubborn head butting the stake to which it is tethered, and this is not—as his parents assume—because he is sensitive to the animal's fate. He is simply furious that it cost so much money. During their early years in France, his parents behave as though, one day, they will regain their former status. They no longer talk about Algeria, about de Gaulle's ruses, about French military prowess, but still they dream of riches, of what they call a "full house"—an expression that comes from the village, and one that already makes them seem old. Hamid listens, and sometimes he, too, believes in the halcyon days that will soon return, but mostly he resents his parents for this outward show of affluence that he and his siblings will later have to pay off. He does not care about the size of the sheep; he would have preferred a new pair of shoes.

When Eid comes, the smell of blood rises from behind every house. The houses are so tightly packed and the number of sacrifices so great that the chorus of bleats is deafening. For the first time, Hamid comes to loathe Eid. For days on end, dishes are brought from one house to another. Hamid refuses to take even a single bite of meat.

When his daughters later ask when he stopped believing in God, he will talk a little pompously about his teenage years, about Marx, but even as he is making a cogent argument, older images will resurface in his mind: the blood, the wool, the holes in his shoes.

A few months after they arrive at the Logis d'Anne, Yema once again falls pregnant. She is as frightened as she was the first time, as though she might have forgotten how to give birth. She thinks about the dark-eyed boy buried up in the mountains. She wonders whether anyone in the family still remembers him, goes to sit for a moment by the tiny headstone carved with a reclining crescent that forms a radiant smile.

"You seem so sad," a neighbor says. "It can't be good for the child. You need to get a grip on yourself."

Yema silently apologizes to the child nestling in her womb. She wants the child, of course, that is not the question; she is happy that he exists, that he is already growing, but she wishes she did not have to let him out, wishes she could keep him inside, protect him. She whispers gently to the child, tells him not to come too soon, tells him she is happy to carry him for years if that is what he wants.

The social worker comes to see her to talk about the future of this baby that is "so special," she says, because he will be born in France. A woman interprets for the social worker, but even in translation her words are not like any language that Yema understands.

"Of course," the social worker whispers, "we have to give this baby every possible chance. Make sure that he feels at home in this country, and especially that French people—sorry, other French people—consider him one of their own."

"That's fine by me," Yema says, "but in that case you'll have to teach me how to make sure he's born with straight hair."

The interpreter glares at her.

"For example," the social worker says, "it's important that you give him a name that reflects your desire to integrate. Have you thought about names?"

"Omar," Yema says, "or Leila."

They are the names of Hamza's and Djamel's firstborn children. Those who stayed behind. Yema thinks that, in adopting their names, it is almost as though she is bringing them back to her, as though she is rebuilding the family against the odds.

"Why not Mireille?" the social worker says, pretending she has not heard. "Or Guy?"

"Because you can't block out the sun with a sieve," Yema says.

This time the interpreter giggles. But that evening, Ali sides with the social worker.

"She knows better than we do," he says with the weary resignation of someone who does not understand anything.

The child will be named Claude and, later, when Naïma tries to draw up a list of her aunts and uncles, it will feel as though she is playing a game of odd man out, as she used to in her puzzle books: Hamid, Kader, Dalila, Claude, Hacène, Karima, Mohamed, Fatiha, Salim.

A curious sort of life develops, for Ali's family and for hundreds of other inhabitants of the Logis d'Anne. A life that is pleasant in spring and in the early days of autumn, a furnace in summer, a long shiver in winter. A life hidden by the pine trees.

"Apart from the employment office," says a man in a video shot ten years later, "I don't know who even knows that we exist."

They keep to themselves, and at the end of the working day the men meet up and play dominoes in front of one of the houses. They carry the table outside, bring chairs and stools, the younger men sit on the front steps. In the evening air, as the scents of the food and pine resin mingle, there comes the sharp clack of dominoes, points being tallied as fast as trades at the stock exchange, the laughter of men making fun of those who are unlucky or unskilled, the angry shouts of bad losers, and the barking of dogs that circle the table hoping someone will toss them food, puzzled at all this attention being lavished on black-and-white tiles that do not smell of anything.

From time to time, one of the men will announce that he has invited a few villagers, or the foreman, and that this time his guests are definitely coming. Empty chairs are set out, but the men do not wait. They start their game. Everyone knows that no one is coming. It is as though no one else can find the path that leads to this spot.

And yet, when the elections roll around, people seem to remember their existence. The local politicians charter buses to take them to polling stations. Mayors, *députés*, and senators come to the camp to shake hands and make promises. If those living in the Logis d'Anne could eat promises, they would all have round moon-faces like the one Ali had in his fairy-tale mountain village.

During these visits, the elected officials and their assistants thank them—always in the same words—for their unfailing love of France, and they respond only with faint smiles. It is a curious thing: to have the right to exist, they must present themselves as having been patriots from the first, champions of the Tricolour who have never entertained a doubt. And yet, many of the men in the camp were members of the FLN, they worked as lookouts or as tax collectors for them, they fought with them in the mountains. There is even a former political education officer—the men, with astonished affection, nickname him "Mao." But now that they are here, now that they have fled, they no longer dare to admit it, because when they arrived they were told it was precisely because of their *unfailing* love of France that they had the right to a home, a job. Their presence here seems so precarious, so dependent on the goodwill of others, that they may even imagine that they would be shipped back if they were to admit that France, well, you know, it's fine, I suppose. They are silent about the complexities of their individual stories; they meekly nod and accept a simplistic version that ends up becoming part of them, burying their memories, so that, when their children try to dig down, they will find that everything has rotted away beneath this armor of unfailing love, and the old men will say they no longer remember.

Sometimes Ali can no longer bear the camp or the forest, and he goes walking through the countryside for hours in search of something else. More often than not, when he comes to a neighboring town he simply sits on the edge of the fountain and watches. From time to time, he goes into a tobacconist's and buys a pack of Gitanes—in Algeria, the government is preparing to nationalize "all assets, rights, and obligations of factories processing tobacco and making matches"—or cookies for the children from the grocer's; the Decree of May 22, 1964, nationalized the flour mills, and the factories making semolina, noodles, and couscous. After each conversation with a shopkeeper, however brief, he feels an overwhelming relief: he is not invisible. In the camp, he sometimes wonders. He has a recurring dream: One of his children is ill and urgently needs to be taken to the hospital. Ali walks down as far as the road and tries to hail a car. In the middle of the ribbon of tarmac, he waves his arms at cars hurtling toward him, but they do not slow down. They drive straight through his hazy body without even registering his presence. Hamid knows this, because he has heard Ali whispering about his nightmare to Yema in the middle of the night, in the darkness of this tiny room they all share. The story that follows he knows because it is one of the few that his father used to tell after they left Jouques, when neighbors asked him about the settlement village. This makes it one of the only stories Hamid passed to his daughters, and one that Naïma will share in turn, though she did not hear it from her grandfather's lips, and cannot be certain that it actually happened.

In early July '63, Ali walks into a bar and sits at the counter. It is the first time he has been in the establishment and the place is rather filthy, even the light seems grubby, but the gloom and the grime are pleasant after the blinding sunshine that has been beating down on him all the way there.

"A beer," he says to the owner.

At least this is what he thinks he says, but to the ears of the landlord, it sounds like "uhbir," and this irritates him. This wound inflicted on the words is painful to him, as though it were inflicted on his ear, hacking at his eardrum. He shrugs nervously and does not answer. When Ali later tells this story, he claims that the man decided not to serve him the moment he saw him come through the door, but it may not be quite so simple. The bar owner is struggling against the wave of anger he is feeling. He wishes he could master it, wishes that he did not feel it at all.

"A beer," Ali says again, without raising his voice.

The pain in Ali's eyes tips the landlord over the edge. They are the eyes of a victim, which casts the bar owner as a murderer even before he has done anything, it strips him of his free will. Eyes that look as though they contain all the suffering in the world.

And the fucking medals he is wearing on his chest. The bar owner cannot believe it: this guy put on his military medals. These are his defense against the French, a free pass given him by the Mother Republic.

"I don't serve fucking *crouilles* here."

The words escape through gritted teeth. Until that very second, he did not know what he was going to say. But now that the words are out, he cannot take them back. So, instead, he stands firm and says it louder.

"Didn't you hear me? I don't serve fucking crouilles here."

Back in the village, Ali would have punched him, and everyone would have thought he was in the right. Here, he feels his towering frame shrivel on the stool, his strength drain away, his blood turn to water, and his legs go limp like a pair of nylons hanging on a line, redundant and grotesque, barely resembling legs.

"Fine," he mutters, "no beer, I'll just rest here for a bit."

"Are you soft in the head or what? Get out! Get out of here this minute!"

"No, no," Ali says softly. "I'm not leaving."

"I-not-leaf, I-not-leaf!" the man behind the counter roars, his face now flushed brick-red. "Where the fuck do you think you are? You think this is your home? Dirty fucking bougnoule! I'm calling the police."

As he takes the few steps to the telephone, he is inwardly praying that Ali will be reasonable and leave, or at least make a move toward the exit. He does not want to pick up the phone. He does not want to have to justify his anger to a third party. It is hard enough for him to persuade himself that he is in the right.

Still Ali does not move. His huge bougnoule frame is hunched over on the stool. He has moved his hands; he is not touching the counter. He does not want to be in the wrong, does not want to cause trouble. He simply does not want to be thrown out. He is convinced that he is in the right. He waits for the local gendarme, retreating into a silence he hopes is dignified, while, on the other side of the bar, the bar owner does the same. No one can know what it felt like for Ali to wait for the police officer to come through the door of the bar. In Hamid's version the gendarme sounds like the bumbling Sergeant Garcia in *Zorro*, with a mustache and a belt, while Naïma pictures him like one of the old-school riot police, all flak jackets and shields.

After the situation has been explained to him, the officer sniffs and scratches the bridge of his nose. Then he stands facing Ali, who still sits motionless on his stool. Ali attempts a smile to show that he means no harm, but the officer does not see the smile; he looks at the floor. Is he trying to avoid making eye contact with Ali? Is he ashamed? Is he about to hit him? Ali regrets having stayed. Then the policeman looks up and says:

"The guy's got ten pounds of metal pinned to his chest and you're refusing to serve him?"

The bar owner blushes but persists in his surly attitude. It is too late now for him to back down. Often, those we think are bastards are simply too scared to ask if they can start over.

"How do I know those medals are even his?"

The policeman shrugs. The argument is so feeble that it does not merit a response.

"Where did you get this?" he asks, pointing to one of the medals.

"Monte Cassino," Ali says in a whisper.

It is a name he has not uttered in almost twenty years. He thought that he would never say it again. Then, suddenly, the officer pounds his fist on the bar.

"Right!" he bellows at the bar owner, who cannot suppress a flinch. "Give us two beers, right now!"

Then, turning to Ali, he says:

"I fought there, too."

And before the mountain man can react, the officer throws his arms around him.

"Monte Cassino, shit . . ."

For a brief moment, the café-bar in Jouques is friendly and welcoming, it feels like he is back in the association, protected by shared memories. He and the policeman drink their beers, smiling, so emotional that they feel as if they might cry. But as they leave the bar, Ali sees the owner give him a poisonous look and knows he will never come back. With a parting glance, he says goodbye to the barstools, to the counter that smells of metal and grease, the Tour de France posters on the walls, the memories of Monte Cassino.

Monte Cassino

Naïma has often said, "My grandfather did Monte Cassino," with just the right note of dread in her voice, although she is unsure about the phrase. It might be more accurate to say that Monte Cassino did him; "it did him over," as they say. To Naïma, the name refers not only to a specific place, but to a five-month period in 1944 and to a handful of memories that stayed with her grandfather all his life, buried deep within his consciousness, a corpse so weighed down with rocks that it would never rise to the surface.

Monte Cassino. A hill rising to a mere seventeen thousand feet, it overlooks the road from Rome to Naples, in the district of Lazio—the very place where Aeneas ended up after his many wanderings—atop which, in the sixth century, Benedict of Nursia founded an abbey.

Monte Cassino. A key position on the Gustav Line that the Allies needed to break through in order to continue the advance into northern Italy. Naïma has watched a number of documentaries in an attempt to understand the military movements that made up this battle (in reality, a series of four battles). She still does not understand.

Monte Cassino. Bombs dropping from hundreds of planes, falling like a downpour, and, below, the buildings of an abbey that has been razed many times through the centuries crumbling once more, sending up a rain of dust and rubble.

Monte Cassino, a sheer rock face that has been stripped of all vegetation so that it is easier to scan, so that it can offer no hiding place, no shelter.

Monte Cassino, or the battle of the stick insects, spindly figures clinging to the rock doing their utmost to appear invisible. Once they have begun the ascent, the soldiers cannot move, eat, or drink anything hot, because the smallest wisp of steam will alert the Germans on the hill to their presence. Submachine gun fire and a hail of mortars.

Monte Cassino, the river at the foot of the hill where the Allies are trying to construct pontoon bridges. Often, it flows red.

Monte Cassino. Whimpers in six or seven different languages. And yet they are all the same: *I'm scared, I'm scared. I don't want to die.*

In the four battles for Monte Cassino, soldiers from the colonies were sent to the front lines: the French sent Moroccans, Tunisians, and Algerians; the British sent Indians and New Zealanders. They provided the cannon fodder, the dead and the wounded that meant the Allies could afford to lose fifty thousand men on a rocky outcrop.

I think the opening scenes of *Days of Glory* are supposed to depict the battle of Monte Cassino. We witness the perilous attack on a mountain. But since this is only the start of the film, they can't sacrifice the characters with whom the viewers have only just begun to empathize, so it is a battle that goes horribly wrong and yet none of the good guys die. I imagine Monte Cassino as being more like Terrence Malick's film *The Thin Red Line*: a long, dreary act of butchery in a place no topographical map can render imaginable.

Among the soldiers from the Army of Africa clinging to the side of Monte Cassino are not only Ali, but also Ben Bella and Boudiaf, the first and fourth heads of state of the future independent Algeria. They never met. If they had, perhaps this story would have been very different.

When the temperature brutally plummets, Yema scrabbles around to find more rugs and lays them over one another on the floor of the cabin to block out the cold damp air rising from the concrete. Ali nails blankets to the walls. Inside this cave, this woolen womb, the mattresses are arranged around the stove, the children are comfortable. In the speech bubbles of his comic books, Hamid can recognize the letters *A* and *H*—the first letters of his name—in other words, he can decode the characters' cries of pain and laughter.

AAAAAAAAAAH!
HAHAHA!

The other speech bubbles have too many words, too much punctuation, to interest him. He continues to make up stories, which he tells to Dalila, to Kader, and to Claude, who babbles as he lies next to them on a cushion, a recent addition to the family, by turns a guinea pig, a chore, or a baby.

"The olive groves are mine," the wicked corporal says as he marches into Tarzan's jungle. "And all your monkeys can't protect you, because I've got airplanes and bombs." But the corporal didn't know that Tarzan had a secret plan . . .

*   *   *

Before night falls, the children roam the hills in search of firewood and, in spite of their parents' instructions, they cannot help but gather the twigs according to aesthetic principles, bringing back only the branches they find attractive, those that are twisted and gnarled, the forked sticks and the tridents, the branches hung with cones that look like Christmas trees. Their clothes become smeared with pine resin, which gives off a lingering scent; smelling of the forest, their hair tangled with leaves, their arms filled with twigs, the children look like wood nymphs. By the time darkness descends over the Logis d'Anne, branches and pine needles are crackling in the stove tended by Ali, Yema, or Messaoud, meaning that all activities in the house are subject to the need of the fire that, again and again, seems on the point of dying, only to be revived by the adults with a nervous or a confident thrust of a poker into its smoldering heart.

For the first time, Hamid celebrates his birthday—the day that accords with his official French birth date—in the camp classroom, encouraged by the teacher, who assures them this is what French children do. It takes them a long time to learn the prescribed song, after which the teacher opens a packet of *petit-beurre* cookies.

That night, to add to the festivities, Cherine, their neighbors' daughter, throws her arms around the boy's neck—it is more of a dive than a hug—and plants a kiss on the corner of his lips, perhaps because she has been taught that this is what French people do, or because this is what children do when they discover that a body can long for another body. Although he apologizes to Annie, whom he still intends to marry (he is blessed with Yema's quiet determination, a virtue that Naïma has not inherited *at all*), Hamid enjoys the fierce, furtive pressure of Cherine's lips against his own. He closes his eyes and stands there, smiling, for a long time after the girl has run away. He is intently aware of his body as the sensations of the kiss course through him, certain that he is branded by this sign of love as by a red-hot poker.

When Naïma asks her family to tell her about the Jouques camp where they spent almost two years, no two answers are the same. Her father, Hamid, talks about the humiliation of being penned. Kader remembers a cave where he used to play, and it is as though the whole of the Logis d'Anne fit inside this cave. Yema talks about the despised social worker. Dalila apologetically says that it was heaven, I'm sorry, but yes, for a kid, it was paradise, the trees, the light, the river.

As for Ali, he can no longer say anything. He was long dead by the time Naïma began to ask questions.

"Paradise?"

"I would have happily stayed there. When we first moved here, I cried and cried, I couldn't stop."

As she says this, Dalila waves the back of her hand toward the cramped kitchen of the public housing apartment and the miserable little playground visible through the window.

They pack up their belongings. They have time. This is not like the head-long rush to flee Algeria when they took only what they could carry (a few wads of banknotes, three silver bracelets set with coral and enamel, a watch, some clothes and shoes, medals wrapped in the folds of a Ber-ber *chèche*, the keys to the old cob-walled house and those to the shed where the machines lie dormant, a photograph of Ali in uniform—the only one that exists, taken in 1944—and a prayer rug). Nor is it like their departure from the Rivesaltes camp, when the fact that they had acquired nothing new since their arrival made preparations ridiculously short and simple. No, this time there are things to be wrapped in news-paper, things to be folded and put into piles: a few plates, a tea service, Hamid's comic books, Ali's new jacket, a herbarium made by Dalila, Claude's Moses basket. This time, they will stow a suitcase in the trunk of the bus and set off to a real house, to the home-for-keeps that is wait-ing for them in a place that is still strange and unfamiliar.

"Where is it?" they asked when the village supervisor brought the news.

"Flers."

No one had ever heard of the town. The supervisor wrote the name on a piece of paper. One of the men recognizes the last letter: it is the let-ter that is at the end of the word "Paris." Somehow, this reassures them. They feel as though they are headed for a miniature Paris, as though the s at the end of the name is a guarantee of stylishness and progress.

Hamid is skeptical about this theory—from leafing through the comic books he has come to realize that letters have no meaning in themselves. They recur in ways that seem random, complicated, absurd—at least to him—and those that look similar can designate contradictory things. The *s* is no more a guarantee of something than *a*, *h*, or *z*—only the illiterate think of letters in French as totems.

Through the back window of the bus, he and Yema energetically wave at Messaoud, who stands by the roadside, as still and upright as the trees with which his receding figure merges.

The local authority has built a number of low-rise blocks for the harki families in an area on the outskirts of the town that, some years later, will boast the pride of the region: the largest Leclerc hypermarket in France. But for now, there is nothing but gray and white blocks of apartments, each of them identical. It is a landscape made up of harsh geometric lines marked out with a ruler: the corners and the outlines of the buildings, the grooves between ceiling tiles, the regular lengths of linoleum on the floors, the oblique handrails, cold to the touch, that encase the stairwell. It is a scheme of parallels and perpendiculars repeated endlessly throughout the buildings. The close-up views of the apartment that the children get by pressing their faces against a wall are comprised entirely of straight lines, as are the views of the neighborhood from the hill behind the apartment blocks. There is no rest, no respite from this world of right angles, except perhaps on the patch of ground between the buildings where the children's playground traces on the ground an oval that is startling in its gentleness. The various pieces of equipment have not been properly bolted down, so the slides and climbing frames rock under the concerted assault of hordes of swarming children.

When the bus drops off the families from the Logis d'Anne in their new neighborhood, it is raining. The ground is muddy, still bare from the building work. It is deadly dull. The problem with this overcast sky, as Hamid will quickly realize, is that you can see everything. There is no need to squint against a blinding glare, no dazzling light to make the surrounding details hazy. The landscapes of Kabylia and Provence were a procession of silhouettes: shadowy trees, mountain ridges, and houses half-eroded by sunlight. They were composed of blotches of color that danced on eyelids it was hard to keep open. And the river snaking down the mountain from the village to Palestro made the mountainside glimmer with blinding flashes as though bandits were using shards of mirror to send signals. People think that light has the power to reveal, to expose every raw detail. In fact, at its most luminous, it is as concealing as shadow, if not more so. But the gray sky of Normandy hides nothing. It is neutral. It allows every building to exist, every pavement, every man walking from the bus to his future apartment, every speck of mud stain that already smears the stairwells and the inside of the apartments because there are no doormats anywhere. The sky is low and yet distant. It does not merge with the landscape. It is simply there, in the background, like the abstract backdrop in front of which children pose for school photographs. It is as though the sky were looking elsewhere.

The family stops in front of Building B: no one dares open the heavy door. Little fingers press against the glass, leaving greasy prints. Yema holds her breath, she is disappointed by the gray, disconcerted by the right angles, troubled by the lock at the entrance to this building, which has to be turned twice. Ali forces a smile and, giving Hamid a gentle shove forward, says:

"We'll be happy here. We'll live just like the French. There'll be no difference between them and us anymore. You'll see."

When they find the bath, the children whoop for joy. They immediately straddle the porcelain rim and slide to the bottom in a heap, Hamid, Kader, Dalila, in a tangle of arms and legs. They beg Yema to turn on the tap, pull off their clothes, their elbows and knees knocking against the cold white walls and the gleaming brass tap, and then watch in an almost religious silence as the hot water fills the bath.

Three children stand motionless, holding their breath, at this miniature tide controlled by their mother.

"I want to live in the bath," Kader whispers.

* * *

As she unpacks the suitcases in their new apartment, Yema allows herself for the first time to think of all the things she left behind: the tabzimt she was given when her first son was born, the khalkhal she was given when she married, her dresses and her smocks . . . Tears well in her eyes as she gazes at the shelves that are still empty when she has placed the contents of the suitcases here and there.

On the days after the move, she repositions, several times, the few objects they brought from Algeria. She sets them on the table, stows them in a cupboard, lines them up at the foot of the bed. She cannot find a place to put what little she has. It looks out of place in the new apartment. It becomes alien, unfamiliar. Those things that, back in the village, were cherished objects to be used every day have become curios here. The Formica furniture, the wallpaper, the pale yellow linoleum create a display case for these objects that isolates them and sets them apart, like a cabinet in a museum. Like the Indian or African artifacts displayed behind plate glass in the Musée du Quai Branly, with a brief explanatory note intended to bring viewers closer to the object that actually keeps them at a distance by marking it out as a curiosity, something that—rightly—needs to be *explained*, like those things so casually used in everyday life (spoons, knives, embroidered textiles) that a museum presents with astonished wonderment, Yema's scant treasures will never blend in with the cookie-cutter housing, whether because they reproach the right angles for their lack of warmth or because the apartment, in turn, calls out their tawdriness, their futility. And so these things that Ali and his wife chose to take with them while leaving thousands of others behind, these things they could not bear to imagine falling into the hands of the FLN or of looters because they meant more to them, because they defined who they were, these things that they believed they would forever cherish as talismans that embodied Algeria and their former life, they gradually forsake, they push them to the back of a drawer, embarrassed and angry, until only the children take them out from time to time, to admire them, to play with them as though they are parts of a spaceship that crash-landed on their planet from some remote and alien civilization.

Despite their best intentions, Ali and Yema do not live in the apartment; they occupy it.

The salespeople who swoop down on them the day after their arrival know what they are doing. They know that these people will buy anything: they know nothing. Better yet: They are afraid of their ignorance. Afraid of these unfamiliar fixtures and fittings. Afraid of being relegated to the margins of society for not knowing how to furnish their apartments.

"My parents were determined that I wouldn't be ashamed of our home if a French kid came around to play after school," Hamid will say later. "That's why they bought the horrible three-piece suite. The nylon duvets. And the paintings. There were so many things they didn't understand. First, French kids would never come back to play with us. Most of them were not allowed to venture into the urban development zone. I was the one who went to their houses—if I was lucky enough to be invited. Second, eight people and all this furniture in a space that size meant there was no place to play even if we had managed to bring anyone over. And third, despite their efforts, I was ashamed. Maybe ashamed *because* of their efforts."

Even after the apartments have been fully furnished, the parade of sales reps carries on: there are the insurance salesmen (in France, an apartment needs to be insured, as does a life), the people selling cars (all French families have one), appliances (you can't just sweep the floor, you need a vacuum cleaner), encyclopedias (they'll impress the neighbors, and they're good for the children's education), the travel agents (Morocco is a lot like Algeria, it would do you good), and still others who pester them with smiles, brochures, promises, and loans.

During the day, while Ali is at work and Hamid is at school, a different type of rep calls, usually women who know that the husbands are not home. Most are Algerian women, "city types," which, to Yema, means that they don't wear the veil, that they wear makeup or even smoke cigarettes. In their sample cases, they carry striped fabrics and silver jewelry of the sort she had back in the village. Yema talks to them about all the things she left behind. The women shake their heads sympathetically and suggest that, maybe, if she were to buy a few beautiful things, it might help her to "heal." At first she politely refuses: she does not want to spend Ali's money without his knowledge. But one day, one of the women comes back and says:

"I know that you're not vain. But when I got these, I immediately thought of you. These are very special jewels. They come from Mecca."

And so Yema goes into the bedroom and takes a few bills from the little nightstand. After all, if they come from Mecca, they can't be tacky. She gives this woman half her husband's salary for a cheap copper bracelet covered with a thin sheet of silver leaf that quickly flakes off, which leaves black and green marks on her wrists.

The French book lying in front of Hamid is intended for toddlers, as is clear from the drawings of puppies with huge eyes, kittens playing with balls of wool, flowers opening to the sun, and loving mothers baking cakes for chubby-cheeked children. The teacher checked out the early readers book from the library for him.

Hamid tries to set aside his shame (he is eleven years old: he likes knights, superheroes, duels with swords, bare-handed fights with lions; he no longer believes in the soft pink world of children's books) and physically wrestles with the French. What he calls "French," and sees as a treasure chest twinkling at him from the steep peaks of a mountain or the depths of shark-infested water, is in fact learning to write the alphabet. Hamid has never parsed his native tongue into words, let alone characters—to him, it is an unchanging, indissoluble substance made up of the murmurings of countless generations. Consequently, the series of lines and circles, of dots and loops he is staring at on the page looks to him like an army on the march, about to invade his brain, where the tip of the *t* and the tail of the *p* will bury themselves in the soft matter waiting inside his skull. Yet in spite of his fear, in spite of his shame, in spite of his headaches, there is a magic to Hamid's slow process of learning. The first sentences he manages to decipher, the phrases he slowly articulates, whose every syllable is weighted with equal importance, the beauty of the sound that parts the lips like a physical object too large to come from his mouth, these phrases will remain with him for the rest of his days.

Auntie pats the mat.

Papa puffs a pipe.

A mirror image: more than forty years later, Naïma will have the same experience with a book in Arabic; she will force herself to choke back her pride, screaming that she is twenty-five years old, so that she can slowly repeat:

Yamchi alrajul. The man is walking.

Yatir alousfour. The bird is flying.

Jak yaqra alkitab. Jacques is reading the book.

She is an adult struggling to pronounce the language her father did not pass down to her.

Hamid is seated at the back of the class with two other boys from Pont-Féron, so that the teacher can come and talk to them without disturbing the other pupils. He stares at the backs of his classmates' heads, the straight lines of hair at the napes of their necks running parallel to their shirt collars. On sunny days, he discovers the cartilage in ears is translucent. There was a discussion about his case when he first went to school: Was it better to put him in a class corresponding to his age or his academic ability? The debate could have been impassioned, a disquisition about the great and noble purpose of education drifting into political considerations, causing the headmaster and the teacher to clash, but this was not the case. Hamid couldn't fit behind one of the tiny kindergarten desks, so he was admitted to fifth grade.

Since neither he nor the other boys from the cité can read the textbook, the teacher gives the other pupils pages to work on, then sits down next to them and patiently explains. From time to time, mocking faces in the front row turn to stare and the three newcomers are made to feel humiliated for the additional support they need. This is why, every evening, when school is finished and forgotten until morning for his classmates, Hamid spends his time struggling to read a children's book, trying to unlock the secrets of the alphabet. He often dreams that he can read. He sees the looks of surprise on his classmates' faces as he fluently reads aloud a poem by Jacques Prévert or a biography of Joan of Arc. The following morning, when he realizes the miracle has not come to pass, and he stumbles over every word, he feels rage burning in his belly.

Hamid does not yet know how lucky he is; it is something he will realize later. His is one of the last families to arrive in Pont-Féron, and the school closest to the cité was already filled with the children of harkis who came on the first buses. There, just as in the camp in Jouques, the teachers have given up on the idea of trying to teach a syllabus that these illiterate children cannot understand. But here, in a school near the center of town, there are too many "real" French children—and therefore too many parents with expectations, if not demands—for the teacher to abdicate his academic responsibility. And because there are only three children from Pont-Féron, the teacher is not daunted. In fact, he considers them brave: not one of them gives up. When the school bell rings, he watches them set off to apartment blocks he has never seen, their books under their arms, and he sometimes cannot help but think that, in their shoes, he would not come back the next day.

Late in April, in preparation for Labor Day on May 1, the teacher instructs his pupils to spend the following Thursday with one of their parents and bring in an essay about the world of work. At playtime, everyone is talking about this particular piece of homework. A barrage of questions flies around the playground, like a ball being passed from hand to hand: What does your father do? What does yours do? (Few mothers have jobs, and even when they do, no one seems particularly interested in the nature of their work.)

"What does yours do?"

"He works in a factory," Hamid says.

"Which one?"

"The one in Messei."

"Yes, but what does he do? What does he make?"

As the boy expected, under the weight of this magic word, Ali finally gives way.

After waking at dawn, Hamid clambers into the car that will take them to Messei, an exercise book in one hand and a carefully sharpened pencil tucked behind one ear. He takes his role as a reporter very seriously. In the metal cabin, he recognizes a number of men from the neighborhood, among them Big Ahmed. He is the idol of the children; he has the looks of a former movie star. The sleeves of his dark green overalls are rolled up to his shoulders, revealing the brawny, somewhat wizened arms of an old tough-guy actor. Ahmed has a face that is not easily forgotten. If he were famous, he would be recognized everywhere he went. People would say: Oh yeah . . . that nose, that jaw, those eyebrows, it's the guy from . . . They would rack their brains for the name of the movie where he plays the gruff, illiterate bodyguard who befriends and protects the brilliant politician, or the old cowboy whose wife has been dead for years but who still has a photograph of her in his log cabin, one that no one is allowed to mention. Among themselves, the kids of Pont-Féron call him John Wine—the forgotten, alcoholic twin of the famous American actor.

"So what do you do?" Hamid asks, standing behind him.

With a disarming smile, Ahmed snaps:

"Me, I burn myself. Him over there, he cuts himself. And that guy over there, he breaks his back."

Hamid pretends to take notes. He writes "me" and "him," and for the rest of the words, the ones that are too complicated, he simply scrawls a series of abstract lines and circles.

He is impressed by the intricate dance of men and machines, by the precision of the workers' gestures, which ensure that parts always appear exactly where the machines require them. To him, their economy of movement (One, two, three! One, two, three!) is something they should be proud of. But as the morning drags on, he begins to get bored. He finds the division of labor within the factory tedious. He does not realize that the workers are not allowed to move from place to place, to change their roles as they please, to follow a single piece through the various processes it requires. After a few hours in the building, the noise

"He doesn't make things. He works in the factory."

Hamid does not understand the question. His father, like most of his neighbors, is a factory worker, and from what Hamid has heard them say, there seems to be only one. They call it the Factory. The one that brought them here to work. It has never occurred to Hamid that the factory *makes* anything, since Ali always comes home empty-handed. In his mind, the factory mostly produces smoke, work injuries, cramps, and the smell of burning that his father trails from room to room even after he has showered.

According to the official documents, the factory was called Luchaire, was founded in 1936, and was described as "the metal processing division of the Luchaire group, specializing in sheet metal, extrusion, and large-scale production for the automotive industry, the Métro, and the aeronautics and the atomic industries." The factory is responsible for "assembly work, fabrication, and surface processing." In reality, it is a vast building that consumes thousands of tons of steel per year, which are digested by gigantic presses, smelting furnaces with blazing mouths, and hundreds of welders who wear astronaut-style masks. The factory employs almost two thousand men, of whom the majority—those with no qualifications—come from Pont-Féron and nearby cités.

"So can I come with you on Thursday, then?"

"No," Ali says.

He does not want his son to see him at work, at the bottom of the social ladder, a nobody, a loser. Sometimes he misses the thin barbed hairs the processionary caterpillars left along the tree trunks. At least he was out in the open air, and the work he did seemed like an achievement he could be proud of . . .

"But it's for *school*, Baba."

Hamid stresses this word, which, he knows, is like an open sesame in his family. It is school that, after several years that seem interminable to the children, is supposed to provide them with a better life, a comfortable social status, and an apartment away from the cité. School has replaced the olive groves as the font of all hope. School is a static continuation of their journey, it will lift them out of poverty.

and the heat make him groggy. He finds it hard to think, the presses and the steel pound inside his head, crushing or melting every sentence as it forms.

During the lunch break, he eats from his father's plate and is surprised to notice that Ali treats his colleagues and his superiors with a deference Hamid has never seen at home. He casually refers to the Arabs as "brother" and "uncle," the French as "sir." Hamid feels awkward in the presence of this softened version of Ali. He wants to say, These men aren't your brothers or your uncles and the ones over there are no more "sir" than you are. Later, as he grows up, he will refine this message that he never dared to address to his father: Why do you humiliate yourself? Politeness should be reciprocal. Friendship is a two-way street. Don't smile or show deference to people who won't even give us the time of day.

He leaves the factory with a dull, nauseating headache that renders him unable to talk. In the car, sharing the back seat with four other workers, he presses his face against the window and tries to fall asleep. He closes his eyes, but cannot doze off: the roar of the factory is still going around and around in his head, chasing away the dreamlike images. Big Ahmed smiles at him:

"You see, son, the problem with this kind of work is that, when you leave, you don't have the strength to do anything except maybe drag yourself to the nearest bar."

"*Khlas!*" the man next to him cuts him off.

"Have you no shame?" Ali says. "Don't you know he's only a boy?"

Under his breath, Ahmed mutters that of course he knows, that it is not as though he were offering the boy a drink. He just wanted to explain why men like him drink—they are not really to blame, but the work is so hard and so numbing that it turns them into donkeys, into dumb animals.

"Why can't you get a different job?" Hamid regularly asks his father after this visit to the factory. "Couldn't you get a job you like?"

"Are you crazy? Or maybe you think I'm crazy?" Ali says.

It is one of his stock phrases, and it is not a nice one. "Are you crazy?" is bad enough, but "Maybe you think I'm crazy?" is worse. It is as though he were asking, Do you want me to beat myself? Do you want me to whip myself? The only thing the children can do is apologize.

"I don't think I want to work when I grow up," Hamid whispers to his mother over dinner.

"Well, you should have been born into a different family, then. In this family, we don't have a choice."

When a letter arrives, it is Hamid who reads it and translates it for his parents. He still stumbles over long words, but it is getting easier. He is proud: *Hear ye! Hear ye! The herald is about to proclaim the news.*

In mid-May, in an envelope addressed to his father, he discovers an invitation to the end-of-year school fete. All the parents are invited, and the letter explains with labored enthusiasm that there will be an afternoon concert and a cake sale. Hamid pictures Ali and Yema, lost among the parents of Étienne, Maxim, Guy, Philippe, busy eating slices of sponge cake from paper plates while discussing the inevitable reelection of de Gaulle . . . (On his one visit to the theater, years later, Hamid will burst out laughing at the aristocrats in white linen suits in *The Cherry Orchard*, struck by the realization that Chekhov's [or the director's] vision is much like his childhood nightmare inspired by the provincial bourgeoisie.) He does not want his parents to come to the school fete: They won't know how to act; they'll talk too loudly, or they won't talk at all. They would not enjoy it, would not understand it. They probably wouldn't want to go anyway, he thinks—they'd be intimidated. But to make sure they do not come, when Ali asks what is in the letter, Hamid says:

"It's just a note from the school saying they've bought a new painting."

His heart is beating fast and hard inside his chest, as though it is an empty space in which the organ can wildly ricochet around.

"That's good, that's good," Ali says, oblivious to the hammering of his son's heart.

He goes out of the room, leaving the boy working on his bed. Helpless and ashamed, Hamid watches him go. It was too easy to lie to him. Two phrases collide inside his head, moving at high speed:

He could be taken in by anybody.

He doesn't know anything.

He considers running after him, telling him that he lied. But what difference would it make? Ali would not be able to check the contents of a letter himself. He is entirely dependent on his son. Does he know this, Hamid wonders, is he conscious of this? In his head, sympathy vies with disgust and contempt, and he realizes, more forcibly than at any point in his life, that he is growing up too quickly. He rips the letter into shreds so tiny that nothing is legible.

Ali is sitting on the sofa, unaware of his son's turmoil. He is listening to the radio, news bulletins and songs spluttered in a language he only half understands. Sometimes, when there is no one else in the room, he giggles and mimics the voice of the announcer, which he finds affected and effeminate.

Although he is not happy in France, at least here he experiences something he has not felt since the summer of 1962: a sense of stability, an opportunity to think about the long term. Order has been restored, an order he hopes will last, and who cares if he has ended up at the bottom of the ladder: at least the long term allows him to imagine that his children might have a future. In order not to disturb this new order, he tries to forget about himself. It is a painful and complicated process, sometimes his pride and his anger well up. But for the most part, he repeats the same gestures, performs the same actions, speaks less and less. He occupies the tiny space allocated to him.

In June 1965, the French voices on the radio, those that, to Ali, sound like a parody, give way to familiar voices. From the news bulletins, partially translated by Hamid, he learns of the coup d'état led by Houari Boumédiène in Algeria. On the various floors of the building, doors open and men call to one another: *Hey, have you heard?* Those with no radio step out and sit in the stairwell, shouting to one another to find out what is happening. In Ali's living room, they convene a djema'a like those they used to hold in the village, or at the association; a gathering of men, their ears glued to the radio and the vociferous debates they barely understand, discuss the news and tear into one another about politics. There is no longer a village hierarchy to dictate whose turn it is to speak: voices are raised; men shout one another down. When a man has something to say, he scratches his stubbly beard with short, square nails, and Hamid, if he happens to be in the living room, wonders what it is about the skin of these men that makes such an unpleasant noise.

In spite of the commotion, Ali and his neighbors are agreed on one thing: to have waged such a war only to end up with neither stability nor democracy is a terrible waste. In the days that follow, when they meet up outside or in one another's homes, they all parrot this same opinion, vehemently condemning the terrible waste. And yet they cannot help but feel a flicker of pleasure: they have so few opportunities to think that they are better off in France. It is something they routinely say ("Well, we're better off here"), as though it is self-evident, and yet, silently, continually, the lost country returns to haunt them and, although they think they are starting to forget, they are simply repainting it in the colors of nostalgia.

The radio does not tell them everything that is going on in Algeria during the coup d'état. It does not mention, for example, that France takes advantage of the change in leadership to broker an agreement with the new government to release harki veterans still being held prisoner. The Red Cross estimates that there are nearly 13,500—Naïma read the report published at the time—but the humanitarian delegation has no choice but to put forward a figure without being able to visit most of the detention centers. Once released from prison, these men will leave the country and they, too, will "return" to a country they have never known. The agreement—decided in secret—also prohibits the harkis from returning to Algeria. The radio makes no mention of this, only talks about the reprisals carried out by Boumédiène's supporters on those of Ben Bella.

*   *   *

It is during this summer that Ali receives the first telephone call from the far shores of the Mediterranean, the first scraps of news from the mountain village that did not cease to exist when they left. Deep down, this is what he wanted: that the country he had left behind would disappear—and it is a feeling Naïma understands, Naïma, who, forty years later, when she bumps into a man she once lived with briefly, realizes that she wishes he had disappeared in a puff of smoke the moment she left his arms, instead of leading a parallel life not far away, about which she knows nothing. But there is nothing they can do, she or Ali.

In 2009, the young man Naïma once loved, this survivor of their shared past, races down the steps of the Métro, heading for his new apartment.

In 1965, the devastation described by Ali's brother simply proves that Algeria has survived, battered and bruised, in the hands of others.

Among the sputter and crackling of the telephone line, Ali exchanges a few stilted words with Hamza. He no longer knows how to talk to his brother, he spends much of his time clearing his throat. Hamza, for his part, sighs and gives long, low whistles between sentences: Djamel is still missing, no one knows anything about his whereabouts. But only last week they released some guys, so, who knows, maybe . . . Insh'Allah. That's right. Insh'Allah. Otherwise, everything is fine. Everyone is alive, thank God. Poor but alive.

"They took almost everything from us," Hamza tells his brother.

But he offers no details, he does not specify the extent of the land seizures. Yema thinks he is afraid Ali will demand that he give back what remains, what is rightfully his as the eldest son. She mutters under her breath that Hamza is a liar and a con man. She is constantly interrupting the brothers' conversation to ask after women in the village whose names mean nothing to Ali. Hamid also skulks around his father, but does not dare ask for news of his cousin Omar, or of Youcef in particular. Ali shoos his wife and son away. Hamid can only listen to him ask questions about things that he does not care about: How many olive trees are left on the mountain? Have you had trouble with fruit flies this season? Did Hamza remember to check that the leaves on the lower branches are not marked with circles that look like peacock's eyes? If it has been raining, it's essential to check because that's a bastard of a fungus. And if there's the slightest doubt when he checks the leaves, he should treat the tree with copper. What is the fruit like? How was the last pressing? Did he allow Rachida to do the winter canning? (He shouldn't, she always uses too much vinegar.)

Ali does not have time to glean all the information he wants: Hamza quickly hangs up, but not before pointing out how expensive the phone call has been and asking his brother to call him next time. There is a telephone in the village, in the offices of the FLN.

As he listens to the uninterrupted tone from the receiver, Ali can almost smell the olive pulp releasing the last drops of oil into the round belly of the filtering baskets.

At the end of the school year, Hamid is allowed to join the eleven-year-olds in sixth grade. At the bottom of a school report that neither Ali nor Yema can read, the teacher has written: *In the past year, Hamid has made remarkable progress.* He underlines the "remarkable" twice. When the last bell before summer break rings, he asks the boy to stay behind, and offers him a few books, picked at random from the classroom shelves. He had not planned to do this, had not anticipated that he would feel so emotional. He piles books into the boy's folded arms: a pictorial dictionary, an atlas, and two Famous Five adventures.

The first pages of the dictionary are filled with the flags of the world, yellow, blue, green, white, and red, with a few black lines here and there. Because the book was published in the 1950s, there is no Algerian flag between Albania and Andorra. Hamid spends the beginning of the break dreaming of the countries hidden behind the eagles, the palms, and the stars. He also forces himself to learn five new words every day, even if he has little opportunity to use them—abeam (adv.), ablation (n.), ablution (n.), abolition (n.), abominable (adj.). He carefully copies them onto the blank pages in one of his exercise books and, thanks to the pale blue lines, can survey at a glance his ever-increasing French vocabulary.

In August, Ali manages to borrow a car for his two weeks' annual leave. The whole family squeezes inside: the parents and their five children, the eldest of whom fight for the window seats. And, almost buried beneath the suitcases and the plastic bags Yema has filled with food, they head for the south. Sitting in the back seat, squashed against the window by Dalila, who blames Kader, who blames Claude, Hamid reads *Five Get into Trouble*. He looks up only when his father asks him to read the road signs. He has the same seriousness when reading about the adventures of George, Julian, and Timmy as he did when first poring over the pages of a textbook. It is something that Naïma will later find fascinating: the attentiveness and the respect Hamid accords any text he is reading, even if it is just a column in a local paper or an advertisement.

They cover six hundred miles in a single burst (they cannot afford a hotel), with Ali driving for a day and a night to the shrieking, the laughter, and the tears of the children. The floor of the car is littered with crumbs and sticky with fruit juice. Hamid puts down *Five Get into Trouble* only when they stop for a picnic or he has to go to the toilet. He spends every other minute reading, blind to scenery flashing past outside the car.

"What's it about?" Dalila asks.

"Dick has been kidnapped."

The little girl thinks for a moment and then says gravely:

"It was probably the FLN."

By the time they arrive at Messaoud's house, Hamid has finished the book and started again at the beginning. (He is reluctant to start on the second book right away.) He finds the story a little disappointing, though. There are no real brawls like there are in comics, the bad guys aren't really scary, and the good guys are so perfect they're almost boring—especially Julian, Hamid can't *stand* Julian. Despite this, as soon as he sets down his suitcase in his uncle's living room, he takes out *Five on Kirrin Island Again* and dives in with rapt attention. He hopes that there is some hidden message in it, some knowledge that he lacks that separates him from others. That summer, he is not really reading the Famous Five books, he is studying reference manuals for small blond children.

When, the previous year, Messaoud decided not to move to Basse-Normandie with them, Yema had cried. She could not bear the thought of the family once again being separated, one piece here, one piece there, and the whole of France in between them, especially since it was such a tiny family, not even a family, a stump, but still Messaoud would not give in. He wanted to make a life for himself, and believed that the warmth he would lose in straying from the herd would be counterbalanced by the time and the space that solitude would offer him. Shortly after his sister left, he found work in Manosque and he quit the Logis d'Anne to move into an orange-colored house in the south of the city. Their reunion is jubilant and raucous, as though—yet again—it is the result of some extraordinary coincidence, some stroke of luck denied to many.

During their two-week vacation, the children will swim in the Durance. (Naïma finds a photograph in which all four are wearing identical swimming trunks, even Claude, who is barely two.) They will play with the one-eyed cat, race from their uncle's porch to the NO ENTRY sign. In a few short days, their skin will tan, returning to an earthy ocher. The adults stay in the little pool of shade cast by the parasol. Yema regularly disappears inside to feed Hacène, who rarely leaves her arms; a sour smell of breast milk wafts around their conjoined bodies. The two men listen to music on the radio. *And even if you came back, I still believe my heart would crack.* In the late afternoon, they open a translucent bottle of rosé. (Ali now sometimes drinks in public and justifies it by saying that they live in France, it's normal—and Yema seems to accept that her husband's God recognizes borders, does not object, simply keeps a close eye on the level of the liquid.) To make his sister happy, Messaoud puts songs by Uum Kalthoum on the record player. *I have forgotten the sleep and the dreams, I have forgotten the nights and the days.* When the children come back, they plead with her to change the music, but Yema will not be swayed. She hums as she cooks dinner for the family. She is delighted to rediscover the small round succulent fruits of the olive tree grow here as easily as they do in Algeria. In Pont-Féron, they can only be bought in small jars, stuffed with anchovies or peppers, useless for cooking, and sold at prices that make them a luxury even for families in wealthy neighborhoods. At her brother's house, she scoops handfuls of olives from a bucket, blanches them until their bitterness is a distant memory, adds them to chicken that has been sautéed with onions and seasoned with saffron. The kitchen is filled with sizzling and smoke. Messaoud greets the green-and-gold *tajine zitoune* with a string of compliments.

"How do you manage when I'm not here?" Yema asks worriedly. "I hope you're not going hungry?"

"I manage," her brother says.

"So, tell me . . . when are you going to get married?"

Messaoud laughs but does not answer. He tells her he is happy living here on his own. From his words, from the way he looks at the little bungalow set in a gravel courtyard, he is obviously proud that he has moved away from the camp. But almost all his visitors still live in the Logis d'Anne. It is as though he has left without actually leaving.

"Why do they spend all day hanging around here?" Yema asks. "Have they nothing better to do?"

"They're just happy to get out for a little while," Messaoud says. "At the camp, all anyone ever does is say a quick hello to their next-door neighbors."

Yema shrugs. She does not like the fact that they are constantly here, under her brother's feet; she especially hates it when they talk to the children. Just yesterday, a wild-eyed old man told Hamid, Dalila, and Kader stories about people having their throats cut in an almond grove. She had come into the living room to lie down on the cushions next to little Hacène, only to find her three eldest children held captive by a grim, horrific tale of twenty-two successive slaughters.

"Shut your mouth, old man," Yema snapped. "These children don't have war in their blood! Why would you want them to have war in their blood?"

But what she is saying is not true, and she knows it. At the age of twelve, Hamid is still having nightmares, he still wets the bed. He has learned to change his own sheets, so he no longer wakes her to ask for help. But she still hears him screaming for someone to *stop, stop, please stop*, and in the dead of night his voice is not that of a little man, but that of a terrified child.

Although Yema would dearly love to erase it from her children's lives, if only for the summer, the war continues to shadow them, the end never comes. It hunts them down and, on September 23, 1965, finds them in their apartment in Pont-Féron. This is the day when Hamza's wife, Rachida, calls to tell them that Djamel is dead.

"At first we were happy," Rachida tells her sister-in-law. "He had come back to us long after we had given up hope. He suddenly showed up one day in a van. We were beside ourselves, we were so happy! But he was in a terrible state. They had fractured his skull; his body was covered with bruises. His whole body looked like a gaping wound. He was so scrawny. And when you looked into his eyes, he wasn't there, he talked, he moved, but he was already dead. He held out for a week and then died sitting in his chair."

"He wanted to die at home," Yema says.

"You're right," Rachida echoes, "he wanted to die at home."

"I'll tell Ali. He'll be devastated."

"Tell him to send money," Rachida says. "The funeral was very expensive."

Yema politely says goodbye and hangs up but, deep down, she is livid. All morning she prowls the apartment like a caged animal, brooding about Rachida, who is now mistress of the three houses in the mountains, Rachida, who probably wears the jewelry Yema left behind, the dresses that cannot suit her. Rachida, strolling through the olive groves whenever she pleases . . . Despite the stories they have heard since they left, of land seizures and devastating fires, in Yema's mind the village on the ridge is frozen in time, unchanged, every centimeter is the same. She looks down at the playground outside, at the broken jungle gym. What exactly does Rachida imagine? That because they live in France, they're rich?

That afternoon, she goes to visit her downstairs neighbor, Madame Yahi. Yema has started to say *Madame* so-and-so, *Monsieur* so-and-so, as the French do, and as her children do—although in her case, the title is not marked by a sense of respect, but almost like a first name. Madame Yahi is about to marry off her daughter, and Yema is helping to make baklava for the reception. It is easy, since their kitchens are absolutely identical, so they never have to ask where to find an ingredient. They simply reach into a cupboard, a drawer. Sometimes they forget which floor they are on, which of them is heading home. As she wipes fingers sticky with honey on a dishcloth, Yema confesses to her neighbor:

"I think I resent all the people who stayed in the old country."

"So do I." Madame Yahi nods, as though it goes without saying.

She is a little older than Yema, and much less timid. She adjusts her headscarf and says:

"I even resent my husband, because if it had been up to me, I would have stayed in Algeria. He was the one who wanted to leave. No one even thought to ask what we wanted. They just drag us around with them. It's the men who make the mistakes, but we're the ones who have to pay."

"Poor us . . ."

And as they grind almonds, they sigh for the country lost by men.

Here, summer does not end abruptly, it dissolves into autumn. Long before the temperature begins to fall, the rainy days sweep in, one following hard on the other—or rather they melt into a single day with no beginning and no end—leading inexorably to winter. The rain does not drum, does not hammer, does not lash as it did in Rivesaltes or in Jouques, no, here it falls as a light drizzle that everyone knows will not stop until March. Hamid follows the chain of puddles that winds between the buildings of the cité. Rainwater soaks into every patch of ground that it can turn to mud, it trickles into cracks beneath the buildings, saturates the grass verges that separate the parking spaces, seeps beneath the concrete to create a murky swamp that even the children avoid. It gives the lie to the apparent modernity of the housing projects. The cité quickly comes to resemble a mud-hut village precariously built on marshy ground. The shift from summer to autumn is all the more deceptive because routines do not change. Ali still leaves for work and comes home at the same time. The younger children go to nursery school, Hamid to secondary school, and, indifferent to the season, the bell rings at the same time. Yema goes shopping, and the shelves are always well stocked, regardless of the weather. Their lives are no longer lived to the rhythms of the earth, the trees, or the skies. Although life is easier, it is also more monotonous. Face pressed to the kitchen window, Hamid wonders how he will hold out until March when the November rains have already worn him out. In the kitchen, Yema sniffs as she stacks the shelves with boxes of tissues that seem to get used up at an astonishing speed. When her back is turned, Dalila uses them to make wedding dresses for her doll and Kader to make bandages that he carefully ties around his imaginary war wounds.

Shortly after Hamid starts secondary school, Ali is asked to meet with his head of year. The teacher wants to talk to him about the signatures on Hamid's report cards, because, well, *cough, cough,* this is a little embarrassing, but he thinks Hamid is signing them himself.

"Yes," Ali says, nodding proudly. "He does it all by himself."

"But he's not supposed to!" the teacher snaps. "You're supposed to sign them."

Ali resolutely shakes his head: Of course he is not supposed to. He cannot write. He is not about to sign his son's neat, clean copybooks with an X. His son is much more talented at tracing the beautiful, alien characters of French.

"He signs them. It's fine."

The teacher changes the subject. "Hamid is a good boy. He works hard."

Ali's heart once more swells with pride. He can tell that his son is intelligent. He can see it in the boy's eyes, in his smile, in the way he invents games for his little brothers and sisters.

"Have you given any thought to his future?"

Ali has to ask him to repeat the question more slowly. Once he has understood, he nods and silently purses his lips. What does this teacher think he is? Of course he thinks about his son's future. He thinks about it every day at the steel press in the factory, in the employees' locker room, at lunchtime, on the bus, before he falls asleep, all the time. He has no control over the future of his son, of his children, and it upsets him. He knows that, in spite of all his efforts, their future is beyond him, that his inability to seize the present means that he is unable to build a future. Their future is written in a foreign language.

"What sort of courses do you think he should take, for example? Have you thought about that? There are some very good vocational courses at the technical school. That way, at least you can be sure that he'll have a trade. But I have to tell you that, if he can keep up his current academic performance, we might consider letting him stay in the general stream and maybe he could work in the public sector."

The teacher says these words with obvious excitement. He is referring to the apex of the social pyramid, or rather to the social pyramid that applies in urban development zones, whose apex has been lopped off, or lost among the clouds.

"He could be a social worker. Now, that's a good job. I know a lot of pupils who go on to do social work. Because it means they can stay in touch with their . . ."

The teacher hesitates. He does not want to be rude.

". . . their indigenous milieu, shall we say."

"What's the best university in France?" Ali brusquely interrupts.

The teacher is surprised.

"I don't know . . . The École Polytechnique, maybe? Or the École Normale Supérieure?"

"My son will go to both," Ali says.

He may be unable to influence the present, to plant the seeds of what he dreams will be his children's perfect lives, but he still has magical thinking. It is impulsive; it is ferocious; it moves by leaps and bounds between two points unconnected by any logic.

When he meets up with Hamid in the corridor where the boy is nervously waiting for the end of the meeting, he says:

"You have to work harder than everyone else. The French aren't going to do you any favors. You have to be the best at everything, do you understand? The best."

"Okay," Hamid says.

"And from now on, I want you to show me your report cards. I want to check them. I'll get Monsieur Djebar to read them to me."

The diligence he demands of his young son is at odds with the slackness he has observed at work. At the factory, Ali often hears foremen use the phrase "typical Arab workmanship," just like that, unthinkingly, without meaning any harm. There may be some truth to the expression, Ali thinks, but the people using it don't understand anything. It is true that the work of the men on the production line is slapdash, but this is not some genetic trait from the Maghreb. It is the despair of those crushed by the factory work that offers them only a means to survive, not to live. There are no Algerians or Turks in office jobs, and they know it. They are offered no path to progress. So the only way that they can protest is to drag their heels at work, half screwing in components, hastily stacking parts, being slapdash in their welding. They don't even boost production; unbeknownst to them, they have already been factored into forecasted losses in a dreary, utterly disheartening way.

In the early days, Ali tried to inject some enthusiasm into his work. If not for the love of the job, at least for the love of money, so that he could make more. It made no difference. The foremen do not offer him overtime. They give it to other Algerians who arrived after him, men who are neither harkis nor French.

"You don't have to send money back home," he is sometimes told by way of apology.

But Ali knows that if the foremen favor migrant workers, it is because, officially, they are here only to work, and they are prepared to work harder than anyone else. They are here to make money for their family, for their village. They are here to break their backs for eleven months and then go home. To a foreman, this is reassuring. They are not going to try to "make a career" for themselves, they are not going to join a union—or at least not for as long as they nurture the illusion that they will soon be going back home. He has no home to go back to. His life is here.

"Is everything going okay, Hamid?"

The school social worker has taken an interest in the boy's future since the first days of term. The files of children from Pont-Féron that land on her desk are marked as high priority. She pays more attention to them than she does to other pupils, as though their small brown bodies are minefields and the school system is waiting with bated breath for them to explode. But she is particularly intrigued by Hamid. She telephoned the head of his primary school to find out more about the boy. He told her that, in a single school year, Hamid had managed to make up for all the schooling he had previously missed—and he had missed a lot—exceeding all their expectations. (Trauma can stunt intellectual development, they thought, with no personal animosity.) Although academically he is no longer falling behind, his social development is more of a concern. The social worker finds the boy too serious. When he speaks, he uses an impeccable but outdated grammar that sounds absurd coming from a child. "He talks as though he's swallowed an old Lagarde et Michard grammar book," she was astonished to realize one day. And there is his drawn face, the dark circles under his eyes, the constant exhaustion. His left eyelid twitches like a broken windup toy. If this were the 1980s, she might worry that this is the result of the crack epidemic that is ravaging the cités, leaving the streets littered with disheveled people constantly itching for a fix. But since it is twenty years earlier, the notion of drugs does not occur to her, it does not even appear in her training manuals, in her pamphlets. This leaves the possibility of physical abuse. Ever since she saw the boy reluctantly undress for his school medical examination, she has been worried that his parents beat him. She imagines a succession of other problems that would allow her to intervene, to save him, to do the things that made her choose this profession.

"How did you get those bruises, Hamid?"

The adolescent stares blankly at the bruises, then looks at the social worker and, in her eyes, he sees the suspicion, the story she has concocted: the brutal father, the beatings (a cane or a belt?), the silence. Hamid laughs.

"Have you ever seen five kids play in a four-hundred-and-fifty-square-foot apartment without banging into doors and furniture? I haven't."

He does not know whether she believes him; probably not. But it is the truth. There is a surfeit of furniture and children in their apartment. It is stuffed to capacity. The slightest jerk of an elbow or bend of a knee is likely to result in a bruise, reminding them that the apartment is too small, or that they are too many. Communication between the residents and the public housing office is a futile tangle of red tape, as Hamid knows all too well, since most of the time he is the one who writes the letters. The families complain: The apartment does not meet our needs. Social services respond (reading between the lines of pompous verbiage): Don't have so many children. It seems a strange response to the families who have come here, since it seems to indicate that what constitutes an apartment is unalterable and it is the responsibility of human beings to adjust to the immutable fact of its surface area. Back home, if a family grew too large, they built another floor, added an annex, extended their living space. In the old country, housing, like life, like family, was in a constant state of flux; here it is a tin can whose size determines how much it can contain.

"Do you sleep well, Hamid?" the social worker asks.

He shakes his head. No, no, he doesn't.

"Is it because you're working too hard?"

A new, slightly contemptuous tilt of the head. It's impossible to work too hard when you have to try to be the best at everything.

"You have a place to sleep?"

"You mean a bed?"

"Yes."

"We've all got beds."

Hamid shares his bed with little Hacène. Claude and Kader sleep together in the next bed. This is the boys' room. Whenever he has nightmares, he wakes his brothers. He is embarrassed. So, it is true that he does not really try to sleep anymore.

"Why are you so interested in my bed?"

The social worker blushes beneath her helmet of immaculately coiffed hair, behind her protective uniform. She is troubled by this boy, this combination of man and child that has not gelled, so that the two appear alternately. Sometimes, in his gestures, his facial expressions, he looks so adult that she cannot think of him as innocent. She feels as though he is mocking her, laughing at her. She feels threatened, as she does whenever she has to deal with a man. (The social worker does not have someone she can talk to about her own fears, no social worker to usher her into an office adorned with soothing paintings to ask her whether she is getting enough sleep.) And besides, Hamid is handsome, and beauty is something that has always overwhelmed her, moved her to tears or to laughter. She would be the first to admit that there is a beauty in Hamid's straight, regular features that disrupt the mass of tight black curls and the fluttering left eyelid. In this town, no one will ever say, Oh, isn't he handsome . . . with that mixture of tenderness and wonder they might use when speaking of a white child. They will say it suspiciously, as though it is an adaptive trait he has developed in order to survive the move to France, to bewitch the local populace and make them forget his innate flaws. They will say it a little nervously, a little excitedly, fearful of getting too close, yet wanting to get closer. They will say it as a reproach.

"Because it's my job," she says curtly, as though brushing off a stranger in a bar.

Then she changes tack; addressing herself to the child rather than to the man who now occupies his body, she hands him the jar of mints that sits on her desk. Hamid smiles, raises his eyes heavenward, and—in a habit that dates back to the camp in Rivesaltes—he takes three: one for him, one for Dalila, one for Kader.

As he leaves the office, he finds Gilles and Julian waiting for him, and realizes that he was right to say nothing. People who have nightmares are given pills, given injections. The stuff of their dreams is replaced with chemicals. He has seen it happen too many times, in Rivesaltes and in Jouques.

The social worker may well be nice, friendly, and well-intentioned, but it would be too risky to tell her what happens in the dark, to tell her that when he closes his eyes, he sees burning olive groves projected onto his eyelids. The burning man, the man with the blazing tire around his neck, visits him every night, and often he is joined by the iron man, with his barbed-wire necklaces and bracelets. Even Hamid does not know where his nightmares come from. He does not remember ever witnessing such scenes, or rather, he *thinks* he does not remember, because the images are not written on that part of his memory to which he has conscious access. And yet, he is wrong to think that they did not happen, that they are not imprinted on him. They are there, in hidden circuits, embedded under the skin. At night, when language barriers give way under the weight of dreams, they come back, they exude a toxic sap deep in his brain.

"What did she want you for?"

"The usual."

"Maybe she's in love with you."

"Yeah, sure."

With a shove, Hamid pushes his giggling friends away. Their friendship is a new and important thing to him, because they are not boys from Pont-Féron. Gilles is a farmer's son; he lives out in the country on a farm filled with cows and apples that, to Hamid, sounds like the reincarnation of the lush, peaceful terrain up on the mountain, with its goats and its olive groves. Julian is the son of a pharmacist; he lives in a mansion in the city center that is almost as large as one of the apartment buildings. The three became friends by chance: they sat next to one another, so the history teacher asked them to give a group presentation on the invention of the printing press. While they were working on it, Hamid could not help but point out to Julian that he had the same name as one of the Famous Five.

"I know," Julian said, "the fucking boring one!"

The three boys laughed, especially Hamid, who would never dare to swear.

"What about your name?" Gilles asked. "Does it mean something?"

"Nope," Hamid said, "it's just my name."

With Julian and Gilles, he talks about bikes (they dream of having mopeds), about comics (they love stories that extol the virtues of groups: *The Fantastic Four*, *X-Men*, and *The Avengers*), about movies (*Batman*, *Jesse James Meets Frankenstein's Daughter*, the endless westerns that have them hooking their thumbs into their belts as they swagger), about girls (if they are not really interested in girls yet, it is because none of the girls they know look like Anjanette Comer, the brunette in *The Appaloosa*). They have deeply serious conversations about music in which Hamid and Gilles—uncomfortably aware that they spend more time looking at album covers than listening to records that neither of them can afford to buy—use a variety of subtle and sometimes surprisingly aggressive ruses to force Julian to agree with their opinions, despite this crucial handicap.

Hamid sometimes talks to Gilles and Julian about his nightmares—the ones he will never talk about with the social worker. He tells them he hates the nighttime, that he is afraid of falling asleep:

"My father says sleep is a wonderful opportunity. I've been listening to him say that ever since I was a kid: 'When you sleep, you forget your troubles.' But for me, it's like the opposite. When I'm awake, I know what I can do to make life better, but when I'm asleep, troubles come down on me like a ton of bricks, and there's nothing I can do, obviously, because I'm asleep."

"Become an insomniac," says Julian. "That way, while everyone else is asleep, you can conquer the world! Right, who's in goal?"

Sandwiched between conversations about the Beatles and games of soccer, his nightmares seem less terrifying.

* * *

Ever since meeting Julian and Gilles, Hamid is rarely at home. He spends less time with his siblings; he is more reluctant to help out. He constantly wants to be outside, talking, playing.

"Can I go out and see my friends?" Hamid asks Yema as soon as he has finished his homework.

She turns around and wipes her hands on her apron.

"What can you possibly have to say to your friends? Surely by now you must have said everything you have to say? What's so interesting that you need to spend your whole life talking?"

After much moaning, she usually gives in and he hurtles down the stairs and runs to the far side of town to meet up with the boys on the community soccer pitch, or in Julian's garage. He gleefully races away from the apartment and the moroseness of his parents, all such a stark contrast to the life he can feel bubbling inside him.

Yema is left sitting in the kitchen, staring at the letters she has brought up from the mailbox, letters that neither she nor her husband will open while Hamid is not here. She waits for him to come home. She thinks that maybe she should stop shouting and nagging when all she wants is to tell him that she loves him, but she does not know how. Her first son. The apple of her eye. Her little Frenchman . . .

Of course she wants him to go out and play like other children. But although she longs to give him back the fragments of childhood that war robbed him of, she cannot deny that she needs him here with her: he is her go-between with an outside world that still terrifies her. Without her messenger, her spindly-legged guide, she is lost.

When the phone rings, for example, there is always a moment of indecision. Ali and Yema are wary of answering in case the person on the other end is French. Yema still does not speak a word of the language. Her husband can get by moderately well, but needs gestures and facial expressions to fill the gaps left by the words he cannot understand. When the telephone rings, he breaks out in a cold sweat. Sometimes, hearing the word "*Bonjour,*" he hangs up for fear that in trying to have a conversation he will make of fool of himself.

As a result, the shrill ringing is usually accompanied by a moment's silence—as though by listening intently to the ringing, they might determine the language of the caller—then a cry:

"Hamid!"

He is the master of the telephone, the secretary of the house. There was a time when this made him proud. Now, as he enters adolescence, he wants to be left alone—for no one to interrupt his dream. Yet still he carries on, because they need him to. Nobody thinks to ask Dalila to take over, because Dalila is angry, she is always, always angry. Her scrawny body contains astonishing reserves of anger. It's apparent from the way she drinks coffee in the morning when getting ready for school, the way she wages war on the breakfast table, the cup, the sugar, the spoon. When the telephone rings, her black eyes look up only to shoot daggers at Hamid, then she shuts herself in the girls' room. It is always Hamid who answers, who passes over the receiver when the caller speaks in Arabic or Kabyle, takes a message if they speak in French. No one has ever taught him telephone etiquette, so he does not even say, "Hello," when he picks up, but, "Who is it?"

Thirty or forty years later, most of Naïma's uncles and aunts still follow his example, and every time she calls them, she is upset by this gruff first question—as though they are criticizing her for calling.

One gray, dull Sunday morning in 1967, one of those winter days in Normandy that seems to stretch from October to April, while the children are doing their homework on the living room table, Ali gets up from the sofa and walks over to the huge piece of furniture that takes up an entire wall of the room—a hideous combination of sideboard and wardrobe that neither Naïma nor Hamid will ever get used to—on which the manufacturer has seen fit to add columns and a small glass cabinet in which to exhibit the best china. To the bottom left is the drawer that houses Ali's medals, the "ten pounds of metal" he brought from Algeria.

On this particular day he gets up without a word from the sofa where he was watching television, goes over to the cabinet, removes the drawer, and disappears into the kitchen. Hamid, Kader, Dalila, and Claude hear him open a cupboard and haul out the large trash bin, then they hear the clatter of the medals as they are tipped out of the drawer and fall in a heap on the vegetable peelings with a muted damp *plop*.

Ali comes back into the living room, reinserts the empty drawer, and sits down on the sofa. He has not said a word. The children carry on with their homework, not daring to say anything.

"Maybe it was a cry for help . . ." Hamid will say later.

"It was an act of rebellion," Dalila will say.

"It was a shame," Kader will say.

"I don't remember that," Claude will say. "Are you sure it actually happened?"

But at the time, they say nothing.

The children speak to their parents less and less for any reason. Language is gradually creating a gulf between them. To them, Arabic is a child's language that deals only with the realities of childhood. What they are experiencing now can be named only in French, it is French that gives it shape; there is no possible translation. So when they speak to their parents, they are aware that they are lacking all their newly won maturity and becoming Kabyle children again. Between the Arabic that, for them, is fading with time and the French that resists their parents, there is no space in their conversations for the adults they are becoming.

Ali and Yema watch as Arabic becomes a foreign tongue to their children, hear the words that increasingly escape them, the growing number of approximations, the French that peppers the language. They see the ever-widening rift and they say nothing, except—perhaps—from time to time, because they feel they should say something:

"Very good, son."

In this apartment that they have never truly felt belonged to them, Ali and Yema make themselves as small as possible to make space in the cramped rooms amid the unnecessary furniture bought to re-create an image in some forgotten catalogue for the generation that has grown up here.

The round table in the middle of the living room chiefly serves as a desk for Hamid and Kader. Not only can both boys read and write, but they have mastered the rarefied language required by official letters and know how to interpret the numbers on a pay slip. They have set themselves up as lawyers, accountants, public letter writers, and social workers for many of the neighbors who come to them with armfuls of assorted paperwork. The care that these illiterate laborers lavish on keeping and organizing documents they cannot read is a source of constant amazement to the boys. They greet the neighbors with a grave expression that does little to disguise the jubilation they feel, and after a few solemn nods they launch into an analysis of the documents as though, like augurs of old, they are cutting open the belly of an animal to read in its entrails some secret higher message.

"They have so many papers, the French," Yema says from the kitchen, shaking her head, "it makes you wonder what you can do in this country without paperwork. Die? I'm sure they would ask you for papers even for that, and if you didn't have them, they would keep you alive until you found them . . ."

Every inch of floor space not occupied by the sink, the stove, and the stout fridge is taken up by wives waiting for their husbands to emerge from their "consultation" with the two boys in the adjoining room. Dalila fumes that she, too, is relegated to the kitchen or to her bedroom, although she is older and more intelligent than Kader. But despite the consistent excellence of her school reports, she finds herself beating her head against the invisible barriers imposed upon the world of women, and all claims are handled by her brothers. The brothers ask for nothing by way of compensation—"Nothing but glory," whispers Kader, who has inherited his brother's superhero comics—but their work is meticulous. The correspondence that eats up most of their time is that with the Department of Social Security. Industrial accidents are common in a district filled with manual laborers, and two neighbors have spent months applying for disability benefits. Over the course of many letters, Hamid and Kader have refined their technique, and their consultations follow a precise format. The men indicate the parts of their body where they feel pain, and the boys, deadly earnest, pose medical questions, ask them to describe the nature and severity of the pain. Then Hamid opens the illustrated dictionary his teacher gave him two years earlier, its cover now coming away from the spine despite his precautions. Turning to the double-page color spread on human anatomy, he and Kader work out which organ, which muscle, which bone is responsible for the pain and argue between themselves, sometimes pretending to adjust their imaginary spectacles.

I feel compelled to request a second opinion, they write, when they are finally in agreement, *since, given the excruciating* (a word they may misuse, but one that they are fond of) *pain I suffer on a daily basis in my*

*spleen/lumbar region/patella/cervical vertebrae, I cannot help but worry that
Doctor X missed something during his most recent examination.*

Years later, Kader will become a nurse. And he will often say that it
was while studying the anatomical diagrams in the battered old dictionary that he discovered his vocation. Even today, he still feels a particular tenderness for patients who have fractured their astragalus; when he
was a child, it was his favorite of all the bones in the diagram.

In the little apartment filled with neighbors and their wives, pain is always greeted with acceptance. This is one of the elementary rules of
politeness that Yema has impressed upon her children: when someone
says that they are in pain, you believe them, you sympathize with them.
According to her, French people do not understand this etiquette. When
you tell them you feel ill, they say, "Don't worry," or "It's nothing," or
"You'll be fine." In the brightly lit living room of the apartment, if someone says, "I've got a pain in my back," everyone present gravely says,
"*Meskin.*" Poor you. There are solemn nods of compassion.

Obviously, this does not mean that, the moment the malingerer has
left, Yema or one of the wives will not say:

"He's always complaining, that man."

But the declaration of pain in itself is sacred.

As a child, Naïma loved the "free zone for pain" her grandmother
created around her. Grazing your knee in her apartment in Flers was
much more comforting than grazing it among French people. If she suffered the slightest scratch, she was showered with hugs; if she cried, her
face was instantly pressed into Yema's generous breasts: "My little one,
my darling, *meskina*, have a piece of cake . . ."

As she grew up, she became accustomed to what her grandmother
always considered French rudeness and got into the habit of mentioning pain only to have it pooh-poohed. The fact that her sufferings are
minimized or dismissed as being temporary has become a necessary
part of conversation in order not to plunge headfirst into despair. Yema's
approach now seems to her strangely destabilizing; with each meskina
she feels as though she has missed a step on the stairs.

It is while in the final years of secondary school—tenth grade, perhaps, or eleventh, he cannot remember exactly—that Hamid stops observing Ramadan. He has had enough of his head spinning, his stomach rumbling, his concentration escaping from his head in random whorls. Ramadan means endless hours of hunger gnawing at his insides, dry heaves. (He has always been surprised that hunger makes him want to vomit up the nothing in his stomach.) Ever since he was a little boy, he has been told that fasting allows the believer to share in the suffering of the poor and the starving, but he sees it as a relic of his parents' lives when they were rich farmers living in the mountains ten years earlier. Here in France, *they* are the poor, so Hamid knows what it means to suffer twelve months of the year. He has no need for a self-imposed crash course in destitution. Besides, he is tired of having to miss out on PE classes, being unable to run for a bus, sitting on the sidelines of the soccer pitch when he meets up with Gilles and Julian—he has had enough of being marked out as weak while he is fasting. Ramadan does nothing to bring him closer to the poor; it does set him apart from the other pupils at school.

He does not want to tell Yema about his decision because he knows that she would be hurt. Her relationship to religion is intimate, emotional, she cannot countenance the idea of Islam as a subject for debate: she is Muslim in the same way that she is four feet eleven; it is something ingrained in her since birth that has grown throughout her life.

Hamid wonders whether he should talk to his father about it. He hesitates: it is contrary to the nature of things for a son to decide rather than simply to obey—this is what he has always been taught. And yet, ever since they arrived in France, his father has increasingly delegated his powers to Hamid. He does not know whether he should feel happy about this. Throughout his adolescence, he has barely had a father to rebel against: Ali is shrunken, diminished. He has grown weak where previously he was a mountain. But just when Hamid believes that his father is no longer a force to be reckoned with, when he tries to develop a relationship that is less strictly hierarchical, Ali's rage suddenly flares—a rage that still simmers within him, pure as a blast of cold air, though his authority has long waned—and the boy feels as though he is four years old and about to get a thrashing. Hamid finds it difficult to be a teenager with a father like Ali. He cannot defy him. He cannot ever be his equal.

And so, it is in secret that he organizes the logistics of Ramadan. For the month of fasting, he does not set foot in the school cafeteria, but, behind the room that stores the balls and the exercise mats and affords cover for all clandestine transactions in the lycée, his friends give him hunks of bread, a few squares of chocolate, a banana, whatever they manage to sneak out from their own lunches. The greater part he wolfs down immediately, but he often keeps something for the evening in case he cannot wait for iftar. The last few hours are the hardest to bear: Yema has already set out the plate of dates from which they will each take one to mark breaking their fast, from the simmering saucepans comes the smell of tomatoes, pepper, and chili. Food is everywhere, yet remains forbidden, and Hamid's stomach can no longer endure these promises constantly deferred. Only the fact that day is already drawing to a close prevents him from crying out in hunger and frustration. And so there follows another rebellion, one connected to the first, yet unexpected. Hamid no longer relies on his parents to feed him, and food has always been the source of their authority: his mother nourished him with her milk, with his first solid food, and with slow simmerings in the kitchen; his father, who once planted olive trees, now brings home the fruits of his labor. From the moment Hamid begins to eat the food given to him by Gilles and Julian, he clearly, if unwittingly, breaks a natural bond, one that he has never considered.

Ali happens on him one day eating a crust of bread in the unlit laundry room. Hamid turns with a start and, faced with the looming figure of his father that fills the doorway, he instinctively puts up his hands to shield himself. But Ali does not seem angry, merely stunned.

"If God does exist," says a wrong-footed Hamid, "I'm willing to bet it's not to make our lives hell."

He has just learned about Pascal's wager at school and is offering his very personal interpretation. Ali nods and closes the door, whispering:

"Make sure you don't leave any crumbs for your mother to find."

Ceasing to observe Ramadan is merely a first step for the teenager to whom the traditions of Islam seem as old-fashioned as the knickknacks from Algeria that are gathering dust in drawers. To what he considers the obsolete faith of his parents, Hamid prefers politics, which he discovers thanks to Julian's older brother. Stéphane is studying sociology in Paris, and when he comes home, he never misses an opportunity to talk about the roiling ferment of ideas at his university. Everyone listens in silence and nods. His long arms and the curiously triangular face that ends with a tiny pointed chin make him look like a praying mantis. Far from making him repulsive, his unusual physiognomy draws people to him like a magnet, and when he speaks, he has the calm, unhurried manner of someone who knows he does not have to make an effort to command attention. Even his parents, who disagree with him on most subjects, seem unable to resist their son's nonchalant charm when he speaks. As for Julian, Hamid, and Gilles, they listen to his words with almost ecstatic reverence. When he talks about the student demonstrations of the previous year, the teenagers are prepared to believe that Stéphane and his friends personally forced the resignation of the elderly General de Gaulle, asleep at the reins of power. *It is forbidden to forbid. If you don't take control of politics, politics will take control of you.* They love the slogans that pepper Stéphane's stories, and clamor for more.

"But without a meaningful discussion," Stéphane upbraids them, "slogans are just lollipops."

Punctuating his words with delicate gestures, Stéphane explains that resistance needs be reinvented in the present, rather than being consigned to the history books. He says it is essential to keep imagining new possibilities and modes of life to thwart the discourse of power, which constantly assures us that there exists only one way to live, which power alone can defend. He asks:

"Have you read Marx?"

A little embarrassed, the three boys shake their heads.

"What have you been reading in philosophy class?"

"Plato," Julian says timidly.

"Pascal," Hamid says.

"A guy who bases his political theory on slavery and a guy who bases his theory on the greatness of God. Good work, guys, you'll really go far with that."

Stéphane lends them thick books with broken spines and dog-eared pages that Hamid treats with the same respect as Yema does the copy of the Qur'an that she cannot read, yet leafs through from time to time, whispering suras that she learned by heart long ago. Stéphane also brings home records. He plays Muddy Waters, the Clancy Brothers, Bob Dylan, because let me tell you, boys, *the times, they are a-changin.* The music and lyrics meld with Hamid's thoughts; politics is like a blues number, a folk song strummed on a guitar going around and around in his head. *Il est interdit d'interdire!*—It is forbidden to forbid . . . There can be no refrain more beautiful. For Hamid, this prohibition begins within oneself, it begins with forbidding oneself to forbid. Hamid travels through his memories in search of proscriptions, challenges his reflexes, questions his habits. He finds them blossoming everywhere, a thick jungle of branches and creepers blocking his path. His mind has been so densely planted with "You should," "You shouldn't," "That's the way things are" that he finds it difficult to move. At night, instead of sleeping, he weeds out his innermost thoughts, hacks at the tangle of branches, digs away the obstacles. Of all the internal prohibitions he identifies, he keeps just one, because he believes that it is helpful, that it is not a creeper but a climbing plant: the prohibition against not being the best.

When he has finished, he feels as though inside him there is a vast clearing, an open space that he can use as he chooses, fill as he pleases. It is in this clearing that he builds his rebellion, one that is personal to him: it combines the words of Marx, the voice of Dylan, the face of Che Guevara, it has—does he even realize?—the youthful grace of Youcef Tadjer, and each time he encounters it, it triggers the same sense of wonder, the same almost delirious joy, the same unconditional love he felt at the appearance of Mandrake the Magician in the comics he read as a child.

Although he continues to work tirelessly at school, he begins to question the logic behind the things they are given to study, the arbitrariness of the knowledge passed on to them—Stéphane says that rote learning is the death of thought. The way he articulates these maxims gives Hamid the impression that his voice is drawing accents over the words. He sometimes stands in front of the cracked mirror of the bathroom cabinet and tries to do the same.

He, Gilles, and Julian toy with the notion of confrontation, all the while knowing that they would never dare provoke one. They revel in stories of what might be, exult in the idea of being heroes. Although they have never uttered a word of refusal, they imagine that their teachers are giving them funny looks, that the prefects are afraid of them, that their rebelliousness is radiating from their rapidly mutating bodies like a purple aura.

One day, in English class, while the pupils are being asked to conjugate irregular verbs and one boy is constantly stumbling, the teacher lets slip:

"For God's sake, Pierre, if Hamid can do this, you should be able to!"

"What's that supposed to mean?" Hamid asks.

He blurted out the question more in surprise than anger. He had not intended to say it aloud, but from the ensuing silence and the wide-eyed stares of his classmates, he realizes that he cannot simply shrug it off. The teacher becomes flustered, stammers, and in the space left by his crumbling authority, Hamid follows the question with another:

"You mean that anything an Arab can do should be easy for a French kid? That if I can manage it with my underdeveloped African brain, a White Man should be able to do better? Is that what you mean?"

Faced with this lack of respect, the teacher forgets his embarrassment and roars:

"Right, that's enough. Now shut up!"

"You're a racist," Hamid says as calmly as he can, though his voice is quavering with a mixture of rage and fear.

Thrilled, Gilles and Julian jump on the bandwagon of his indignation. They shout much louder than Hamid, perhaps to make up for lost time:

"He's right, monsieur, you've got no right!"

"It's disgusting!"

A few other pupils join in with them, pressing for the teacher to apologize. The voices swell, fueled by an astonished joy. It is more uproar than revolution, but the teacher is livid, bewildered, panicked. He goes on saying, "That's enough," and "Pipe down!" but cannot regain control of the class.

"He probably subscribes to *Minute!*" Julian shouts, laughing.

"Get out!" the teacher shrieks. "Hamid, Gilles, Julian, out of my class!"

Giggling, they leave the classroom, followed by a handful of classmates. They head off to the nearest café and collapse onto the chairs, tossing their schoolbags aside as though shrugging off the yoke of a conservative education. They are convinced that "all hell broke loose"; they are thrilled to have been a part of it; the beers and *diabolos* taste like champagne. The girls look at the rebellious trio with a new interest in their eyes that blooms like the first buds of spring.

"My father's going to go mad," Gilles says, pulling a face and leaning back in his chair. "I don't think my heroic revolutionary deeds are going to make him happy."

He says this with the knowing air of a boy whose convictions are not to be shaken by a dressing-down or even a thrashing. He says it for the girls and their vernal smiles. For the same reasons (the breasts, the smiles), Julian also calmly announces that he is not afraid. In his family, Stéphane has paved the way with much more serious screwups.

His parents are no longer shocked by anything, he says with studied nonchalance. It is also for the girls that Hamid tries to maintain an expression that is serene and heroic. He stretches out on a bench, lets out a yawn in an ostentatious display of indifference. As he lets his arms fall, they brush against Chantal's shoulders, her back, her waist. He pretends the contact is accidental but, not having the nerve to take advantage of the situation, immediately pulls back his hand. She flashes what he assumes is a mocking smile, so he grabs his bottle of beer and swigs. With girls, he is always at a loss. The girls at school and those who live in the cité are so completely different that understanding one teaches him nothing about the other.

Gilles suggests another round, eager to prolong this moment of glory and the presence of the girls. Julian hesitates, glances at his watch, but Hamid loudly agrees, stepping up his show of bravado: *Come on, boys—to us, and to the revolution!*

In reality, he is annoyed with himself for taking things as far as he did, and with his friends for encouraging him—they have less to lose than he does. If he were suspended from school, he has no idea how Ali would react—he does not understand what triggers his father's sudden, illogical bursts of anger. But aside from his father's reaction, he is already anticipating the disastrous consequences: if he is not allowed to sit his baccalaureate, his hard work will have been for nothing, he will be packed off to the factory. I'd rather die, Hamid thinks, clenching his fists under the café table.

When he gets home, he says nothing about what happened at school. He does not know how his family might react to his new rebelliousness, whether he can share it. Dalila is fifteen. She is in love, her skin blistering and breaking out in spots along her temples, her fury entirely directed at her own body. She has no interest in politics—this, at least, is what Hamid imagines, being unable to see that, in itself, her rage is a form of rebellion, the rebelliousness of a teenage girl who is tacitly forbidden any public display of freedom because she was born a girl and because, here, in the teeming, serried buildings of the cité where neighbors spy on each other, *people will talk* the moment a girl does something that seems to break with tradition. Kader is thirteen and bursting with such electrical energy that his mother has to send him out to run around the grounds every evening just to calm him down. He does not have the attention span to listen to Hamid for more than two or three minutes. He constantly wants to be playing, jumping, dribbling, climbing. The others are too little: Claude is six, Hacène four, Karima three, and then there are the new arrivals: Mohamed, who has just had his first birthday, and Fatiha, who has only just been born. More than a playmate, Hamid is a father of this new tribe. If he wants to talk politics in the apartment, he has only his parents, but Yema immediately stops him with a "Leave me in peace" whenever he asks her about her lot as a woman. Once, she even said:

"It's disgusting. A son has no business seeing his mother as a woman, he should see her simply as a mother. So leave me in peace."

Hamid prowls around Ali, excited and yet afraid. It is Ali he really wants to talk to. He has never asked his father what he did that forced the family to flee Algeria. He has not even asked himself the question until now, because a father's choice is sacred, and when he makes a decision, it is binding on his wife and his children, regardless of the reasons that prompted that decision. He has never asked him anything because the self-imposed prohibition that forbade him from questioning his father's choices has meant that there were no other possible choices, no hypothesis of how their lives might have been different if his father had chosen otherwise. Now that Hamid has taken a scythe to the jungle in his mind, he would like to know how he wound up in Pont-Féron, what happened in the first part of the book that he has since forgotten except in his nightmares. And yet he dares not ask the questions buzzing inside his head: he is afraid of uncovering a past he cannot forgive. These days, Hamid is in favor of independence, of all forms of independence—especially that of Vietnam, where, as Stéphane has explained, South Vietnam is being shamefully manipulated by the United States for the benefit of the military-industrial complex—and he is also becoming a retroactive partisan of Algerian independence. The right of nations to self-determination seems to him so obvious that he cannot understand how Ali could have thought otherwise, given that he was on the side of the oppressed. When someone opens a prison cell, who would say: No, thanks, actually. Thank you but I think I'll stay here. What happened in his father's life for him to turn away from his own independence? How can someone *flunk* such an important turning point in history?

One evening, he asks the question, as though jumping on his father's back.

"Were you forced?" he asks.

"Forced to do what?"

"To collaborate with the French? Did they forcibly enlist you?"

His Arabic vocabulary is too scant to discuss politics, and his questions are peppered with French.

"Did they threaten you?"

Ali looks at his son—for whom the language of his ancestors falters and slips away, who speaks the language of the former oppressor even as he claims to understand the oppressed better than his father. It might even make him smile were it not that he is being directly challenged. Why is his pride still the size of Algeria? he wonders as his face flushes with anger. He says nothing but instinctively clenches his fists until they are two balls of flesh and bone containing all his rage; distraught, and frightened by their involuntary contraction, he stares at his fists as though they are inanimate objects, as though they are weapons taken from a drawer and he is afraid of what might happen, because if his fists can clench against his will, who knows what they might do next, so, to prevent the worst from happening, to force his hands to bend to his will rather than to their own mute logic of violence, to catch his fists off guard, perhaps to surprise them, with a sweeping movement he scatters his son's schoolbooks from the table, muttering between clenched teeth: "You don't understand anything, you'll never understand anything." In truth, Ali does not understand, either. He knows this, but he cannot admit it: it is easier to lose his temper in the hope that one day someone will see his anger as a confession. No, Ali does not understand anything: neither why, in the first instance, he was asked to prove his unfailing love of France, thereby creating a clear ideological path, nor why his son is asking him to prove that, on the contrary, he merely submitted to an all-pervading polymorphous violence. Why will no one allow him the right to have hesitated? To have changed his mind? To have weighed the pros and cons? Are things really so simple for everyone else? Is it only in his mind that nothing comes with a single possible explanation? For good measure, with a vicious tug, he rips the oilcloth off the table. Then he looks at the bare table and at his son as if to say: Look what you have made me do. The teenager turns on his heel and, picking up a few books as he goes, stalks out of the living room with all the dignity he can muster.

"Out!" Hamid roars at his little brothers as he bursts into the bedroom.

The boys are playing at being pirates, trying to capture each other's beds.

"Go on, fuck off!"

Claude and Hacène drop the forks they have been using as cutlasses.

"I won't have you speaking to your brothers like that!" Ali bellows from the living room. "At least they are good sons."

From the kitchen, Yema echoes him with a long keening, and Kader sticks his tongue out at his big brother as he leaves the bedroom. The apartment is ringing with angry cries. The plasterboard walls quiver. Hamid throws himself on the bed, muttering that his father is a bastard. He deliberately puts his shoes on the garish desert-island-themed duvet. But seconds later, he takes them off, thinking about Yema and the loads of washing that punctuate her day.

He is furious and embarrassed that, just as he is beginning to understand the broad political sweep of history, his father's choices represent not just a minor obstacle, but an illogical and opaque barrier to his understanding. He wishes that, like Julian and Gilles, he had parents with a coherent, recognizable way of life—a peasant outlook, a bourgeois mindset—that he could reject outright. Instead, he is lumbered with an evasive father he wants to defend but who refuses to be defended.

It is like the shriek of fingernails on a blackboard.

That night, in the stifling bedroom, he listens to the wheezy breaths from the small warm bodies all around him (impossible to jerk off and think about Chantal, impossible to jerk off at all, it is a chronic problem, one of the problems of the poor that he will never hear mentioned at a political meeting, as though no one thinks it is a problem—and yet he cannot be the only teenager to feel the desire, the need, to masturbate every day, only to find himself thwarted by a crowded bedroom), he composes press releases in which he announces a clear and decisive *ideological rift* with his father, and formally *disassociates* himself with his father's past choices. Comrade Hamid herewith reaffirms his support and his commitment to the struggle of all oppressed peoples in France and throughout the world.

When the school issues its verdict on the "incident" in English class—what the pupils are calling a "revolt," and the governors have dubbed "scandalous behavior"—Hamid, with practiced ease, fishes the envelope from the slot on his way to school, signs his father's name to the letter announcing that he has been given detention for the remainder of the the school year, tears up the envelope, and tosses it away. He feels nothing like the panic he felt the first time. Duping his father has become a habit.

On May 8, 1970, while Hamid is struggling to read *Das Kapital* on the advice of Stéphane, and the little ones are helping Yema peel potatoes, the radio announces that Fauchon, the famous Paris delicatessen, has been raided by a Maoist commando group. Hamid leaps up, runs over to the radio, and turns the volume all the way up—it is the only way to drown out his brothers and sisters. Ali nervously asks him to translate.

"They've raided a luxury deli and handed the food out in the streets," Hamid says, trembling with excitement.

"Nothing but crooks," his father says, scowling. "They belong in prison."

Dragging himself from the sofa, he turns off the radio; the gesture is irrevocable. Yema and the little ones focus more intently on the potatoes. Not for the first time, Hamid mentally disassociates himself from his father's reactionary attitude. He resumes his reading of *Das Kapital*, but the text is elusive, he finds it dry and dull, and he so wants to love it that he cannot bear the distance that still exists between him and Marx in spite of his efforts. He tells himself that it is this apartment, his family, that is preventing the great truths of *Das Kapital* to blossom, that they are crushing everything that is great and beautiful in this world. No one could be deeply moved by the words of Marx surrounded, as he is, by the crackle of bubbling oil, the giggles of the children, the smiling silence of his submissive mother, and the thinly veiled hostility of his father.

When Yema asks what he thinks of the meal, he says sulkily that it is bland, and, as he says it, it feels as though the words encapsulate his whole life and that he has found the most succinct, most luminous allegory in the world. He spends the rest of the meal repeating the phrase "My life is bland," separating out the words, and does not speak to anyone else. His parents see his lips move silently and shrug. When she is sixteen, Naïma, too, will marvel at the private epiphanies she does not share with anyone but that seem so intense, so complex, that they are enough to give substance to her life. By that point, Hamid will have forgotten the inherent fervor of adolescence and, finding his daughter exasperating, will wish she would grow up a little.

After dinner, a number of Ali's colleagues come up for a "consultation" with his son. There is Mokhtar, the husband of Madame Yahi (though, strangely, no one ever refers to him as Monsieur Yahi), the two Ramdane brothers from Building C, and Big Ahmed, who looks less and less like a Hollywood actor, and who has come around only for some company. While Hamid leafs through the documents they have brought, Yema anxiously asks whether the newcomers have eaten and, refusing to believe their answers, returns to the kitchen she has only just left.

"They're not here for dinner, Maman," Hamid grumbles, embarrassed to see her working herself to the bone.

For his troubles, he receives only a "Shame on you": Yema would never allow anyone who came through her door at mealtimes—an incredibly flexible time period—to go away hungry. So her son's consultations are accompanied by the sounds of rattling pans and bubbling sauces; they smell of coriander and ras-el-hanout and crushed garlic. Mustaches tremble in anticipation at the aromas drifting from the next room.

Mokhtar plans to apply for a pension next year and cannot work out how many years he has been paying contributions. He has gathered together a sheaf of pay slips, which Hamid looks through, frowning worriedly at the numerous gaps he finds in the paper trail.

"They make us work for far too long," wheezes one of the Ramdane brothers, to whom retirement seems as remote as a Pacific beach. "Honestly, they work us to the bone."

Over Hamid's bowed head, the men nod vigorously, a mixture of weariness and resentment. The boy looks up.

"Have you ever thought about going on strike to protest?"

Mokhtar shrugs. Yeah, they've thought about it. And not just about striking. They have dreamed of destroying the factory, of escaping on a forklift, of kidnapping the boss. Around the table, the men laugh heartily. It's the truth, it's the truth.

"But these strikes and these—what do they call them?—these *manifestations*"—he uses the French word—"only really happen in Paris, don't they?" Ahmed asks.

"Of course not," Hamid says. "You are among the most exploited workers in the country. You have every right to protest!"

His father's face becomes expressionless, but Hamid forces himself to ignore the consequences and insists:

"You have the right to disagree."

"Disagree about what?" Ahmed asks vaguely, his gaze shifting between Ali, silently gritting his teeth, and Hamid, beaming with barely contained excitement.

"There's lots of things that I don't agree with," one of the Ramdane brothers says with the eagerness of someone who keeps a list of grudges handy in his jacket pocket.

"Your left hand doesn't agree with your right," Mokhtar sighs.

The others laugh, but Ali still looks somber.

"Anyway," the younger of the Ramdane brothers says, not remotely flustered, "it would be good if things changed. I'd like to be promoted. I'm sick and tired of watching even the dumbest roumis being made foremen, and what do we get? *Ouallouh*."

"And then there are the accidents at work," his brother adds. "Someone needs to do something. When you're working with metal, they happen all the time."

From under the table, Mokhtar lifts up a slender, chapped hand. One of the fingers is missing. He wiggles the stump in a series of movements that Hamid finds repulsive.

"Every time we're injured," he says wearily, "the bosses call us stupid."

"Stupid?" One of the Ramdane brothers chuckles. "You're being kind. Lazy bastards, maybe. Or liars . . ."

"I'd like to see them welding, since they think it's so easy," says the other. "They can take my job . . ."

Ahmed mimes the boss's panicked reaction if he were called on to operate the machinery. He imitates the man's reedy, pompous voice, mimes getting his tie caught in the workings, letting out shrill screams of terror. Even Ali loosens up a little and ventures a smile. Yema sets on the table a steaming ragout and a huge golden disc of flatbread, and the men immediately begin to tear off hunks.

"The accidents happen because we're all exhausted," the younger Ramdane brother explains to Hamid, who is still surreptitiously looking at Mokhtar's missing finger. "They need to cut the number of hours we work on the machines. If I went on strike, that would be my demand."

"I'd demand a proper lunch break," Ahmed says with his mouth full. "Because what we're given is ridiculous, it's not even a break. You hardly have time to turn around and you're back on the job."

"We'll draw up a communiqué," Hamid says decisively, grabbing a pen and a sheet of paper. "That way you can give it to the management."

He imagines telling Stéphane how, with his impassioned words, he galvanized the proletarian masses of Normandy. Suddenly not being able to understand *Das Kapital* does not seem so serious. He looks around the living room from one man to another, ready to take down their every demand. According to their usual ritual, the elder of the Ramdane brothers repeats what his brother has just said. Ahmed reiterates the importance of a midday break, but he is more hesitant, his eyes fixed on Hamid's pen. Ali turns away without a word.

"To be honest"—Mokhtar sighs—"I'd be happy just to get my pension. That would be a start."

After the men have left, Hamid helps Yema clear the table, then slumps into a chair opposite his silent father. The list of demands lies between them on the table. On the left-hand corner of the paper there is a tiny sauce stain. For a few moments they silently appraise each other, then Ali abruptly asks his son:

"Why are you trying to get us all riled up? Do you want us to lose our jobs?"

"They can't fire you just for asking for something," the young man responds just as curtly. "That would be illegal."

"Oh . . ."

Ali finds this strange. He remembers the old days, the fairy-tale kingdom in the mountains where he was the boss. He used to fire men who slept under the olive trees, those who spoke crudely to women, those who stole, those he thought had shifty eyes. He had every right. After all, they were his fields, his olive trees. Why had French bosses agreed to limit their powers?

The following morning at the usual hour, Ali sets off for the factory in Mokhtar's car. As soon as they arrive, they go up to the secretary's office, knock at the door, and timidly, but in a single breath, Ali says:

"Hello, we're here about the workers' demands."

The secretary sighs, removes one of the large clip-on earrings that frame her face, massages her earlobe with two fingers, and says wearily:

"What is the problem with you people?"

Ali might have answered: Our sons.

Eyes fixed on the ground or on the steering wheel, farmers till the neighboring fields, their noisy tractors assailing the rounded flanks of the hills. Lying on a tall stack of hay bales, away from prying eyes, Hamid is smoking a spliff with Gilles and two of his cousins. He does not really like the two slightly older boys, who regard him as a curiosity, call him "the Arab" behind his back, and bombard him with questions about life in the cité in Pont-Féron, as though it were a place so remote or so carefully guarded that they could not venture there themselves. But Gilles, who grew up with them, still sees them as his childhood playmates and insists that they are "okay guys." And besides, today they are the ones who have the dope. Hamid tries not to let them get on his nerves. (He knows that if he starts to get annoyed, the spliff will simply make things worse and push him toward paranoia.) He closes his eyes and tells himself that he is fine. He feels the sun on his skin, and the almost imperceptible sway of the stack of bales when one of them moves. He is in his straw castle, his tower of hay. Stretching away on all sides is the lush green Normandy landscape that has never been scorched by the sun, and on the far side of the road, cattle, slow as prehistoric animals, are lined up along the fence, chewing their cud.

They have just taken their baccalaureate and are waiting for their results in laid-back apathy. They help Gilles's father on the farm whenever they can, in order to save a little money for the impending summer break, and spend the rest of their time finding someplace where they can relax and dream about that break. Julian is being kept home by his parents, forced to review for the oral exams he will probably have to take, because his grades have been slipping. For once, Stéphane does not stand up for his little brother. Over the phone, he simply said tiredly:

"The old man's doing you a favor. Left to your own devices, you're just dumb enough to end up having to repeat the year."

The June sunshine beats down. The reclining boys feel beads of sweat trickle from their armpits across their skin to be soaked up by wisps of hay, the ticklish promise of the coming summer. Even so, Hamid is not entirely calm. If Julian were here, they would have had their own dope, and if they had had their own dope, he would not have to put up with the cousins. So his missing Julian is threefold, Hamid thinks—his absence, multiplied by the two tiresome consequences of that absence. Gilles is not so sentimental, he claims that Julian's temporary incarceration is the price to be paid for being bourgeois, one he had to pay sooner or later.

Suddenly—although in reality the boys move very slowly, but the lack of reason gives the impression of suddenness—one of the two cousins props himself up on one elbow, looks over at Hamid, and asks:

"So your father brought you all with him when he came to work in France?"

They have exhausted all possible questions about the present and have begun to delve into the past.

"Yeah," Hamid says. He does not have the energy to explain that his father is not an immigrant worker, but a French citizen.

"That's good, that's good . . ."

Hamid passes him the joint, hoping it might stop the boy's reply there, but, after a long toke, the boy continues, his voice slurred but careful:

"I mean, it's more humane, isn't it? Because . . . you can say what you like, but when you look at the number of Arabs who come over here leaving a wife and kids back in their village . . . you can't help thinking that these people don't have the same sense of love that we have. Like they don't know what it is. 'Cause if they really loved their wives and kids the way we do, they wouldn't be able to spend all that time away from them, would they? I mean, I've just had my first kid, and I can't imagine not watching him grow up. So the way I see it is, if they can cope with that, then we're obviously not made the same way. These guys, they've got no feelings. But I'm glad about your father. What he's done is . . . it's civilized. And it shows that he has confidence in France, you know?"

Gilles slowly rolls over on the straw mattress and shoots Hamid an apologetic glance, his face flushed by the spliff. Hamid props himself on his elbow and stares at the two cousins lying on the hay bale above his.

"It's kind of surprising . . ." he begins (and as he affectedly modulates his opening phrase, Gilles slumps back, pretending to be bored), "no, honestly, it's surprising how, to amateur anthropologists like you, the way that people go about things in the cité—because they have no choice, because they're poor, because they're destitute—are seen as *proof* that they are different by nature. *They* don't need the same things that you do. *They* have a completely different notion of comfort. *They* like living with their own kind. Do you really think we like having to squeeze eight people into a beat-up old car? Do you think we like the fact that our mothers never venture beyond the steep embankments that separate us from the town because, even after ten years living here, they're still afraid of what's on the other side? Do you think we like wearing clothes made of shitty synthetic fabric that rips easily? Do you think we like the fact that Yema buys our underwear in bulk, in packs of fifty, and that young and old, boy or girl, we all wear the same underwear?"

One of the cousins sniggers—he finds the image highly amusing. It reminds him of the Dalton brothers in the *Lucky Luke* comics.

"Now, obviously," Hamid continues, "I can understand why it's easier for you to pretend that it's all the rage in Algeria to accept that this country treats people in the cités like shitty second-class citizens."

"Shitizens," Gilles mutters vaguely.

Ever since he met Stéphane, ever since he discovered political discourse, or perhaps—in a superficial way—ever since he stood up to the English teacher, Hamid's relationship with the French language has changed. It is no longer about usefulness, about respect, or even a form of camouflage; these days it is about pleasure and power. He speaks as though every sentence is the first line of a poem, as though he can see himself writing or printing verses on the pages of a collection of his loftiest thoughts. When he speaks, he is both himself and his own radiant future. He is intoxicated by the bridge across time that appears whenever he opens his mouth. Gilles calls him the Man of a Thousand Faces.

His tirade has had no marked effect on the hated cousin. It dissipated with the smoke from the spliff and the clouds shaped like animals scudding above their heads. But for Hamid it inscribed itself somewhere, in flowing letters—his conception of mektoub is diametrically opposed to that of his father: for Hamid it is not about deciphering a fate already written in the heavens, but about writing the present as a history for future centuries to decode. This period of his life has offered few opportunities for him to write brilliant epics—he knows this—but soon, with his baccalaureate under his belt, he will get the hell out of here. That is the only thing that matters. And the chapter that commences when he leaves will begin with one of those huge, intricate illuminations, like the ones that mark a new letter in the old dictionary his teacher gave him.

The night is dark, a thick blue-black darkness, one of those nights when it's impossible to tell whether the inky blackness above is the sky or the invisible branches of the trees. The night is calm and deep, and Gilles's little car moves forward along roads that spool out, six feet at a time, in the beams of the headlights.

Suddenly the dark fabric is broken by a burning hole of light: flames of yellow, orange, red rip through the night and puncture it with sparks.

"There, the bonfire, the bonfire, turn left!"

It is Kader who is shouting—thrilled to be the first to have spotted it. Gilles does as he is told, and as they approach, the bonfire looms, vast and roaring. The tower of branches set ablaze for the feast of Saint John soon makes them forget the hour they have just spent lost, performing clumsy U-turns, looking for the party at La Ferme Jolie that everyone has told them is the most amazing in the region. When their eyes grow accustomed to the painful glare of the blazing *charibaude* (Julian's father taught them the word when he agreed to allow his son out for the evening, and they repeat it with exaggerated formality), they can see strings of lights around the makeshift bar and the spotlights that illuminate the dance floor.

They clamber out of the car, hastily parked by the side of the road. Hamid puts an arm around Kader's shoulder, takes him aside, and says again:

"I don't want you embarrassing me, okay?"

"You've already said that, like, a dozen times," Kader complains.

About a hundred people are gathered around the bonfire, the bar, and the speakers, bodies of all sizes and all ages. But Gilles, Julian, Hamid, and Kader see only the girls. Some are already bronzed by the early June sunshine, others flaunt legs that are still wintry white. As it moves, their hair catches the light in a cascade of gold, and when they twist and twirl to the music, it lags a second behind, whipping their faces, streaming across their mouths, their eyes, while a few unruly strands linger here and there, caught in the sweat of their foreheads. The music lurches without warning from Claude François to Thiéfaine and Bob Dylan. Sometimes you can hear the crackle of poorly connected sound cables and the roar of the generators. As such festivities go, it is slightly pathetic, and yet, being so long anticipated, then appearing out of nowhere, to the four boys it is like a paradise. Kader is dazzled.

"Tonight, my little Muslim friend," Gilles says, giggling, "we're getting you plastered."

"Stop teasing him."

At first Hamid tries to stop Kader from going near the bar. He intercepts the glasses Gilles and Julian try to give him. But, having to knock back himself the drinks intended for his little brother, he loses the will. All too soon, the four of them are drunk and happy.

At this point in his life—something Naïma knows because of a single photograph in which he can be seen standing outside their building in the cité—Hamid is sporting a magnificent Afro. Lithe, slender, and topped by this jet-black orb of hair, wearing a pair of red flares, a tank top, and a wide-collared white shirt. Because the photo was taken from a distance, he looks like a disco doll. The god of disco. Although she cannot make out his face, Naïma knows that he is very handsome.

"When I saw him for the first time," Naïma's mother, Clarisse, says, "I though he looked like Dionysus."

"And what does Dionysus look like?"

"Um . . ." Clarisse hesitates, caught off guard. "He looks like your father."

Hamid-Dionysus, Kader-getting-plastered-for-the-first-time, Julian-just-unleashed, and Gilles are dancing wildly to a Led Zeppelin song.

Over Robert Plant's voice, electric guitars blast through the demented drumming, sounding like a racing car driven by an epileptic. It jolts through them, jangling their nerves. From the side of the dance floor, a group of boys about their age watch and sneer. When the trance is broken and the music moves on to Michel Delpech, the dancers head off, laughing, toward the bar. A quick jerk of their heads and their long hair flicks drops of sweat all around. The boys who were watching follow them. There are five of them, they walk bowlegged like cowboys from a western, as if they have just climbed off their mopeds. At the bar, one of the boys stands next to Hamid, raucously calls the bartender by name and orders a pint of beer, then, without even turning to the young man next to him, he whispers:

"Hey, Mohamed, you do know this is a Catholic festival?"

Hamid starts and glances around. It is at this point that he realizes he and Kader are the only two Arabs at the dance. It is strange: in general he always checks. He has developed a sort of automatic radar that kicks in the moment he enters a space and gives him a rough idea of how mixed the crowd is. Tonight, he forgot. He was too excited that they had finally arrived. Instinctively, he takes two steps back, brings his hands in front of him to signal that he is not looking for a fight. Sometimes this is enough. But tonight, the guys have decided not to back down. They are not openly aggressive, they don't push or shove, but they are determined to say their piece. Whether Hamid and his friends leave the dance floor for the bar, or leave the bar to sit at a plastic table, the guys follow.

"You guys don't belong here, you don't belong anywhere, and everyone feels sorry for you. But we're the ones who are being invaded and no one gives a shit. You think that's okay?"

They use words that wound and seethe, pretending to themselves that they are angry when in fact they are simply bored to tears. They don't want to dance with these girls, they know them already, and have already been the objects of their affection or their contempt. They're not into the music. The beer is like cat's piss. They're bored to death and it feels good to be angry, or to pretend to be angry—in the quivering hope that maybe something will kick off.

"Hey, bougnoule, I'm talking to you! Didn't they teach you to respect the White Man? Who do you think fucking feeds you?"

It is Hamid who throws the first punch. He would like to say it was the other way around, but his fist was the first to fly. The fists that came afterward may have punched more accurately or more often, but nothing can change the chronology of the blows. It was he who initially gave them the gift of violence. Gilles immediately piles in with the furious joy of someone who is confident of his strength. Fired up on alcohol, Kader does not hesitate for long. He lashes out wildly, too uncoordinated to aim, and takes more punches than he lands, but he roars enthusiastically because this is his first fight. Julian pushes and pulls: he does not want to fight, simply to separate the combatants, looking for spaces he can open up, blows that are slow enough for him to stop. His policy of appeasement does not mean that he is spared. He, too, takes a beating—one that is all the more painful since he refuses to punch back. What exactly the other side has in mind, I don't know. But one thing is certain: they don't pull their punches, they leave their mark.

The following morning, despite the clever ruses they use to conceal them, Hamid cannot hide the gash above his eyebrow, and Kader cannot hide his crooked nose, or the blue bruises beneath his eyes. When their parents demand an explanation, Hamid shrugs and says that it is not his fault, that the French are racist, or those boys at least, as though the five of them wanted to be the only French people in the world. He sets his bowl on the table, lays his hands flat, and presents the family with a clear view of the ragged, bloody gash above his eyebrow. He assumes his parents will understand his logic, that he will earn the sympathy accorded to any pain or illness in this house, but Ali throws a hunk of bread in his face and calls him an idiot. Of course there's racism out there . . . Does he really think they need him to tell them that? If he wants to avoid it, he simply has to stay with his own kind instead of gallivanting around the countryside and dragging his little brother along with him. Kader does not say a word, but stares more intently at his bowl of coffee.

"What's racism going to do, if you stay put? Climb over our walls and come through the window? Leave racism in French people's houses where it belongs, don't go looking for it. That's all. It's like your sister, going around with that roumi boy . . ."

Faced with this accusation, Dalila stalks away from the breakfast table with the air of an outraged queen. Ali carries on, raising his voice so that she will hear him from the bedroom . . .

"She thinks I don't see him hanging around waiting for her on the other side of the playground. Well, she's looking for trouble. What does she expect? Does she think the boy's mother will be happy to have an Algerian for a daughter-in-law? Why do you all go looking for fights? Morons, that's what you are. You wear me out."

And he does look tired. With a wave of his hand he indicates that he is finished. Yema clears the table, then sets it again for the little ones who will be getting up soon. Hamid and Kader head off for their showers and, as they take their clothes off, reveal new cuts and bruises.

"He thinks that he's still back in Algeria," Hamid protests, stroking his bruised ribs, "that we can all live in our own little world. He doesn't understand anything. Well, I don't give a shit about his little world. I don't want to live there."

The scalding spray of the shower drowns out any further insults. Kader waits, hopping from one foot to the other on the bathroom floor. It does not occur to either of them to associate this morning's tirade with Dalila, just as—despite the open-mindedness they boast of—it did not occur to either of them to invite her to the dance the night before.

In the kitchen, Ali stands, silent and motionless. The bathroom pipes rumble and shudder in the walls. He knows that he will not be able to keep the children close. They have already strayed too far.

They do not want to be part of their parents' world, a tiny world that extends only from the apartment to the factory, from the apartment to the supermarket. A world that grows a little bigger in summer when they go to visit Uncle Messaoud in Provence, only to contract again after a month in the sun. A world that does not exist because it mirrors an

Algeria that no longer exists, one that may never have existed, refashioned on the margins of France.

They want to live a full life, not merely to survive. And more than anything, they don't want to go on saying thank you for the few crumbs they are given. This is what they have had until now: a life made up of crumbs. He has not been able to provide his family with anything more.

Bare feet dangling in the fountains of the Sacré-Coeur, hands rummaging through the secondhand bookstalls on the Boulevard Saint-Michel, body stretched out on the lawns of the Tuileries, silhouette lost among the tourists taking snapshots of a Louvre without its glass pyramid, throat hoarse from shouting at a concert in the back room of some bar, head pounding from the effect of alcohol and sunshine, pockets laden with little gifts picked up along the way for his brothers and sisters, multicolored stickers plastered all over his saddlebag, ears filled with the deafening roar of engines, Hamid wallows while he can in the intoxication that is Paris. He wishes he could shoot it directly into his veins: he loves this city; he is *in love* with it, which he did not believe was possible; he never wants to leave. Here, all the buildings are famous and all the faces anonymous. Through photographs and films, Paris seems to belong to everyone and, as he wanders through it, Hamid realizes he has been missing the city long before he ever set foot in it.

He wants to absorb every moment of the city—vary his comings and goings, try to catch it sleeping. He is fascinated by the fact that, in the dead of night, regardless of the district where he is wandering, his feet invariably lead him to a lit window, to the intimation of a life about which he knows nothing. Julian, who is already accustomed to the city, and Gilles, who is impossible to wake up, don't accompany him on these nocturnal expeditions. He is alone with the mysterious windows. He wants to serenade them. He feels a kinship with all the sleepless people; Paris belongs to them.

Stéphane's two-room attic apartment near the old city gate at Strasbourg-Saint-Denis is perfect for a student. For three boys in search of adventures, however, it is a little cramped. The heat is stifling. They move around, doubled over, with one hand on the beams to make sure they don't bump their heads. Books spill out from under the bed where Stéphane has piled them. The shower is an oddity: wedged into a cupboard. It opens into the kitchen—there is no shower cubicle, let alone a bathroom to protect people from prying eyes. You open the door, step straight under the shower, and step out the same way, with no space in which to wrap yourself in a towel. The three boys gradually become accustomed to this peculiar arrangement that forces them to appear naked in front of whoever is brewing the coffee or cooking spaghetti. In fact, they are fascinated by the opportunity offered by the apartment to parade naked in front of one another, simultaneously embarrassed and proud. The exhibitionism—disguised as modesty—of their boyish buttocks and their manly cocks constitutes proof of their friendship. For the first time, they are confronted with the nakedness of another person, a real person, not the brothers and sisters who are flesh of their flesh and thus an extension of themselves, not the girls—those potential conquests where bravado must compensate for lack of experience—but a simple otherness that they can survey, one where they can show themselves, aware that something important is at stake, a trust they will not often feel, an affectionate competitiveness that is not threatening. Gilles and Julian make fun of Hamid's circumcised penis. He responds by heaping scorn on their useless foreskins, which look like wilting flowers.

Before setting off for Italy, Stéphane left them a list of addresses: cafés, restaurants, the offices of organizations where his friends usually hang out, all the nerve centers of political debate. He does not realize that, having left school and the feeling of incarceration behind, the three boys are—suddenly—much less interested in the overthrow of society. They visit these places all the same, if only to meet people other than the tourists who flood Paris in the summer, obscuring it with baseball caps and cameras in the same way that fat can obscure the features of a face. Hamid and Gilles envy Julian when they see him shaking hands with everyone, emphasizing the fact that he feels at home here. They discover that the anonymity of the big city, however liberating, creates the paradoxical need for places you can go where you are known.

In what remains of a summer not taken up by task forces, neighborhood associations, tribes of squatters, and union meetings, they settle on a vacation routine of beers on café terraces and soccer matches in parks where they are chased by officious whistle-blowing park-keepers who quickly tire in the heat. They spend several desultory evenings traipsing around with a mythomaniac student they met on a bench near Montparnasse who promises to introduce them to Bourdieu and eventually disappears in the corridors of the Barbès Métro one particularly sweltering night. They try to pick up Parisian girls precisely because they are Parisian, but cannot stop themselves from apologizing every time they open their mouths for living in the godforsaken département of Orne. Often, they pretend that they are older so they don't have to admit to Stéphane's friends, who staged sit-ins at the Sorbonne, ripped up paving stones in the Quartier Latin, made thunderous speeches at l'Odéon, and now hang out on the benches of the Bois de Vincennes, that they were still at school during May 1968. They help organize a barbecue for immigrant laborers in a hostel in the *banlieue*, during which they witness a heated argument about the standing of religion within La Cimade. Hearing the name of the organization for the first time in more than a decade, Hamid briefly finds himself back in the time of canvas tents whipped by the tramontane, the time when he was the one standing in line when food was being handed out. The room is spinning, but he stands firm, turning with a wan smile to the volunteers milling around him who mistake him for those holding out their empty plates: them, me, them, me . . . A pretty volunteer from ATD Fourth World sits him down on a plastic chair. Since he does not say a word—the faint smile is still plastered on his face—she talks enough for two. He falls asleep on her shoulder while the argument is still raging a little way away. The following day, he tells Gilles and Julian that they went off into a corner for . . . you know—wink, wink—and that she gave him her phone number.

His friends are convinced that Hamid is a hit with the ladies. Whenever they go to a party, he is instantly surrounded by girls. Gilles and Julian give him envious looks, wondering what he can possibly have to talk to them about. They are intimidated by the feminists in Paris; they don't know how to talk to them. Hamid, on the other hand, seeks them out. Like him, they have been labeled by society as flawed—because they are women. When he talks to men about discrimination and injustice, he finds that they often forget that as white males—even if they are young and working-class—they already belong to the subsection of the population that controls society. They forget that things are not the same for those who look like him. With girls, there is a shared experience; they compare notes about that first condescending stare—men staring at their breasts, men staring at his dark complexion. They talk about the impossibility of being seen as an equal, even for a second, when faced with the enemy, although much of the time they would like to withdraw from this grueling war. On rare occasions, Hamid ends up with a kiss on the lips from these girls, but more often he is rewarded with a friendly arm around his shoulder, and he is more than happy. The apartment is too small, he thinks, philosophically. When the three of them are lying next to each other in Stéphane's bedroom, with the skylights wide open, he, Gilles, and Julian whisper the names of girls they have met, conjuring their spectral forms whose smiles, whose dresses, seem to glide toward them in the darkness.

One night, in what he will claim was impetuous haste, but Gilles and Hamid interpret as smug exhibitionism or, at best, a clumsy pooling of pleasures, Julian arrives back at the apartment several hours after his friends with a girl whose face the two boys never see. The shadowy figures tiptoe through the dark room and slide into the bed.

Gilles and Hamid pretend to be asleep. They listen to the giggles, the sighs, to the girl frantically whispering, "What the hell are you doing?" (Gilles has to bite the pillow to stop himself from laughing), the panting breaths, the sounds of their skin sticking like a suction cup, the little cries, the gasps, their friend's name whispered over and over like an incantation, the muffled wails, and the final groan of relief. When they wake up, the girl is gone and Julian is smoking by the window in the kitchen with a smile like a badge of honor plastered on his face. All three of them will remember this as the night that they made love, even if Gilles and Hamid do not know who with.

Not far from Stéphane's place is a smoky café so cheap the three boys have taken up more or less permanent residence, in the hope of adding an additional room to the apartment, making it feel less cramped. The bar owner, a Kabyle from Fort National, wears a jazzman's hat, is all mouth and broad smiles. If the boys have not eaten (which often happens, since food is a secondary consideration in their budget), he fills three bowls with glossy salted peanuts and sets them on the bar in front of them. He calls it "the poor man's stew":

"Because it costs nothing, fills your belly, but leaves your mouth so dry you'll spend your last franc on a drink."

During the various visits, he tells the boys that he came to France in the fifties with his parents, lived through the period of the notorious Nanterre bidonville, that place of filth and misery at the gates of Paris. He boasts that he spent several years as a vagrant before settling down and "taking over" this bar. He says these words as though the event were akin to storming the Bastille. When he drinks too much, he suddenly becomes maudlin and starts telling Gilles and Julian that the region he hails from is the most beautiful place in the world. He describes the white roofs, the oleanders, the steep slopes covered with hundred-year-old trees, and constantly asks Hamid: "Am I right or am I right?" To Hamid, his descriptions sound more like dusty postcards rather than actual memories, but, because he likes the bar and the owner's hat, he nods vigorously and pretends that he still remembers Kabylia. One evening, in the course of a homage to the homeland, the bar owner asks when he arrived in France and Hamid naively replies:

"In '62."

Beneath the brim of the hat, the smile suddenly vanishes. The bar owner's face becomes expressionless. Hamid wishes he could take back the words he has let fall on the counter. He smiles nervously at Gilles, who does not understand. Later, he will tell Naïma never to answer this question, unless she wants the whole story of her family to be swallowed by the abyss opened up by that date.

"What did your father do?" the owner asks belligerently.

Hamid finds the question particularly painful, because he has no answer. It is not the truculent, aggressive political insinuation that upsets him, but the fact that this man is summarily demanding to know what lies behind his father's silence, a silence Hamid has never been able to penetrate, trampling over years of misgivings, of vain attempts to get his father to talk, of heated arguments—the fact that he is drawing attention to a void Hamid already finds unbearably painful.

"What about you?" he asks, aware that it sounds as though he is defending his father. "What exactly did you do during the war that was so great?"

He doesn't know why he is prepared to be an advocate for Ali's choices. This is not how the conversation is supposed to go. Hamid should be agreeing with the bar owner; he should be trotting out all the carefully penned justifications he has used to dissociate himself—if only privately—from his father's history. But nothing comes to mind, none of the carefully rehearsed slogans, and he is reduced to the level of the bar owner, asking spiteful questions. Unfortunately for him, in the late fifties when he was only a teenager, the bar owner was a bag carrier, something of which he is very proud. He talks about the wads of banknotes slipped into a schoolbag that he would carry from one apartment to another, about the roadblocks, the police who never managed to capture him, about the risks he took for his emerging country. *That* is what he did during the war. The two customers propping up the bar give him a cheer and tap out a triumphant drumroll on the zinc counter. At the back of the bar, the Polish laborers juggle coasters, utterly uninterested in the conversation.

"Your father sold out his country," the heroic Kabyle taunts Hamid, who grits his teeth. "He's a traitor."

Gilles gestures to his friend that they should leave. Julian is already outside smoking a cigarette and staring intently at two streetlights as though playing Spot the Difference. But Hamid refuses to leave:

bad-mouthing his father is something that only he has the right to do. He is enraged by the bar owner's neat, carefully ordered memories—Hamid's only memories of the war are blurred and confused. It is easy to justify yourself with memories; too easy.

"Okay, maybe you didn't betray Algeria," he roars into the smug face, "but tell me something: When was the last time you went back, huh? You say you're Algerian, but you've been here in France for twenty years. Why lie to yourself? Because you're planning to go back there to die? What difference will that make? Okay, so Algerian maggots will get to eat your body—and I guess that's enough for you to be happy."

"Yes, I am happy," the man bellows, his face flushing crimson. "At least I have a country!"

Hamid applauds derisively.

"And in the meantime, you don't live anywhere. You don't live here, you turn your back on everything that happens here because you're Algerian so France is none of your business. But there's nothing you can do for Algeria because you're far away. Your whole life is 'tomorrow,' it's 'back there'!"

The bar owner says something, but Hamid is not listening. He turns away, pointedly picks up a newspaper lying on the bar, and pretends to leaf through it, giving the man a weary shrug as though he is no longer interested in the conversation. He knows he should pay for his drink and leave, but, as he turns to the sports page, he looks up again and waves the newspaper in the man's face.

"I suppose this is what you call being Algerian—standing behind your Paris bar reading the results of soccer matches between a couple of godforsaken shitholes in Kabylia?"

In a flurry of punches and smashed glasses, Gilles and Hamid are ejected from the bar by the owner and his two faithful disciples. As they are being shoved toward the door, they throw a few wild punches over their shoulders. Their adversaries unceremoniously toss the boys onto the pavement, knocking over a couple of chairs that clatter and clang, prompting the few pedestrians on the street to hurry past. As Julian rushes to help, he gets an elbow in the chest that sends him sprawling on top of his friends with a ridiculous, childish wail.

"Fuck!" Gilles howls as Julian lands on them.

As they struggle to their feet, groaning, the bar owner reappears and tosses the contents of the huge washing-up basin over them. The greasy, reddish-gray water hits them with a soft splash.

Drenched and reeking, they wander the streets of Paris, unable to find a bar prepared to serve them the last drink they desperately need. They wander around the Place de la République, along the Canal Saint-Martin, heading toward Châtelet. In parks engulfed by darkness, shadowy figures install themselves on the benches in a clamor of whispers and broken glass, but the boys are too scared to scale the railings and join them. A bar on the Rue Saint-Denis agrees to let them in, but they are put off by the heavily made-up faces of women in the neon glow, monstrous masks waiting to devour them. They turn and head back toward Stéphane's apartment. Gradually their shoulders slump, their bodies bend like creased cards. Hamid throws surreptitious glances at his two friends but cannot decode their silence. The only sound is that of their footsteps, as their soles wear thin on the concrete and pick up wads of chewing gum. All along their route, windows turn dark and metal shutters roll down. Before going back up to the apartment, they sit on the steps of the Métro station and smoke a last cigarette.

"Gotta say," Gilles mutters, "that was all a bit grim. Hanging out with you means we get beaten up by French guys *and* Algerians."

He spits on the pavement, a gob of pinkish saliva still tinged with blood.

"Can't say we're not having fun!"

The gleam in his eyes indicates that he is not being entirely tongue-in-cheek.

"Woe betide the vanquished," Hamid says laconically.

"Woe betide you and your thousand faces," Gilles says, punching him on the arm.

"Pair of fucking idiots," Julian says, smiling.

The smell of Bolognese and warm beer from their clothes mingles with that of melted tar and gas fumes. They gaze up at the bas-reliefs on the Porte Saint-Denis in which battles that they have never heard of are still being waged and acclaimed in song in long Latin inscriptions. It is a summer night in Paris and the three boys sit on the steps, indifferent to the beating they have just taken, perhaps even happy to accept the beating as one more adventure that can only bind them closer, one of those incidents that instantly becomes a founding memory, one destined to be endlessly recounted to unite the group.

The summer of '72 is almost over when Hamid meets Clarisse. Already the boys have stopped scattering their belongings all over Stéphane's apartment. Now they toss them closer to their rucksacks, ready to head home. They start talking about September as though it begins tomorrow and is not some dim distant future in which anything is possible.

On that particular night, they go to a party given by Beaux-Arts students in an abandoned railway station in the banlieue. Beneath the vaulted steel arches, in the evening glow that struggles to filter through the murky windows, Hamid sees her for the first time. She is pinned between a wall and a rickety pile of coolers by a guy vaguely dressed up as Andy Warhol who is calling her a bad feminist for choosing to do manual activities traditionally reserved for women.

"But I *like* doing them . . ." Clarisse says irritably.

"That's what they *want* you to think," the faux-Warhol says.

He continues to try to convince her she is wrong, citing endless examples and quotations, oblivious to her increasing irritation. With a sigh, she turns her head, and, as she weighs up the difficulty of squeezing past the multicolored coolers, her eyes meet those of Hamid, who is gingerly moving toward the beer supply. Suddenly she flashes him a broad smile, pushes Warhol aside as though moved by an irresistible urge, throws her arms around Hamid's neck, and exclaims: "I've been waiting *ages* for you!" Hamid plays along, pretends to be an old friend, and leads her away. Later, when they talk about it, she will grimace slightly, to acknowledge that she is conscious of the half-baked romanticism of her phrase (while hoping he agrees), and say:

"Maybe it was true, maybe I really was waiting for you."

As soon as they have moved away from the boy with the bleach-blond mop, Clarisse apologizes for throwing herself at Hamid. He is not sure whether she is embarrassed or whether she is joking: she rapidly strings together words like "horrifying," "appallingly," and even "to death," smiling all the while. She talks a lot, as though trying to quickly kindle an intimacy between them that will make her initial impulse authentic. She explains that she was dragged here by her friend Véronique, who was meeting up with her boyfriend, but that she is sorry she agreed to come. She can't stand students from the École des Beaux-Arts, who look down on her. Having spent the past two years studying arts and crafts at the Atelier des Arts Manuels, she has had her fill of condescending remarks from students at the École des Beaux-Arts.

"They can't bear the fact that both colleges have the word 'arts' in their names. They're desperate to prove that they're the only ones who deserve to use the word. I don't care, they can say what they like, I give up . . ."

Then she comes out with a phrase that puzzles Hamid—but perhaps curiosity is the first stage of love?—and she says:

"Personally, I'm not interested in just being a good old-fashioned girl."

Clarisse weaves, she sews, she sketches, she paints, she sculpts, she models, and she cooks. With her hands, she fashions the world into whatever she wants, regardless of materials. She has no pretensions beyond that, which, in itself, is astonishing.

After a "happening" that they both laughingly admit they did not understand at all, they decide to leave. They take a bus that jolts them back toward the center of Paris. She lives near Bastille, something she mentions several times, as though afraid that he will take her somewhere else, as though she might forget. But when they get off at the Gare de Lyon, instead of walking toward her apartment, they head down toward the Seine. In the dusty, antiquated glow of the streetlights, they reach the dark ribbon of river and follow it downstream to the west. Unbeknownst to them, they lightly run their hands along a section of stone wall where, ten years earlier, were daubed the words:

HERE WE DROWN ALGERIANS

Clarisse walks a few steps ahead, swinging a sort of beach bag containing nothing but two twenty-franc notes and a pack of cigarettes that rattles like a snake. He follows, hands in his pockets. When she stops to pretend that she is looking at something on the bank below, he comes and rests his head on her shoulder. (They are almost the same height.) He does not dare put his arms around her. He breathes in the scent of her neck, her hair, the warmth of her skin. They stand motionless until a cramp sets in, watching a rat shred a packet of cookies on the broad paving stones.

"Do you want to kiss me?" Clarisse asks, as though offering him a cigarette.

It is at this point that he realizes they probably have different notions of what constitutes *a good old-fashioned girl.*

In the last days of August, Gilles, Julian, and Hamid pack their bags in the tiny apartment they already look on with nostalgia, as the stage set for *Summer in Paris,* a play that will never be performed again. On the station platform, they hug each other warmly. Gilles and Julian board a crowded train of vacationers leaving the city. Gilles is going to work as a waiter in a hotel in Granville. Julian is to begin studying biology at the University of Caen. Hamid is staying. He has decided not to take his suitcases back to Pont-Féron. He will move them into the apartment Clarisse shares with Véronique. Since their first kiss on the banks of the Seine ten days earlier, they have barely been apart, and when Clarisse suggested he come and stay with her at the end of the summer, he said yes without a second thought, perhaps simply so that he could dream, so he could imagine that it might be possible. Clarisse smiled and whispered, "Good," and changed the subject and, since it all seemed so simple, he longed, for once, to believe that it was.

In Arnaud Desplechin's film *My Sex Life . . . or How I Got into an Argument*—which Naïma and her friend Sol will later watch over and over—Jeanne Balibar comes out with a wonderful, twisted line: "Jesus, I wish I had been spared like all of you." Hamid feels something similar when he watches Clarisse live. His longing to be like her is sometimes tinged with bitterness, but for the most part he admires her, and tries to emulate her.

When he phoned his parents to tell them that he was still in Paris, he felt the same crazy pounding of his heart as when he first lied about the contents of a letter from school. This is a decision he has taken without consultation, an additional rupture of the family. And yet he knows that it is one he had to make there and then, that if he went home, if he were confronted by the joyous tribe of brothers and sisters he has cared for, he might never find the courage (the selfishness?) to leave them again.

"What are you going to do?" Clarisse asks.

"Work," he says.

She pulls a face. The word comes spontaneously and is utterly devoid of enthusiasm. Work, it is nothing more than the simple mechanism through which to access money. With no passion. No excitement.

NEVER WORK

was another graffiti slogan daubed all over the walls of the capital a few years earlier. This is one that she read and liked.

"It's not a problem," Hamid says. "My whole life has prepared me for this. And besides, I can't sponge off you . . ."

Clarisse persists, tries to persuade him that there is no hurry, that he should study. She talks about men holed up in factories—although she knows less about this subject than he does—for whom work is a life sentence. She quotes Marx, laughing as if it were a swear word or a dirty joke: We must once again storm heaven. This, perhaps, is the moment when Hamid truly falls in love, when he realizes that, to Clarisse, he has a right to greatness, like everyone else.

In the weeks that follow, he falls further. Love is like an endless tunnel, like the rabbit hole that leads Alice to Wonderland. At any moment, he expects to find some flaw in Clarisse, something that might halt or slow his descent, but he finds none, and so he falls, terrified, exultant, amazed. She does not change after they move in together. Hamid cannot abide the sudden changes he has seen in other girls—especially Julian's girlfriends—who, when a relationship turns serious, stop being the charming, exuberant partners they were at first, begin to nag and sulk, turn into temperamental children who demand attention by constant whining or sudden orders. Clarisse remains precisely herself, she is still the same girl she was on the banks of the Seine the night they met, as though she feels that being someone's girlfriend gives her no special prerogatives, as though she has no mask to drop, no quagmire into which to sink. Clarisse is Clarisse to the core.

When he first goes home to Flers, he cannot stop saying, "Clarisse says . . ." "Clarisse thinks . . ."

"Who exactly is this girl?" Yema asks suspiciously. "Is she a witch or something?"

Who exactly is this girl? It is a question Hamid often asks himself. He studies her, hoping to find answers. He could watch her go about her life and never get bored, could spend hours in a darkened cinema watching a film made up of close-ups of her hands, her face.

Clarisse has short, spiky hair, like a silken hedgehog. Clarisse has blue eyes speckled with navy. Clarisse has only one dimple. Clarisse wears his T-shirts and jeans, and he wears Clarisse's clothes.

"You're so slim," she whispers admiringly, "you're beautiful like a girl."

He savors the novelty of such a phrase in his ear, this compliment that in Pont-Féron could be said only as an insult.

Clarisse has pale, creamy skin. Often they press their arms or legs together and compare their complexions.

Clarisse is his strength, his backbone. Being with her, he can toss aside every last vestige of those roles he never wanted, as elder brother, as head of the family. She does not expect power or protection from him, nor—and this still surprises him—does she expect advice.

"I know what I'm going to do," she often says when he proposes a solution to a problem she has confided.

"Then why are you telling me all this?"

"So we can share it," Clarisse says cheerfully, as though the problem were a cake she has just taken from the oven.

With Clarisse, he is free to think, to take his time, to be inefficient. He is convinced that anyone who was with Clarisse would aspire to being an artist, would believe that it was possible. Her hierarchy of professions is different from that of ordinary mortals—or at least those Hamid has known before now. Clarisse has the free spirit of those who have been told, not that they must be the best, but that they should do what they love.

Despite her misgivings, he signs up with a temping agency and criss-crosses the city, doing manual work for a few hours, a few days—like his father when he was simply an itinerant farmworker before the torrent brought the olive press, like Youcef, who was always scouring the mountains for small jobs. The time he gets to spend with Clarisse between his jobs is enough to make him feel as though his life is more than just drudgery. She tries to teach him to paint. He paints Clarisse. Tries to teach him to sculpt. Using a bevel and a cake of Marseilles soap, he sculpts Clarisse. Tries to teach him to mold. His fingers are tainted red with clay as he tries to replicate the curve of her hips. When he has finished, they agree that she looks like a heron, like Georges Marchais, or the whale that swallowed Jonah.

"Maybe art isn't your thing," Clarisse gently whispers.

She says it with the confidence of someone who knows that there is "a thing" out there for everyone and Hamid will soon find his.

With Clarisse, he discovers a very different Paris from the one he discovered over the summer, a city of antique dealers, craftsmen, and materials. Clarisse loves to go to the flea market at Saint-Ouen, where she picks up old things that her hands bring back to life. When Hamid first goes there with her, he feels as though the belongings of freshly plundered corpses have been laid out along the streets. Everything smells of skin. He cannot understand why anyone would want to occupy the place a stranger's body once did, be it in clothes or on a piece of furniture. Seeing these objects laid out on blankets or on the concrete pavement, he thinks of the piles of clothes spilling from humanitarian aid trucks in the camp at Rivesaltes, and the feeling of revulsion makes him choke. Clarisse desperately wants to make him a present and is insisting that he choose something, so he settles on an old Tarzan comic, with a cover depicting the King of the Jungle swinging on a vine just above a burning train that has been derailed and is about to hurtle over a cliff. (Catastrophes come in threes.) His hand is shaking as he flips through the pages and sees the *Hahaha*s and *AAAAAAAAAAH*s he remembers from his childhood.

"Are you okay?" Clarisse asks worriedly.

The walls of their bedrooms are plastered with photographs of Clarisse at different stages of her life, smiling, smeared with chocolate, sobbing. He appears in the most recent photos, as though he were born at age twenty. Of the past, and of his early years in France in particular, he says nothing. He responds to her questions with a shrug, a smile, an evasion. Sometimes he thinks that he is like his father, that in spite of himself he is bowing to the exigencies of *sabr*: master the tempests in your soul, forbid your tongue from all complaint, do not claw at your cheeks when life puts you to the test. Since he does not like the thought, he tries desperately to find some other explanation for his silence: Clarisse would feel awkward. She would pity him. She would suddenly realize the yawning gap between them. Can someone who has been spared ever understand someone who has not?

Twice a week he goes down and calls home from the telephone booth on the corner. More often than not, it stinks of piss. Sometimes it stinks of death and Hamid wonders whether, in the middle of the night, someone crawled in here to die like a sick animal. The telephone in the apartment is in Véronique's bedroom. Hamid does not want to be seen when he regresses and becomes once again the little boy from Pont-Féron. Although neither Clarisse nor her friend understand Arabic, Hamid feels it would be somehow obscene for him to expose himself to them in his other language. The Paris apartment is no place for such things, it is a place where he can reinvent himself.

He goes downstairs to face the stench of the phone booth and the passersby peering at him through the glass walls. He calls with a machinelike regularity, always the same day, the same time, driven by a sense of duty whose power surprises him. The family uses his distance to register their grievances and list the quarrels between neighbors, the little ones' problems at school, the sullen moods of Dalila, who wishes that she could escape as he has done but is being forced to finish school by their parents, the sporting achievements of Claude, who won the long-distance race, but whose coach has refused to send him to the regional finals.

"That's good," he says, without really listening, "that's good."

Just as his father did before him, just like a patriarch who no longer understands his family but refuses to abdicate his position of authority.

After a few weeks working as a temp at the Sécurité Sociale as an "advanced writing technician" (a job title that is intriguing in theory, since it makes him sound like Champollion deciphering the Rosetta stone but in practice involves sorting files), he is offered the opportunity to take a management training course.

"You must have an amazing talent for sorting files," Clarisse murmurs dreamily, "to be so quickly singled out for promotion." Hamid gratefully accepts the offer, convinced that, though the course may not offer intellectual stimulation, in the long term it will at least give him a social life so his loneliness does not weigh entirely on Clarisse. From time to time, he meets up with Stéphane, who treats him more like a little brother than a friend, unable to understand that, since the end of the summer, Hamid believes he has become a new man and finds any allusion to his previous life hurtful. He sometimes sends Gilles and Julian postcards he finds in the flea markets Clarisse so loves, postcards commemorating scenes from their Parisian odyssey: not of famous monuments but of streets, squares, parks, slivers of night, streetlights reflected in puddles. On the back, he writes laconic phrases that he hopes sound mysterious and adult. He misses his friends, and, though he refuses to admit it, he misses his brothers and sisters. Everywhere seems empty when it does not echo with their constant clamor, their cries and laughter. He finds himself thinking of people from Pont-Féron he was convinced he would forget as soon as he left. It is not the individuals themselves that he remembers, but the groups who used to hang around outside the housing projects, the reassuring thought that, whenever he went home, he would find so-and-so at such-and-such a place and someone else here or there, this comforting geography of meeting places that never changed. He is bewildered by the whirl of faces on the streets of Paris, the perpetual motion of interchangeable passersby in which a few familiar figures appear: the man who runs the kiosk, the old woman who reads *Paris Match* at the same café table, the concierge in the building opposite, the wino who sleeps off his hangovers in the launderette . . .

He learns to recognize those who, like him, explore the night, including those whom he at first assumes are of little interest, being like their shirts: neat, clean-cut, well turned out. He drinks a few beers with them. There are two girls with biblical names from Martinique, the Corsican who overplays his Corsican heritage. They ask where he comes from, and when Hamid says from Normandy, they all pretend that this was the answer they expected.

He gets to know the gang who hang around with Véronique and Clarisse, a curious assortment of nice girls who are proud of the fact and young men who like to think of themselves as bad boys. He sometimes thinks that Clarisse's male friends play at being tough guys for his benefit, prompted by what they imagine of his past, embellishing and inventing brawls they have just won as though trying to turn their mundane existence into a lawless jungle that fits with their fantasies of Hamid's life.

One night one of the girls giggles as she runs her fingers through the tight curls of his Afro.

"It's like moss," she laughs.

Hamid hunches a little, not daring to protest. The hand lingers, toying, poking into the tight curls. He feels hot. People are staring. He tries not to move.

"Stop that," Clarisse curtly tells her friend.

Dumbstruck, the girl removes her hand. She doesn't understand Clarisse's reaction. Later, with aggrieved astonishment, she will claim Clarisse is jealous. After her friends have left, Clarisse tries to console Hamid:

"People did the same thing to me when I cut my hair short."

He pretends to accept the parallel, although he knows that the two situations have nothing in common. (Years later, Naïma's youngest sister, Aglaé, will provoke a passionate argument over a family meal by wearing a T-shirt emblazoned: YOUR HAND ON MY AFRO, MY FIST IN YOUR FACE.)

He listens to the sounds of the city that drift up to the half-open bedroom window, the squeal of brakes, the nocturnal conversations, the music of a distant neighbor, the chirrup of birds so confused by the streetlights that they no longer know when to sleep. Paris, beyond these walls, is immense, and yet the awestruck love he feels for the city is not enough to drown out his bitter feelings of loneliness.

For the first time he finds himself with no one who shares his history. His earliest memories of Clarisse are barely a few months old and they have worn them out already, constantly recalling every second of their first meeting, trying to squeeze out every drop of magic. No one in Paris knows what happened before that evening at the warehouse party. When he left Pont-Féron, Hamid hoped that he might become a blank slate. He believed that he could reinvent himself, only to discover that others are simultaneously reinventing him. Silence is not a neutral space, it is a blank screen on which everyone is free to project their fantasies. Because Hamid remains silent, he exists in a multitude of versions that conflict with one another and, more importantly, conflict with his version of himself—yet continue to exist in the minds of others.

In order to be understood, he would need to tell his story. He knows that this is what Clarisse is waiting for. The problem is that he has no desire to tell his story. She watches anxiously as he drifts away on a sea of silence.

"I can't tell you over the phone, you have to come home," Ali interrupts him.

In the background he hears his mother's voice, pleading and cajoling. Good cop, bad cop, he knows the routine. But today the stench of the phone booth is unbearable and he is desperate to end the call. He agrees to go home for the weekend, hangs up the phone, steps outside, and takes a deep breath.

"Can I go with you?" Clarisse asks.

Hamid hesitates, then shakes his head.

"Some other time," he says.

If Clarisse spoke Kabyle, she would respond with Yema's phrase: *Azka d azqa*, "Tomorrow is the grave."

"Maybe his parents want him to marry one of their own?" Véronique says.

Clarisse shrugs. So what? This is what parents do. Since she left home, her mother has tried to set her up with two lawyers, a doctor, and a mathematics professor in Dijon.

"So, have you introduced her to Hamid?" Véronique asks, although she already knows the answer.

Clarisse mutters that if Hamid does not want her to meet his parents, she is not going to introduce him to hers. She clings to this idea of reciprocity so she does not have to examine the real reasons she has never mentioned Hamid's existence to her family. The fact that she spends her time carefully refashioning the world with her hands often allows her to ignore the questions going around and around inside her head. But she cannot quite silence her thoughts, and from time to time fragments of answers flicker through her mind, waiting for her to have the courage to consider them. Her uncle Christian did his military service in Algeria and brought back a seemingly never-ending string of epithets for the local people: *crouille, bicot, l'arbi, fatma, ton, raton, melon, mohamed, tronc-de-figuier, fellouze* . . . He says them for a laugh, to provoke a reaction, but although Clarisse's parents scowl, she has never heard them criticize his comments. Not that she believes that her parents are *racist*, a heinous word that seems somehow remote and applies to Nazis in uniform, to skinheads who are ready to say anything to differentiate themselves from hippies, to the new political party chasing votes of which Jean-Marie Le Pen was recently appointed president. The problem is not that Hamid is an outsider: on the contrary, the fact that he comes from Algeria means that, like it or not, he is already part of Uncle Christian's history and the history of Clarisse's family. And in that story, he is not one of the good guys. Clarisse would need to create a palimpsest, to overwrite Christian's earliest inscriptions with the story of her love for Hamid. She does not know whether she is capable of that.

The train speeds through the lush countryside where cows flaunt their mottled coats of black and white. Hamid ignores them just as he ignores the person sitting next to him and his attempts at conversation: he is not interested in anything other than Clarisse. He does not understand why he has to continue being the family secretary once he has left home. (In his night classes, this is referred to as "dereliction of duty.") He is afraid this means that he will never truly leave Pont-Féron and treats this first enforced homecoming as though it were a permanent state of affairs—one that he will dread for years to come. His sullen mood is his way of making his parents pay for the things they have not yet asked of him.

Once he is settled at the living room table and Yema has set out the coffee and a plate of *kaab el ghazal* that leave his fingers and lips white with powdered sugar, Ali lays a large manila envelope on the table and warily points out the official stamp of the Algerian government. It is because of the stamp that they have not dared ask a neighbor or the little ones to read it—Hamid uses "the little ones" to refer only to his youngest brothers and sisters, while Ali and Yema use the phrase to refer to all their children—except Hamid—since, in their eyes, the others will never quite be adults, never quite responsible.

Hamid tears open the envelope and, one by one, takes out a sheaf of documents of various colors, careful not to look at any until he has them all arranged on the table. The documents they have been sent are in two columns, one Arabic, one French, each running toward the opposite margin, each superbly oblivious to the other, two systems of writing the world that are utterly different.

Hear ye! Hear ye! Hamid hears his inner child proclaim as he begins to read the contents to his parents: *By the power vested in these documents, and in the name of the Agrarian Revolution, Sieur Ali is hereby enjoined to ratify the transfer of his lands to those working the aforesaid lands.* He struggles to find the right words to translate the bureaucratic language into Arabic, but Ali and Yema quickly realize what it is about and their faces fall. The letter requests that they give up the olive groves, the fig trees, the houses, and the stores to Hamza and to Djamel's family. According to the revolution, private property no longer exists except as usufruct. He who tills the land, owns the land; it is as simple as that. Ali must also give up a number of his fields because their total area exceeds that permitted under the new agrarian policy. The surplus land will be transferred to a farming cooperative and later redistributed to *khammès*—peasants too poor to buy their own plot who, until now, have paid rent to landowners in order to be allowed to cultivate some of their acreage. (In fact, the documents Hamid reads are more succinct—it is Naïma's research that fleshes out the aims of the revolution.)

In one of the drawers of the monstrous dresser, Yema has kept keys to the old house and the barn. Her first instinct is to go and fetch them, as though the letter is demanding that she send back these keys she has taken with her everywhere. She stares at them, clasps them in her plump fist, not saying a word. It is not as though she thought she would ever need them again, but these worthless keys strung on a frayed length of cord did keep alive the notion that they were landowners, the notion that there were fields on the far side of the Mediterranean that belonged to them, were waiting for them—perhaps just as they themselves were waiting, motionless, quiescent.

Hamid can see the distress of his tiny mother and his aging father, but he does not share their pain. He can only endorse the principles of agrarian reform, which conform to those in a book lent to him by Stéphane. He tries to tell his parents that the program of reform is a means to a more just world, but Ali shrugs and Yema turns away. Hamid changes tack: They have not even set eyes on these fields for ten years. What do they care whether the fields belong to them, to his father's brother, or to a tenant farmer? What difference does it make? He insists because he knows his parents are powerless against the relentless march of the revolution. The bureaucratic civilities of the letter do nothing to hide the fact that there is no alternative to dispossession.

"You'll have nothing to leave to your children," Ali says sadly.

Hamid laughs. He finds it difficult to imagine what his hypothetical children would do with groves of olives and figs a thousand miles away.

"Your father planted those trees for you, for them," Yema says reproachfully. "You don't understand anything."

He has heard this phrase so often that he doesn't stop to think, doesn't search his heart for some compassion. One day he will draw up a list of all the things that his parents do not understand.

"Fine," he says defiantly, "if the trees are mine, I will be the one to give them back to Algeria. That way, everyone is happy."

As he reaches for the pen, Hamid receives the last slap he will ever get. Ali half rises from his seat and lashes out across the table with all the weight of his clumsy posture. His large hand hits Hamid on the chin.

"Show a little respect," he mutters. "Just a little respect."

Hamid feels the pain radiate from his jaw through his whole face. He has bitten his tongue and it is bleeding; he can taste copper in his mouth. Yema quickly brings him a damp tea towel. He does not notice her concern or her panic. He picks the pen up off the floor and, in a triumphant rage, signs the documents in his father's stead.

"*Li fat met*," he says, pushing the papers into the middle of the table.

The words resurface from an ancient past and, in the process, they consign it to limbo. *Li fat met*: The past is dead. Hamid has just signed its death certificate. He does not spend the night as he had promised his mother and the little ones, but storms out of the apartment.

As he slams the door, he hears Yema sobbing—that strange dove-like cooing she makes when she cries—but he refuses to be moved. He paces around the cité, head down, saying nothing to anyone. He vows never to come back here, and for long months he keeps his promise. (Ali, for his part, will not get in touch with his son when he travels to Paris the next month.)

From this moment, Hamid will cherish the miles separating him from Pont-Féron. At the station, he waits a long time for a train to finally arrive and take him back to Paris, scrolling back the dreary landscape that he ignored a few hours earlier, whose expanse he savors now that he is determined never to cross it again.

He arrives home at nightfall. The blow to his jaw has flowered into a bruise. In the narrow hallway, he takes off his coat and his shoes, pretending not to notice Clarisse's anxious looks.

"What happened?" she asks finally.

"I don't want to talk about it."

She insists. She trails after him as he goes into the bathroom, the bedroom, the kitchen. She has a right to know, she says, then corrects herself, says she needs to know, please. She feels humiliated, being forced to plead for information. She carries on only because, having started, she can think of nothing else, not even of saying nothing (especially not saying nothing). When she blocks his path in the hallway, he angrily asks why she's so fascinated by his family. Is it because she finds them quaint and exotic?

"Because let me warn you right now: there's no camel."

Clarisse's lips begin to tremble, her face crumples. Hamid lights a cigarette and smokes in silence, refusing to look at her.

"I'm sorry," he says eventually.

As she is drifting off to sleep as far from Hamid's arms as the bed will allow, Clarisse wonders whether she should break up with him. You can't be in love with someone's silence, she thinks, it doesn't make sense. She shouldn't care about the things Hamid refuses to talk about, she should accept that his past is not part of their present, that he's free to do as he likes. But because she feels that he carries it with him constantly, that his past affects him, affects *them*, she cannot bring herself to consider it a closed book. To her, it is like a secret life that he is living in parallel to the life they live together. It is more hurtful than another woman, she thinks, or some shameful addiction he refuses to acknowledge, simply because it has been going on for longer, because with every second he spends with her, he is silently reliving twenty years that are closed to her. Maybe, Clarisse thinks, her skin chafed by the sheets as she tosses and turns, maybe she should break up with him. But when she sees him sleeping, and imagines that this might be the last time she will ever see his face, the closed eyes, the narrow chest swelled by the calm, regular breaths of sleep, she feels like crying, the very thought of a breakup crushes her heart like the hand of an ogre. What can she do? She decides to stay with him but to share less with him, to keep secret certain thoughts of her own, certain memories, certain achievements. She decides to establish a level playing field, one that might make Hamid's silence less painful.

In the morning, when he wakes, Hamid finds Clarisse looking at him. Something in her face alarms him—he can make out the resolution made that night in a deep furrow carved between her brows, in the fact that the corners of her mouth are drooping a little more. He longs to talk to her, but none of his thousand faces seems prepared to open up, none is practiced in the art of intimacy. He closes his eyes again without saying a word.

"Who is it?"

The voice on the other end of the line answers in Kabyle. Kader hands the telephone to his father and simply says:

"Mohand."

He does not know who this man is, he has no memory of the members of the association in Palestro, but from his father's face he can tell that the call comes as a surprise.

"Salaam Alaikum," Ali says, taking the receiver.

He says nothing else, not, It's been a long time, not, What do you want? He leaves Mohand to explain that he is in France, in Lyon, staying with his nephew, but that he is planning to head north to see his cousins. Maybe they could meet up.

"Of course," Ali says. "Let's meet in Paris."

He says it as though it is a town close by, a place he knows intimately and visits regularly.

"You shouldn't see him," Yema says. "He's a vile man. A murderer."

"He's one of us," Ali says.

If the letter about the Agrarian Revolution had not provoked a quarrel that has made the silence between father and son even more opaque, Ali might have asked Hamid to join them and, at the same time, through Mohand, given him back a sliver of the Algeria they had left so abruptly. Hamid might have recognized Mohand as one of the guests at his circumcision, might have been pleased to see him again. And if that happened, perhaps Hamid might have spoken about him to Naïma, about the man on the far side of the Mediterranean who had the courage, the clarity of mind, or the good fortune to fight on the right side. But Ali is too proud to take the first step and contact his son. He goes alone to this meeting that—were I not to write about it—would sink, with his death, into complete oblivion.

On the appointed day, he dons his best suit (his only suit) and takes the train to Paris. He meets Mohand at the Gare Montparnasse. Mohand is waiting on the windy platform, wearing his best coat (his only coat). The two men awkwardly shake hands. It has been more than ten years since they last saw each other. Now in their fifties and graying, they search each other's faces for the ravages of time they do not notice in their own reflections. And when they walk, they throw back their shoulders, trying to look like the memory they think they left behind.

Ali, in his role as a French citizen, treats Mohand as a tourist, which means that by extension he must pretend to be Parisian. He vaguely points out various monuments that all look much the same to him. Meanwhile, all he can think is: Does my son live nearby? Is this a familiar sight for him? Together, they wander the streets, saying little or nothing, and, when it is time to eat, Ali stops in front of a restaurant with windows lettered in gold and a velvet interior. The doorman looks at them in astonishment. Much as Ali would like to pretend that he is a habitué of such places, he is ill at ease from the moment they step inside. He does not know how to move, how to speak, where to look. He doesn't know how to sit down without jostling the other diners. He doesn't know what to order or—worse still—how to order. He can tell that Mohand has noticed his discomfort, and this simply makes matters worse. As the waiter brings a first course that he did not want, Ali asks in a tone he hopes sounds casual how things are going back in the bled. Mohand sighs and, his mouth full of herring, says things are not good.

"We're draining the country and filling up France. There are no men left in the village. The only men left are the cripples and the lunatics. The ones who can't work. The ones who are happy to let their mothers cook for them. Or the ones who've come back saying France has broken them, worn them out, that they're not fit for anything anymore. Which is probably true. When you look at their faces, they seem very old. You, too, Ali, I'm sorry to say it but you look old. It's something France does to people, that's just how it is. You'd have been better off staying at home."

"I couldn't."

"You don't know that. Maybe they'd have killed you, maybe they wouldn't. Look at Hamza, he's still in the bled. They didn't even arrest him. A lot of harkis stayed in the old country, and they're still standing."

"They killed Djamel!" Ali's voice chokes on the words and people at the surrounding tables turn to look. "They killed Akli! And thousands of others! Why would I risk it? It was obvious that Algeria didn't want us. They pushed us out the door to the sound of machine gun fire . . ."

Mohand's bad faith has taken away Ali's appetite. He pushes aside a plate of tiny, carefully arranged vegetables he does not recognize and did not expect to enjoy.

"Maybe, maybe," Mohand admits. "You know, sometimes I don't know what it was all for. Independence is all well and good, but when you see the village now, you realize we're still consumed by France. Completely. Young people don't even try to find work in the country. They ask for their papers and they head for France. And then when they come back, they think they're too good for the place. They throw money around, pretend they don't remember how things work in the village. All they can talk about is France. To listen to them, you'd think they lived like kings there. But I went to visit my nephew in Lyon. Last summer, he told me that if I came he could put me up. But then I get to Lyon, and he doesn't answer his phone. He pretends to disappear. But I know where he works, so I go looking for him. He's really embarrassed. He says, 'Uncle, what a surprise!' And starts telling me that it's not a good time, that things aren't easy for him right now. Obviously he can't leave me out on the street like a dog, so he takes me back to the apartment. When he opens the door, it is pitch-black inside. There are four of them, all men from the village, sharing a tiny room. That's what life in France is like. I end up sharing a mattress with him. He says to me, 'You've come for the money. That's fine. I'll get it for you.' But I know he can't. He hasn't got a centime in his pockets. Even to go to a café he has to borrow from his neighbors. And when I'm leaving, he says: 'Maybe it is better not to talk about this, uncle.' I don't even ask him what he means. I know he means his life. Because next summer, when he comes home, he will be strutting around like a peacock again. He'll make France seem just a bit more attractive to the village boys and they'll want to go, too. That's all the village is now: an echo chamber for the lies brought back by emigrants. They hang on his every word, but every word is a lie. Maybe you're lucky after all. You might not see it. I can understand. But at least you don't have to lie, because you never go back. And besides, you have your family here. Back in the village, we see women and children who have no husband, no father. They live like widows and orphans, even though the man is still alive, but he is working on the far side of the Mediterranean. Algeria is constantly counting its missing. Did you know that when they did the census in 1966, they included all those who were absent? What will they do next time? Include the dead?"

When the bill comes, Ali insists on paying. He will regret it at the end of the month, but he cannot help wanting to show Mohand that he is doing well. Or rather—since he knows that Mohand won't believe that he is rich, that Mohand has worked out what life is like for most North Africans here—he simply cannot give up the pretense, cannot help but play at being successful even though they both know that it is a game. And Mohand, out of politeness, plays along.

They wander through the streets of the 3rd arrondissement and eventually sit on a café terrace.

"I feel like an anisette," Mohand says.

For the first time that evening, the two men smile. They sip the pale cloudy liquor as cars pass on the boulevard, their yellow headlights growing scarcer.

"Are they good sons, your boys?" Mohand asks suddenly.

Ali's hand tingles, he can almost feel Hamid's jaw, which he slapped with all his might a month earlier.

"Yes," he says finally, almost surprised.

"That's good."

"I spend my life telling them the opposite."

They order another round, and this time Mohand insists on paying. He pulls a wad of crumpled notes from his pocket.

"My sons are entitled to apartments, to loans, to jobs, all because I was in the maquis during the war. Everything is easier. That's all we ever wanted, isn't it? When we chose one side or the other, all we wanted was for life to be easier for our children . . ."

"Yes," Ali says.

"My sons are just like all the others: they want to go to France, or even to South America. Whenever they talk about Algeria they sneer, and yet they are not prepared to give a minute of their time to improve the very things they sneer at . . ."

The waiter sets down two fresh glasses of anisette.

"I'm doing all the talking here," Mohand remarks, pouring a little water into the clear liquid. "Tell me something about you. I'm boring myself . . ."

Ali hesitates, then, out of the blue, he says:

"I'm *jayah* now."

It is the first time he has admitted to how he feels. He knows that although Mohand is not a friend, he will be able to understand. "Jayah" is the word for an animal that has strayed from the flock, for an emigrant who has cut his ties with the community. Jayah is the black sheep. The one who has nothing to give to the group, whether it be the family, the clan, or the village. Jayah is a state of disgrace; it is a decline, a disaster. This is how Ali feels. France is a trap in which he has lost himself.

"I'm not proud of anything anymore . . ."

"But you have a job, my friend?" Mohand says with sudden gentleness.

Ali nods slowly.

"I'm afraid of losing my job at the factory. Everyone's talking about the economic crisis. Everything is closing. If they lay me off, I don't know what I'll do. My arms don't have the strength they once had, my hands don't know how to make things anymore . . . I'm just one of a thousand useless men . . . If I lose this job, who will give me another?"

Since Mohand looks at him encouragingly, he carries on, he explains. *An idle shepherd must whittle his own crook.* What was possible back in the village is not possible here. Here, there are people who have no work. Here, people throw out rather than repair furniture because it is not made to last. Here, there is television. Those with no job watch it. That is how things are in France. But how can a man remain head of the family when he sits watching television with his children and his wife? What distinguishes him from his children? From his wife? The television and the sofa put an end to family structures and hierarchies and replace them with a uniform inertia.

Back in the village, Ali had "earned" the right not to work. If he did not till the land, it was because he had become too important, he had assumed the purely symbolic roles of head of the family and of the business (which were one and the same). When he rested, he was leaning against a house he had made strong. Here, he fears leisure time because it is called unemployment. In an empty house idleness palls and has the bitter taste of rose laurel.

"I remember my mother, when I was young and first trying to make a living," Ali says. "I remember the look on her face when I used to say it was too hard. She'd say: 'Outside a man must prove himself a man; at home every man is assumed to be a man.'"

"To tell the truth," Mohand says, counting his change (there is enough for another anisette), "I never really understood that proverb."

Ali says nothing. The words go around in his head.

"Maybe it's complete garbage."

As they sink a little further into drunkenness, they transform into pure language. Their bodies are utterly still, as if all that remained on their chairs were a heap of winter clothes, a shape that would collapse if someone were to flick it with their finger. They have finished the pack of cigarettes. They no longer move at all. Words alone attest to the fact that they are still here, still awake.

"When you went up to the maquis, did you never worry that it was a bad thing?"

"Why?"

"Didn't it worry you, the stuff the FLN had done?"

"No."

Mohand responded instantly but regrets this a little. He does not want to be disrespectful to the dead body of Akli, left naked in the winter cold. Everyone was fond of the old man, despite his dusty stories, and Mohand wishes he could have died a natural death in old age.

"Akli would have understood. He was never opposed to independence."

"Opposed to independence? *Ya hamar*, was anyone actually opposed to independence? I've spent the last ten years surrounded by harkis and I've never met one of them who said they were against independence! Is that what you told yourself when you were killing for the FLN? That the people you killed were against independence?"

"I didn't kill anyone."

"Even in 1962, during all the reprisals?"

"No. I arrested people."

"But you knew what would happen to them . . ."

"Like everyone else, I suppose . . ."

"And you thought that was acceptable?"

Mohand hesitates.

"No . . . Or maybe . . . yes. These days I think it was a tragedy, I don't understand it anymore. But at the time, it was normal. You . . . you think that after the accords were signed, we were left to our own devices and we had the option to calm things down. But that's not true. We still had to deal with the OAS. And when they struck, we struck back. It wasn't personal. I never believed that the reprisals targeted this guy or that guy because he, personally, had betrayed the cause. We had to kill someone; it was tit-for-tat. So it was you, you, you. Neighbors would tell us things, sometimes we knew they weren't true. But we had to prove we weren't afraid. It was our way of saying to the OAS: You think you can teach us about terror? We invented terror! It was necessary, that's all, even if it seemed unfair. You should have seen what was happening . . . there were bombs exploding everywhere, all the time. Suddenly the whole world seemed fragile; I'd look around me and think: That might explode, he might die tomorrow. Building or human, the simple fact that something remained standing would fill me with love. I swear, I used to say thank you to the buildings of Palestro, to the old men still breathing, to the kids still being born. You can't possibly understand."

"You can't understand, either."

And it was like being back at the association, but the rift that once separated the veterans of the First World War and the Second had been replaced by the chasm that separates two camps in the same conflict. It is a problem they understand. And if they cannot understand each other, they can at least understand why they cannot understand. And that is reason enough for them to shake hands as they leave the café terrace, for them to say—without pretense—that they are happy to have seen each other again.

In January 1974, at the end of Hamid's military service—another period of his life he never talks about, months of silence occasionally punctuated by terms like "racism," "solitary confinement," "orderly officer," "guard duty," and "barracks"; a silence so impenetrable that, years later, his daughters will imagine that their father was actually conducting secret missions like James Bond or Largo Winch—he and Clarisse move into an apartment on the Rue de la Jonquière near the municipal swimming pool whose glass doors regularly stand open, releasing clouds of chlorine. In their blue smocks and their plastic shoes, the pool staff look like a tribe of nurses as they troop out of the building. The Bar de la Piscine opposite owes its name solely to its location, since the regulars who prop up the bar, with their weathered faces, red noses, lungs lined with tar from Gitanes Maïs, have never swum the length of a pool in their lives, and have no intention of starting.

A few yards from the entrance to the building is a telephone booth that Hamid passes without a second glance. He calls home rarely, and only when he knows that Ali will not be there. They are brief exchanges, his brothers and sisters talk to him, their words vague and rushed, as though clandestine. He and Yema repeat the same platitudes, unable to address the estrangement between father and son. And, like a melody, the words "do not understand" recur, conjugated and declined in every possible form, a parade of mutual incomprehension, available in every style and every color.

Clarisse no longer asks questions. She allows Hamid to live in his silence while she tries to create one of similar size for herself. Insulated from her curiosity, Hamid should feel better, but this is not the case. He is upset by the distance she has put between them—the distance he has forced her to adopt. He longs to ask her to go back to being the woman who shared everything, but he knows that he has nothing to offer her in return. They love each other while respectfully keeping each other at arm's length. Neither is happy with the circumstances, but each is convinced that only the other person can rectify the situation. Each spends sleepless nights wondering whether they should end the relationship, whether it is going anywhere. Neither can bear to finish it, because they feel that love is still there, behind this barrage of silence, and it cannot simply be diverted, in the way that an agricultural engineer might divert the course of a river to irrigate other fields. For each, this dammed-up reservoir of love has only one beneficiary, it is Hamid, it is Clarisse. And so, despite the silence, they move forward, they go through the motions.

The new apartment is a narrow warren of cramped, low-ceilinged rooms. It is made up of several *chambres de bonne* that the landlord has knocked together, taking a sledgehammer to partition walls whose previous existence is hinted at here and there by fragments of plaster cornice. The lives of the previous tenants can be read in the blackened grooves in which seams of crumbs and dust have accumulated. The toilets are outside the building, at the far end of the courtyard. To get there in the night is an escapade involving stairs and winding corridors of the kind that Kader-the-magic-rabbit would have loved back in the days of his red pajamas. Clarisse shivers as she trudges there. Although he denies it, Hamid pisses in the sink when he is sure that Clarisse is sound asleep. In order not to risk waking her, he sometimes leaves the dirty dishes where they are, spraying them with a muffled yellow jet before turning on the tap and letting the water run for a long time, erasing the evidence of his crime.

Some months after they move in, Hamid passes his civil service exam and starts working at the Office for Family Allocations. The building is a vast ocean liner on the outskirts of the city. The offices on every floor are identical, with the same vertical blinds, the dark carpets, the steel shelving units, the Formica desks, the colored spines of the box files. Huge boxy computers rumble like turbines. On the upper floors, everything is well-ordered. Employees wear jackets and shirts, if only because the solemn office furniture seems to demand it. By contrast, downstairs, where benefits claimants are interviewed, there is pandemonium. Long lines reveal a range of languages and degrees of poverty, like shades on a color chart. Hamid avoids walking through the area; he always takes the rear entrance. He prefers not to see the people whose files he deals with because, when he focuses on the documents, he feels as though he is helping, whereas when he hears the people downstairs talking, the feeling is reversed: there are only stories of benefits being unpaid, of illogical demands for payments to be refunded, of hundreds of francs missing, of people whose lives are already precarious being forced to wait. And often, among the hulking bodies of the adults, he sees the frail face of a child interpreter, a child scribe who reminds him of himself, a child he cannot face without feeling ashamed.

When Clarisse asks him whether he is happy working there, he says yes, if only because it is not the factory, because he can earn a salary without having to strain his body every day on machines that are too heavy, too hot, too dangerous, because—despite his dark skin and the mass of black hair he will soon cut in order to look more serious—he is upstairs working in one of the offices rather than down in the reception area, waiting in a line that inches forward toward the claims desks, carrying a plastic bag, his damp hands crumpling a sheaf of forms against his chest. Perhaps if his childhood had been like Clarisse's he would have done something else, he would have taken the time she suggested to discover what he truly loves, what he wants to devote his days to doing, but he has not been able to shake off entirely the obligation of the utilitarian, the efficient, the concrete, nor has he been able to shake off a notion of the civil service as a grail where he is fortunate to be allowed to work. At night, as he sets his alarm clock, he sometimes thinks that it takes much longer than he expected to escape, and that if he has not put as much distance between himself and his childhood as he would have

liked, the next generation can carry on where he left off. He imagines
that what he is really doing in the stifling little room that serves as his
office is amassing shares in freedom that he will be able to pass on to
his children.

One night, after she has hurried down the stairs, thighs squeezed together, a hand pressed against her crotch as a last resort, Clarisse sees
a rat calmly creep under the toilet door without giving her a second
glance. She stops dead in the middle of the courtyard, her knees pressed
so tightly it is painful, shaking from head to foot at the thought of following the rat into the dark cubicle. She paces in front of the door, unable to make a decision. Her lower abdomen feels hard as concrete and
about to explode, but she still thinks she can hear the rat scrabbling
around inside.

   Standing in the middle of the courtyard, she pisses, her legs still
pressed together, forcing the urine to find its own escape routes, streaming down her thighs in rivers under her nightdress.

   In the moment, the pleasure is intense, her whole body erupts with
joy, with relief. But no sooner has the flow stopped than Clarisse wonders
how she could have done such a thing. She stinks. Her nightdress drips
and clings to her body. To clean herself up a little would mean pushing
open the door and stepping into the rat's domain to get some toilet paper.
She cannot do it. Nor can she go back upstairs and risk Hamid seeing
her—she knows that she woke him when she got up, that he is lying
there, staring into the darkness. Panicked, and crazed by the smell of her
own urine, she stumbles and jerks around the yard like a broken mario-
nette. Her body is shaken by ragged sobs. She will have to wait until Hamid falls asleep again before slipping into the bathroom to wash herself.
She sits down on one of the trash cans in the courtyard, but immediately
gets up again, unable to bear the feeling of the cold, wet nightdress clinging to her buttocks. She goes around and around in circles. There is nothing she can do. She flaps the hem of her nightdress in the hope that it will
dry more quickly. She feels so ashamed that she wonders whether she
should just leave, push open the great wooden door and disappear into
the streets of Paris. This paralyzing shame is new and overwhelming,

and she cannot help but wonder whether its sudden appearance in the dead of night is not proof that her relationship with Hamid is a mistake. But immediately she reconsiders, blames herself entirely for the pitiful situation in which she finds herself. She would like to slap herself. Clarisse cannot understand why, for the first time, she finds herself visiting the depths of Clarisse, a palace in the sewers, made of silt. She loathes this inner world, she longs to escape it, but she tells herself that there is no way out—nothing to be done—not until Hamid goes back to sleep. The walls of her nightmare echo with the mocking laughter of a crowd that is no less cruel for being imaginary. I can't do this, Clarisse thinks, without knowing to what this damning certainty refers. I can't do this.

Worried when Clarisse does not come back, Hamid finally leans out the bathroom window overlooking the courtyard. He sees Clarisse curled up in a corner, shivering, the pale flash of her nightdress against the dark walls. For a moment he thinks that she is leaving him, that she is gathering her strength, marshaling her words before coming upstairs to tell him that it is all over, and he is horrified to realize that perhaps she is right. He longs to close the window, to pretend that he has seen nothing. But he overcomes his cowardice, forces himself to lean out a little farther and call:

"Is everything all right?"

Clarisse starts, looks up, her eyes meet his and she collapses. Clinging to the trash can as if it were a life buoy, she howls: No, no, no, it's not all right. Hamid runs from the apartment and races down the stairs to her.

Clarisse feels a surprising wave of relief at the thought that Hamid has seen her in a state that is acceptable only in babies and perhaps the elderly (although in the elderly, it provokes a brief involuntary spasm of revulsion), that she has allowed him to see her like this: filthy, weak, and sobbing. She tells herself that Hamid will love her now no matter what, that she has no dark desires, no memories more disgusting than the cold piss he has seen her drenched in. She is still sobbing as they climb the stairs, but now it feels liberating.

The shower, long and scalding—and yet not long enough, not scalding enough for Clarisse, who wishes she could strip away her skin to be sure she has eliminated the stench—leaves her steaming and red as a lobster. Hamid wraps her in a large bath towel, pulls up a chair, and sits her down while he boils some water.

"I should have gotten a real job right away," he apologizes. "If I'd started saving as soon as I got here, we'd be able to afford a real apartment, not this jerry-built hovel with a toilet in the yard."

"It's my fault," Clarisse says. "I was being stupid. I'm at least twenty or thirty times bigger than that rat, but I let it scare me."

"My father was terrified of caterpillars," Hamid says with a smile. "He used to see them everywhere when we were living in the south."

"In the south?" Clarisse says, puzzled. She has always assumed that Hamid grew up in Normandy. "When did you live in the south?"

Embarrassed that he has let slip this piece of information, Hamid gives a dismissive wave that means it was years ago.

"Was it nice?"

Clarisse's efforts to make the question sound offhand, to give it a nonchalance barely flecked with curiosity, are blatant: her voice quavers and the corner of her upper lip trembles. Hamid cannot bring himself to reject her again, not while she is sitting on the kitchen chair swaddled in a towel like a child, frail and tender. He tries to find a few words to describe those years. He babbles drivel about the pine trees and the cicadas, about the sunshine, the River Durance, a sort of photo essay devoid of memories, a travel brochure. He couches the period in words so impersonal they have no more value than silence, he strings the words together so as to have something to say, so as not to disappoint Clarisse. But the more he talks, the more he finds the eager look on her face unbearable, so he stops and focuses all his attention on the teapot filled with fragrant herbs, as though making tisane demands the precision of a surgical procedure.

"When was this?" Clarisse asks.

There is a moment of silence. The little room is filled with steam that blurs the outlines of the objects. Hamid hopes that she cannot see his hands trembling.

"Sorry . . ." he mutters, "I don't want to talk about it."

Clarisse realizes that she was wrong to think that things would be better simply because, after a night like this, she can no longer keep secrets from Hamid. She never really had any secrets. Hers is a life with no shadows, only a few faint smudges, things she wishes she had not done, regrets that she stayed silent when insulted, intermittent dreams of greatness; but these are not things she hides, they are simply of no interest. The one who needs to open up—to let the piss of all the pent-up years, however ugly, however painful, stream down his legs—is Hamid, not her.

She walks over to Hamid and holds open the towel to welcome him inside. She enfolds his slender body in the slim fluffy cotton. She presses herself against him, and he can feel the heat of her skin from the shower. But just as he is about to take her in his arms, grateful for the easy way she affords him her forgiveness, Clarisse takes a step back and says:

"I can't live with you if you're living alone."

Her tone is not harsh, but it is filled with all the seriousness she can muster. She stands there naked and flushed in the middle of the kitchen, the towel thrown back like a useless cape, and Hamid finds her beautiful and absurd, beautiful for this absurdity that does not frighten her, of which she is not even aware, and which ultimately magnifies her. Exposed in the cramped kitchen, the shimmering light, the steam-filled air, Clarisse's whole body strains toward the only two possibilities she can envisage: surrender or separation. Her body quivers with expectation, it is a living question mark, fearful of being misinterpreted.

"We came to France when I was just a kid," Hamid says in a tone he hopes is neutral. (And what follows is probably closer to the speech he hoped to give than to the one that he actually gave at the time, which was more disjointed, more hesitant, more vague.) "We were housed in a resettlement camp, kept behind barbed wire like dangerous animals. I don't remember how long we spent there. It was the kingdom of mud. And my parents said thank you. Afterward, we were dumped in a forest in the middle of nowhere, near the blazing sun. That's where we saw the caterpillars. And my parents said thank you. After that, we were sent to live in a housing project in Normandy, in a town where I don't think anyone had ever seen an Arab before we showed up. And my parents said thank you. They're still living there. My father worked, my mother had babies, and, like every guy who grew up around there, I could tell you that I love them, that I respect them because they gave us everything, but I don't think that would be honest. I hated the fact that they gave me everything while they stopped living. I felt stifled; it drove me insane. I spent my last few years there dreaming of escape, and now that I've escaped, I can't even bring myself to feel guilty. The last time I saw my father, he slapped me across the face and I hated him with all my heart but, at the same time, I understood him. Because he stopped living so that I could live and I go around doing whatever I like and he must think I'm the most selfish person in the world. And maybe I am . . . But sometimes I think that, even if I'd followed the path they wanted, it wouldn't have made any difference to them: maybe they would have said thank you *very much*, but apart from that . . ."

When he has finished speaking, when the words die on his lips and he knows that, for the moment, he is incapable of going any further, he looks hard into Clarisse's eyes, telling himself that if he should see pity there, if he sees that she now thinks of him as a humanitarian cause, or sees her gloat at winning the battle against his silence, he will walk out of the apartment. But she wraps herself in her towel again and says:

"It's true, there's a serious shortage of camels in your story."

To her family, Clarisse has always pretended (though she prefers the term "implied") that she is still sharing an apartment with Véronique. When her parents announce that they are coming to Paris, Clarisse and Hamid carefully tidy up and camouflage the apartment—hiding the men's clothes, the shaving kit, all the documents bearing his name, in a small bedroom cupboard. Véronique kindheartedly agrees to sleep on the sofa and scatter a few representative objects here and there to throw them off the scent. She kisses Madeleine and Pierre on both cheeks, asks them how they have been, talks about her future, sprawls amid the cushions with the contented air of someone who genuinely lives there, or a large cat. As soon as Clarisse's parents have left, she stuffs the clothes, the toiletries, and the magazines she brought into an overnight bag and goes back to her own apartment, without passing judgment on the favor that was asked of her. Véronique likes to think that she has seen much stranger things in her life, and that she is not easily shocked.

In a long interview, Emil Cioran's long-term companion, Simone Boué, admitted that she, too, hid their relationship from her parents for years. At first she rented a room next to the one where the philosopher lived; a room she visited only when her parents came to Paris. Later, when she and Cioran moved together into an apartment on the Rue de l'Odéon, she got into the habit of rearranging the furniture to block one of the doors and persuaded her mother that she was living with a "foreign roommate," but that the apartment was strictly divided into two separate spaces. I don't know whether she stopped lying at some point, or what triggered her confession—she makes no mention of it.

Naïma has never managed to understand why, one day, out of the blue, Clarisse decides she has had enough of sparing her parents' feelings. (Neither Clarisse nor Hamid has ever told their daughters about the night their mother pissed herself and the war of silence ended.) All Naïma knows is that, after two years of keeping the relationship secret, Clarisse decides that it is time for Pierre and Madeleine to face the fact that she is in love with an Arab.

"People from Kabylia aren't Arabs."

"I meant with an Algerian."

"I'm not Algerian, either."

"You know what you are? You're unclassifiable . . ."

Hamid pulls a face and throws up his hands: there is nothing he can do. Clarisse is not the first person to have to deal with the absence of a label that fits him. Perhaps it is this very absence that led to the years of silence—when you are missing the main noun, how do you build a story?

"I'll introduce you to my parents," Clarisse says, "you introduce me to yours. Fair's fair."

She cannot so easily dispense with the principle of equality she has advocated for the past two years. She is afraid of finding herself back at square one, afraid that the war of silence will have been fought for nothing. She prefers to continue her careful but stubborn system of trade-offs. At first Hamid rejects the idea: he reminds her of the quarrel that set him against his father and has kept him from going home. She replies that she will have to face up to the racism she senses in her parents, but (for want of opportunity) has never actually witnessed. They have the same conversation again and again with only minute variations. The responses come automatically, without their having to think, it is a familiar pas de deux, a choreographed exchange. And then, one afternoon, sitting cross-legged on the couch, Clarisse changes tack.

"You know, this isn't easy for me, either, Hamid . . . although you obviously think otherwise."

Flustered by this sudden variation, Hamid is silent.

"I need space, too," Clarisse goes on. "Just a tiny bit of space for my concerns . . . It doesn't have to be much—maybe a quarter the size of this coffee table. That should be enough . . ."

She traces a vague square on the table.

"This is the space where I can put my worries without you sneering or belittling or ignoring them. Okay?"

Hamid stares at the corner of the table.

"Keep in mind that this still leaves you the rest of the space."

He is amused by the seriousness of her presentation and smiles, gesturing for her to carry on.

"Okay, so let's say you're angry with your father and, in order to introduce me to your parents, you have to overcome that anger. That represents a huge effort, easily three-quarters of this coffee table. Now, take me. I love my parents, I've got a good relationship with them—I never had a rebellious teenage phase, you know, I've always been a good little girl . . . But I'm afraid that if I introduce you to them, we will finally fall out, because my parents aren't brilliant, they're not extraordinary, in fact they are pathetically ordinary. But they're my parents . . . And I spent my whole childhood thinking they were amazing."

Clarisse's voice is oddly choked as she says the last word. Hamid forces himself to look up from the coffee table. There are tears in her eyes, a fine film of liquid that clouds the irises and that she tries to ignore or to blink away while keeping her face perfectly still. He comes and sits next to her.

"Okay," he whispers softly, "we'll do it together. Besides, what's the worst that can happen?"

"Our parents could disinherit us," Clarisse says with mock theatricality.

Hamid slumps back into the soft cushions and, with a sweeping gesture, puts his feet up on *his* part of the coffee table.

"Mine couldn't," he says with a dazzling smile. "They've already lost everything."

Round 1

It is not a good day to see Pont-Féron for the first time, if the cité can ever be said to have good days. Hamid and Clarisse are greeted by a guard of honor made of decrepit towers, a tangled forest of television antennas, uneven pathways, old men sitting outside the blocks with gummy smiles or mouths filled with gold teeth, surrounded by plastic bags containing food and medication. It looks to Hamid as though, in the year that he has been away, the cité has crumbled under the weight of its old age. It is one of those housing projects that look good only when they are brand-new, that rot as they age. This, combined with the flaws in the architecture, has caused the walls to crack: the economic crisis has signaled the end of the postwar boom, crushing this working-class neighborhood in which work is increasingly scarce. Inflation and unemployment are rising exponentially, twin curves that frequently appear in brightly colored graphics on the proliferating television screens. Soon the government will start beaming a public service campaign into every living room about "eliminating waste," offering tips on how to save fuel: drive your car slowly, avoid braking suddenly, keep the thermostat in your home set at sixty-five degrees. Soon the old men in the neighborhood will suggest that people turn off their central heating and go back to using an individual kanoun because they cannot afford the bills. The young, who have been raised in an area bounded by the community playground and the stairwells, will stare in wonder at these old men who manage, by some magical feat, to persuade themselves that they are back in the old country. In the cité, people begin to rack up debts, it is easy to justify because everyone believes that the economic crisis will be short-lived, and all the more necessary because the principle of "full house," as practiced in the mountains of Kabylia, has survived for fifteen years in France and, when the refrigerator is full and the cupboards are overflowing, there are few who see the danger of a negative number at the bottom of a bill or a statement from some intangible bank. As Clarisse and Hamid are parking the car outside the block where Ali and Yema live, they cannot imagine the debts to friends or family, the bank loans, the credit agreements looming invisibly over the heads of the inhabitants, like glittering fiscal swords of Damocles, but they can sense that the place is bleak and the men are worried.

The stairwell smells of beer, of *chorba* cooking slowly; on the banisters boys have used house keys to carve their insignificant identities.

To Hamid, every squalid detail seems to jump out. He doesn't know whether to use his body as a screen to hide the smashed mailboxes, the broken windows, the overflowing plastic bags next to the trash cans, or whether to draw attention to them, to throw them in Clarisse's face and say: You see? This is where I am from, take it or leave it.

Feeling as though she is being watched, Clarisse scarcely notices her surroundings because, although she forces herself to look straight ahead, she is entirely focused on what it is that Hamid expects of her, something she cannot define. They are both nervous and wordlessly communicate this irritation: their necks tense, their shoulders stiffen, their fists clench.

When Yema opens the door, Clarisse is struck by how small she is. She cannot be taller than four feet ten. Her brown hair, burnished orange by years of henna, pokes from beneath a flowery scarf tied around her head. There is something Asian about the almond-shaped eyes fringed with long lashes. The round face beams when she sees the young woman in the A-line dress on the doorstep, and she blurts out one of the few French phrases she has ever learned:

"Hello, hello, my, how you've grown!"

As Clarisse stands there dumbfounded, Yema takes the girl in her arms and hugs her. Clarisse bends her knees so that they are at the same level. She smiles foolishly as the embrace drags out, looking over Yema's shoulder at a dark-eyed girl staring at her from the kitchen. Given her age, she can only be Dalila. She has a handsome face, stern with delicate features, like her elder brother, and a mane of thick black hair that falls to her waist; although she straightens her hair, she cannot hide the thickness.

Yema finally releases Clarisse, but throughout their stay she seeks out ways to make physical contact with her. She uses any pretext to touch Clarisse, take her hand, squeeze her arm, press against her, hug her. There is maternal tenderness to these gestures, but also something of a horse trader evaluating a broodmare, thinks Clarisse, who finds it uncomfortable to be given into the hands of this little woman. She prefers the chilly aloofness with which Dalila greets her.

*   *   *

Aside from the two women, the apartment is empty, and Clarisse is surprised by the silence. The little ones have been palmed off on a neighbor so that Clarisse will not be overwhelmed, Dalila tells her. As for Claude and Kader, they are at a sports event in the neighboring town.

"I'm the only one who is never allowed out," she says, shooting her mother a reproachful look.

"What about Baba?" Hamid asks, ignoring his sister's complaints.

"He's on his way . . ." Yema mutters. "He should be here by now."

Hamid shrugs and, as he guides Clarisse into the living room, he whispers that his father's lateness is deliberate, it is his way of punishing Hamid. They sit around the big table, which has already been laid with plates patterned with small flowers and glasses rimmed with gilt, a riot of color that contrasts starkly with the dreary gray that extends outside the apartment.

"We won't wait for him," Hamid says.

He immediately launches into a rambling conversation with his mother and sister in Arabic, asking a series of questions whose answers he rarely translates for Clarisse. Whenever Yema attempts to speak to her in French, she sees Hamid screw his face up at the mangled sounds emerging from his mother's mouth. She can barely understand the little woman and, blushing with embarrassment, is forced to ask her to repeat what she has said. Hamid frequently interrupts, but even when he is speaking, Yema and Dalila keep their eyes on Clarisse, as though expecting her to join in the conversation in Arabic. Clarisse nods, she smiles, and in her flushed face, her blond, almost white eyebrows and her dark blue eyes stand out like sandbanks and pools.

Hamid does not stop talking until Yema brings the couscous and their mouths are entirely occupied by food. Clarisse eats greedily, drowning the couscous in the spicy red sauce from the *marga*, cheerfully spearing chickpeas with her fork. Seeing her plate empty, Yema serves her again and again and Clarisse cannot bring herself to refuse. She considers that politeness dictates that she clean her plate. Yema, on the other hand, believes that politeness dictates that she refill her guests' plates until they eat no more. The ladles work constantly, and, before long, Clarisse feels like the wolf in *Little Red Riding Hood*, its belly bloated with the little girl and her grandmother.

When Ali arrives home, he pretends to be surprised by the fact that his son is here, as though he got his days mixed up, as though it is not a big deal, and Hamid, irritated by his unconvincing pretense, squirms in his seat. Clarisse stares in astonishment at this man-mountain next to his little ball of a wife. She cannot help but wonder how they manage in bed (after all, they have had ten children), and the very thought— without any attempts to picture it—makes her blush all the more.

Ali eats quickly at one corner of the table while the others are having coffee. He barely speaks, but smiles awkwardly whenever Clarisse's eyes meet his. Next to her, Hamid continues to writhe in embarrassment—he will later explain that his father was giving her his best *French smile*, the one Hamid hates. She does not notice this, and responds to each smile with a broader smile, surprised to discover that the father Hamid described as a stern, authoritarian patriarch is a slightly shy man with graying hair who is embarrassed by his size. When he finishes his meal, Ali gets up and excuses himself; it is time for his nap.

"We're about to leave anyway," Hamid says.

"Aren't you going to wait for your brothers?" Yema asks, her eyes wide. "They'll be home soon."

Hamid shakes his head.

"No, no. It's time we made a move."

Clarisse, who is so stuffed that she wishes she could sit motionless for hours, watches as he gets hastily to his feet. She struggles to follow him, bumping against the furniture because, once the chairs are pulled back, it is clear that the room is too small to host a family lunch. (She cannot imagine how Hamid can have lived here with five or six other children; it seems physically impossible.) Yema's hugs begin again, Dalila kisses her on both cheeks. Ali does not get up, but solemnly shakes her hand as though she were a foreign dignitary. Just as they reach the door, he calls after Hamid without looking at him:

"It was good of you to come."

Although Clarisse does not understand a word of Arabic, she realizes, from the way Hamid's whole body relaxes, that he came simply to hear these words.

Round 2

The encounter with Clarisse's parents takes place a month later in a Paris brasserie. Madeleine and Pierre are gray, white, and blue, very respectable, and *terribly* sorry they're late. To Hamid they look like brother and sister, and he wonders whether the years of marriage have given them this patina, or whether they already looked alike when they first met, with those same gestures, those same facial expressions. As they arrive, they make clear their surprise at discovering Hamid's existence and their disappointment that they have been kept in the dark for so long, but each interrupts the other with warning glances and their sentences trail off well before the end. It feels as though they have agreed (perhaps as they drove here, or perhaps just after Clarisse's phone call) not to criticize the young couple over lunch and to try, in spite of the "unprecedented" situation, to show themselves in a favorable light. But, once they are seated at the table in the restaurant, they find it difficult to stick to their resolution. They mask their discomfort with constant, impersonal conversation: problems with traffic, the cost of living, the shops in Dijon. They ask vague questions as though afraid that if asked about their life together, their daughter and her partner might reveal something obscene, and in a sense they are right: any mention of their life will strike her parents as obscene. Whenever Clarisse tries to talk about Hamid, her mother flashes a nervous smile.

"Yes, yes, darling, you told me on the phone."

Then she goes back to whatever she was talking about, and Pierre chimes in, or vice versa. Hamid and Clarisse can do nothing but nod their heads every now and then; they have the curious impression that they are sitting at the wrong table. Over dessert, Pierre and Madeleine speculate about the health of President Pompidou, whose swollen face has been worrying them. Glancing at each other over their *îles flottantes,*

Clarisse and Hamid do not know whether to laugh or cry. When the coffee arrives, they talk about the weather, and seem prepared to discuss every cloud formation of the past few months to get them to the end of the meal. Clarisse is biting the inside of her cheek while Hamid is staring at neighboring tables.

When the bill arrives, Clarisse's father insists on paying. He does so with a solemn, almost sacrificial gravity, as though taking upon himself the terrible burden of this meal. He goes to the counter; Clarisse gets up to go to the bathroom and Hamid is left alone with Madeleine. He smiles as he stirs the dregs of his coffee, but Madeleine turns away, stares out the window, mutters, "It's very busy around here," and then starts to count the cars. Hamid self-consciously stares at the grains of sugar sodden with brown liquid. He is astonished when, as they are walking them back to their car, Pierre and Madeleine invite them to Dijon for their next vacation.

Naïma was not present for any of these meetings, but she can easily picture them, since it seems to her that even now, years later, the relationship between her parents and their in-laws has not changed. Yema and Clarisse still hug each other, saying nothing, or almost nothing, since the language barrier means that they cannot even try. Meanwhile, Hamid and Madeleine exchange polite, insubstantial platitudes as though they have only just met.

Even if the twin encounters were conducted according to the principle of equality favored by the couple, their outcomes are completely disproportionate. For Clarisse, it means the occasional invitation to Dijon, and the mention of Hamid's name in phone calls to her parents, usually just before she hangs up. ("Give him our regards.") But for Hamid, the encounter sealed the tacit reconciliation with his family, and a stream of brothers and sisters who were not present at lunch come to visit the couple, eager to spend a weekend in Paris. Clarisse, being an only child, finds this constant stream of visitors funny; it is like those cartoons where a dozen different characters climb out of a tiny car. Kader is now studying nursing. He still has the ebullient energy he had as a boy and, for

Clarisse, he transforms the childhood Hamid is so ashamed of into a series of anecdotes that make her laugh until she cries. Dalila is bored, taking a marketing course that is too close to Pont-Féron for her to leave her
parents' apartment. She spends the weekend pointing at buildings where
she would like to live. The city interests her only because she might move
there one day. She is less fascinated by the Gothic filigree of a church than
by a little balcony on which a girl like her is smoking a cigarette or hanging out laundry. Claude is unlucky: he is arrested on the Rue de Turbigo
by a police officer who believes he has no right to a French first name, that
it must be a lie or a prank. He is taken to the *commissariat*, where Hamid
bails him out, and Claude leaves Paris with the memory of a racist city he
never intends to set foot in again. Karima never arrives: at the last minute,
she changes her mind and goes to a friend's birthday party—a Moroccan
girl, Yema says with a mixture of surprise and reproach when she calls,
though Hamid cannot tell whether this has to do with the canceled trip
or the nationality of the friend. Over time, Karima's endlessly postponed
visit becomes a family joke, one that Naïma heard often as a child: to her
aunts and uncles, the phrase "sending Karima to Paris" has become syn-
onymous with "moving heaven and earth." Little Fatiha and Mohamed
make the journey together. Hamid is waiting nervously on the station
platform—he has repeatedly reminded the little ones which coach they
should sit in, terrified at the thought that he won't find them, that they'll
get off at the wrong stop—and is wondering what he'll do if they do not
emerge from the train pulling into the station, but no, here they come,
hand in hand, skipping along under the tender gaze of a female passenger who says to Hamid: *They're adorable. I'd love to adopt them*, as though
she were talking about little animals. Having to cope with a six- and
seven-year-old turns Hamid and Clarisse into parents. She watches in
astonishment as he calms their tears, bathes them, dresses them. He is
both brother and father to his siblings, she thinks, and there is an ancient
strangeness to this phrase.

This leaves only Salim, the tenth child, back in Pont-Féron, cradled
in Yema's arms. She rocks him gently and smiles, imagining that she
will soon be holding Hamid and Clarisse's baby, and the endless succession of children she has pressed to her breast will go on.

In the crowded café where he is drinking with his colleagues, Hamid sees a young woman with long brown hair confidently elbow her way through the throng, arms raised in front of her face like a boxer with her guard up. She blindly forges ahead, laughing at her own brutality, and Hamid stands motionless, his mind a blank, watching spellbound as this faceless figure comes toward him, bumps into him, lowers its arms, and starts. They stare, neither daring to pronounce a name that might be immediately rejected. ("I'm sorry, you must be mistaken.") They waver, suspended between doubt and hope, then Hamid splutters:

"Annie?"

The sound that comes from her is like a roar, and her face twists into a smile.

"Hamid!"

She throws her arms around him, heedless of the other drinkers' feeble protests. Dazed and stunned, they step back, look at each other again, repeat the other's name just to hear the response, grip each other's shoulders to check that they are here, that they are real, to gauge how much they have both grown. Some minutes later, as they are trying to elbow a space at the bar, Annie whispers:

"I can't believe we recognized each other . . ."

Hamid smiles and says nothing: strictly speaking, he did not recognize her. It was not the little girl he used to play with that he saw walk in, but her aunt, Michelle, a woman he thought he had forgotten fifteen years ago. Annie's appearance is like a memory he did not know he had, and he is astonished by the discovery.

She tells him that he hasn't changed a bit, and is immediately annoyed with herself at having said something so clichéd. Obviously, he has changed. When she left him, he was a little boy of eight or nine, she cannot remember.

"But you grew up to be the man I always thought you'd be. That's what I meant: you look like the person you were going to be."

She is keyed up. She trembles, cries a little, but mostly she roars with laughter, just as Michelle used to do behind the counter of the grocery in Palestro.

"Meeting up with you tonight is a sign," Annie announces. "Well . . . not a sign, I never really believed . . . A coincidence, an amazing coincidence!"

For some reason he does not understand, she bursts out laughing, fishes a pack of cigarettes from her bag, takes out two, brings them to her lips, and lights them before offering one to him. It is something he has only ever seen in a movie, and he is convinced that, perhaps unwittingly, she is mimicking the gesture of an American actor from back when they were teenagers. Between small, quick puffs, she tells him that, after hesitating for a long time, she is going back to Algeria next month with a few members from her group (she does not mention who), to help build a socialist Algeria.

"I thought that after a while I'd stop missing it. But I didn't, every day for all these years I've thought about the old country. There was nothing to be done. People in France don't understand the pieds noirs. 'Let them go and readapt somewhere else.' Talk about a welcome. The only thing that scared them more than us was you, the bougnoules. Stupid fucking country."

"You'd rather Boumédiène?" Hamid grimaces.

"You'd rather Pompidou? Don't tell me you're right-wing?"

"Are you telling me you approve of coups d'état? Are you a fascist?"

"You want my fist in your face?"

They smile, happy to discover that when they are together they go back to being the little brats who knocked jam jars off the shelves and squabbled in the wreckage. Since they cannot attract the bartender's attention, Annie leans over the bar and refills their beers from the pump. He remembers her in her father's shop, climbing up on the shelves and helping herself, supreme ruler of the jars and the bottles.

"What about Claude, what does he think about you going back?"

"Claude's dead," Annie says bitterly. "Cancer."

Suddenly holding his glass steady seems to require superhuman effort. Even so, he trembles and spills a little beer on the counter.

"It's strange," Annie says, staring intently at the little golden pool of beer, "but in the end I accepted it. Not that I had any choice, you'll say. On the other hand . . . I still can't get used to the idea that he is buried so far from my mother. It's unbearable. They're on different sides of the Mediterranean . . . I don't think he ever forgave himself for leaving her there, under that little white marble slab. He thought about it all the time. He tracked down friends, people who had stayed behind, and asked them to visit her grave, to leave flowers, to make sure that no one else bought the plot. And in the end, he passed that fear on to me. I don't care if I never see the house again. But the idea of never seeing her grave is something I've never been able to come to terms with. It's stupid. Have you ever played that game 'What would you take with you to a desert island?'"

"Of course."

"As far as I know, no one has ever said 'my dead.' But since we came back here, they're the ones that we miss."

Hamid nods. He does not tell her that he has never thought about the graves up on the mountain, not even the grave of the little brother he never got to know, the brother he sometimes thinks he invented, or confused with Dalila or Kader. He does not want to exclude himself from Annie's "we," even if it means lying by omission.

Another serpentine movement ripples through the warm mass of drinkers. Bodies press against them from behind, forcing them to lean over the bar. Annie's glass slops foam and bubbles. Calls of "Sorry!" go up to no one in particular. With a wave, Annie dismisses the dead she has just conjured, who still hover around them. As she traces figures of elaborate curves in the spilled beer, she tells Hamid about her project, about the friends she is going with, the people who will meet them over there, the fields that they will till together. She is thrilled by the Agrarian Revolution that Hamid witnessed through a plain brown envelope, that earned him a slap from his father. She studiously says Lakhdaria every time the name Palestro is on the tip of her tongue—the town has been renamed since they left.

"Do you want to come?" she asks suddenly, already enchanted by the idea.

He shakes his head and smiles. "I don't think they'd want me there."

"You don't know that."

"A country that drove you out is not your country anymore."

"They didn't drive us out, Hamid. We left. Our parents left because they were afraid. We ended up in Picardy . . . If Picardy is what safety looks like, I think I'd rather be afraid."

He laughs and says:

"We ended up in Orne."

She pulls a face and, in a comedic pied-noir accent, says:

"I want to go back to my roots."

"My roots are here," Hamid says. "I brought them with me. It's bull-shit, this thing about roots. Have you ever seen a tree grow thousands of miles from its roots? I grew up here, so my roots are here."

"But don't you remember how beautiful it was?"

Her eyes grow wide as if to make space for all the beautiful vistas she remembers, or to make space for Hamid, so he can enter the world of her memories through the portholes of her eyes. For a moment he imagines . . . He pictures the mountain, the valley, the tall grass speck-led with poppies, the dark trees with their twisted trunks, and then he pictures a huge white house with a flat roof, young men tilling the field and breaking bread together in the shade of a fig tree to the sound of cicadas, Annie running through the olive groves in a summer dress call-ing his name a single note that hangs in the air for a second then swells to become the shrill screams of men and women and the olive groves are burning black smudges against the sky the smell of burning tires burnt flesh a man ablaze stumbling a man ablaze sprawled as voices howl we'll come back for you for your father we'll come back.

"I can't . . ." he says. "And besides . . . I can barely speak the language anymore."

A few minutes later, Annie is joined by a group of friends and Hamid quickly slips away. He leaves the bar with the impression that he is completely drunk, drunk on beer and on years of memories exploding inside his head.

In the months that follow, Annie will send him postcards from Algiers and later from Mitidja, the early ones enthusiastic, the later ones less and less so.

He replies to one of them, telling Annie that he is going to be a father. Clarisse is pregnant.

The ultrasound tells them they are having a little girl, and as they are leaving the hospital Clarisse cannot bring herself to confess that she is disappointed: she wanted a child who would be Hamid in miniature. She is less interested in having a daughter: she knows herself too well, and pictures a little girl as another Clarisse who would follow her path. For his part, Hamid is overjoyed. Until this moment, he has not wanted to admit it to himself, but now he knows: it would have been too complicated to raise a boy, to instill in him values different from those he learned, to stop thinking about the role of "eldest son" that was imposed on him, to do things not in accordance with, but contrary to, his own childhood. A daughter is different. In his family, in the villages on the mountain, fathers take no role in raising their daughters. He has a clean slate.

When they phone Yema to tell her the news, she congratulates Clarisse and says that she hopes her next child will be a boy. Her prayers will not be answered: Clarisse will bear only daughters, four daughters, nature will thumb its nose at patriarchal tradition.

Shortly afterward, Clarisse, Hamid, and little Myriem leave Paris to settle in the country. It is here that Pauline, Naïma, and Aglaé will be born. The mix of cultures in the names of the four girls fails to capture the way in which their mixed heritage fragments into multiple variations that never cease to amaze their parents, given that Myriem and Pauline have curly ash-blond hair, while Naïma has black hair and dark eyes; given that Aglaé inherited her father's Afro and her mother's delicate hands, while Myriem inherited her nose from no one in the family and Pauline is a tomboy; given that Aglaé is a chatterbox and Naïma moody; given that all of them, at an early age, demanded that Yema teach them to ululate, but they speak Arabic only as a silly gibberish intended to make themselves laugh; given that Pauline will tell her sisters that she is adopted—based on the fact that she is the only one with a beauty spot at the corner of her mouth—and will invent a Russian family for herself, while Naïma, over the years, will grow to look like a portrait of her mother painted with all the wrong colors. Hamid and Clarisse watch them as they grow and become different from one another, encouraging them with joyful, timid gestures. And given that, from this point, they become parents, that is to say unchanging figures completely taken up by the constant attention demanded by their children, Naïma finds it inconceivable that they still have a story to tell. While their daughters take their first steps on the green carpet of grass and moss, they ossify within this house, become images of themselves, motionless, immutable.

Part III

A MOVEABLE FEAST

When at last he made it home
to his own land, wise Ulysses
His old dog remembered him
Next to a fine-weave tapestry
His wife was waiting.

—Guillaume Apollinaire, "La Chanson du mal-aimé"

The time has not yet come for harkis to visit, I have to say. It is exactly like asking a Frenchman from the Resistance to shake hands with a collaborator.

—Abdelaziz Bouteflika, President of Algeria, June 14, 2000

From a distance, if it were possible to step back far enough without bumping into the plate-glass window or the white wall at the far end of the gallery—impossible on a night like tonight, when there is a private event—we would see a shifting mass of black dresses, tweed jackets, anthracite jeans worn over block-heel ankle boots, checked shirts, champagne flutes filled to different levels, some smudged with traces of lipstick, glasses with broad frames, meticulously groomed beards, and the blue or whitish glow of smartphone screens. It would be possible to make out that the crowd is moving in two perfect spirals, one centripetal, the other centrifugal, one slowed by dawdlers who linger in front of the paintings, the other by the difficulty of getting to the buffet table.

Moving farther back, leaving the gallery guests behind the large plate-glass window of the gallery, we would be able to take in the tranquil street in the 6th arrondissement where it is located, the clothing shops where sales assistants are turning the lights out one by one, the patisserie whose almond-green blinds have been rolled down, and, in the half-light, leaning against a car, we would be able to make out Naïma, smoking a cigarette, staring at the people in the gallery.

This is where she has been working for the past three years. When she first finished her studies, she spent two years on the editorial team of a cultural magazine, where the open-ended working hours, having initially generated exciting surges of adrenaline, left her in a state of exhaustion and fragility she had never before experienced. Eventually she resigned, ashamed by what she considered her own weakness, but encouraged by Sol, who repeatedly told her that the EU working-time directive exists for a reason. She spent several months unemployed, alternately panicked and apathetic, then found a job here. She never imagined that one day she might be working at this gallery, which she knew very well. She had seen numerous amazing exhibitions here, mostly photography: the bound, naked Japanese women of Nobuyoshi Araki, exposing the flowers of their vulvas and of their kimonos, the dignity of their hieratic faces; Raphaël Neal's self-portraits taken in the Icelandic wilderness; Dutch photographer Piers Janssen's studies of exhaustion, dark circles under eyes photographed in such close-up that they are reminiscent of lunar landscapes . . . Naïma was able to mention at least a dozen when she came for her interview with Christophe; she gushed ecstatically, and although her passion was genuine, it was also (she realized) excessive. She evoked certain images with awestruck precision, suddenly remembered another series, and, even as she urged herself to shut up, to stop talking right now, she described this, too, and said again that it would be a dream to work here, a dream, honestly. Christophe simply smiled: he had already decided to hire her. He liked:

"the energy she radiates," he told his employees, his clients, his wife;

"her smile and her tits," he told his friends.

They have been sleeping together for two years now. She does not quite remember how it began.

Between twenty and twenty-five, after a few romances that were just like those promised her in magazines (and which she had, perhaps unwittingly, fashioned to be just like them), Naïma decides she prefers sleeping with strangers. Which does not mean any random guy. They are always men she finds attractive. They are simply men she finds attractive at first glance, without having to justify that attraction by a mutual, often disingenuous, trawl through their respective CVs.

Sometimes, joking about her family background, she says:

"My grandmother got married when she was fourteen. My mother met my father when she was eighteen. At least one woman in this family needs to break the mold."

And yet, at twenty-five she decides to put the brakes on this. It is not that her desire has waned, or that some ancestral form of morality has caught up with her, it is that suddenly she has the impression that her actions have been rendered so banal by American TV series—particularly *Sex and the City*—that they have become the norm. There is no longer a flicker of surprise in the eyes of the guys who, after a few drinks, she invites back to her place, and there is no longer any real lust: they go with her because this is what they're *supposed* to do these days, and they assume that she is doing it for the same reason. She feels as though desire has been spoiled or perhaps sullied by this sudden obligation to sleep with people. As though women (as a whole) are now required to prove they are equal to men (also, as a whole) by adopting the predator/prey approach to sex ascribed to men, in something that is no longer a skilled hunt, but a massacre. She no longer feels free to choose; on the contrary, she feels like she has fallen into line with those who do not choose, but simply make do with whatever is within reach. Naïma is also embarrassed by the realization that, in promoting women to the role of sexual consumers, contemporary society has made them consumers, pure and simple. The bars and restaurants where women are not treated as "guests" and offered menus with no prices were among the first to realize: women foot the bill. They were followed by the sellers of sex toys, the beauty parlors that offer time-conscious pricing (a Brazilian wax in your lunch hour, make the most of every minute!), and the pharmaceutical laboratories that sell eye-wateringly expensive potions intended to delay menopause, or at least its effects, so that "women" can go on consuming sex and its derivative products for a few more years. Ever since every poster on the streets of Paris, every magazine article, has insisted that she be a sexual predator and shell out the money that this entails, Naïma has all but lost her taste for one-night stands.

For the past two years, she has mostly slept with Christophe. Sometimes she sees other men, but, strangely, it is her relationship with him that has become central. He is forty years old and married, with two children. She does not really understand why it has lasted. One day, when she was confiding in Élise (when Christophe is around, she continues to pretend that no one at the gallery knows), Élise offered the opinion—it was hardly very original, but she was a little distracted that day—that guys like Christophe are all the same: they promise to leave their wives but they never do. It was at this point that Naïma realized that Christophe had never promised her any such thing. He had never pretended that their affair might ever be something more. She decided that she was going to stop. She started again. She does not know whether she is in love with him or whether she is simply motivated by the desire to have him fall in love with her, whether it is her ego that has decided to wear this man down until he is hers, or whether it is the beating of her heart. Maybe a little of both.

She knows that in this she behaves as she does in many other areas: she refuses to accept that she is not entitled to something. Over the years, she has pushed at many doors just to check that they were open to her, doors of organizations and doors of bedrooms. If she was afraid that schools, galleries, museums, and foundations might reject her, she is equally afraid that men from more cultivated backgrounds would not see her as a woman. And just as she is put off by the principle of quotas since it devalues her work, she does not consider herself accepted if she thinks that she is nothing more to a man than an exotic interlude. So she lives with fear constantly gnawing at her belly. When she sleeps with a man, she is always waiting for a sign that he feels contempt for her, and if she finds one, she feels contempt for him. Contempt is the reason previous relationships have soured.

Yema said to her one day:

"If you carry on like this, I'll never get to see you married. Find a nice man. That's the most important thing. Someone who doesn't leave you to kill yourself working at home."

"I want a man who understands me, Yema," Naïma said with a laugh, cradling a glass of scalding tea between her hands.

"You might as well search for the roots of the fog . . ."

When one of her cousins told her she was marrying an Algerian from Draâ El Mizan, Naïma realized that she had never had a relationship (sexual or otherwise) with a North African man. Worse, she had never felt attracted to one. She wondered whether she had developed a form of racism common to certain children of immigrants: she cannot imagine having a relationship with someone who comes from the same region as her family. It would go against the logic of integration, which is also, secretly, the logic of upward mobility, which requires that a woman procreate with the dominant majority in order to prove that she is successful. She has not confided this doubt to anyone. And if anyone should ever suggest that she is racist, she would angrily splutter—throwing a few Arabic words into the mix—that it's impossible, not her, no, not with her dual heritage.

Dual heritage, my ass. When she was ten, she baked *makrouds* with her grandmother. And she knows how to say: *thank you, I love you, you're beautiful, I'm fine*—and the obligatory variant: *thanks be to God I'm fine*—*fuck off, I don't understand, eat, drink, you stink, the book, the dog, the door.* Although she refuses to admit it, that is the extent of her knowledge.

"Sometimes you're as dumb as the kids I teach at school," Romain tells her. "I hear it all day long: 'But, sir, I can't be racist, I'm Black!' 'I can't be racist, I'm an Arab!' And then they go and spew insults at Asians, Christians, Eastern Europeans . . . But they're convinced that the color of their skin has vaccinated them against racism, that racism only exists in other people."

"Go fuck yourself, roumi," Naïma says, and gives him a big smile.

As always, they argue and end the evening saying how much they love each other. From her earliest years in Paris, Naïma has gathered around her a new family to which she is unswervingly loyal. Romain and Sol are the two steadfast pillars of that family. In this, Clarisse thinks though she does not say so, Naïma is like her father: she has inherited his need to reinvent himself in order to feel he truly exists. And Clarisse sighs, because just as Hamid's choices placed her at the center of everything, so Naïma's choices have just as irremediably banished her mother from the heart of her life.

When it comes to her friends, Naïma has developed a theory that people can be grouped into two tribes, the Sad and the Angry—and there is no point in saying that there are also happy people, that does not count: only when happiness disappears is it possible to recognize these distinctions, to see a person's true self. Everyone breaks down at some point or other, you just have to wait a little while. There are days when you think you're fine—according to Naïma, or Romain, or Sol—and then bend down and see your shoelaces are untied. Suddenly your feeling of happiness evaporates, even your smile crumples like a tower demolished by a controlled explosion: it collapses like a building. In fact, this is precisely what you have been waiting for, these shoelaces, this tiny niggle. Everyone secretly longs to be either furious or miserable. It makes things interesting.

Romain belongs to the tribe of Sadness. Sol, like Naïma, is a child of Anger. Sharing an apartment, as they have done for years, had its difficulties in the beginning, rage facing down rage. Sometimes they wouldn't speak to each other for weeks, there would be a kind of Berlin Wall running across the apartment. And then one or the other would finally relent. They would organize international celebrations to commemorate the détente, drink vodka straight from the bottle. Now that Sol's job as a journalist means that she is not living in the apartment much of the time, they no longer have these epic rows.

Naïma has never understood where Sol's rage originated. She barely talks about her parents, and gives the impression that she ran away from home rather than simply leaving in order to go to college. She fiercely defends her independence, as though it were the only thing that helped her survive a traumatic childhood, as though her independence is an old Swiss Army knife she has always carried with her, one that has helped her out of many a tight corner. When Naïma met Sol's family, she was baffled to discover that nothing about them justified Sol's behavior. Her parents are charming, her little sister is a tiny Goldilocks, their house is lovely. It is impossible to work out the root of her anger.

"What about yours, where does it come from?"

"*Ssurfet-iyi*, I have lost my roots," Naïma says, imitating her grandmother's accent.

"Have you tried down the back of the fridge?" Sol says (a Ewan McGregor line from *Shallow Grave*, one of their favorite cult films).

Naïma never thought to go in search of her roots, other than in novels, because for a long time she thought that she had, in fact, lost nothing at all.

"Do you know Algeria? Have you been there?" Christophe asks her one night.

He is naked, his body stretched out, his eyes half-closed. In his crotch and his lower abdomen, covered by a gold or reddish shock of pubic hair, his penis is slowly shriveling, deflating as though it has sprung an invisible, irreparable leak. In a complex, sinuous movement, the skin covering his testicles shifts. It looks like an animal curling up beneath the epidermis before going to sleep. Christophe, silent, waits for his body to finish withdrawing from desire, to finish clearing the scene and disposing of any traces.

In the beginning, when she would see him lying completely abandoned on the bed after making love, Naïma thought that he might fall asleep there. But the impression that his body is relaxed is only superficial. After long minutes lying utterly still, he gets up, gets dressed, and leaves. They have never spent the night together. Christophe claims that he never cheated on his wife before Naïma. She finds this difficult to believe.

"No," she says.

After sleeping together, they struggle to find words, and the silences between sentences drag out. Sometimes Naïma attributes these to shame, sometimes to contentment, to the drowsiness that surprises them, sometimes to the difficulty of going back to ordinary conversation after so much time panting and moaning.

"Why?"

It is like a sort of slow-motion game of Ping-Pong, word, pause, word. And yet the response that follows is a well-rehearsed refrain. The usual speech comes to her without her even having to think:

"My father was waiting until my sisters and I were a little older so he could take all four of us. But in 1997, during the 'Black Decade,' my cousin and his wife were killed at a fake roadblock and my father changed his mind. He said he would never go back to the old country."

The speech avoids the need to wade through the deep, murky waters of history, of which Naïma has gleaned only snatches: a harki grandfather, an abrupt departure, a father who grew up terrified of Algeria. The speech is practical; it has just enough tragedy that no one questions it, and it has the advantage of being true. Until Azzedine—Omar's son and Hamza's grandson, about whom Naïma knows nothing—died in a hail of machine gun fire somewhere near Zbarbar, Hamid had always given his daughters to understand that they would one day see the country he had come from. They waited, disappointed every year to be sent to Pierre and Madeleine in Dijon for summer vacation and never to the far shores of the Mediterranean. "Patience," Hamid would say, "patience, you're too young." How old do you have to be to go to Algeria? Naïma and her sisters sometimes wondered as they drove through Burgundy in their maternal grandparents' car. Maybe Hamid genuinely believed that he would one day make the crossing, maybe he was simply waiting for an excuse to declare it impossible, Naïma is not sure. But since 1997, he has categorically vetoed any attempt by his daughters to raise the prospect of a trip. Myriem quickly recovered from her grief, replacing her father's lost country with the more distant, more glittering America, where she has been living now for several years. Pauline went to Morocco five times, she rubbed herself against the Algerian border like an old cat against a cushion. Aglaé claims that she doesn't give a damn: she's an internationalist. She caterwauls a song by Brassens mocking the "happy half-wits who are born somewhere." For her part, Naïma protested, but half-heartedly. During her years at university, she took a course in Arabic until she realized that the literary language she spoke painfully and falteringly bore almost no resemblance to the dialect that

Yema speaks. Despite their differences, she knows that, when asked why they know nothing about Algeria, her sisters give the same speech that she has just given Christophe. The speech is as much a part of their upbringing as the precepts "Don't talk with your mouth full" and "Don't put your elbows on the table."

"My father took me to visit Tipaza when I was little," Christophe says dreamily.

His penis is now so shrunken that it no longer extends beyond the triangle of hair toward his navel. It is half-buried in his public hair, curled up, delicate. Naïma does not much like it when it is like that. One of the reasons why she finds Christophe attractive is because his erect cock looks like him: long, straight, maybe a little too thin. It is not the penis itself she finds attractive, but its resemblance to the body and the character of the man it is attached to. Last year, Sol wrote an article about how porn has determined what genitals are supposed to look like for men as much as for women, a specific size, specific color variations, fixed proportions. Naïma thinks this is absurd. All the men she has found arousing have had cocks that look like them—so making love with them has been like a continuation of their conversation.

"The sea stretched away beneath the sun," Christophe whispers, "it glistened like a shield, and there was the stela carved with that quote from Albert Camus . . ."

Almost automatically, Naïma chimes in:

"*Here I understand what is meant by glory: the right to love without limits . . .*"

She slightly regrets saying these words in front of him. She would not want him to think she is making a demand. It is a point of honor with her not to ask for more than they have. In this moment, for example, she is thinking that she would like him to sleep here, for them to make love again when they wake in the early hours. But she says nothing.

"Would you like to go someday?" Christophe asks.

He looks at her and smiles. He has the smile of a little boy, a mischievous, naive grin. Her heart beats a little faster because she is imagining them going there together. He would tell his wife it was a business trip, or one of the lies used by married people who do not have the honesty to admit that desire is plural, and then they would cross the sea. Solemnly, as though he were asking her to marry him, she replies:

"Yes."

But he does not say more. He smiles again, strokes her face, then gets up and begins to dress.

The Christophe Reynie Gallery exhibits contemporary art; this is what is inscribed on the plate-glass window. There is a lot of photography, but also sculpture, installations, paintings ("Figurative only," Christophe insists, "abstracts really piss me off. I want people who know how to make something with their hands, not guys who've come up with a concept"), and not much video ("It doesn't really sell"). Artists of all ages from all over the world exhibit here. This is what Naïma likes about the place: it is a gallery that belongs to no particular generation, no particular school, it is not a refuge where a particular group of artists can hide out, remain oblivious to what is being done elsewhere, and crow about being in the vanguard of something, or the rear guard of everyone, the last bastion of a society that, after them, has lost its soul.

Nevertheless, Christophe has a particular passion—he prefers to say a "specialism." He is interested in works of art produced in colonial countries during the years of decolonization (violent or otherwise). He refers to his specialism as "non-aligned aesthetics." In his office, on the first floor, there are books by Fanon and Glissant.

"I assume you've read them," he says to Naïma one day.

She shrugs. "I don't see why."

She was not born into a family that gave her the books Christophe read when he was young, those that were a springboard that later led him to discover these. Hamid reads only newspapers and, very occasionally, a historical biography. Clarisse reads hippie books about the environment and education. They have bushes on the cover, complicated embroidery, and smiling faces. Naïma never set foot in a gallery as a child. Nor did she ever set foot in a theater. She has spent years trying to adapt to the dominant culture (which, for a long time, she simply referred to as "culture," before meeting Sol and Romain and becoming politicized, without really doing anything, by osmosis), terrified that she might miss some of its codes. Once one had infiltrated the host culture, one might be able to explode it from within, she thought when she was at university, not knowing whether "one" in this case referred to women, to young people, to the children of immigrants, or simply to the still-hazy person she was in the process of becoming. But the dominant culture turned out to be ever more vast and she eventually gave up on her intention of subverting it. Simply understanding it, moving within it, being comfortable like a fish in water, is a goal that requires a whole lifetime to achieve.

Naïma is proud to have studied subjects that had no purpose beyond feeding her intellectually, did not prepare her for a profession, and which, on her CV, have never impressed anyone. When she and her sisters were young, Hamid would anxiously check their school reports and constantly push them to do better. He dreamed of excruciating university courses that, to the girls, seemed to stretch out their time studying to old age or death. In the end, none of his daughters went to the École Polytechnique or to the École Normale Supérieure. Over the years, their father's obsession became a joke among the girls, a catchphrase they no longer heard. Myriem and Pauline, the two eldest, attended business school, and Aglaé, the youngest, qualified as a secondary school teacher a year ago. Naïma spent five years studying art history at university. She says that she wanted to include useless beauty in her studies: useful studies are the obsession of poor people, the terror of immigrants. She did not want to take her father's advice on this.

Christophe took the same course she did, but finished earlier: he left after he had his undergraduate degree—he told her this at her interview. She wanted to tell him that their career paths had nothing in common. Christophe inherited the building where his father had created a gallery specializing in primitive art and transformed it into a gallery of contemporary art. Christophe grew up in an apartment a stone's throw from here, amid the antique marbles and the African statues that passed through his parents' living room before ending up in a display case. He chose his studies the same way he probably chooses which shirt to wear in the morning: from a vast swath of possibilities, knowing that each can be replaced by the next.

"You do realize that you represent pretty much everything these guys are against?" she taunts, pointing at the books.

(The real question that she does not ask: You do realize that you represent pretty much everything that *I'm* against?)

"On principle," Christophe says, not rising to the bait, "or maybe to piss my parents off, or because I figured that everyone's got the right to reinvent themselves . . . I decided to side with the oppressed."

Looking at him sitting in the expensive armchair behind his desk, Naïma cannot make up her mind. Do struggles *belong* to someone? Do they more properly belong to those who are directly oppressed than to those who lead the struggle without ever having suffered oppression? Could Christophe's rebellion be anything other than a veneer? She hesitates.

"You should at least try," Christophe says, handing her the copy of Frantz Fanon's *The Wretched of the Earth* before calling a taxi.

As she watches the shiny black car pull away, she is thinking that Christophe spends so much of his life in taxis that he has developed a kind of indifference to the world. Every news story (personal, national, international) reaches him in the fragrant, comfortable, dimly lit cocoon of the car. None of these news stories disturbs the calm that reigns on the back seat, or the composure of the driver, or the feel of soft leather against his fingers. Christophe has the impression that he is unshakable, that he is possessed of much greater fortitude and emotional stability than is actually the case, since these qualities belong, not to him, but to the atmosphere on the back seat, which has been expertly engineered by the taxi company to make its passengers feel relaxed.

"I'm not afraid of anything," he says sometimes with a tinge of regret.

Naïma wishes she were not afraid of anything. But this is not the case. She feels that she is doubly afraid. She has not only inherited her father's fears, she has created her own. Clarisse, her mother, passed on no fears to her. Clarisse seems to have no fears. Naïma sometimes thinks that life is like a dog: if it senses no fear, it doesn't attack. Life is kind to Clarisse and she glides effortlessly through it.

As an exercise, before she falls asleep, Naïma sometimes lists her fears—her own and those she inherited. Among the fears that come from Hamid, she includes:

- The fear of making mistakes in French.
- The fear of telling certain people her name and surname, especially people who are older than seventy.
- The fear that someone will ask when her family arrived in France.
- The fear of being lumped in with terrorists.

This last is obviously the worst, but Naïma became aware of its presence only a few years ago, in March 2012, and since then the fear has continued to grow. After the shootings in Toulouse and Montauban, before the killer was identified and while journalists were speculating about whether he might be an Islamic fundamentalist or a right-wing fanatic, Naïma would come home, turn on the television, and spend the whole evening watching rolling news on BFMTV ("Thanks for insulting my work," Sol would say), keeping her fingers crossed that the suspect would turn out to be a white supremacist. And she knew that a few hundred miles from her Paris apartment, Hamid was doing the same thing. This is something he passed on to her, this feeling that she would have to pay for every crime committed by other immigrants in France. She takes their antics personally, whether it is cars being torched for no reason or machine gun attacks. She believes what she has done, the career path she has forged, is within the grasp of everyone. She is contemptuous of the culture of victimhood that claims it is understandable that the children of immigrants grow up to be criminals. She is equally contemptuous of the strong-arm conservatives who claim that it is an outrage but come to the same conclusion: the children of immigrants grow up to become criminals.

On January 7, 8, and 9, 2015, when the *Charlie Hebdo* massacre is followed by the hostage crisis at the Hyper Cacher kosher supermarket, which in turn is followed by a sordid police chase, Sol spews her guts in the bathroom between news bulletins while Naïma, stock-still, splutters angrily at the television. After these three days of terror, Naïma begins to notice the suspicious looks directed at Kamel, one of her colleagues at the gallery, or at the Tunisian who runs the newsstand outside her building. She imagines the same hostile looks directed at her father, at Yema, at uncles, aunts, and cousins she has lost count of. When directed at people she knows, these looks are unbearable, and yet she herself cannot help feeling frightened whenever a bearded man gets into the Métro car with an overstuffed sports bag slung over his shoulder.

On November 13, Naïma spends the evening at the cinema. She sees the latest James Bond, a movie that will later seem to her like an obscenely flippant choice. One of her former colleagues from when she worked at the culture magazine dies at the Bataclan. She finds out in the early hours and collapses on the cold tiled floor of the kitchen. She mourns her dead friend and then, despising herself for being selfish, she mourns herself, or rather the permanent place she thought she had carved out for herself in French society, which the terrorists have gunned down in a scene of carnage now playing out on every channel in the country and beyond.

Naively, she believes that the people who commit these atrocities do not realize how impossible they are making life for a whole section of the French population—that nebulous minority that Sarkozy referred to in March 2012 as *Muslim in appearance.* She despises them for claiming to liberate her when in fact they are contributing to her oppression. In doing so, she is merely following a historic pattern of delusion started by her grandfather sixty years earlier. At the beginning of the Algerian War, Ali had not understood the plan of the separatists: he saw the crackdown by the French army as a terrible consequence that the FLN, in its short-sightedness, had not envisaged. He never imagined that the strategists of independence had anticipated and even hoped for a wave of repressions, knowing that this would make the continued French presence intolerable to the populace. The masterminds of al-Qaeda and of ISIS have learned from the struggles of the past, and they know all too well that in killing in the name of Islam they incite a hatred of Islam, and beyond that a hatred of anyone with dark skin, beards, or veils, and this in turn results in unrest and violence. This is not collateral damage, as Naïma believes, it is precisely what they are striving to achieve: they want dark-skinned people to find life in Europe impossible, so that they will join them.

After the November terrorist attacks, Naïma stumbles through the following weeks in a state of shock and, without realizing, finds herself catapulted into December. She loathes December because it is a month consumed by night that falls unexpectedly before she feels she has really woken up, a month consumed by Christmas so that it seems to end on the twenty-fifth, after a vast, orchestrated crescendo of garlands and fairy lights, a month consumed by hunting for gifts as though nothing else has any importance and, this year, a month consumed by the fear of terrorists and the fear of, one way or another, being lumped in with terrorists.

One afternoon in December, while outside it is pitch-dark, freezing, and windy, she is leafing through magazines with Élise in the deserted gallery. Élise has just opened the copy of *Charlie Hebdo* on the reception desk—Christophe, like more than two hundred thousand others, took out a subscription in January.

"It has to be said that the Muslims haven't really condemned the attacks," Élise comments. "It's hardly surprising that the rest of the population thinks that maybe they support them."

Élise has the special gift of seeming so fragile that no one gets angry with her, no matter what obscenities she comes out with. She is one of those tiny individuals with huge eyes in whom everything, even rank stupidity, takes on a childlike charm.

"What do you expect them to do?" Naïma asks, surprised to find she is not yelling. "You want them to walk around with a little sign saying NOT IN MY NAME every time they set foot outside? Do you want me to phone my grandmother and put you on so she can personally apologize?"

Élise raises an eyebrow and says calmly:

"That was stupid. Forget I said it."

They spend the rest of the afternoon talking listlessly about the articles they are reading, carefully avoiding those about the attacks. Naïma is disturbed that Élise thinks "the Muslims" are a homogenous community capable of speaking with one voice, and is also disturbed by the fact that she was so quick to spring to their defense, as though—if, hypothetically, such a community exists—she is inescapably part of it, or at least vaguely associated with it. Nor is Élise the only one to confront her with this dual problem: the television, the radio, the newspapers, and social networks are buzzing with the phrase "the Muslims of France"— one that Naïma has never heard before now. And during discussions about Islam, which flare up in conversations now like wildfires, one of the participants will often turn to her for support, for an opinion, for clarification. While firmly insisting that she is not religious (the descendants of immigrants have as much right as anyone to be atheists, thank you), she finds herself talking about her grandmother, or those of her aunts and uncles who are still practicing Muslims with varying degrees of strictness (and Mohamed's remarks come back to her: *your daughters who act like whores, who've forgotten where they come from*). She claims that she is not in a position to give an *insider's view*, although she often, vehemently, does just that. She feels lost, unsure. She has never spent so much time thinking about her relationship with religion. She remembers the curiosity she felt as a child when she saw Yema praying. Her grandmother prayed discreetly: she would slip away without a word and come back a few minutes later. Naïma discovered what she was doing only when she accidently opened her bedroom door. She was surprised by the density of the silence that pervaded the room. There was Yema, kneeling, forehead pressed against the floor, on a prayer rug. She was just on the other side of the bed, but to Naïma she seemed very far away.

"Mommy, what's Yema doing?" she had asked Clarisse.

"She's praying, darling."

Naïma did not understand, in part because she did not hear the comma and so thought that her mother had said something like "she's prayindarling," a verb she did not recognize. When her grandmother reappeared, Naïma asked:

"What were you doing, Jaddati?"

Yema said something in Arabic, and Dalila translated:

"She was with her God."

As a girl, Naïma had liked the simplicity of Yema's relationship with Allah. It was nicer than the masses that her maternal grandparents sometimes dragged her to, where she was expected to talk to God in public in a cold church for far too long. What Yema did was a little like what Naïma did when she played with her dolls, she thought, a journey into imaginary worlds that could take place only in the silence of the bedroom. She remembers trying to pray herself after that. But nothing happened, so she stopped.

At the end of 2015, Naïma makes a list of her new fears:

- Fear that Yema will be attacked in the street because she wears the veil. (There is not much risk: she ventures out less and less frequently, and goes less and less far.)
- Fear of dying while having a drink on a café terrace.
- Fear of realizing that, in the years since she last saw him, her uncle Mohamed has been training in Syria or in Pakistan.
- Fear that she is beginning to lump people together by including this last fear in her list.
- Fear that the twenty-eight percent of French people who say they understand why Muslims are attacked after terrorist incidents will continue to rise.
- Fear that a civil war between "them" and "us" will break out in which Naïma will not be able to choose a side.

Standing by the window, Naïma makes herself a third cup of coffee in the hope that the scalding liquid will loosen the viselike chill that gripped her as she walked back from the Métro station. Outside, a few snowflakes are falling. The stark white meeting room, lit by a soft glow, looks as though it has already been buried by snow. Naïma shivers and goes over to sit next to the radiator. At the conference table, Élise and Kamel are gently flirting, recounting extravagant stories of their Christmas holidays punctuated by cries of, "You should have been there!"

As he does at the start of every year, Christophe gathers his team together "to take stock" and "talk about next steps"—an exercise not unlike Naïma making New Year's resolutions, and one that she has sometimes seen turn into score-settling. Ordinarily, it is a meeting she enjoys, since it allows them to go over the past year, to rewrite it with ellipses and embellishments (two things at which she excels). They replay the greatest hits, transform failures into "learning experiences," and, in the process, bad-mouth one or two particularly tiresome artists behind their backs. This year, it is a little different.

"We have to face facts, no one goes into galleries in the wake of a terrorist attack. People don't give a shit about art."

People don't give a shit about a lot of things. On the other hand, in the wake of the January 7 and November 13 attacks, there was a net increase in the sale of adult coloring books. The results are gloomy; Christophe focuses on the future.

"For the start of the academic year next September," he announces, "I'd like us to do something about Algeria. I think that would be good. Lately, the media have been pushing a deplorable view of the Arab world, whether about the destruction of Palmyra, the Bardo Museum in Tunis, or the attacks here in France . . . People are going to end up thinking that Arabs despise art, culture, journalism, and I don't know what else. So it occurred to me that this is the moment to fight the fear, to showcase the powerful art emerging from these countries. We'll probably be called Islamic apologists or snowflakes, but it will allow me to fulfill one of my dreams: the first major retrospective of Lalla."

Around the conference table, the team is guardedly enthusiastic. Lalla is a Kabyle painter; Christophe included a number of his paintings in a group exhibition entitled *The Mirror Wars* ten years ago. They were large oil paintings of sand-colored buildings that merged into an ocher background, somewhere between palace and tombstone. Naïma leafed through the exhibition catalogue shortly after she started working at the gallery and was not particularly impressed by them. She felt that the most interesting part of the catalogue was the artist's biography. Lalla is not his actual name, but a pseudonym adopted in the 1960s shortly after Algerian independence as a tribute to Lalla Fatma N'Soumer, the "Joan of Arc of Djurdjura." Over the years, the name has been truncated until now it is simply Lalla—"Madame"—a curious moniker for an artist who, from the little photograph in one corner of the page, looks like an old man with a bushy mustache stained yellow from smoking. Born in 1940, Lalla was also the pupil, the acolyte, and the friend of the artist Issiakhem, and through him came to know Kateb Yacine. This means he is at the epicenter of Christophe's passion: non-aligned art, revolutionary aesthetics. Threatened both by the Islamic Salvation Front and by the Algerian government during the Black Decade, the artist reluctantly sought refuge in France and is now close to death, eaten away by the disease of the century, in a maisonette in Marne-la-Vallée. Lalla has painted very few large works, and these, it has to be said, are not exceptional, Christophe admits to his team. On the other hand, few people know that he produced an incredible series of tiny ink drawings throughout his life, using them as a means of payment, as visiting cards, as coasters, drawings that are now scattered far and wide on both sides of the Mediterranean. Christophe saw about thirty of them when he visited Lalla a month ago. Once he had finished them, Lalla tended to use the drawings as part of his daily routine, so some are scribbled with shopping lists, and others are drawn on scraps of colored fabric he uses as dusters. Most were in very poor condition and could not be exhibited in the gallery. Christophe would like to try to track down others and gather together as many as possible. He can already picture the exhibition:

"We'll hang a number of large paintings in the middle of the walls. Not the ones we exhibited from *Mirror Wars*. We would need to find other, older works, maybe from the period when he was studying at the Beaux-Arts with Issiakhem, for example. It doesn't matter if they're not for sale, we could get them on loan from Algiers. And all around, displayed with a brutal simplicity, we'll hang the tiny little ink drawings."

"Getting works on loan? That's a very museum-based approach!" Kamel protests. "Is that what you think a gallery like this is here for?"

"To do something that a museum won't ever do? Yes, that's exactly what we're here for. Don't worry, once it's over we'll go back to exhibiting photography. Probably a Chinese artist. Élise, could you find out whether S-Tao might have something to exhibit next spring?"

"What about the Korean artist who works from old slides—are you giving up on that exhibition?"

Kamel is worried: this is his pet project, the first time Christophe has agreed to exhibit work he did not personally discover. Besides, he does not like it when the gallery showcases work by North African artists because some woman will invariably come up and congratulate him.

"Yes, of course we're still doing it. You keep working on that. Maybe it should be a group show. I'm a bit worried that, on its own, the work seems a little weak. Do you think you can convince him?"

Before Kamel has time to respond, Christophe turns to Naïma. She is not sure whether it is out of embarrassment, out of a fear of exposing their relationship, but at meetings Christophe always addresses her last.

"Naïma, can I leave you to work on Lalla? See what you can dig up from his friends and acquaintances?"

"Are his details in the Bible?"

The Bible is Christophe's huge shagreen address book. He brings it with him every morning and takes it home every evening, as though the addresses and telephone numbers of the artists were highly coveted information. To Naïma, he seems like a little boy who mistakes a piece of dull glass for a precious stone and cannot imagine that others— including grown-ups—are not trying to steal it from him. At first Christophe's employees mocked him for the practice, but before long they, too, handled the Bible only with great caution. Naïma thinks that this is perhaps why Christophe is the boss—not because he inherited the premises, but because his madness is contagious. But, on the other hand, there are times when she thinks that his madness is contagious because he has always been in charge and has never had to curb his lunacy in order to meet the expectations of a boss. Christophe nods and says:

"You'll probably need to get in touch with his ex-wife. From what Lalla has said, she kept a lot of his works. He doesn't even want to speak to her these days, but he thinks that she would be prepared to give them to us if she got a percentage of the sales."

Naïma frowns. Divorces in the art world are something she cannot abide. They are invariably messy—and almost always full of thorny legal clauses she cannot circumvent. She focuses on the little cup of coffee in front of her, turning it between her fingers so as not to reveal her annoyance. Once, a year ago, she complained about a task she had been assigned and Christophe accused her of demanding to be treated as though she were special—he might even have said "like a princess," *you expect me to treat you like a princess.* She could not bear the implication: It's not enough that you're sleeping with me, you have to make it obvious, you cut yourself off from other people, from ordinary mortals, deep down you're a romantic. So these days she bites her tongue.

"As for travel expenses, try and keep them to a minimum. We're a little in the red right now."

"What travel expenses?" Naïma asks gloomily. "The train from Paris to Marne-la-Vallée?"

"Very funny. To Tizi. Someone has to go to Tizi. That's where most of the drawings are. I've talked to Lalla, he'll give you the list of people."

Her coffee reflects the meeting room's fluorescent lights, so when Naïma starts, it creates a ripple across the surface. The coffee no longer reflects anything, it spills over the side and spreads across the table. She looks up, convinced that she has misheard. Christophe is beaming at her like Father Christmas: Naïma, I am giving you back Algeria; Algeria, I am giving you back Naïma.

Obviously, she cannot deny that, from time to time, she has dreamed of making this trip. When she took a few Arabic lessons at university, it was with the intention of putting them to good use when she crossed the Mediterranean. But over time, she has accepted Hamid's refrain about the Black Decade as a justification for not fulfilling her dream, she has accepted that Algeria is too dangerous for her.

It has been years since she traveled in order to explore exotic countries. Her work at the gallery gives her the opportunity to discover distant lands through the works they exhibit and the artists' biographies she edits for the catalogue. She enjoys becoming variously attached to some godforsaken little town in Nevada, to a Japanese skyline, to a series of rusty hangars on the outskirts of Manchester, and to feel, when looking at each landscape, that it is home. Perhaps it is no more than a consolation prize, perhaps there is something she is still missing, something that is sending out feelers that run through her, but she believes that it is for her to decide whether or not she wants to fill these little voids. In sending her to Tizi Ouzou, Naïma has the impression that Christophe is taking it upon himself to write her history for her, or rather is forcing her to fall back into line with a family history from which she extricated herself the better to write her own.

"The bastard, the fucking bastard," she rages, pacing around her cramped, cluttered kitchen.

"So you don't want to go?" Sol calls from the living room.

"Of course I do! But I always thought I'd go later, when I was ready."

"Yeah, in ten or fifteen years," Sol scoffs, "who knows, maybe thirty or forty. And if you die in the meantime, no big deal."

"That's right," Naïma says, coming to join Sol in the living room. "That's pretty much what I was thinking."

"What have you got to lose by going there now?"

Naïma cannot answer. Perhaps she would lose the absence of Algeria, an absence around which her family has been built since 1962. It would mean replacing a lost country with a real country. The implications seem enormous.

"What if it's dangerous?"

Sol raises her eyebrows, the cap of a ballpoint in her mouth. She has reported from Afghanistan, from Mali, from Egypt, from a host of countries that Naïma has forgotten or would be unable to pinpoint on a map. She has never shown any fear when setting off.

"A country is only dangerous if you don't have the right contacts," Sol says, spitting out the pen cap.

As she lies in bed, Naïma rephrases the terms she will use a dozen times, a hundred times, to turn down Christophe's offer. She wants to be sure there is not the slightest chink that would allow him to claim that this is a whim, so she rephrases it again. She even considers mentioning Ali, but she has nothing to say about him beyond the fact that he turned the Mediterranean into a wall that none of his descendants has dared scale since he left. On the alarm clock, the orange digits tick by too fast. They hover in the darkness of the room, shortening the time left for sleep every time she looks at them. Still she tries to edit her response, but the words are less and less cooperative.

As sleep gradually dulls her thoughts, absurd and vivid elements begin to disturb the laboriously prepared sentences and they explode and dissolve into violets, into dinosaurs, they stretch out into a trail of dots . . .

Through the vast windows, a triangle of light glides across the parquet floor and licks the back wall. Élise stands in the pool of light, eyes closed, arms hanging limply by her side. On the other side of the room, in the shadows, the narrow stairs lead up to the second floor, which seems utterly silent.

"Is Christophe not in yet?"

Élise stretches but at first replies only with the muffled cracks of her vertebrae, then she turns to Naïma.

"He is. He left something for you on the desk."

She returns to her exercises, to the meticulous counting of her muscles, indifferent to the stares from passersby or perhaps happy to make an exhibition of herself. Naïma opens the plastic folder and takes out a sheaf of photographs of the ink drawings Christophe mentioned the day before. She spreads them out on the smooth white surface, studying them as a whole and then individually. She is surprised by their quality. Lalla's sketches are marked by both a delicacy and a brutality: there is nothing calm about his work, even the most recent drawings. Naïma likes people who age without relenting. To decide to remain standing, stiff and bolt upright, is to run the risk of the bones or the ego shattering. And so, in most people, the spine slowly curves with the years and a sort of calm takes hold—one Naïma thinks of as an abdication— transforming the late works of aging artists into nostalgic vignettes that do not interest her.

When Christophe comes down from his office, she watches him move around the huge bright room without saying anything to him beyond a few trite remarks. Before turning down the task he has given her, she can handle the preparatory work: she can go to meet Lalla. There will be time enough to wriggle out later, she thinks. But she wants to meet him. She wants to meet the man who still draws like this, though he is past seventy.

As she leafs through the Bible for the artist's telephone number, she manages to convince herself that, if the meeting goes well, she can handle the whole thing from Paris: bring together the necessary contacts and expertise to have the works shipped without her having to leave this reassuring space of white walls and vast windows.

"Come by tomorrow," says the woman who answers the telephone.

Sitting in the train, Naïma cannot shake off the strange impression that she is heading into a trap. She pictures those scenes in movies where a small group marches forward, all too vulnerable to an ambush. As children, she and her sisters would scream at the characters:

"Turn back! For God's sake, turn back!"

At the time, they were convinced that you had to be as stupid as a movie hero to carry on in spite of the gnawing atmosphere of menace, and that they themselves would be much more sensible. And yet Naïma does not get off at the next station and turn back. She settles deeper into her seat and bites her nails, staring out at the snatches of suburban scenes that flash past between the tunnels.

When she arrives, she finds only a series of small beige pebble-dash houses and streets named after obscure ministers from the Third Republic, as devoid of danger as it is of exotic charm. She sets off on foot for the cul-de-sac the woman mentioned on the telephone, which bears one of those names that exist only in leafy suburbs: Hazel Grove Mews or Great Oaks Way, she can't remember, a clumsy or perhaps derisive attempt to make residents believe that they are living in the countryside. The artist's house is identical to the neighboring houses and to those on the next road. There is nothing to suggest that an artist lives here, not the slightest square inch of beauty or folly in this functional, faux-charming building.

Nor are there hazel groves or oak trees. Lalla opens the door and, after briefly looking her up and down, says with a smile:

"Fantastic, they've sent me the Arab!"

"Kabyle," Naïma automatically corrects him.

Lalla bursts out laughing.

"Even better! Come on, come in!"

Inside, the house looks as though it were renovated by someone who never planned to live here. Everything is neutral and matching, from the walls to the furniture and the knickknacks. Yet, on closer inspection, the dog-eared books, the piles of letters, the Aït Menguellet CDs, and the drawings strewn between the magazines on the glass-topped coffee table gradually reveal that this really is the home of Lalla Fatma N'Soumer. These objects nudge the little house into another realm, extirpate it from the French suburbs, from a life stretched between Paris, almost beyond reach, and Euro Disney.

Naïma cannot help but compare the house with her grandmother's apartment, where Algeria is all on display, glaring and garish; Algeria is present in the Muslim calendars pinned to the wall (calendars her grandmother cannot read, Naïma was stunned to realize late in life), the copper trays embossed with Arabic calligraphy, the photo of Mecca in a gilt fame studded with paste stones, the tea service, the packets of sticky dates piled up in every cupboard, and—Yema's pride and joy— the panoply of pots for making couscous that take up every shelf in the storeroom. Algeria is present on the giant flat-screen television, always on, always tuned to an Arabic channel. It is present in the jewelry on her fingers and her wrists, in the red-and-yellow scarf that covers Yema's hair, which in itself is marked by Algeria, being carefully hennaed every month. But there is no depth to it. Naïma's family has been orbiting Algeria for so long that they no longer really know what they are circling. Memories? A dream? A lie?

"Apologies for my rude welcome," Lalla says as he pours her a coffee. "It's just that—have you noticed the French tendency to presume that all Algerians understand each other? Twenty years I've been here, and it feels like every time I have to deal with an institution, they dig out the duty Arab and send him to meet me."

"In his office, Christophe Reynie files all the applications he gets from the job center by country of origin," Naïma says. "And he takes on temporary staff according to the nationality of the artists he's exhibiting."

Lalla laughs so hard it triggers a coughing fit. Naïma thinks that he looks like Hemingway with his white beard, the repulsively stained mustache, and the dark eyes that never smile—the smile appears in the lines around his eyes, but there is no warmth in the irises.

She had expected to spend an hour or two with him, that they would exchange contacts, telephone numbers, addresses, and brief descriptions of the works, after which she would make a dash for the train. She had imagined a professional conversation of the kind she usually has with artists, who generally reserve their more artistic conversations, their view of the world, and the outpourings of their souls for Christophe and provide her only with logistical details. But Lalla talks to her randomly about everything and nothing (the expression is misleading; he talks about his life) with a surprising volubility that prevents her from steering the conversation. He confides to her that he sees this retrospective as connected to his imminent death (cancer) and that he finds the prospect as frightening as he finds it appealing. He is not sure that he wants to live long enough to see it.

"Imagine," he says to Naïma, "this will be the first time I've been confronted by everything I've done, from the sixties to today, a distillation of my life in scrawls of ink and colors. What if, at the last moment, when it's too late to create something new, I end up thinking it's shit? That really scares me."

She offers a few hackneyed compliments that he dismisses with a sigh. A little later, as he empties a packet of speculoos biscuits onto a plate, he returns to his fears.

"I've come to terms with my death, that wasn't too difficult. But I don't know if I could face discovering that my life was mediocre and die knowing that."

"How can you come to terms with death?" Naïma asks.

She is convinced that it is simply a figure of speech, a brave man's vanity. As he sits there in his gray-and-beige armchair wearing a baggy sweater scattered with dog hairs, the artist looks too old, too frail, not to fear an end that is bound to come soon.

"I've spent a long time rubbing shoulders with death," Lalla says, sipping the last dregs of his coffee.

In his youth, he made several attempts to kill himself. It was complicated, he says, suffering from depression as he did in rural Algeria in the 1950s, because the old people simply told him that it was the work of a djinn and no one wanted to talk about his sadness because that would have been tantamount to talking to the djinn and no one was prepared to do that. And then everything changed with the war, when death truly entered his field of vision. He would have been about fifteen. His older brother quickly joined the maquis, and he found himself running messages for the FLN. For Lalla, it was a stunning reversal: when life had been offered to him on a plate, he had not wanted it, but now that it was threatened, he wanted it desperately. He experienced incredibly powerful rushes of adrenaline when he encountered army patrols, and he remembers racing headlong through the woods with a laugh that erupted from his chest, one he could not stop until he had shaken off his pursuers. He has never loved life more than he did in that moment, he says, and he has never again experienced that strange laugh. And so, when the whole country began to breathe again after seven years of horrors, he felt terrified. Terrified that, now that the risk of danger was gone, his death wish would return. This was how he found himself a little later fighting with the Kabyle rebels and how he finally managed to antagonize both the government and the Islamists. Obviously, it was a matter of principle, but it was also a way of reinforcing his fragile existence. Lalla believes that he manages risk in the same way a diabetic manages his insulin. Too little, he wants to die, too much, he will actually die. In 1995, he went into exile, because the Black Decade threatened the precarious equilibrium he had created.

"I'm a suicide case who would be prepared to live forever as long as I felt at risk every day," he says.

Illness, in the end, is a risk like any other. It is one of the things that encourages him to rejoice in the fact that he is alive. And when death comes, he will have toyed with it so often that it will be entitled to take him once and for all. He knows this: death must be frustrated, given how often he has danced with it, only to slip away.

"Life is violent. My life, at least . . ."

This last phrase seems to shake him from his thoughts, and he returns his attention to Naïma.

"Was your family involved in the war? When did they arrive in France?"

Hamid told his daughters over and over that to answer this question is not simply a matter of giving a date, it opens a door to a history that still provokes violent reactions. Ordinarily Naïma never specifies the year, only the decade. But she feels at ease here amid the smell of the old dog and the aroma of coffee, and perhaps part of her is hoping that, if she quarrels with the artist, she will be spared the imminent trip to Algeria.

"In '62."

His eyebrow rises only slightly.

"Harkis?"

"Yes."

It is the first time Naïma has heard the word pronounced with an Arabic accent, and the *h* that takes up so much space gives it a certain additional gravity. Lalla sits back in his chair and looks at her, his face expressionless.

"What about you, what do you think?"

"I don't understand."

"What do you think about independence?"

"I'm in favor, obviously."

"Obviously . . ."

He says nothing more. The ambiguous silence is broken by a jangle of keys. Céline comes in laden with shopping bags and cheerfully greets them. This is the woman Naïma spoke to on the telephone. On subsequent visits, she will come to understand that since the old painter fell ill, Céline has been his lover, his nurse, his model, and his assistant, a polymorphous yet discreet companion with gray eyes and an unwavering love. When Céline suggests she stay for dinner, Naïma realizes that she has let the whole afternoon slip away. She leaps up from her chair, brushing biscuit crumbs from her skirt.

"You'll have to come back," Lalla says. "I'm too tired now to get my thoughts in order. I've talked too much."

And from his sly smile, Naïma wonders whether he did this deliberately, whether he is not trying to defer the exhibition by swamping it in a torrent of stories, as though, in spite of his protestations of acceptance, he would like to dance with the devil one last time and make his escape.

The following week, *langues-de-chats* have replaced the speculoos biscuits on the little plate sitting on the coffee table. It is a box of mass-produced cookies of the kind supermarkets sell by the thousands every day, and yet, as she bites into a langue-de-chat, Naïma thinks of Yema. At some point in her childhood she cannot precisely place in time, her grandmother decided to include Western food in her pantry and in her recipes, as though to prove to her grandchildren that she could move with the times, or because she feared that their little French palates would crave foods that they could not find at her house. Yema tried couscous with fries, mutton pizza, hamburgers in kesra buns, and, of course, every brand of cookies available in the largest Leclerc hypermarket in France. She was so proud of her purchases—entirely based on the images on the packaging—that Naïma and her sisters never dared to tell her that the supermarket cookies were dry and bland and they longed for her to go back to serving honey pastries. Naïma doesn't know how many langues-de-chats exactly like the one offered by the old painter she choked down, smiling so as not to upset her grandmother. She takes a second bite—the flavor, or rather the absence of flavor, has not changed.

Today, Lalla is wearing a pale yellow shirt and a thick jacket of an old-fashioned style. He looks a little like an elderly uncle in a wedding photograph, or one of those fogyish gentlemen who put on their best suit to go for a drink on Sundays down at the PMU—not to bet on the horses, nor to see the handful of old soaks they are likely to find there, but because it is Sunday, a day for suits and patent-leather shoes. Naïma, determined to be more efficient than she was on her previous visit, immediately steers the conversation to the ink drawings that Christophe wants to procure.

"When did you start working in this form? When do the earliest examples date from?"

Lalla pinches his lower lip between thumb and forefinger.

"In '65, maybe a little earlier. I can't really remember. I do know it was a few years after independence . . ."

He smiles dreamily at this word and, despite urgent (or perhaps slightly panicked) looks from Naïma, he picks up the story of his life where he left off last time, as though it were a book he had carefully bookmarked and slipped under the coffee table waiting for her to come back so that he could easily open it at the right page.

"Independence was . . . it was a magnificent, tragic shambles. There were wonderful moments, truly wonderful moments. Life was changing. Thanks to socialism, we suddenly had heaps of new friends. Algiers was teeming with foreigners who spoke languages we had never even thought about before. Intellectuals and artists from chilly, far-flung countries who came to give lessons. We were taught to use machines. In almost every sphere of life, whether agriculture, mining, or the plastic arts, the machine was king—or rather we were told that, with them, we could be kings. At first I studied photography and filmmaking. I met René Vautier several times—you know who I mean?—with his obsession for filming truth, of capturing every image of what he called 'our people on the march.' He sent me to document a military parade once, I saw former mujahideen on crutches, their stumps on display, I watched wide-eyed, but I didn't shoot a single second of footage—I completely forgot I had a camera."

He laughs and, on his upper lip, the whitish mustache squirms like a little animal.

"I don't think I was ever cut out for machines. Actually, I thought that dreaming about machines was a peasant farmer thing. It reminded me of my father saying to me, One day maybe we can get a tractor, as though this in itself was a goal in life. So I went back to painting and drawing. That was something I enjoyed. I went to the École des Beaux-Arts in Algiers, and that's where I met Issiakhem. I was impressed by him, obviously, but not for artistic reasons (I never understood what it meant to say someone was good or bad at painting, I'm not sure I really understand it now), no, I was impressed because I knew he was the person who had designed the five-dinar banknote, to me that was the epitome of success. I mean, you paint something that gets hung in a gallery, good for you, it'll look good on your CV. But a five-dinar note! They're everywhere, all the time. Everyone gets to see them. What you've painted is spilling from wallets and scarves and socks, *ka-ching*, your painting is in cash registers in shops, it gets deposited in banks, hidden under mattresses. I think one of the reasons I've never liked painting large works is because I was so impressed by Issiakhem's damn five-dinar notes."

This time Naïma laughs with him. Céline appears in the doorway. She does not ask what they find so funny, does not try to join the conversation. She simply stares for a moment at the two faces lit up by laughter, then, with a little frown, she goes back to her work. Naïma wonders whether, like her, Céline is aware that the painter is pouring out secrets that, at first blush, seem spontaneous and random—those ramblings of old people that seem to proceed like a ship with a broken tiller—but end up creating an impenetrable wall of words that prevent her from broaching what she is here to talk about. Or perhaps it is not that he is actually building a wall of words—this is another possibility—but it is Naïma who is turning a sweeping conversation into a heartfelt monologue because her responses seem so insignificant that she forgets them as soon as they are uttered, while Lalla's stories hold her spellbound, as though he is Scheherazade and she the sultan—since, if the sultan in his palace of arabesques and fountains actually did ever interrupt the storyteller, the various versions of the *Thousand and One Nights* make no mention of the fact, the tales are not punctuated by their incidental conversations, which Naïma, like the sultan, promptly erases from her memory to preserve only the intoxicating nectar of the stories. The artist glances at the doorway, empty now that Céline has disappeared, and carries on:

"Anyway . . . the problem is that it wasn't long before people realized that independence wasn't everything. Power is never innocent—who said that, Shakespeare?—so why do we go on believing that we can be governed by good people? Those who want power badly enough to seize it are those with monstrous egos, overweening ambitions, they are all potential tyrants. If not, they wouldn't seek out the role . . . As soon as Ben Bella was elected, people claimed that the vote had been rigged, that he should never have been president, that he had circumvented the internal negotiations. I didn't listen, because I wanted independence to be a beautiful thing. But by 1965 it was difficult to believe we were living in a democracy . . . Has anyone ever told you about Boumédiène's coup d'état?"

Naïma shakes her head, and Lalla's eyes immediately light up, filled with the anticipatory pleasure of telling the tale. He leans forward.

"You're an artist, you'll enjoy this. So, imagine, Pontecorvo was in the middle of filming *The Battle of Algiers* at the time, so people were used to seeing tanks and soldiers and the whole panoply of war in the streets. When people saw Boumédiène's men, they thought Pontecorvo was shooting a particularly big scene that day. 'He's good,' they said. And in fact the soldiers took advantage of the confusion: 'No need to panic, it's just a movie.' Except it was a real-life coup d'état and the next morning they started to hunt down their enemies. And the whole thing started all over again, the arrests, the disappearances . . . It's terrible to disappear like that. I was painting like a madman, hoping that this would stop me from disappearing. I wanted to be famous so that my name at least would live on after me, even if my body disappeared . . ."

He offers the plate of cookies again, and Naïma, whose mouth is still coated with soggy crumbs, takes another. Eating langues-de-chats and listening to stories of another era, she feels as if, for a few hours, she is a child again.

"Anyway, in those first years, people were creating all over the place," Lalla continues. "It was as though art was an itch we had to scratch. The theater world in Algiers, for example, was bubbling with ideas. There were performances every night, theater companies sprouted like poppies in the fields, there was Kateb Yacine's company, obviously, but . . ."

Something seems to occur to him, something that stops him mid-sentence. He allows the words to trail off and gives Naïma an apologetic smile.

"I'm sorry, I'm rambling, I'm sure you already know all this stuff."

It is at this moment precisely—although this is also the last of a long succession of less significant moments that began ten or fifteen years earlier—that Naïma realizes how little she knows about Algeria, its history, its politics, its geography, what she will call the real Algeria as opposed to Yema and Pont-Féron, which constitute her personal, empirical Algeria.

When she gets home, she picks up the copy of *Larousse* lying on a shelf. (She still regularly consults the encyclopedia, despite the existence of the internet; it is a habit she inherited from her father.) She opens it at the letter *H* and reads:

> harki, n.:
> A soldier serving in the Harka auxiliaries.
> harki, n. and adj.:
> A family member or descendant of a harki.

"No way," she says to the book. "It's out of the question."

That night, she telephones Clarisse and tells her she is coming to visit this weekend. She can tell from her mother's voice that she is worried: Naïma usually only goes home if she has been dumped by a boyfriend, is temporarily unemployed, or—more rarely—if there is a public holiday and she has a long weekend. Naïma reassures her mother that she's fine, that she just wants to talk. As she hears herself say these words, she realizes how ominous they sound. These are the words that precede a breakup, they are the lie used by bad guys in movies to get someone to open the door . . . Is it really so difficult to *just talk*? When someone says they just want to talk, do they always have an ulterior motive? Isn't it just a ruse—Naïma concludes—since what she really wants is to "make them talk," an even more ominous phrase, one usually snarled in a German accent?

Between each of her visits, her childhood home seems to shrink. It no longer has anything of the vast farmhouse with the endless paddock in which she believes she and her sisters played. The pond at the end of the garden that, when it froze in winter, served as a skating rink looks more like a puddle. Each time she goes back to visit her parents, Naïma is surprised that the dimensions of the place jar with those in her memories.

As she carries her suitcase upstairs, she looks again at the family portraits that hang on the staircase. Through them, she can explore the family tree back through the generations preceding Clarisse and trace the surrounding branches. Of Hamid's family there is only a photograph of Ali that dates from the Second World War and another, in which he is with Yema in the little kitchen in Pont-Féron, printed in black-and-white to give it an antique patina. The paternal branch never provided Naïma with great-grandparents, or with great-uncles or great-aunts posed in front of silk flowers or richly colored drapes.

In the first few hours following her arrival, she does as she always does: she walks in the garden despite the biting cold, helps her mother defrost apples for a tart, shares news of her sisters with her parents. She is careful not to broach too soon the subject that has brought her here. Getting Hamid to talk is no easy task, this is something she knows. He has only two modes of speech: the great orator and the Pierrot, that is to say mute. When he wants to talk, he talks—too much he holds forth, it is impossible to stop him, to steer the conversation. When a subject is uninteresting, or intimidating, when it saddens or angers him, he crawls off into a corner of his mind and plays dumb.

Naïma waits until the two of them are in the kitchen before cautiously explaining Christophe's project. She tells him about her first meetings with Lalla, tries to make her father laugh, retelling some of the old man's anecdotes, mentions the drawings on the other side of the Mediterranean. In doing so, she repeats the name of the country where the drawings are to be found, at first timidly and then a little louder, but the name elicits no reaction from Hamid, it is a word like any other, as though she were saying "table" or "apartment" or even "peony," but she continues to repeat it, hoping that the repetition will cause his mask to slip. Her father is preparing a tray of snacks, not saying a word, as though waiting for her to get to the point, as though he knows—maybe she is being paranoid?—that this is just a long preamble. She babbles on constantly, helplessly plunging back into the torrent of words, she feels as though she is losing her footing, and so, confused and irritated, she blurts out:

"I'm going to go. To Algeria."

She thinks she is saying it simply to get a reaction, but as she hurls the words in his face, she realizes that she is not lying: she is going to go there. She doesn't know when she made the decision, perhaps at the very beginning when she did not immediately reject Christophe's suggestion, perhaps in Lalla's living room a few days ago, perhaps a split second ago when she realized that her father's silence left her no choice.

He finishes carefully slicing a saucisson, and the dry clicking of the knife sounds like a pendulum, stretching time even as it measures it. He places the thin slices in a porcelain bowl and finally turns to look at Naïma.

"Is there anything I can do to stop you?"

"No."

Hamid gives a shrug that says, in that case, she should not have told him.

"What I'd like is for you to help me."

"I don't see how."

"You've never told me anything about Algeria," Naïma whispers.

When she imagined this conversation, she heard the phrase slipped casually into a conversation on a summer evening, she accorded it the weightlessness of those gossamer words spun around a glass of white wine and slices of saucisson. (Alcohol + pork; sometimes she thinks her father feels it is his duty to prove it is possible to be from the Maghreb without being Muslim.) But her tone now is angry, filled with reproach, and outside the garden is shrouded in January frost.

"What did you want me to tell you?" Hamid asks without looking at her. "I first worked out the shape of Algeria when I saw it on a map here in France. I saw Algiers for the first time as I left the country. So what did you expect me to tell you? The color of my bedroom walls? I don't know anything about Algeria."

"What about your childhood?"

"Children are the same everywhere."

To stop him from retreating into sullen silence, she does not insist. She decides to steer the conversation toward superhero movies, a passion she has always shared with Hamid and that sometimes seems like an inchoate longing for someone to come and save them, although from what, she does not know. They spend the rest of dinner classifying the members of the X-Men according to personal preference, scorning Superman for his near-absolute invincibility and his permanently perfect hair, praising Spider-Man for his constant moral crises, and making fun of Clarisse, who has never managed to take an interest in these characters and continually mixes them up.

The following day, she agrees to a morning stroll through the woods, although she has always found the mud that mires the paths through the trees from November to March depressing. In silence, the three of them walk through the forest, which has also shrunk in comparison to her memories, and has lost its precious secret places: the Fairy Glade, the Deer Path. While Clarisse falls behind, looking for the paint marks on the trunks that indicate the next felling area, Naïma resolves to bluntly ask her father the question that has been nagging at her.

"What did Ali do during the war?"

Hamid's head explodes with a sound he has not heard since adolescence. It is like the shriek of nails on a blackboard. The sound seems so loud that he is convinced that Naïma can hear it, too, that it is being transmitted from his skull to his daughter's, drilling into her ear.

"I don't know," he confesses finally. "Not much, I think . . ."

In his eyes she can see that this is a hope he longs to believe is the truth.

"You'd probably need to ask your grandmother," he says. "I don't remember anything."

"Very funny," Naïma says.

He knows full well that this is the sort of conversation she cannot have with her grandmother. After all, he is the one who did not want to teach his children Arabic. When his daughters asked him about it, he said, as he did about almost anything concerning Algeria, that he remembered nothing, especially not the structure of this language he nonetheless still speaks, increasingly haltingly, with his mother and his brothers and sisters. He argued that to teach a language required understanding of how it works, how it is constructed. Naïma was never convinced by these arguments. She feels that he has confused integration with a scorched-earth policy, leaving his daughters only the narrow strip of no-man's-land created by Yema's poor French and the incomplete translations by the uncles and aunts who still visit their mother. By the end of the walk, she is dragging her feet like a petulant child.

As they are taking off their muddy shoes outside the door, Naïma asks her mother the same question, though she holds out little hope.

"I don't think anyone knows," Clarisse says. "But one thing I do know: your father will spend the rest of his life feeling guilty that he doesn't know."

And Naïma hears the unspoken second sentence slipped beneath the first: *Maybe you should give him a bit of peace about that.* But Naïma cannot comply, simply, easily, as she used to do back when her parents seemed to her, if not heroes, then endowed with an absolute authority to which she had to submit because there was a deeper meaning that she did not understand and she trusted them to interpret it for her. She mutters her thanks through gritted teeth.

Inside, the telephone starts to ring, and Clarisse, her socks still crumpled around her ankles, rushes to answer. Although Hamid is sitting in the living room, he makes no attempt to pick up. In the past few years, he has stopped answering the telephone. He has decided—Naïma does not know exactly when, probably shortly after Mohamed with his Day-Glo misery set himself up in her parents' garden—that he would no longer take the time, or the risk, of talking to his brothers and sisters. All he wants is to be left in peace, in his shrinking house, with his wife and his daughters, the daughters whose numbers grew at first, settled at four for a long time, then gradually dwindled as their studies took them away, and, in due course, in peace with his wife, his garden, and the thought of his daughters living their lives in cities more or less distant.

When she was a child, Naïma often saw her father on the telephone, bowed beneath the weight of what he and Clarisse laughingly called his family's "compendium of troubles." (She laughed, he scowled.) There were Mohamed's spliffs and his cans of beer and Yema's despair of ever making a man of him; there were Salim's health problems (the perfect youngest child, he remained the most delicate); there was Fatiha's succession of doomed romances as she searched for a loving, faithful husband among men uninterested in fidelity or perhaps in love; and there were Dalila's interminable phone calls in which she barely paused for breath in her long tirades against city bureaucrats trying to swindle the family, doctors who didn't know how to cure her brother, the economic crisis, rising unemployment, the government of champagne socialists who had never seen a poor person—in a tempestuous rage, Dalila would call down the wrath of heaven on employers, other members of her family, the rich, the lost, the sun, the air, the water, the morons, the fascists, and, most especially, Yema's neighbor, the old crone with the lavender hair, One of these days I swear I'll blow a fuse, *ouallah*, one of these days I'll kill her. Each time, Hamid would sigh and say:

"Yes, yes, calm down, what do you expect me to do, if that's how you feel, don't talk to her, calm down, don't go setting them against each other, yeah, no, okay, okay."

Dalila's war against the downstairs neighbor had seemed to Naïma much like the Trojan War, which she was just discovering at the time in expurgated versions written for children. It seemed just as long and just as brutal. The downstairs neighbor was a Frenchwoman—She's probably dead now, reflects Naïma, who has always thought of the woman in the past tense—who couldn't believe that she had washed up in Pont-Féron, according to Dalila, and was determined to prove that she was better than the Arab tenants in the cité, and that the public area belonged chiefly to her, since she was *properly* French.

"Why do you say that?" Hamid would ask. "Has she ever said anything like that to you?"

"No," Dalila would say, "but you only have to look at her. She lets her dog run around the playground, shitting everywhere and digging up the flower beds, but if any of the kids go there to play, she comes out and says they're making too much noise. As if her dog, not even her grandson—not that anyone ever comes to visit her, to be honest—her *dog* has more rights than the little bougnoule kids of Pont-Féron. And she's forever writing letters of complaint about how we make too much noise and how we shouldn't be hanging laundry out the windows. It was some woman down at the town hall told me. She said, next Ramadan, if we celebrate iftar late at night, she'll set fire to the place. Torch the place, Hamid! And we're the bad neighbors!"

"It's just fear," Hamid would say. "When she sees she's got nothing to be scared of, she'll soften up."

But there was no letup in the war.

"It's people like her who spread a negative image of the projects all over France," Dalila would rage, "writing letters to the newspapers, or telling her friends that the place is a jungle, that everything around here gets vandalized or stolen or looted."

Sometimes Hamid would try to get his sister to understand that the old lady had every right to complain about the vandalism, and Naïma would listen as he tried to shoehorn a few phrases into the ceaseless torrent of words from his sister, who did not understand and did not want to understand. Although, at the time, Naïma wanted to side with her aunt, she, too, felt that, by the late nineties, the cité was bleak, ugly, and forbidding to anyone who did not know it, and likely to terrify an elderly woman. When Dalila sensed that her brother could not bear listening to her talk about the old crone downstairs any longer, she would abruptly change the subject, peppering her conversation with the names of the rioting banlieues in Lyon: Vaulx-en-Velin, Givors, les Minguettes, Vénissieux, Rillieux-la-Pape, Bron, Villeurbanne, and Saint-Priest. Riots that rippled out in concentric circles through the angry youths of neglected housing projects every time some kid was beaten up by the police, and these riots seemed to infect Dalila's body, creating another knot that made it impossible for her to sleep or caused dry patches on her skin, and she would rail that they were bastards, the lot of them, though it was never clear whether she was referring to the youths or the cops, probably both, Why don't you say something?

"Because it doesn't concern me," Hamid would say, "it's got nothing to do with me."

Whenever there was a report about the *banlieues chaudes* on the television—and there were many; the media seemed to revel in them—Hamid would quickly turn off the television so that his daughters did not see the shocking images, only for the radio to take up the baton when they were in the car. It was at this point that the media first began to talk about "the problem of the banlieues" (they would never stop), as though it were a recognized fact that these various and diverse suburbs made up a single no-go area and, to listen to them, the blame for the violence rested jointly with city planning and the morals of the residents. News anchors adopted a concerned, almost compassionate tone—"the *problem* of the banlieues"; perhaps unwittingly, while fueled by good intentions, they permanently stigmatized a whole population whose chief misfortune was to find themselves living on the margins of real life, that of property owners. On news bulletins, footage of clashes between young men from the housing projects and the riot police in their gleaming uniforms proliferated. On the speakers of the car radio, vehicles were constantly being burned.

"Why am I supposed to feel that this has got anything to do with me?" Hamid would ask wearily.

And—doubtless to prove that it had nothing to do with him, Naïma now believes—he stopped answering the telephone.

On Sunday evening, he walks her back to the train station with the same stubborn defiance. Algeria has nothing to do with him.

The light of an early spring can make everything seem beautiful, even Marne-la-Vallée, swathing the roadsides with lush green and obscuring the houses beneath groves of budding trees. The tentative sun conjures a quivering golden dust in the air. In the course of her conversations with Lalla, Naïma will sometimes note down another name and address, but mostly she simply listens and stares out the window at the town as it is transformed. Sometimes Céline joins them, and she, too, listens to this man, who was old and worn-out when she met him, talk about a time that seems as remote as that of fairy tales. Occasionally Naïma will leave them to talk to each other, like a Shakespearean go-between withdrawing discreetly, except that she remains in the room and becomes lost in contemplation of the view outside. In time, she comes to enjoy the fact that from Lalla's window she can see only houses identical to the one she is in, as though rather than a window it were a hall of mirrors.

"Have you noticed all the satellite dishes in the neighborhood?" Lalla asks. "Not long ago there were none. They all arrived at once. And with them the religious channels broadcasting from Saudi Arabia, from Qatar, from I don't know where. Islam streaming into the houses via satellite dishes . . . Even my son, my youngest, suddenly started going to the mosque. He grew a beard. I didn't say anything, I wanted to give him space. Then one day, down at the market, I saw him begging. I couldn't believe my eyes. There he was, calmly collecting money for the mosque in broad daylight. For the first time in my life, I felt like slapping him.

At least I don't steal money from you, he said. I think I would have preferred that. Your money is haram, he told me, like your paintings, like your whole life, I'll have nothing to do with it. Can you believe that, Naïma, can you believe it? Is this what we fought for? We wanted to give our children a free country, that's why we fought the French, why we fought the fanatics in the Islamic Salvation Front, why we fought among ourselves, and now our children turn their backs, they turn into morons I wouldn't give ten euros to, let alone a country."

He twists and tugs at the ends of his mustache. For a brief moment Naïma thinks he will rip it off.

"Obviously," he says spitefully, "his love for God lasted as long as his love for his hamster or his dog when he was little. Six months later, he moved on to something else. The only thing he truly despises is me. I'm the one constant in his life."

He waves his hands wildly, as though shooing a swarm of flies. *Khalas.* His hands are covered with patches of white hair and liver spots. With fascinated disgust, Naïma studies the patterns out of the corner of her eye.

"Have you sorted out the paperwork to go there?" he asks.

"No."

She is waiting for the official letter from the museum in Tizi Ouzou that will vouch for her during her stay, which, together with the letter Christophe wrote back in January, which is lying in one of Naïma's desk drawers, will allow her to apply for a business visa. The museum has promised on several occasions to send the letter, but nothing has yet arrived at the gallery. Sometimes Naïma hopes that the letter never comes. She has read somewhere that there is a blacklist, a list of harkis, and that some people who apply to return to Algeria are refused a visa. She is afraid that her family name might be on the list, and confesses her fears to the old painter.

"But what exactly did he do, your grandfather?" Lalla asks, not knowing that this is precisely the question Naïma has been asking members of her family for weeks without getting a response.

When she called on Dalila to help, she could tell her no more than Hamid and Clarisse.

"Probably nothing," she said vaguely. "Maybe it was his brother. I don't remember, but I do know they killed Baba's brother not long after we left. Your father had nightmares for ages . . ."

To avoid having to answer the painter, Naïma stares out through the living room window.

All she has ever known of Ali's life is a silence that she never thought of as a gap but that, now that the trip is beginning to seem real, feels like a void inside her body—not a wound, but rather a vast expanse like the images of black holes taken with a telescope you sometimes see on the covers of science magazines. She regrets the conversations she never had with Ali and she blames herself—irrationally, since he died before she was old enough to ask him to relate his life story. She was eight, maybe nine—she cannot really remember—when he died in his bed. She has very few memories of him, and when she tries to put them in order, she is horrified to discover that most of them are from his long agony.

In Naïma's memory, Ali looks ill. He has been bedridden for weeks. He is covered in bedsores. The pain is excruciating. He cries out. He cries out in Arabic. He has forgotten his French. The aunts translate for Clarisse, and Naïma overhears snatches of their conversation. Ali screams that the FLN is here. He screams that they are killing him, slitting his throat, to beware the barbed wire. He wails that the houses have been lost, the fields have been lost, the mountain ridge has been lost. He howls that he does not want them to burn the olive groves. He calls on Djamel with his shattered skull. He calls on Akli with his slashed throat. And he sinks deeper and deeper through the layers of memory that illness has made porous, moving through them in his delirium as though his foot were crashing through rotten planks. He says the Germans are coming. He talks about a prisoner-of-war camp in eastern France. He sees Nazi uniforms beneath the sad icing of snow. He shouts that they have to hide. He swears at Naïma for opening the door because she will give away their positions. And after that, there are only insults that gush forth from his foam-flecked mouth. Insults whenever someone changes his dressing or tries to get him to drink something, when the bed creaks, when a tree branch taps on the window, when shadows dance across the ceiling.

And Yema, in a tiny voice, says:

"The poor man is mad, it's because he's in pain."

But perhaps Ali was not mad, Naïma thinks as she looks back. Perhaps pain gives him the right to cry out, a right he has never exercised before. Perhaps, now that his decaying body is in agony, he has finally found the freedom to scream that he cannot bear anything, neither what has happened to him, nor this place where he has wound up. Perhaps Ali has never been as lucid as when he insults people for opening his door. Perhaps he has been stifling these cries for forty years because he felt obliged to justify his flight, his settling in France, obliged to mask his shame, obliged to be strong for his family, obliged to be a patriarch to those who understood French better than he did. Now that he has nothing left to lose, he can howl. On the other side of his bedroom door, Hamid's four little daughters ask if they can go outside and play. They cannot bear to go on listening to the screams.

"I didn't go to his funeral," she suddenly tells Lalla.

The detail has just resurfaced in her memory.

"No women were allowed. I stayed in the apartment with my grandmother, my mother, my aunts, my sisters, my cousins . . . I didn't see him lowered into the ground. I know nothing about his life, and I missed his death."

The painter slowly turns to Céline:

"You're not planning to skip it, are you? I want you there, I want you to cry enough for ten. My postmortem reputation will be based on your tears."

"I'll cry so hard," Céline says, "that everyone in Marne-la-Vallée will think you must have been an amazing lover, even in old age."

"That's good," Lalla whispers with a smile. "Isn't that good, Naïma?"

She smiles back at him.

"You can come, too, you can be my artistic endorsement."

Her laptop lies open on the coffee table, a rectangle of gray light in the dark apartment. She stares at it as she finishes a bowl of soup, deferring the moment when she has to go back to the keyboard, slurping the thick liquid in ever smaller sips.

If her family has nothing to offer but death, silence, and wishful thinking, Naïma still has the tentacular memory of the internet with which to learn about the history of the harkis. Typing her grandfather's name into Google gives her nothing, which is already a relief, since websites about the Algerian War are teeming with denunciations and vindictive personal attacks. Apparently no one has seen fit to nickname her grandfather the Butcher of the Atlas Mountains, or the Hyena of Palestro, or to devote a page to a list of his atrocities.

One after another, she Googles the following search terms:

> harkis
> activities harkis war Algeria
> tasks assigned harkis
> reprisals harkis Algeria
> harkis in Kabylia
> harkis departure 1962

Her searches return thousands of images, pages and pages of text, a mess of headlines, and assorted spelling mistakes on which she clicks, not knowing what she is looking for, through which she tumbles, that night and in the nights that follow.

Her evenings now are all the same: she does not stay behind for a drink with Kamel and Élise when they leave the gallery, she does not call anyone, does not reply to Christophe's text messages, which manage to be insistent while remaining extremely terse. She stays at home, watching documentaries on YouTube, eating Chinese food from the downstairs deli that has so often been her salvation on days when she has had hangovers. She binge-watches all three episodes of Patrick Rotman's documentary *L'Ennemi intime* while eating cold noodles from a cardboard container, falls asleep at dawn without leaving the sofa, her head filled with stories of torture and of slow submission to pervasive violence. She listens to presenters and guests sitting serenely on futuristic chairs saying that the Algerian War continues to this day as a war of memories. She hears them say "open wound," "anguish," "trauma," "mindless violence," and, in spite of the compassion they try to demonstrate for the stories of others, Naïma often thinks that they are about to rip each other apart from their comfortable little chairs in the television studio. She watches, without really understanding, the footage shot in 1955 showing reprisals carried out by the French army on the population of Aïn Abid following the murder of seven Europeans. Strange images in which the victims do not run or panic. The soldiers calmly arrive, shoulder their rifles, and fire. By a curious coincidence, all the bodies fall facedown in the footage. It looks like one of those animal documentaries where one of the gazelles is drugged to make sure that the lions will catch it and rip away a mouthful of flesh in close-up.

Quickly Naïma becomes fascinated by the comments section under the videos. Not a single image of the Algerian War can be posted online without triggering a series of reactions that inexorably leads—with varying degrees of swiftness depending on the site—to invectives against the harkis. No matter the starting point of the discussion, it ends up in this explosion of hate. This variation of Godwin's law, according to which "as an online discussion grows longer, the probability of a comparison involving Nazis or Hitler approaches 1," plunges her into a world of horror.

> You say you dream of going back to Algeria, you dirty harki bitch.
> Come on! I'll be waiting to slit your throat.
> Harkis, batars and collaborators: allah hate you and so do I

And this one, which seems almost personally directed at her:

> The french fought to keep algeria and they have every reason
> to feel proud the pieds noirs wanted to keep all the money and
> the farms and they have every reason to feel proud the Algerians
> fought for their independence and they have every reason to feel
> proud but this whore this daughter of harkis is the problem she
> should be ashamed of her traitor father and let me tell her we people
> of algeria we long to slaughter the children of harkis

Between the insults and the threats, she finds comments defending the former auxiliaries in the French army—in terms as virulent as
those of their detractors. But the commenters who refuse to accept the
equation that harki = traitor, like the equation that the only good traitor is a dead traitor, and who might briefly ease the vise-like grip of
fear and disgust Naïma feels in her throat, often turn out to defend the
methods of the French paratrooper units and even those of the SS Char-
lemagne Division. At the foot of their comments are images and slogans
she glimpses as she quickly skims down the page:

YOU WILL UNDERSTAND US

THE OAS IS ALWAYS WATCHING

THE OAS STRIKES WHERE IT WANTS WHEN IT WANTS

She feels as though somewhere beneath her computer is a vast
subterranean cavern filled with warring monsters, their faces twisted
with hatred, from which the fiber-optic cables draw these insults, this

hostility, in order to inject them into every website. Deciding what is reliable information and what is simply rage or grief spewed out, belched out, takes her too much time. She prefers to fall back on the calmer, less angrily participatory medium of books.

Between the yellow, red, black, or white covers of the books she has ordered, there is explicit use of the word "harki"—this word the dictionary claims applies to her, this word the internet uses, like a hot key, as an insult. She is aware of just how much she has been affected by the online comments when she finds herself covering up the titles of the books when she reads them in cafés, in the Métro. She is not even sure that she did not lower her voice in the bookshop when she ordered them. She does not know quite what she fears, but she is now conscious of the hitherto unimaginable number of people armed with cut-and-dried contradictory opinions on the role of the harkis. At night, in bed, she downs books in the same way she might down a glass of rotgut.

To make their sufferings heard, the former harkis and their descendants have crunched the numbers. In their accounts, the desire to be taken seriously takes the form of statistics. And yet, they are incapable of preserving the dispassionate precision of these numbers. They scream them, sob them, splutter them. But this is not what numbers are meant for. They are meant for calculation. Numbers eat away at pathos and, in turn, pathos tarnishes them. Naïma watches the statistics of suffering dance in a savage round, a round that does not mean anything.

The numbers supplied by the harkis are added to those that tally the atrocities committed by the French army, which the more general history books repeat and explain in detail. Naïma is aware that some of the authors would like these to cancel each other out, but this is not the case: a massacre does not disappear when faced with the scale of the reprisals, and the demand of an eye for an eye and a tooth for a tooth, in its infinite variations and applications, simply leaves more people one-eyed and toothless, without the remaining good eye of the first victim and that of the second ever forming a pair. The numbers reached over the course of the pages are so great that Naïma finds herself bogged down in arithmetic, in calculations, she swallows dozens, chokes on hundreds, her throat is congested by several blocks of thousands that will not go down yet continue to pile up, steadily climbing, chapter after chapter, such that she can no longer take in the numbers, nor imagine the people they represent, she simply reads them and later merely stares at them; they no longer mean anything to her.

The official invitation to Tizi Ouzou has finally been delivered to the gallery. But still Naïma has not applied for her visa. She is still lost in the books that are multiplying all over her apartment in piles like cairns, marking the progress of her research. More than once Christophe has told her in an exasperated tone that it is time she dealt with the bureaucratic paperwork necessary for her trip and, without paying him much heed, she mutters that of course she will, tomorrow probably, Monday, soon. Ever since she stopped sleeping with him, he has treated her with a coldness that she would like to ignore but that she actually finds flattering, since it is proof that he has been affected by the fact they have stopped having sex. (If she were honest, she would admit that it has affected her, too. Whenever she speaks to him, she constantly flashes him nervous smiles. Since he is taller than she is, she has to look up slightly in order to catch his eye. Since they stopped sleeping together, this simple gesture has come to seem like the beginning of a dangerous process.) Tomorrow, Monday, soon, she repeats, and, as she postpones getting a visa, she also keeps Christophe and his desire at arm's length. But when she sees the precarious columns of books waiting for her in her living room, she tells herself that he is right: even if she wants to, she cannot wait until she has absorbed the complete history of contemporary Algeria before going there.

She opens her laptop again, her movements slow and fearful, as though the comments she read on previous visits might jump out at her.

Come on! I'll be waiting to slit your throat

She sighs, shakes her head, and forces herself not to think about it. She focuses on the practical problem: the difficulty of going back to Algeria for harkis and their descendants, which means—although Google will never *directly* answer this question, which is the only one that matters—whether, because of her grandfather's past, it is possible that Naïma may not be able to travel to Algeria.

She is unsurprised to read that a number of former harkis have recently been refused permission to enter the country. A man was arrested at the border for actions committed by his brother; this she finds more troubling, since it implies that responsibility, that blame and punishment, can be transferred indiscriminately between members of a family. She thinks about the great-uncle that Dalila mentioned, the one who died at the end of the war, the one the FLN made pay for something—though no one on this side of the Mediterranean seems to know precisely what. *Maybe it wasn't Baba, maybe it was his brother.* The idea that an action committed by her grandfather or her great-uncle fifty years ago might have consequences for her today seems absurd—but she is only beginning to understand just how enduring anger can be, she is not sure about anything, so she goes on searching, looking for cases of children and of grandchildren to discover how many generations are tainted by this infamy.

In 1975, she finally discovers, Algeria prevented the son of a harki from leaving the country. This is a situation that had not even occurred to her: that she might be allowed in, but not allowed out. But this is what happened to seven-year-old Borzani Kradaoui, who traveled with his mother to visit family in Oran that year. The Algerian authorities claimed that the boy did not have "the necessary paternal authorization to travel abroad." According to other versions, as his mother was released, someone whispered to her: "Tell your harki husband to come and fetch the boy himself." There were a number of similar cases in the 1970s, but if the Kradaoui case is the one that crops up most often in the articles Naïma finds, it is because it played an important role in the uprisings in the harki camps in France at the time. Naïma allows herself to get caught up in this story, which distracts her from her initial question, and takes her back forty years. It is almost by accident that she discovers, in the national radio and television archives, the first images of the icy French camps that her father has never wanted to describe. In the spring of 1975, before the Kradaoui affair, the children of harkis began protesting behind the barbed-wire fences and, for the first time since their parents arrived in the country, the cameras of the French media were trained on them.

In May, at the Bias camp, they stormed the administrative buildings and occupied them for a fortnight. They ransacked the offices and burned the records.

On Thursday, June 19, 1975, at 4:00 p.m., four harki sons armed with rifles, dynamite, and cans of gas took hostage the director of the Saint-Maurice-l'Ardoise camp, and holed up in the town hall of neighboring Saint-Laurent-des-Arbres. "We do not wish Monsieur Langlet any harm. But, to us, he represents the government with which we have struggled in vain to assert our rights as French citizens." Twenty-eight hours later they released him and returned to the camp, where they were welcomed as heroes. They were accompanied by a journalist from the *Nouvel Observateur*, who was horrified to discover "the camp of shame." *Of course, he wrote, on the face of it, the harkis do not easily command sympathy, our sympathy, but even so!* For a few seconds, Naïma stares at the words "of course" that casually appear at the foot of the first column of the article, then forces herself to carry on reading.

The unrest spread throughout the month of June and suddenly, in an online video Naïma is watching, she sees a familiar name: the residents of the forest hamlet called the Logis d'Anne occupy the administrative buildings and, among other things, demand the withdrawal of the soldiers patrolling the village. All too briefly, she sees an image of a rusty sign and the abandoned, crumbling bungalows amid the pine trees. Her mind sketches in the figure of Hamid as a boy, something she has never seen in any photograph.

Some days later, the walls of Pertuis are plastered with posters urging the harkis to carry on with the struggle.

In early July 1975, M'hamed Laradji, president of the CFMRAA

(Confederation of French Muslims Repatriated from Algeria and Their Allies), calls on French Muslims doing military service and those about to be called up "to cease to carry out their duties as citizens as long as the state considers them and their families to be second-class citizens who have only duties to their homeland." As far as Naïma knows, her father completed his military service shortly before this. She wonders whether he considered refusing.

On Sunday, August 3, M'hamed Laradji demands "the closure of the transit camps and the resettlement of families, who should be provided with moral and financial support, the return of those families still detained in Algeria, fair and swift compensation, and the creation of a commission of inquiry at parliamentary rather than administrative level."

Naïma watches archive footage of teenage boys protesting between rows of bleak identical shacks and, though obviously Hamid is not among them, she cannot shake the idea that one of them could have been her father, or her father could have been among them. Some of the boys say they have hardly set foot outside the camp in fifteen years: "Every time, every time, they'd say, what are you going to do out there? It's swarming with fellagas. They'll cut your throats. And like idiots, we believed them." They talk about the years spent living under a quasi-colonial administration that cut off the electricity every night at 10:00 p.m., where it was forbidden to own a television, years of depending on the Red Cross to come and dispense condensed milk and potatoes, years spent going around in circles. A few were daring enough to cut holes in the fences and venture into the neighboring fields; those who were caught ended up in a reformatory. On the jerky footage, these boys with black hair and young, furious faces are dressed in old men's clothes, rags that date from a time long before 1970.

Not long ago, Sol was writing an article about the refugee camps run by the UNHCR and, looking up from her computer, she asked Naïma:

"Do you know the average length of time a refugee spends in a camp?"

Naïma shook her head.

"Seventeen years," Sol said, before going back to her work.

As Naïma watches the children of harkis in the Bias or Saint-Maurice-l'Ardoise camps condemning their indefinite incarceration with pained surprise, she already has an advantage over them: she knows that, despite official terminology, there is no "transit," nothing "provisional" about the reception camps.

In the middle of the summer of 1975, when the young men in the camps are already volatile and angry, Algeria manages to incense them by detaining Borzani Kradaoui and, in doing so, demonstrating that it holds sons responsible for the crimes or the mistakes of their fathers.

On August 6, harki sons at Saint-Maurice-l'Ardoise abduct a number of Algerian workers from the Keller et Leleux factory and hold them hostage.

The following day, four armed harki sons burst into the Café de Bourges and take the owner and a number of customers hostage, all of them Algerian. Three hours later, they release the hostages.

Naïma finds the frequency and the brevity of the kidnappings unsettling. She does not know whether it means that the rebels were panicking at the enormity of their actions, whether they naively believed the promises made to them, or whether they were simply demanding to be seen.

"Before, we lived in the shadows. Now all France knows," says a young man with sad eyes filmed by FR3. Perhaps, but who is watching television in the sweltering days of August 1975? Naïma wonders. Sprawled on the beaches of the English Channel, the Atlantic, and the Mediterranean, most French people are building sandcastles, they are not reading the newspapers. She makes a quick mental calculation: at the time, Clarisse would have been pregnant with Myriem. As they were busy preparing for the arrival of their first child, did her parents see footage of the unrest? Did her father recognize anyone in the footage?

Monday, August 11, a commando unit once again occupies the administrative offices of the Bias camp, where since May there has barely been time, Naïma assumes, to right the heavy metal filing cabinets and hang new maps of France, carefully divided into neat, color-coded départements. Unlike the previous occupation, this time the young men are armed with hunting rifles. At dawn, the préfet agrees to meet with the intruders and "communicate their demands to the ministry in charge," and the young men withdraw.

Saturday, August 16, Djelloul Belfadel, director of Amicale des Algériens, is kidnapped near his home by four young French Muslims (three men and a woman, Naïma notes with interest, since this is the first time she has seen a woman involved in the commando units). They take him to the camp at Bias and issue a demand for free movement for harkis between France and Algeria. A communiqué from the Confédération Musulmane warns the French government against the use of strong-arm tactics: "If an attempt is made to rescue the hostage by force, he will be shot." The Bias camp is in a state of siege, surrounded by gendarmes and riot police. Helicopters buzz across the sky like huge deadly dragonflies. Television cameras set up all round the camp by FR3 are filming close-ups of the kidnappers, who, being novices in the arts of guerrilla warfare, do not even think to try to hide their faces. On Monday, August 18, at 5:30 p.m., the hostage is released after negotiations between the préfet of Lot-et-Garonne and members of the harki community.

This last uprising sounds the death knell of the Bias camp, and the process of closing it begins that same year. From that moment, harkis who so choose can settle outside the ghetto. Perhaps it has come too late for them to rediscover the taste for freedom, perhaps France is too vast, or perhaps they are sick and tired of being moved from place to place, whatever the reason, the fact remains that many of the ex-auxiliaries' families settle near the camp, while others remain in the homes they had within it.

Naïma closes the laptop and pushes it into the middle of the coffee table. In the bathroom, the insistent yet comforting drip, drip of the leaking immersion heater continues through the night. She is exhausted, her eyes are stinging and burning. She is not sure whether the fact that she has been able to watch videos of these rebels and listen to their demands proves that they were successful, as they claim, in breaking the silence surrounding their existence. Everything she has seen in the past

few days, she has had to search for. She knew nothing about it before-
hand, although her family lived in one of the camps. She tries to remember whether, when she briefly studied the Algerian War at school, her
history books even mentioned the harkis. She thinks so, she thinks she
remembers seeing the word leap off the page and smiling at first, as if it
were a direct reference to her grandfather, then feeling a vague but persistent unease when she realized that he had played a minor role that no
one—not the writers of the textbook or her teacher—seemed interested
in exploring further.

She looks at the piles of books teetering next to her laptop and wonders why not a single line from them has found its way to her before
today. With her toe, she pushes the glass top of the coffee table and the
books collapse in a muffled rush of paper and card. They scatter randomly, mingling accounts by harkis and those by mujahideen.

History is written by the victors, Naïma thinks as she drifts off to sleep.
This is an established fact, it is what makes it possible for history to
exist in only one version. But when the vanquished refuse to admit defeat, when, despite their defeat, they continue writing their own version of history right up to the last second, when the victors, for their
part, write their history retrospectively to show the inevitability of their
victory, then the contradictory versions on either side of the Mediterranean seem less like history than like justifications or rationalizations
sprinkled with dates and dressed up as history. Perhaps this is what
kept former residents of Bias so close to the camp they loathed: they
could not bring themselves to break up a community that had reached
an agreement on the version of history that suited them. Perhaps this
is a foundation of communal life that is too often overlooked yet absolutely essential.

On March 22, Naïma wakes to the sound of Sol swearing and the almost inhuman monotone of the radio broadcaster. Shortly before 8:00 a.m., suicide bombers set off two devices in the departure lounge of the main airport in Brussels, in Belgium . . . Naïma gets up and listens distractedly to the bulletin as she drinks her coffee. She does not know anyone in Brussels. She does not have any urgent text messages to send. A victim who we do not know dies a little less, she thinks.

Naïma is—and I find it interesting to highlight this even if I do not know what to make of it—the first person in her family for generations not to have heard the howl of a man who is suffering a violent death, a howl that, in Hollywood movies, is only a pale imitation, a truncated part (what a lump of beef is, for example, to the grazing animal), or a misguided fantasy, because it is impossible to know this howl, let alone replicate it, unless one has heard it, or perhaps even uttered it, in which case one knows it for only a split second and then one knows nothing more.

On the radio, a handful of journalists are discussing the reward that the *shahid* believe are promised them if they die in a terrorist attack: seventy or seventy-two virgins, from what they are saying, although the source of this figure is unclear, since the only text that exists simply describes "an abundance." In any case, one of the guests argues, it is a misinterpretation of the Qur'an, since the Holy Book actually uses a

Syriac word, meaning not "virgin," but "grape." The panelists all seem fascinated by this piece of exotic, erotic religious lore brought to the debate, but none of them asks the questions Naïma wants answered, namely: Do these young terrorists truly believe in a paradise where they would be comforted by seventy-two virgins for all eternity? And, if they do, what do they imagine? That they will all be in one vast room, thousands of ISIS fighters with an exponential number of virgins? Or do they believe that paradise is made up of individual cells, like a student dormitory, like a brothel, and that they will be able to enjoy these women without having to suffer the bragging and the farting of their former brothers-in-arms? She indulges this daydream, picturing cubicles carved into the clouds scudding across an immensity of ageless sky, each hosting a pornographic movie where sex meets sequins.

Some days later, as she is getting off the train on her way to Lalla's house, Naïma sees a bus shelter daubed with a slogan that seems to have come from the depths of the internet:

DEATH TO MUSLIMS
THE SUITCASE OR THE COFFIN

When Naïma mentions it to Céline, she is told that, the night before, the doors of the local mosque were found smeared with pork fat and slices of ham.

"It's a monstrously stupid rage," Céline says, "a . . . piggish rage."

From the way she says these words, Naïma can tell that Céline is a Daughter of Sadness. It has been years since she last thought of her old classification system, but she finds that it still works. Lalla, on the other hand, is in a foul mood, which proves that he belongs to the other tribe, the one Naïma knows best, the tribe of Anger.

"Racism is crass stupidity," Lalla growls at his partner. "Don't tell me you're surprised. It is a debased, degraded form of class warfare, it is the moronic blind alley of revolution."

Céline sighs and rolls her eyes to heaven.

"Not that again!"

"Yes, that again," Lalla roars, "again and forever! That's precisely the problem: you young people have allowed yourselves to be convinced that these arguments are hollow, dusty, outmoded. No one wants to talk about class war these days, it isn't sexy. And what have you been offered—worse, what have you accepted as the epitome of modernity? A return to the ethnic. The question of communities instead of classes. This way people in power think that they can ease tensions with a pretty little cabinet of minorities—put a face like theirs in government, and that'll calm young men in deprived projects. They parade government ministers like Fadela Amara, Rachida Dati, Najat Vallaud-Belkacem. But it's not enough to have dark skin and an Arabic name. Of course, it's amazing that they're successful—it can't have been easy—but it's also the problem: they're successful. They have no business talking about those who failed, about the dispossessed, the desperate, about the poor in general. And most of the North African population of France is exactly that—poor. And just look at the ones who have been successful, all they can afford . . ."

With a wave, he gestures to the serried houses of Marne-la-Vallée that look as though they are dying of boredom.

"But these women, they're sending out the message: 'If it can happen to me, it can happen to anyone.' And the corollary: 'If it hasn't happened to you, it's because you weren't prepared to do what was necessary.' All they do is make the poor feel guilty."

He is interrupted by a coughing fit that leaves him doubled over in his armchair.

"I do, too," Naïma says pensively.

"What?"

"I send out that message."

"Then you'd do better to keep your mouth shut."

Naïma freezes, dumbstruck. The old man starts coughing again, more violently this time. It is a terrifying sound of rending flesh. When she sets a glass of water on the table next to him, he whimpers, groans, and waves for her to leave. A little spittle of indefinite color has formed a drying wave on his lower lip. She obeys without a word. As she closes the door, she sees Céline's desolate look, and, by responding only with a shrug, Naïma makes her pay for the wound inflicted by the old man, which is completely unfair but, an offended Naïma tells herself, it is human, unjustifiable but understandable, or at least excusable. She strides past the cloned houses, the flowering hedges, and walks along the railway line. The cables and resistors strung along the track give off a dull hum. It is possible—she is not sure, she does not want to be sure—that Lalla was telling the truth, that for years she has been part of a sham that goes beyond her, one aimed at creating a stereotype of the "good Arab" (serious, hardworking, wreathed by success, atheist, with no discernible accent, Europeanized, modern; in a word, reassuring; in other words, as un-Arabic as possible) to contrast with the others (just as she contrasts herself with the others). But if she committed herself so firmly to this path, it was in order to avoid what her father held up as the most certain path to failure: seeming like a "bad Arab" (lazy, dishonest, even violent, speaking a French littered with shrill *i*'s, religious, old-fashioned, exotic verging on barbaric; in a word, terrifying). And she seethes at finding herself trapped between two stereotypes: one who, Lalla believes, is prepared to betray the cause of immigrants poorer and less fortunate than she is and one who would see her excluded from the mainstream of French society. There are moments—like this, like now—when she feels that it is profoundly unfair that she cannot simply be Naïma, but has to think of herself as a dot on a graphic representation of integration, with the archetype "bad Arab" at the bottom and at the top the exemplar of the "good Arab." Furious, she kicks the railings that run alongside the tracks and they clang faintly, almost inaudibly. The insignificance of this act brings on a sudden, nervous laugh: "Quake, France, for I have kicked your public property with the tip of my toe!"

A few minutes' walk is enough to dissipate the irritation caused by Lalla's brutal words. Naïma is astonished; usually she is more tenacious in holding a grudge. She tells herself that there are lots of reasons why it is difficult for her to resent the old man. First, because he already has a host of official and important enemies who forced him into exile, next to whom Naïma pales into insignificance. Second, because it is quite possible that he is right. Last, because his harsh words came between two coughing fits and she cannot be angry with someone in whom death is patiently carving out cancerous tunnels.

Just as she reaches the RER station, she realizes for the first time that, if she does not hurry up, Lalla will die before his retrospective.

In the first week of April, she finally goes to the Algerian consulate near the Arc de Triomphe, in an area of Paris she never visits because, in the capital, money traces invisible yet solid borders, and getting lost in one of those areas, or having to wait for someone there, means spending at least ten euros on a coffee, unless you are prepared to sit at the molded tables of a McDonald's or a Starbucks—that is to say, to deny the very fact of being on the Champs-Élysées by seeking refuge in a branch of a franchise that, by virtue of being multiple and identical, appears on no map and exists only in itself: whether the window offers a view of an avenue in Paris or a square in Cairo, you are *first and foremost* in a McDonald's.

Naïma goes around in circles, unable to get her bearings, reading the names of the streets that branch off like spokes from the Place de l'Étoile. *Who the hell lives here?* she cannot help but wonder as she looks at the beige buildings sheltered by trees coppiced at right angles. Nothing here is on a human scale, especially not the streets. Any attempt at ordinary life is attacked, lopped off, amputated, and eventually destroyed—so it seems to Naïma—by the breadth of the thoroughfares teeming with growling vehicles. She heads down the Avenue de la Grande-Armée, turns into the Rue d'Argentine, walks past the carved marble signs for Au Petit Matelot that promise, as they have done for generations, SPECIAL CLOTHING FOR HUNTING AND YACHTING. She goes into the modern building located at number 11, outside which the Algerian flag is flying. (The Algerian flag always reminds her of football matches.) She greets the security guards flanking the metal detector with strained politeness, and they respond with a curt nod. The desks on the ground floor deal only with recent arrivals from Algeria, and there are many waiting, sitting on plastic chairs, on suitcases, sometimes on the floor. Most have an air of seething patience, a calm that is not stoic, but focused on its future eruption. An employee glances at Naïma's French passport and gestures toward the stairs down to the basement.

She stands in one of the most chaotic lines she has ever witnessed—and even as the thought occurs to her, she dismisses it, because she does not want to have a clichéd, racist view. But it is difficult not to notice how people are jostling for places in the line, brusquely stalking up to a counter to complain that they've been waiting too long, unceremoniously handing someone else a baby or a bag so they can rest their arms for a few minutes. Naïma does the best she can to participate in this series of impetuous movements that at least gives the impression that things are moving. She lends a few coins for the photocopier at the far end of the room, picks up dropped papers, defends her position in the snaking line. When, finally, it is her turn to present her documents, the woman sitting behind the counter wearily mutters that she has made a mistake, official visas are dealt with upstairs.

"But I was told to come down here."

"Probably because you look like you're Algerian," the woman says. "They probably thought you were going back to visit family."

Hearing that she has come to the wrong counter, the couple behind Naïma push past her and, without giving her time to complain, launch into a conversation in Arabic with the woman as though Naïma were not there. Reluctantly, she leaves the room in which she has been hanging around pointlessly for more than an hour, and as she is going back up the stairs she suddenly thinks of abandoning the whole thing—the door is right there, to her left, and she can just make out the street through the tinted windows. She can still give up; she can blame the Algerian administration. Incompetent bureaucrats. She will look annoyed. But the image of the elderly painter hunched up in his battered armchair stops her. She goes up to the second floor, vowing that if she has to stand in line again, she will leave. Upstairs, in a white room adorned with curved, polished wood furniture, there is no one except the official behind his window. He gestures for her to take a number from the dispenser; Naïma takes ticket 254, and the number immediately starts flashing above his counter. She steps forward.

"Am I the only one?"

It is an absurd question, given that the room is empty. The man nods.

"It's weird . . . I mean, given what it's like downstairs . . . Why did you get me to take a ticket?"

"I feel very lonely," the Algerian civil servant says with a sort of theatrical melancholy. "I probably see three, maybe four people a day . . . When I'm leaving work and I see that the ticket dispenser has decreased by a few numbers, at least I feel as though something has happened. What can I do for you?"

Hesitant and nervous, she hands over her papers, trembling at the thought that, when he types her name into the computer, an alarm will go off and WANTED will appear in huge letters on the screen. But when he sees her father's birthplace on the form, he smiles and says:

"I'm a Kabyle, too. Have you ever been to Kabylia?"

"No."

He shakes his head sympathetically, as though she has just told him she never had a childhood or that her parents had never loved her.

"It's nice to go there in spring," he says, delicately opening her passport. "That's my favorite season."

"What if I'm going in early summer, is that nice, too?" Naïma asks, not taking her eyes off his computer.

"Everything's nice in Kabylia," he says. "But the heat will be murderous."

She does not really know what she is saying anymore. She feels like a spy trying not to blow her cover. Every time she smiles at him, she feels as though she is brilliantly deceptive, that she doesn't look anything like the granddaughter of a harki—though she would be incapable of describing what that might look like. She emerges from the second-floor room with the feeling that she had him *completely taken in.*

* * *

A couple weeks later, following the recommendations on the website, she comes back to the consulate, where she is given a small plastic folder in which she finds her passport, newly Arabized with a fresh visa. The melancholy clerk has been replaced by a middle-aged woman with flabby jowls. As Naïma stands motionless, staring at the official stamp, looking distraught, the woman asks:

"Is there a problem?"

Naïma does not know how to answer this question. Algeria is opening its doors to her for a month. She does not know whether she is relieved, disappointed, or terrified.

As she leaves 11 Rue d'Argentine, she calls Lalla to give him the news. No one answers. With a wave, the security guard makes it clear she cannot pace up and down outside the building. She walks away quickly, trying to contain the unidentified apprehension that gripped her while she was inside the consulate. Before descending into the Métro station surrounded by mutilated trees and trapezoidal buildings, she tries again to call the painter. Céline answers, her voice distant and shaky, slowly repeating, "Naïma." Lalla was admitted to the hospital the previous night suffering from respiratory distress. The doctors say he's out of danger now, but he won't be allowed home until the end of the week and, besides, "out of danger" is meaningless given the state of his health, there's no "outside" of danger, Céline stammers, there's nothing but danger, they're drowning in it. After a pause, she adds that Lalla drew up a list of drawings just before "it" happened, for her to give to Naïma. He also photocopied pages from his address book. Céline's voice is so desolate that to Naïma it sounds as though she is talking about his will—though that may not be altogether untrue.

"I can come and see you right now," she says.

"No," Céline murmurs, "I'll meet you in Paris. The house is unbearable without him."

Naïma dreamily leafs through her passport as she waits for Céline in a café near République. Despite her genuine concern for Lalla, she sees the aggressive advance of his illness, or rather the synchronicity of his illness and her getting the visa, as an opportunity, which she feels a little ashamed of. (She wishes she could think of another word, she hates to think of it as an "opportunity," but the word keeps coming back.) The fact that the artist might die means that she must make the trip, it gives the journey a new significance, a new impetus, a human dimension that is hers alone, it has nothing to do with her family and goes far beyond simply carrying out Christophe's wishes. It means that the trip is fraught with meaning without forcing Naïma to wonder what there might be *for her* on the other side.

Céline comes into the café, her face drawn, and sits on the banquette.

"Are you all right?" Naïma asks.

She immediately regrets this question, this trite platitude. She should behave toward Céline as Yema would. She should have put her arms around her as soon as she came over to the table, hugged her to her heart, and whispered, Meskina, meskina, as she might to an injured child . . . But she has forgotten how to deal with suffering without resorting to everyday words that keep it at bay and dictate a code of good conduct.

From her handbag, Céline takes a thin sheaf of papers and hands them to her; while Naïma quickly thumbs through them, Céline orders a coffee that she does not drink, she simply toys with the handle of the cup. She continually checks her telephone, nervously tapping the screen with her fingernails. She apologizes several times, explains that she is *not really here*, then starts talking about the hospital, about the tubes, the drips, the doctors who treat her like an intruder, the nurses who treat her like a child, and about Lalla, fatalistically making his last will and testament.

"He'll never admit it, but he wants to be buried back in the bled. I don't know why he's stubbornly insisting on a grave in Marne-la-Vallée. It's as though he thinks by doing that he can punish Algeria: You didn't want me when I was alive, you can't have me when I'm dead. It's infantile. He's the only one it hurts. Apart from me and the son he doesn't talk to anymore, there's no one here in France. From time to time, he sees a couple of exiles who are miserably unhappy and try their best to hide it. They talk about the freedom of expression they have here as though it were fresh air filling their lungs, but not one of them will admit that it's a useless freedom given that the French aren't interested in what's happening in Algeria, and no one listens to them."

After Céline leaves, Naïma stays in the café for a while. It gradually fills as people leave work. The increasing clamor of the conversations around her seems only to delineate a zone of silence around Naïma's table that nothing can disturb.

She thinks about the Mediterranean, the little waves that lap at the Côte d'Azur, the islands that rise up from half-forgotten books of mythology: Rhodes, Lesbos, the Crete of Minotaurs and labyrinths. She thinks about the microplastic particles glittering like sequins, of the bodies that must come to rest on the seabed, shipwreck after shipwreck, about the fish that see everything, about the wrecks of Turkish corsairs being joined by those of people-smugglers, about the polymorphous sea, at once bridge and boundary, crucible and dumping ground. She wonders whether she will cross it by boat or by plane, whether she will see it from above, the tiny hemmed-in sea that maps have always shown her, or whether, for the first time, she will get a sense of its vastness.

In a little more than two hours a plane could take her from Paris to Algiers, or rather—and she finds the thought amusing because it warps the history she has been reading—from Roissy-Charles de Gaulle to Houari Boumédiène. The boat is much slower—in a work context, it is probably a waste of time—but to travel by sea is to make the journey in the company of the poor and the burdened, the drivers of the "cathedral cars" photographed by Thomas Mailaender, it is to take the slow and heavy journey of an ant in the belly of a metal whale. To take the boat would mean returning to Algeria by the same means her family left it.

When she thinks about their departure in 1962, she imagines it like the scene in *War of the Worlds* in which Tom Cruise and his two children are trying to board a river ferry heavily guarded by soldiers. The dark coats and battered suitcases of those waiting on the jetty recall migrations that are anything but futuristic. The dark mass of bodies wrapped in wool and leather is punctured by three pale ovals, the faces of Ray Ferrier (the character played by Tom Cruise), his teenage son, and his little daughter, who are looking the wrong way: not at the ferry that might save them, but at the hill that, all too briefly, masks the threat. Suddenly the alien fighting machines appear, perfect in their murderous technology, and people begin to scream. Despite the frantic scramble, the longshoreman's family manages to get aboard the boat. Tom Cruise turns to lend a hand to his neighbors stranded on the quay only to see the soldiers pulling up the ramp before the boat is even full. He starts shouting hoarsely: *There's still room on the boat! There's room on the boat! There's room on the boat!* The injustice of the situation sends him into a fury, he is screaming in the name of others, but no one is listening and the boat pulls away. Naïma imagines the same cries tearing Ali's throat. *There's still room on the boat!* The blows of the soldiers pushing him away from the rail. *There's room on the boat!* The blows of rifle butts. The ship's siren.

But maybe it was the opposite, maybe he stood silently on the deck of the ship, hugged his wife and children to him, maybe he simply felt relieved that they could all be together. Naïma has never been able to imagine the crossing except with her family outside, on deck, standing facing the city and then the sea. She has never thought that it was unlikely that they would have stood there, exposed to the elements, for more than twenty hours. In fact, she has no idea of the time it takes to travel from Algiers to Marseilles by sea.

In the early morning, in the blinding white light that flattens the city of Marseilles, Naïma slowly follows the metal barriers that zigzag from the departures lounge to the gangway of the ferry. She grips the handrail tightly as she boards, the dark sea lapping between ship and wharf a narrow ribbon beneath her feet. She walks along corridors painted in dated colors, glimpses vast rooms filled with armchairs, most of them empty, goes up and down the companionways that smell of bleach, and finds her cabin. She imagined that there would be a porthole, but it is a blind wall. She must be below sea level. The steel sides reverberate with all kinds of sounds. She lies down on the narrow berth and closes her eyes.

She chose the ferry as one last deferral to her arrival, so that she would have twenty hours to come to terms with the idea that she will soon be on the other side. An airplane would simply have shattered the years of silence.

In her bag, which lies open on the floor of the cabin, is the list of names, telephone numbers, and addresses given to her by Lalla, a map of the country, another of the region, antibacterial gel, sunscreen, long-sleeved smocks she bought more or less at random, two long skirts from her hippie phase that she dug out from the back of her wardrobe, and a scarf to tie up her hair. As she was carefully folding her collection of "respectable" clothes, she felt a little like Thomson and Thompson in the Tintin adventures, when they go to China disguised as mandarins, or when they arrive in Syldavia dressed in Greek folk costumes. At the last minute, she added a pair of jeans and a hooded sweatshirt. Stuck to the jeans, like chewing gum to the sole of a shoe, looking entirely out of place, is a Post-it note scrawled with a number. It is the telephone number of Yacine, a distant cousin who lives in Tizi Ouzou, which her aunt Dalila insisted on giving her before she left. At the time, Naïma noted it down without asking any questions, and made sure she did not forget it when she was packing her bag, but now that she sees the little yellow tongue sticking out, she finds there is something absurd about this single scrawled line. Her family lived in Algeria for centuries, but all the guidance they could offer when she was leaving is contained on this tiny slip of paper.

On the eve of her trip, she finally responded to Christophe's text messages. As usual, within an hour of getting her message he rang her doorbell. Christophe is always punctual; Christophe is always efficient. After he had left, she looked at the bluish condom lying on the floor. She asked herself why she had done it. Because she is afraid to die, maybe. To take her mind off things. Out of habit. Because she still finds him attractive.

Because she has not the first idea of what it means to be a woman on the far side of the sea.

The white flanks of the huge ship rise out of the waters; orange life-boats cling to the sides, like a clutch of young held out of reach of the waves. Its size does not make it immune to the swell, and when Naïma goes up on deck after a night of shudders and creaks, there still lingers an acrid stench of vomit. At first she spies only the Mediterranean stretching as far as the eye can see, then, some hours later, the coastline appears, quivering on the horizon, more mirage than country. As the ferry enters the Bay of Algiers, Naïma thinks of a line from a fairy tale: *I see only the sea shimmer blue and the houses shimmer white.* There is not a cloud in the sky, and the expanse of water reflects the sun, golden, silvery, carving out the crest of each wave. As her eyes adjust, she notices that Algiers the White is white only in the foreground.

Farther back, as it scales the hill, it is tinted ocher and yellow and, farther still, brick buildings of reddish brown blend into the distant outline of a peak.

Fishing boats setting out, trailing nets behind them, pass the ferry as it approaches the quay. Naïma can make out the craggy, curious faces of the fishermen, shifting their tillers to avoid the huge wake opened up by the ship.

Naïma is sorry that she is alone, that she has no one with whom to share the ambiguous emotion washing over her. It is a block stuck inside her chest that refuses to resolve itself in joy, fear, relief, or even indifference.

She is sorry that she is alone, but she cannot think of anyone who could have made the journey with her. The conjured image of Christophe refuses to stand next to her, mocks her, slips away.

In the customs hall, she opens her travel bag for a female officer who barely glances at the contents before asking whether she will be going into the desert.

"No," Naïma says.

"That's good," the officer replies.

Around her, the parcels and packages of other passengers disgorge presents of every sort onto the conveyor belts and the officers rummage through them, frowning. A little farther away, just past the checkpoint, a man is waving to her. This must be Ifren, Lalla's nephew, whom the painter has arranged to drive her to Tizi Ouzou. Naïma zips up her bag and walks toward him flashing the exaggerated smile she always adopts when meeting someone for the first time. The customs officer quickly scuttles ahead of her and stops in front of Ifren.

"She's not going into the desert?" she asks.

"No," he says.

The woman heads back to the counters and the tidal wave of perfume bottles and vibrant clothes. Puzzled, Naïma watches her go, then turns to Ifren.

"Why does she want to know that?"

"Ever since the hostage crisis at the Tigantourine gas plant, French people have been warned not to travel in the south. It's a pity, since it was about the only place where we still had something that resembled tourism."

Outside the harbor buildings, on the road consumed by dazzling light, families hug; cars set off, laden with packages and boxes that have crossed the sea; drivers hurl insults at each other. The air is thick with dust that leaves Naïma's mouth and nose dry. Through the thin soles of her sandals she can feel the heat rising from the pavement and the potholed tarmac. It is still early and already she feels hot in the outfit she put on before disembarking. Ifren is just wearing shorts and a multi-colored short-sleeved shirt. She waits for him to point to where his car is parked, but he simply stands on the pavement, his face turned to the sun.

"I lent my car to a friend who needs to move a fridge," he explains. "He was only supposed to take an hour, but he's got stuck in a traffic jam."

He shrugs, as though this holdup is part of the rhythm of everyday life, then says:

"Do you want to see a bit of the city before we set off?"

Naïma nods and adjusts the heavy rucksack that is biting into her shoulder.

She follows Ifren through the streets, glancing in every direction. Algiers constantly eludes her gaze with its multitude of decorated flights of steps that rise in jagged lines, mounting an assault on the hills whose peaks she cannot see. The striped awnings of the shops hang over the windows, casting small, shadowy, and secretive pools over the wrought-iron balconies. On either side of the streets, electric cables mingle with the washing lines and the leaves of the intermittent palm trees. Naïma is discovering a new continent, and she is sorry that on her first glimpse of Algeria she is hobbling, her right shoulder all but dislocated by the short strap of her rucksack.

"Lalla told me that you're a painter, too," she pants as she trots behind Ifren.

He smiles and shrugs. "Not officially."

"What does that mean?"

"I paint out-of-doors," he says, his answer cryptic or absurd.

They walk as far as the Grande Poste, a post office as beautiful as the palace of a caliph, its pristine white facade broken by three vast arched doorways. They walk around the Jardin de l'Horloge, with its floral clock and benches where young Black men lie sleeping, their belongings in bundles under their heads, and past the Ministry of the Interior, whose forbidding facade cannot be softened even by a row of lush green palm trees. The streets are teeming with a noisy, bustling crowd. Naïma continually has to stop so as not to collide with other pedestrians, while Ifren, a few steps ahead, seems to instinctively know which way to sidestep to avoid collisions without slowing his pace. She trails around Algiers after him, taking tiny steps, like an old Chinese woman.

They leave the broad avenues for streets that twist at curious angles. Behind the massive shimmering buildings on the avenues, the city wears its finery like an old threadbare suit. The buildings are cracked and peeling, crudely stitched together with television antennas; if she viewed them in isolation, Naïma would probably think them ugly. But their dilapidation cannot change the fact that they face out toward the sea and the sweeping curve of the bay, glimpsed by a sudden tumbling of steps, which offers a vista of such beauty that it defies all human structures and adds its luster to each.

Murmurs in Arabic surround Naïma, the sound is familiar to her ear, though she cannot make out the meaning. Neither the days spent with Yema, immersed in the language, nor the hours spent poring over a textbook are enough for her to understand what is being said in the streets of Algiers. She recognizes the sounds just as, as a child, she recognized the song of the bird that had built its nest near her bedroom window, but the sounds are meaningless. She tries to concentrate, to pick out individual words from the torrent. Meaning struggles to reach her brain and dies along the way. A rattle of meaningless sounds like the dull clatter of bones. The conversations of the passersby, the slogans on the billboards, are not intended for her. Nothing reaches her except for the occasional French word that rises to the surface of the Arabic and leaps to her ear.

"Do you have money you need to change?" Ifren asks.

Thinking about the wad of banknotes in her wallet makes her nervous. Ordinarily she never carries cash with her. She likes the idea that the pickpocket who will eventually rob her—whose proximity is regularly announced on the Paris Métro—will find that she has little in her pockets.

Ifren leads her through the bustling streets glutted with market stalls where fruits and vegetables, beneath the sweltering sun, give off a sweet scent of rot. Everywhere, standing behind the stalls or sitting on upturned buckets, men are smoking with small, jerky movements. They move their crates with one hand so they can continue to puff on their cigarettes, or clamp the smoldering stub between their teeth when they need to free up both hands, screwing up their eyes so that the smoke does not get in. The ash falls on the fruits and the vegetables, into the half-melted tub of ice containing shellfish, into the basins of tiny, slimy squid, and the butts float on the gray water.

Naïma would like to light a cigarette herself, but when she dips her hand into her bag to fish out a pack, Ifren gives her a disapproving look.

"Not here, not in the street."

"I'm not allowed to smoke?"

"It's not a question of being allowed. There's no law against it. But people will stare, they'll make remarks . . ."

"I don't care about that," Naïma says blithely with a shrug.

She is playing the girl who has seen it all before and, in doing so, she knows that she is imitating Sol and her past littered with dangerous journeys.

"Are you sure?" Ifren asks with a dreamy smile. "Do you know what it's like to feel that everyone in the street despises you? That if they had the chance, they'd slap your face? Do you want to try it?"

She pushes the pack of Camels to the bottom of her bag.

"Wait till we get to Tizi. Things are different for women there."

Under the market stalls, deep in the square, there is a gallery with modern shops whose displays are almost empty—the rents are too high for the merchants who continue to sell their wares outside from stalls made of cardboard and wooden crates. Ifren takes her into one of the few shops that is open, a shop with luminous walls selling leather goods. With his pointed beard and his weary doe eyes beneath coal-black eyebrows, Naïma thinks he looks like a vizier from a comic book.

"Give him your euros," Ifren says. "He offers the best exchange rate in Algiers."

The banknotes in her wallet are replaced with a different wad of notes, which feature elephants, buffalo, antelope, and ancient ships with sails swelled by the wind. Naïma looks for the images painted by Issiakhem that Lalla mentioned, but those notes are probably no longer in circulation. She feels a brief, sharp twinge of disappointment, one that will recur throughout her trip, at the thought that Algeria, as it has evolved and modernized over the decades, has divested itself of what, for Naïma, would have been an important marker, one of the rare reference points gleaned from a few vague stories.

They meet up with Ifren's friend on the Place de l'Émir Abd El-Kader, formerly the Place du Maréchal Bugeaud. The Milk Bar still exists, and still offers up its sorbets and sodas through the large open windows. The statue of the French Maréchal—governor of Algeria from 1840 to 1847 and famous for his unconventional military tactics, such as pouring smoke into caves where hundreds of villagers were hiding, leaving them to die of asphyxia—is no longer there. It was shipped back to France in 1962 and, much later, erected in some little town in the Dordogne. The grim statue depicting Bugeaud with his hand on his heart has been replaced with one of Abd El-Kader, mounted on a mettlesome horse, holding his saber aloft. The emir, whom the French Maréchal battled for almost ten years before exacting his surrender, went from being a loser to being a hero after independence, and the plaque beneath the statue describes him as a "humanist, philosopher, and founding father of the State of Algeria." Naïma absentmindedly reads the words, but her attention is focused on the car held together with Scotch tape whose trunk Ifren has just opened. For her, Algiers is just an introduction, like the zone between the airport and the city center in a foreign capital that she watches flash past from the back seat of a taxi, vaguely trying to work out what sort of country it prefigures. If she knew that in the late summer of 1956 her grandfather stood on this square, just a few meters from where she is standing now, caught in a shower of glass, plaster, and blood, she might consider the scene more intently, substitute familiar faces for those of passersby, ask Ifren for a few more minutes so she can try to imagine the noise and the fear. But she knows so little that she is eager to leave the capital, and with no regrets she climbs back into the old car.

As they slowly head eastward out of the city, Ifren offers to show her some photographs of his works. On the screen of his phone she sees a succession of walls, police stations, town halls, and political party headquarters covered with huge faces and Amazigh symbols. Later, she sees the facades of opulent villas painted with shadowy figures, fleeing, screaming, writhing between lines of darkness. Ifren does not have his uncle's precision, she thinks as she swipes through the images, but he is clearly much more comfortable with large-format works. The way his gigantic paintings invade the city make the viewer forget the weakness of his lines. Some of them take her breath away.

"Do you ask for permission before beginning a mural?" she asks.

"Of course I don't." Ifren grins. "They simply appear. And pretty often they disappear again the next day. I can't claim them as mine, I can't exhibit them, I'm like a painter without a painting."

He seems to find this amusing.

"And the police don't try to arrest you?"

"Of course they do."

He says this in the same gleeful tone, as though he thinks it is completely normal for the police to try to arrest him—he's got his job, they've got theirs. He has done several short stints in prison, he says, though as yet he was there for no *official* reason: a painter without a painting, a prisoner without a sentence, he seems to enjoy these absences. He is dancing above the abyss. The psychiatric hospital is the only thing he could not endure. He refuses to be sent back there.

"I felt like I was in an old Russian horror movie. And, from what Lalla says, it was a lot worse in his day. Apparently I'm lucky . . ."

They talk a little about the old man, about his departure from Algeria and the ambivalent relationship he has had with his country ever since.

"It's as though he's given up hope of ever seeing a positive development," Naïma says.

Ifren sighs: his uncle is not the only one in that position. Ifren knows a host of intellectuals and artists who left a decade ago, at the end of the civil war, because just at the moment when the country might have been reborn, might have improved, they saw only regression.

"The thing is, a lot of people don't seem to understand that Algeria is still in the process of construction, that all the problems it inherited after independence are not permanent. A lot of people thought that if things were shit, well, that's just the way things were. I don't believe that. I believe that a country has to evolve, otherwise it dies."

When she has finished looking through the photographs, Naïma surreptitiously glances at Ifren. Tall, with fine, sharp features, a vaporous mass of blond hair already peppered here and there with gray, he looks like the gilded statue of a warrior. She thinks back to everything she has recently learned about the origins of the Kabyle people. Ifren could be a living advertisement for those who claim that the Amazigh tribes are genetically descended from the Vikings or the Vandals. Sensing himself observed, Ifren turns and stares at her, smiling, not troubling to look at the road—a common practice here, as Naïma will quickly realize. Embarrassed, she lowers her eyes.

On a number of occasions, when the line at a junction or a traffic light seems too long, Ifren hops out of the car and dashes into a little shop, or wanders around the makeshift stalls on the hard shoulder. He comes back with bottles of water, almonds, cigarettes, wrapped in more plastic bags than the layers of an onion. He never switches off the engine.

"Gas doesn't cost anything here," he explains when Naïma comments. "This is the kingdom of the car, it's probably the only luxury that most Algerians can afford, so, honestly, when it comes to the environment . . ."

As if to underline his words, a plastic bag flutters out the window

and becomes caught in the scorched fronds of the palms that line
the road.

Ifren drives, seemingly unperturbed by the military sentry boxes dotted everywhere, or the metal teeth used to narrow the lanes. For her
part, Naïma stares in astonishment at the succession of uniforms and
guns and the gloomy boys brandishing them, who look as though they
would rather be anywhere else. In Paris, every time she encountered
soldiers participating in Opération Sentinelle, after the attacks in January 2015, she anxiously glanced at the red or blue caps, the black barrels
of their assault rifles, which seemed to turn the streets of her neighborhood into a war zone of the kind that, until recently, existed only in
movies or on distant continents. From the awkward way they smiled
at residents, she suspected that they knew the effect they were having
and were almost attempting to apologize. They, like her, seemed to be
convinced that their presence was only temporary, and that this uneasy
coexistence was something that had to be accepted for a short period.
In contrast, the Algerian soldiers they keep passing look as though they
sprang up with the landscape, and the sullen expressions that distort
their adolescent faces prove to Naïma that they know they will be here
for years, perhaps for centuries.

They pass Bordj Menaïel, where once the cork factories and the tobacco
warehouses were set ablaze, then drive along the Oued Chender. Storks
in black and white plumage as elegant as evening dress from another
century are perched on the minarets, the satellite dishes, the telegraph
poles. Their huge round nests, like chefs' hats atop buildings, give Naïma
a curious feeling of serenity. She cranes her neck the better to see them,
hoping to spot an egg.

   In Hassen Ferhani's documentary *Roundabout in My Head*, which she
watched in the middle of the night a month ago, a worker in an Algiers
slaughterhouse told a story about a stork from the days when Algeria
was still a colony. The bird stole a French flag to line its nest. Furious
when they discovered their emblem missing, the French soldiers arrested and tortured half of the villagers, but to no avail. The culprit was

revealed only when someone spotted a corner of the Tricolour hanging out of the nest. The French arrested the stork and kept it in prison for several months. They regularly tortured it, but the bird did not confess to anything. In the end they released it.

"This is a true story," the man telling the tale says several times, smiling proudly.

Ifren drops Naïma off in Tizi Ouzou at the Maison de l'Artisanat—the Museum of Traditional Arts. Mehdi, her host for the next few days, comes out to greet them as soon as he sees the car pull up. While preparing for the trip, Naïma had been thrilled to discover that Lalla's contacts were prepared to go out of their way to welcome her. Now that she is here, she feels like an awkward package being palmed off from person to person. She watches as the golden-haired driver behind the wheel of his battered car pulls away, waving at him until the car turns the corner. (This is what Yema always does when her children are leaving, and since, to Naïma, there is no distinction between Algeria and her grandmother—Yema *is* Naïma's Algeria—it is hardly surprising that, now that she is here, she should copy Yema's gestures.)

Mehdi is a little man whose excitability makes him seem ageless. He hops about like a sparrow or a small child, he blinks a lot. (She will later find out he is nearsighted, but can't stand the weight of glasses on his nose.) He met Lalla when they were young and studying photography together, and clearly loves him like a brother, though his love is tinged with concern. When Naïma updates him about Lalla's health, he sighs and shakes his head reproachfully, as though Lalla has deliberately decided to be at death's door, as though this is just one more example of the artist looking for trouble. He leads Naïma to his house, and insists on carrying her rucksack, though he is at least four inches shorter than she is and his constant restlessness causes the bag to bump against the back of his head just where a bald spot reveals a patch of pale, almost bluish skin. Hardly have they stepped through the door of his house than he asks the same question as Ifren:

"Do you want to see the town?"

*   *   *

Naïma is disappointed by the architecture of Tizi Ouzou. The town center is mostly new buildings that could have been built anywhere and, despite the promise of its name (the word *ouzou* refers to flowering broom), the town has more boulevards and cars than shrubs. Naïma pays little attention to the buildings, focusing instead on the passersby. The streets seem to belong to the young, to schoolchildren and students. Laughter and jeers erupt from groups of young people huddled around benches. Unlike in Algiers, there are bareheaded young women wearing short skirts in the streets. M'douha, a district just outside the city center, is known for its university campus filled with young women, Mehdi explains. He does not know exactly how many of them there are, a thousand, two thousand, maybe more.

"Obviously, it attracts perverts," he says with a sigh. "My wife's niece studied there, but she decided to go home to her parents. She said that at night there were creepy men prowling the campus."

Naïma, on the contrary, finds the men's stares less insistent than they were in Algiers. Here, they seem more like jokes or compliments than acts of appropriation.

Music is everywhere, streaming from cars, from radios balanced on windowsills, or blaring from the telephones of people walking by. Naïma asks Mehdi what young people in Tizi listen to and he shrugs and scowls. A few yards farther on, he ushers her into a music shop whose window is plastered with hundreds of record sleeves. After a brief conversation with the salesman, he hands her a stack of CDs and says:

"This is real Kabyle music."

Naïma studies the face of the handsome man on the cover of several of the albums.

"Who is he?"

Mehdi and the shop owner roar with laughter because, to them, not recognizing Matoub Lounès is like not recognizing Che Guevara or Jesus. Wounded in 1988 when he was shot five times by a gendarme, kidnapped in 1995 by an armed Islamist group that was forced to release him due to public pressure, Matoub Lounès long seemed invincible. For almost two decades he released a new album every year, seemingly untroubled by the enemies he made with each new release. In the end, it took a sordid and mysterious roadside assassination in 1998 to silence the champion of Amazigh culture, the advocate of freedom and secularism, the hero—almost twenty years after his death—of a whole swath of the Kabyle population.

"But you people in France, you don't understand," the shop owner says. "What's the name of that newspaper everyone reads?"

"*Libération*," Mehdi says.

"That's it. In *Libération*, they said that Matoub Lounès was a fascist because he didn't like Arabs. France doesn't understand anything."

"You mean, because . . . he *did* like Arabs?" Naïma asks, a little confused.

"Absolutely not," says the owner.

"It's complicated," Mehdi prefers to say.

By the time they go back to the Maison de l'Artisanat, Naïma is exhausted and the straps of her sandals are biting into her swollen feet. But she smiles sweetly when Mehdi suggests they visit the collection of craftworks, and as they wander around the display cases she allows herself to be adorned with pieces of jewelry she does not recognize: khalkhal, tabzimt. She repeats the names as though they were magic spells. Weighed down with silver more than a century old, she looks to see whether these pieces transform her into a Berber princess, but what she sees in the mirror is simply her usual face, the face of a thirty-year-old Parisian woman garishly dressed up. Embarrassed, she allows Mehdi to photograph her ("for your family," he says) and, as she strikes a pose she imagines is Oriental, she thinks about Thomson and Thompson.

The following day, Naïma begins to follow up the leads that should guide her to Lalla's drawings. Mehdi and his wife, Rachida, an editor with a beautiful, stern face, help her with an enthusiasm she finds astonishing. They flesh out the fragmentary information she has been given, drive her from one end of town to the other, take the lead in many of the conversations such that she feels like a little girl being dragged into meetings with grown-ups where nothing she can say will be taken seriously, or, rather—since everyone listens to her, attentive, smiling, knitting their brows, making little guttural noises of approval—where nothing she can say is likely to have unfortunate consequences. She finds it restful and allows herself to be led from house to house, from one long-standing acquaintance to another, studying the sketches shown to her, making no attempt to hurry things along. She makes an initial selection of the ink drawings, puts aside those she finds most interesting. Among these is a series of self-portraits she particularly likes: the features of his face merge into lines of text and traditional motifs that cast pools of shadow. The texts are sometimes snippets from newspapers, sometimes political slogans, sometimes lines from old poems, and sometimes, in minuscule characters below the eye or along the ridge of the nose, shameful or brutal memories, set down in few words. Naïma tells those she meets how the gallery works, explains that she has not come to *buy* the works but to ask that they be loaned for the duration of an exhibition during which they are likely to be sold. It is a complicated process, because at this point the owner will then make a different selection, taking back works he does not want to part with and suggesting others. The negotiations remind Naïma of the games of Monopoly she used to play with her sisters during the summers. *I'll give you the Rue de la Paix for your two orange ones. You can have my train stations and I'll give you fifty thousand on top.*

She is beginning to understand Kamel's opposition to the project: it really is the sort of approach taken by museums, one the gallery is not accustomed to. The works to be exhibited will come from a range of owners, and each of them wants to set a different price—either because his fondness for Lalla encourages him to part with the drawings in his possession for nothing (Lalla gave it to me, I'm not going to sell it), or that same fondness leads him to demand exorbitant sums (he's a great artist).

Some of the names given her by the elderly artist lead nowhere: more often than not because the family has moved without giving a forwarding address, or left for France, Italy, Spain, or Morocco during the 2000s, disgusted by the fact that, after the Black Decade, freedom did not return as they had hoped it would. On one or two occasions, even Mehdi and Rachida are surprised when a door is opened by a complete stranger. "He was someone I never thought would leave," one or the other whispers, Mehdi forlornly, Rachida angrily.

But most of the time the search proves surprisingly easy. Lalla's friends are charming, amenable, and, more than anything, they seem to have been waiting for years for Lalla's genius to be recognized and for him to be accorded the kind of retrospective Naïma is describing.

"It's about time," they mutter, taking from a wardrobe, from a shoebox, from their wallet, the delicate ink sketches Lalla gave them as gifts.

She likes all the people she meets in the days spent negotiating, particularly Mehdi and Rachida, who shower her with attention. She discovers a host of characters that she never expected to find here, given that she inherited only a few scant memories of a rural Algeria where everyone worked in olive groves. In the search marked out by Lalla, she meets intellectuals, artists, activists, journalists, and with every word they say, Naïma's inner Algeria extends in unexpected directions. All the people she talks to seem to have fought for independence, whether for their country, for Kabylia, or for the freedom of artists from state control. As she bonds with them, she naturally tends to conceal her family's past. (With half-truths and omissions, she introduces herself as the descendant of emigrants.) She is not sure whether this is a bad thing: she is exercising her freedom, she thinks, and she is refuting the dictionary definition, which is somewhat exhilarating. Rather than following in the footsteps of her father and her grandfather, she is creating her own connection to Algeria, a connection that is not about necessities or roots, but about friendships and possibilities. She has thrown away Yacine's telephone number, she knows she will not use it.

"What about Tassekurt?"

The question rouses Mehdi from his doze. Naïma sets down the thick file in which she has carefully placed the works she has gathered and pulls a face.

"Tomorrow . . ."

She has saved what she considers the most delicate phase of her mission for last: the meeting with Lalla's ex-wife. The artist has never spoken about her, it is a line of silence he has walked very carefully. Rachida described her as a viper. Mehdi simply sighed and said, *C'est compliqué.* (When he is uncomfortable, his usually perfectly articulated French reverts to something that reminds Naïma of how Yema speaks—an accent where words run together and the French *é* sound becomes *ee: see compleekee.*) Neither Mahdi nor Rachida wishes to come with her this time. With a knot in her stomach, Naïma sets off to meet the viper.

Tassekurt lives in Haute-Ville, the historic district of Tizi Ouzou. She owns a modern apartment in the city center, according to Rachida, but has arranged to meet Naïma in the family home. It is in an area of narrow streets and the kind of low houses typical of traditional villages— something this quartier has not quite ceased to be. The stone walls are cracked and there are tiles missing from the low red roofs, yet, despite the superficial dilapidation, Naïma is overjoyed to explore the neighborhood peppered with little squares in which fountains, most of them now dry, create cool, colorful grottos.

As she wanders aimlessly, circling the house, putting off the moment when she will ring the doorbell, she notices Tassekurt at a second-floor window, watching silently from behind the mosquito screen. Naïma meets the woman's agate eyes, trying not to blush.

Inside, the light filtering through the *mashrabiyas* casts filigree patterns on the tiled floors. Naïma nervously follows this woman, who walks like a queen, through rooms devoid of any ornamentation other than that traced by the sun's rays. The little courtyard where they sit is so completely sheltered by the broad leaves of a fig tree that one might almost think that night was falling. Tassekurt serves them both coffee and chain-smokes long menthol cigarettes.

She has the faded beauty of those large flowers that seem at the height of their perfection when the slightest touch will cause every petal to fall. From her body, from the folds of her neck—and from the house itself—rises the sweet, dusty scent of age, and she exudes the troubled sensuality of a statue about to crumble. Her gray-blond hair is tied at the nape of her neck in an intricate chignon that reminds Naïma of pictures of Uum Kalthoum on the sleeves of her parents' old vinyl records.

Contrary to what Naïma expected, Tassekurt does not criticize her ex-husband in conversation. She does not even mention their relationship. She talks about him as an artist whose works she was fortunate—or intuitive—enough to buy at one of his early exhibitions. She takes a keen interest in what Naïma has to say about the retrospective, as though she were expected to offer advice rather than put the works she owns on sale.

"Who came up with the idea for the exhibition? Was it you?"

Naïma talks about Christophe, about *The Mirror Wars*, about how the Arab world is perceived, the unique nature of Lalla's work, but Tassekurt is no longer listening, she is engrossed in her own thoughts.

"Do you realize that you—I mean your boss, the gallery, the art world in general—can decide who has the right to go down in history and who doesn't?"

Naïma mumbles that she has never thought of it like that, that surely it's more complicated. (In spite of herself, she finds her voice taking on Mehdi's intonations, which are those of Yema.)

"What do you think about the notion of deservedness?" Tassekurt asks. "All the Algerians I know in France are obsessed with the notion of deservedness. Personally, I find the idea repellent."

"I . . . well . . . yes . . ." Naïma begins, but cannot come up with a coherent response.

She is intimidated by this woman, with her large eyes painted with turquoise and azure eye shadow, the heavy gold bangle that encircles her wrist, her overelaborate coiffure. She looks like an actress in the twilight of her career playing the role of Cleopatra one last time.

"I don't deserve the things I have," Tassekurt says, paying no heed to Naïma's stammerings. "Lalla does not *deserve* this retrospective. Things simply happen, some of them can be prompted, others are the result of luck or chance . . ."

She stacks the cups without even leaving Naïma time to finish the thick, sweet coffee, and in doing so signals that she is dismissed. "As for the drawings, I shall have to think about it," she says. "I am not sure whether I am willing to part with them."

Naïma gets to her feet and hates herself for doing so, for meekly obeying this woman's wordless command. She longs to shatter this mask of haughty majesty, to disconcert Tassekurt, and this is doubtless why, as they leave the little courtyard, she says:

"He's in the hospital. If we don't move quickly, he may not live to see the retrospective."

She knows that Lalla would hate her for saying such things, for using his illness to stir pathos in order to further what is essentially a business transaction. From the way Tassekurt slowly raises her eyebrow, Naïma can tell that the woman has precisely the same reaction as the ailing artist. For a split second she can see how the two of them must have made a daunting couple, uncompromising, untroubled by good manners.

That night, Mehdi and Rachida take her to dinner at a little restaurant just outside the city center. At her instigation, they regale her with stories about Lalla's gilded youth. Naïma is surprised to learn that Rachida knew him before Mehdi. Lalla would sometimes draw cover illustrations for the publishing house where she had her first job. The wistful, sensual smile that plays on Rachida's lips leaves little doubt about the nature of their former relationship. It occurs to Naïma that she would like a man to speak about her like this, when her hair is gray and her skin looks like a suit of rumpled clothes too big for her. Mehdi does not seem upset by his wife recalling these tender memories, he smiles, he blinks, he orders himself another drink. When he goes to the toilet, Naïma admits to Rachida that she is astonished by how brazenly she talks. Visibly flattered, Rachida gives a deep, throaty laugh.

"That little game of pretending to be pure and chaste, pretending, 'My life began the day I got married,' never appealed to me," she says. "It kills me to see girls today being taken in by this gibberish. Things have clearly regressed for women in this country."

She looks around and, seeing many all-male groups, sneers:

"Most of the things that women don't do in this country aren't even forbidden. They've just accepted the idea that we're not supposed to do them. You saw the café terraces in Algiers where there are only men? Women are not forbidden from going into those bars, there's no sign saying we're not allowed, and if I walked in, they wouldn't throw me out, but you'll never see a woman sitting on those terraces. Just as you won't see a woman smoking in the street—and don't even get me started on the subject of drinking alcohol. My attitude is that, as long as I'm not forbidden to do something by law, I'll keep on doing it, even if I'm the last Algerian woman drinking beer and not wearing a veil."

Later, she picks up this conversation again, as though the subjects discussed in between were mere parentheses:

"But it's not always possible to resist things, sadly. Part of the reason they won is because they managed to get it into my head that I'd rather have been born a man. I hated it when I hit puberty, hated it, I still remember it perfectly. I got breasts at thirteen, and it was like I'd caught a disease or had something grafted onto my body by a mad scientist while I was asleep. I went to bed flat as a board, I looked quite boyish, almost a double of my brother, and I woke up with bumps and curves everywhere, transformed into a mother, I was visibly a woman who could be raped or married off, and I was squashy, I had to protect my breasts from any impact, I couldn't run without wearing a bra. A few weeks later, I got my period and then it was the end of everything. I cried for hours."

In the restaurant, diners turn their heads at Rachida's sudden outburst and Naïma notices Mehdi, from time to time, gently laying a hand on her arm. When she feels his skin against hers, Rachida lowers her voice without pausing.

After dinner, they are joined by a group of friends and move out to a large table on the terrace where bowls of sorbet and bottles are passed around. To those who have not met her yet, Rachida and Mehdi introduce their guest as an envoy sent by Lalla and as a prodigal daughter who is returning to her country after a long absence. Naïma is greeted by approving nods she is not convinced she deserves. (She has not admitted to anyone that for a long time she thought about refusing to undertake this trip.) One of the newcomers asks where her father is from. She gives the name of the village, of the seven hamlets strung like beads along the mountain ridge, assuming no one will recognize the name. (No one in France, not even Kabyles, has ever recognized it.)

"That's over near Zbarbar, isn't it?" the man says.

"Just above the dam," says the person sitting next to him.

Naïma doesn't know. She tells them what she does know (from her searches on the internet):

"It's in the Bouïra region."

"Well, yes, but not really," someone corrects her. "It's close to Palestro."

"Have you ever been?"

No, she admits with a shake of her head.

"Of course she hasn't been," Rachida says. "When exactly do you think she could have gone there? The place is swarming with fundamentalists!"

At this point, Naïma feels it appropriate to quote the Speech, the one that justifies her never having visited the village her family is from:

"My father planned to take me and my sisters there when we were old enough. But in 1997, my cousin and his wife were killed at a fake roadblock and my father changed his mind. He said he'd never go back to the bled."

A number of people silently nod, as though they have already encountered this situation. Rachida says:

"They should have slaughtered the bastards like dogs when they first came down from the mountains, instead of giving them apartments and opening bank accounts for them."

The conversation quickly becomes heated; voices are raised. Around the little square in which a ragtag group of children are chasing a colored ball, several other café terraces offer similar scenes of boisterous, quick-tempered diners. Naïma listens to the heated exchanges taking place around the long table, unable to participate, since the Black Decade that wounded Algeria and the other guests reached her only as the faint, feeble ricochet that is the Speech. Mentally, she takes notes so that she will be able to relay the conversation when she gets home. She is witnessing—she thinks—a slice of Algerian life, the sort of scene we like to experience since it is one that ordinary tourists never see, and, for a moment, makes us feel like a native. Naïma assumes the subject of her village has been forgotten in the cut and thrust of the discussion, that her origins have been noted but do not matter. She is wrong.

"The Islamists won because, even today, people are afraid of going into the mountains. With tourists, it's understandable. They never come back. But even Algerians are afraid. Take you, Rachida, telling the girl she shouldn't visit her village because it's too dangerous!"

"That's not what I said," Rachida says defensively.

"Oh, yes, it is! This is her first time in the country and you're telling her that her village is full of terrorists!"

"The thing is, Rachida's got a point," Mehdi says. "I don't know anyone who'd be prepared to drive her there. Everyone knows the place is dangerous."

Once again, voices are raised and no one is listening to anyone else. There are now two camps: those who think the village is perfectly safe, and those who think going there means taking your life in your hands. Somewhat surprisingly, it is taken for granted that Naïma *wants* to visit the village; they are merely discussing the feasibility of the journey.

"Well, I'm not afraid," one of the men says. "I go up there on business all the time."

"And you've never had any problems?"

"No."

"In that case," Mehdi says, "you can drive Naïma up there tomorrow."

They shake on the deal without even consulting the interested party. Naïma's self-appointed chauffeur turns to introduce himself: he is Noureddine, a distant cousin of Mehdi's. She stares at him fixedly but does not hear a word he is saying. He has the same triumphant smile she saw in Christophe when he decided to send her to Tizi Ouzou. Why are all these men so determined to send her back to her roots? Naïma thanks him for the offer, but declines: she has too much work to do, sorry.

"You mean Tassekurt's drawings?" Rachida interrupts. "Don't worry. She's enjoying making you stew, but she'll let you have them all. She's long since realized that she loves money more than her memories of Lalla . . ."

Rachida's lips curve into a contemptuous sneer when she talks about Lalla's first wife.

"None of us could ever work out what he saw in her."

The men around the table stare disinterestedly at their shoes. There are some wounds that even decades cannot heal.

"You're sure it's not dangerous?" Naïma asks after a moment.

The others do not seem to understand what she is talking about. The conversation has already moved on. Rachida is lost in thought.

"Oh no," says Noureddine, "the terrorists are a lot more considerate of women these days. They prefer to kill cops."

The table, littered with empty bottles, glimmers beneath the ropes of colored lights. Naïma cannot think of another objection. The fear she feels gnawing at her belly is only partly about the terrorists on the mountain ridge. What really frightens her is the thought of setting foot in a place that has been frozen in her family's memory since 1962, and in doing so bringing it brutally, jarringly back into existence. It seems to her that what she is about to do is akin to the careless act of the explorer in "A Sound of Thunder" who crushes a butterfly in the Jurassic era and thereby destroys the present to which he hoped to return. How could she possibly communicate this fear to the gang of tipsy revelers gathered around the table? How could she even begin to express it coherently?

That night she barely sleeps, her head is filled with the rumble of machines juddering in the darkness. In her wanderings through the city, she has noticed the sometimes weeping blisters of air-conditioning units that project from buildings, a pervasive rash that infects office buildings and houses alike and, at night, when the hum of traffic and the voices of passersby have faded, she has only to listen to hear the muffled, monotonous hum of these machines that rattle each time they stop and start without ever keeping time. At every clank, Naïma is jolted awake and lies there, tossing and turning on the thin mattress.

The blare of Noureddine's car horn forces Naïma from the kitchen, where she has been drinking an umpteenth cup of coffee, scalding her lips, trying to buy time before she has to leave the house. Worried that Noureddine will wake the whole neighborhood, she quickly grabs her rucksack and, seeing that she has forgotten to fix the strap, she worries that her shoulder will ache tomorrow, worries that she is getting old, worries that if the Islamists kill her she won't get much older, then jumps into the car, which takes off at top speed.

As soon as they move away from the main roads, Noureddine's driving becomes frenetic. Frustrated at having to negotiate bumpy roads pitted with potholes and that weave between boulders, whenever he sees a few yards of straight, flat road, he floors the accelerator with a whoop of joy, one hand on the steering wheel, the other hanging out the window, toying with his hair or bringing a cigarette to his lips. At every burst of speed, Naïma clutches the handle above the passenger door, feeling the plastic slip between her sweaty fingers.

To take her mind off the prospect of an accident, she forces herself to concentrate on the landscape. There are the same houses, permanently under construction, the same trees hung with plastic bags, the same military checkpoints she passed on previous days, but, knowing that she is on the road home (she cannot help but think this word "home," even if she does not even know where she is going), she studies them with renewed interest, as though she might recognize them.

*   *   *

The farther they drive, the more Naïma notices that women are scarcer and more covered up. The flip-flops and sleeveless T-shirts worn by girls in Tizi give way to traditional smocks and *fatas*. Farther still, the Kabyle scarf becomes the Islamic veil. In the streets of Lakhdaria (formerly Palestro), not a single woman is bareheaded. Naïma asks Noureddine to pull over so that she can open the trunk and get the scarf she brought to cover herself with, which, until now, has remained at the bottom of her rucksack. Glancing in the rearview mirror, she realizes that her colorful scarf does nothing to make her blend in with the women on the streets wearing the hijab and often a full *jilbab*. She looks less like someone respecting a religious commandment than like a girl going to the beach. On her forehead and her neck, stray black curls stick out from beneath the scarf. She shrinks as far away from the window as she can, unable to apply the precepts that Rachida mentioned the night before, to proudly assert her right not to cover herself.

At the junction of the Rue du 5-Juillet and the market square, a small grocery shop sheds its peeling green and white paint onto the pavement. Sitting at the window, the owner pensively moves a toothpick in the gaps between his incisors. He sells tomatoes, chickpeas, olives, and onions. It is much the same produce that Claude once sold, except that on the shelves inside there are no bottles of pastis, of Picon or Fernet-Branca. Naïma bows her head so that no one will reproach her for brazenly looking a man in the eye. Even if she had stared long and hard, she could not have recognized Youcef Tadjer, the childhood friend and hero of Hamid's when he lived up on the mountain ridge. She has never even heard his name. The car flashes past without even slowing.

Despite what Noureddine said at the restaurant, he clearly has no idea where the village is. As they leave Lakhdaria, he stops several times to ask soldiers for directions, and each time they say:

"Oh, so you're going up to visit the terrorists?"

Noureddine laughs and gives them an appreciative thumbs-up. To Naïma, however, it sounds much less funny. And yet, she feels a kind of joy as she cranes her neck to look up at the peaks. For the first time since she arrived in Algeria, she knows that this landscape is one that several members of her family have seen before. In a surge of mingled fear and excitement, she telephones her father:

"I'm on my way to the village."

Hamid immediately responds with a series of questions:

"Why? Who with? Have you let someone know? Do they know you're coming?"

"Everything's fine," Naïma says in a tone she finds curiously calm. "Don't worry. I just wondered whether you could help me find the house."

"I don't remember a thing, Naïma. Not a thing! What do you expect me to say?"

Naïma doesn't know. Perhaps she simply wanted him to say thank you.

The battered old car begins its ascent of the narrow mountain roads toward the ridge that is no longer visible, lost among the pines, the flowers, and the fig trees. The village is twenty miles from Lakhdaria, it takes an eternity to reach it via this tortuous road. Noureddine no longer lets go of the steering wheel. He focuses on the hairpin bends that promise the careless driver a leap into the unknown. They pass no more soldiers, only a few shepherds from time to time. After a while, Noureddine notices that Naïma is cowering in her seat.

"What's wrong? Is my driving that bad?"

"Ever since we left Lakhdaria, I haven't seen a single woman," she whispers.

He shrugs, and says bitterly:

"It's true that around here has been pretty heavily Islamized . . ."

Half an hour later, they finally spot a woman, leading a handful of goats. They think she has her back to them until, as they pass, they realize she is wearing a black niqab that makes it impossible to tell which way she is facing.

"Batman in the mountains," Noureddine says, and they both giggle.

The scent of the pine forest that penetrates the shuddering vehicle seems as heavy and sticky as the resin itself. As they approach Zbarbar, the sentry boxes reappear and, behind them, tall watchtowers.

"Around here was the VIP section for Islamists during the Black Decade," Noureddine says laconically. "The army had to torch the forests to flush them out . . . Acres of trees went up in smoke."

Naïma can see no scars left by the fires; the forest seems to have once again enfolded the mountain. The dense vegetation is surprising. Naïma has always imagined the area as a range of barren mountains, vertical deserts, a mural of the Sahara pasted over the sheer rock face, and yet there is something familiar in what she sees. Eventually she realizes that the landscape reminds her not of her family's memories, but of scenes from the film *Manon des sources*, steep hillsides thick with gnarled shadowy trees and groves of juniper and rockrose. But she knows that there is no Manon here, no naked woman dancing beneath the cool water of a nearby waterfall.

Finally, the first houses on the mountain ridge appear and Noureddine pulls over to ask a group of men sitting on large rocks above the village whether they recognize the surname of Naïma's family.

The first group says no. In fact, they say nothing, they simply wave for the car to drive on, that they have no information, and Naïma doesn't know whether the gesture signifies that they have nothing to say to the driver and that he is wasting his time and his breath talking to them, or whether it is they who would be wasting their time talking to him.

A little farther on, a second group nods when they hear the name. "They've got a shop in the next village," they say.

"Not this shop," a third group tells them. "The other one. In the next village."

Naïma feels as though she is being rebuffed in a bid to test her already fragile desire to find her family, but now that she is here, she feels an electrical energy that will not allow her to give up. Her whole body is tensed, her face tilted imperceptibly toward the windshield, as though her energy could propel the car faster.

In the next village, Noureddine pulls up outside a small grocery shop, its window filled with buckets of olives of every size.

"Let's go," he says.

Inside, the shop is also filled with buckets, bowls, and jars. The counter glistens with the silver and gold wrappers of chocolate bars. This, it seems, is all they sell: olives and sweets. A chubby teenager shifting his weight from one foot to the other looks surprised to see them come in. (It seems clear that people rarely make a detour to visit the shop, even less so with a tourist.) Noureddine launches into an explanation in Kabyle of which Naïma understands nothing aside from her family name, which crops up a number of times. The teenager shifts his gaze from Noureddine to Naïma and echoes listlessly:

"Zekkar?"

"Zekkar," Noureddine says curtly, irritated by the boy's apathy.

"Zekkar, that's me," the fat boy says, pointing to himself to make sure that Naïma understands.

Slowly, carefully, she copies his gesture (it's like a scene from *E.T.*) and says:

"Me, too."

They smile happily at each other.

The boy's name is Reda. Naïma cannot quite work out the precise relationship between them, but he launches into an excitable babble and closes up the shop.

"We're going to see the family home," Noureddine translates, climbing behind the wheel of the car. "He says his father speaks some French and is bound to know who you are."

Young Reda guides them while making a series of telephone calls. Naïma has no idea what he is saying as he talks incessantly, his face unsmiling. The only thing she understands (or thinks she understands) is that he calls her "the French girl." This annoys her for no apparent reason, as though the otherness he is drawing attention to were necessarily an insult.

A few miles farther on, they pull up in front of a huge metal gate that Reda pounds with his fist. Soon the gate screeches open and Naïma sees three houses painted pink, yellow, and white, arranged in a crude triangle on a patch of bare land on which a few chickens are scratching around. As the gate closes, a gang of children rush from the houses to greet them. In the midst of this boisterous, ragged horde, Naïma suddenly sees the face of her elder sister Myriem, or rather a face that looks like it has come from a family photo album when Myriem was seven years old. The features of the laughing girl approaching her are exactly the same.

"Shems," Reda says by way of a monosyllabic introduction.

Hearing her name, the little girl starts to babble, tugging at Naïma's hand, and to Naïma there is something surreal about seeing a familiar face uttering these alien sounds. She cannot take her eyes off Shems: This is my flesh and blood, she thinks. She pictures the combinations and convulsions of chromosomes (images inspired by vague memories of a school biology textbook) that somehow, separated by thirty years and by the wide Mediterranean, managed to produce two strangely similar beings, Myriem and Shems. Never has biology seemed so tangible.

The girl leads her into the white house and sits her down in a small living room on the long bench upholstered in an old-fashioned fabric that runs along three of the walls. Inside, a crippling heat builds behind the closed doors. Gradually, they are joined by an old man, a couple in their sixties, a woman whose age is impossible to determine—perhaps because her blue eyes are so arresting that the rest of her features seem to disappear—and two young women who— Naïma is relieved to see—are wearing sheer, colored scarves. The children, with the exception of Shems, stand in the doorway and giggle, elbowing each other as they stare at their unknown cousin.

Noureddine stands outside, chain-smoking and watching the chickens' abortive attempts to fly. The interior is a private space to which, as an outsider, he is not permitted access. He is condemned to the no-man's-land between the metal gate and the door. He did not even attempt to follow Naïma, and she feels his absence keenly. The moment she sits down, she is struck by the sheer impossibility of conversing with the people around her. There is no place for her eyes to wander in this spartan room whose only window is too high to afford a view. She cannot pretend that her silence is a spellbound contemplation. She looks at them. They look at her. Self-consciousness vies with infinite kindness. The old man does not smile, perhaps because the delicate, wrinkled skin of his face might crack, but the others never allow the corners of their mouths to droop. And then, suddenly, as though a single thought has suddenly occurred to all of them (This silence is *really* awkward), the conversation starts up, in a cacophony of mingled languages. To Naïma's surprise, these even include English:

"The family, all is *bien*?" one of the young women asks, and laughs at the sound of her own words.

"All is *bien*," Naïma says.

And, in concert, they add:

"*Alḥamdulillāh*."

Quickly, Naïma finds herself miming, sketching her family tree in the air. She draws a circle, representing her grandfather Ali and her grandmother Yema, and the line connecting them to her father, Hamid, next to whom she traces a series of circles before intoning the litany of her aunts and uncles: Dalila, Kader, Claude, Hacène, Karima, Mohamed, Fatiha, Salim. Then she comes back to the beginning, to the circle that represents Hamid (as if he has been hovering there since she first traced him with her hands), and sketches the line that leads from him to her and to her sisters Myriem, Aglaé, and Pauline. The children in the doorway laugh and mimic her, tossing out circles, lines, and names. But the young woman who incongruously speaks English gets to her feet and steps toward the invisible family tree with the cautious care owed to objects so fragile that the slightest clumsy gesture might sweep them away. She points to the first circle, the one that represents Ali, and traces a horizontal line, adding his brothers Djamel—whose name is followed by a mournful silence—and Hamza. All eyes turn to the wizened old man who slowly twirls his ivory-handled cane, apparently uninterested in his place in this insubstantial diagram. The young woman next to Naïma continues to gesticulate: from the circle representing Hamza she draws lines to Omar, who is sitting nearby with his wife and his daughter—the little boy Ali hated for having the temerity to be born before Hamid is now a gray-haired patriarch with an impressive paunch—to Amar, who is not here, but the apprentice genealogist is his daughter Malika, and to a dozen other circles that hang from the invisible threads of family ties. Among them is Yacine, the unknown cousin whose telephone number Naïma threw away, and Fathi, the father of Reda. Hearing this name, the chubby boy in the doorway mimes the thin line that connects them. From the circle representing Djamel she traces others representing Azzedine, then Leila with her blue eyes, who is ageless and husbandless, and Mustafa. Djamel's line of descendants is so short that it becomes clear to Naïma that he was the man in Hamid's nightmares that Dalila mentioned: the man murdered by the FLN in 1962, the man who put the full stop to the tale of Algeria as a country of the dead.

Everyone gazes at the nothingness that has been traced in the air as though it were a cathedral made of lace. Naïma and Malika look at each other and smile through the floating fragments of family they have managed to assemble, then they take a step forward and embrace. Leila, in turn, gets up and takes the newcomer in her arms, and Omar's wife follows suit. For the first time since she came through the gate, Naïma feels at ease. These hugs are such that they can make up for everything, even the lack of a shared language. The women here hug in the way that only Yema does, a real bear hug, not some token gesture. Naïma feels their breasts press against her, the beads of their necklaces dig into her skin, leaving small red marks, she breathes in the smell of their flesh, their sweat.

Malika says a few words to Shems, and the girl goes off and reappears with a collection of old photographs, which Malika firmly places in Naïma's hands.

"For you."

Naïma blushes and says thank you. She realizes that she has brought no photographs, no gifts—not even a bar of chocolate for the children. Yema would reproach her for daring to show up at someone's home empty-handed. (Naïma remembers that, on the rare occasions Yema visited her house, driven by one of her other children, she always brought pounds of sweets and almonds—this is not a figure of speech: literally pounds—and Hamid would always sigh at this antiquated tradition, yet always accept the bulging bags.)

To try to make up for this lapse, Naïma scrolls through some of the photographs on her phone: Hamid and Clarisse last Christmas (flutes of champagne in hand), Myriem in the bar downstairs from her Brooklyn apartment (beer taps clearly visible), Pauline and Aglaé picnicking in the Buttes Chaumont (bottles of red wine on the grass). Until this moment, Naïma has never noticed just how much alcohol is a part of their daily lives. She has no idea what her relatives here on the ridge think about alcohol, but no one handed her an ice-cold beer when she arrived (although right now she would love one). The next photo dates from the last exhibition launch at the gallery; she and Kamel are posing in front of a dragon made from rusty nails. He has his arm around her shoulders.

"Your husband?" Malika says.

Without even thinking, Naïma says yes, hoping that a little marital morality will make them forget about the omnipresent alcohol. When she leaves, she does not want her family—whom she knew nothing about until today, and whose approval she has never needed—to describe her as *a whore who's forgotten where she comes from* like her uncle Mohamed. Yet—and this fills her with a sudden pride, like a breath of fresh air—she is the one standing here with them in their stifling living room. She and not Mohamed, whose diatribes about Algeria have never taken him beyond the boundaries of the département of Orne.

By pointing at the phone, then at the assembled company, Malika suggests a group photograph. They all get to their feet and gather around Hamza, taking little sidesteps, arms hanging limp. The children clamber up onto the bench, the adults crowd in around the motionless old man. Just as Naïma is about to take the photograph, Reda takes the phone from her and gestures for her to join the rest of the family. As she squeezes in between Leila and Omar's wife, she feels Shems's hands, like little animals, on her shoulders. They stand bolt upright, smiling, tense, waiting for the liberating click of the shutter that never comes. (Another of Naïma's memories: one of the first videos shot by Hamid after he bought a camcorder. The living room of the apartment in Pont-Féron, her aunts and uncles screaming and pulling faces for the camera while Yema stands, stiff and motionless, staring into the lens, despite Clarisse's cheerful voice calling from off-screen: "It's a movie, not a photo, you can move.") Just as he is about to press the button, Reda sets down the phone, runs out into the yard, and shouts something. Three men and two women, whose proximity Naïma was unaware of, suddenly appear from the pink and yellow houses next door. In the noses, their eyes, their stature, there is a something of Ali, of Hamid, or of Dalila—little details that could easily pass unnoticed, and further emphasize the strangeness of Myriem-Shems's features. Smiling, they join the group, and it is as though the family tree traced in the air is becoming real, each circle replaced by a head, each line by a hand that reaches for its neighbor's hand. Not all those who live in the three houses are present, some are working, some may not have heeded the call, and then there is Azzedine, the phantom cousin, who died in 1997 in a fake roadblock, the cousin who is invoked several times in the Speech about the impossibility of going back, but Naïma does not see the gap that represents his absence. She feels only the heat radiating from the mass of bodies in this small, cramped room. Reda takes several photographs and the people once again disperse and wander back to their houses.

From the courtyard comes the voice of Noureddine:

"I need to head back, Naïma. I want to be home before dark. What do you want to do?"

"Stay tonight," Omar's wife suggests so quickly that it is as if an automaton is speaking through her.

Naïma understands the words. She has heard her grandmother and her aunts make the invitation so often, usually in vain, since Hamid is reluctant to spend the night in the Pont-Féron apartment where he grew up. She glances around at the members of her family waiting for an answer, at the warm smiles of the women and the children, the indifference of Omar, and the stony face of old Hamza, who mumbles:

"Did anyone see you come here?"

Malika translates the question as best she can, and Naïma nods. Everyone on the mountain ridge knows that she is here. She senses that he is nervous and annoyed. He says nothing because he has no right to revoke the hospitality offered her, but it is clear that he would rather Naïma did not stay. She can only imagine what it is that scares him, that is to say, she projects her own fears onto him: a group of armed men bursting into the house, followed by a kidnapping, a murder, or a stoning. Here—she assumes, because these isolated villages have always been fearsome archives in which little is forgotten or forgiven—everyone knows the role her grandfather played during the war, and knows that this young woman who has suddenly appeared, asking men by the roadside how to find her family, can only be a descendant of Ali's. She is French and the granddaughter of a harki; qualities that, she imagines, make her an excellent candidate for having her throat cut.

> . . . and let me tell her we people of algeria we long to slaughter the children of harkis

Even so, Naïma decides to stay—perhaps because she does not want to seem as though she is running away from the family she has only just rediscovered, perhaps because she sees the old man's disapproval as a challenge, perhaps because the prospect of her death, though terrifying, is still unreal, perhaps stirred by the same hope that makes her stay at parties in Paris until dawn: the hope that something wonderful might happen, and she might be there to see it. The roar of Nourredine's engine fades, making her heart pound, just as it does when she realizes she has missed the last Métro: she is now there *for real*.

Shortly afterward, Reda's father, Fathi, arrives, a man in his forties whose chubby, friendly face looks so much like his son's that the difference in their ages is barely noticeable. As his teenage son proudly told her, his French is better than that of others in the family. With him, she can have a halting but coherent conversation. He also knows something about Yema and Ali's family, since, for the past twenty years, he is the one who has made the occasional telephone calls.

"What's the name of the girl who's always shouting?" he says with a tired smile. "I forget . . ."

"Dalila," Naïma says.

At the last moment, she bites her tongue and does not use her aunt's nickname: Angry Dalila. But Fathi responds as though she has.

"She's harsh," he says, "but it runs in the family. She's carved from the same stone as my father, as Omar and Leila. They can't abide weakness in others."

"Is that why Hamza never smiles?" Naïma asks.

Fathi shakes his head, amused. "Don't you realize that he's afraid of you?"

"Why?"

"He's afraid that you will come home."

Naïma bursts out laughing. It never occurred to her that her visit might produce such an effect. But, thinking about it, he has a point: she is the daughter of the eldest son of the eldest son and she could therefore be seen as representing the property rights of Ali's branch of the family. Looking around at these three houses, sheltered by a metal gate and the walls bristling with barbed wire, built on a mountain ridge where no woman walks abroad, she wonders what exactly she could do with such a place. She has no desire to own it, let alone to live here.

Shems and Malika lay out a mattress for her in the girls' bedroom in the yellow house. As she sets her rucksack on the floor, Naïma notices the little girl's eyes gleam. She lets Malika open the bag, take out the clothes that the girls seems to find disappointing, a toiletry bag from which, with the care of a surgeon, she extracts a lipstick, a small palette of eye shadow, a tampon that makes her giggle, and, lastly, a single earring, which has been caught in the lining for years. It is a cheap, tarnished reproduction of Damien Hirst's diamond-encrusted skull that Naïma bought at the Centre Pompidou. Shems seems very taken with the pathetic little earring, and Naïma says:

"You can keep it."

The girl does not need a translation. With a beaming smile, she slips the earring into the pocket of her dress. Her joy rekindles Naïma's sense of shame: After more than sixty years of silence, she arrived here empty-handed. All she will leave to the family she has rediscovered is this little piece of jewelry that represents everything she despises about contemporary art. All she has to offer is a shard of market forces.

That evening, Naïma helps three generations of women prepare couscous with black-eyed peas and potatoes. Flies swarm around the smallest scrap of food left on the kitchen counter or at the bottom of the sink. To mocking laughter from the other women, Naïma disgustedly shoos them away and pulls a face whenever an insect lands on her.

"You don't have bzzzzz fil Francia?" Malika asks in the language of Babel on which their scant communication depends.

Naïma cannot help but smile at the thought that, because of her visit and her phobia about insects, the people living in these houses on the ridge will forever imagine France as a country with no flies. As a fantasy, it is no more absurd than any other, she thinks. For the past two to three years, television news channels have been filming migrants who, the moment they arrive, describe France as the birthplace of human rights. The ISIS press statement after the November 13 attacks referred to it as "the capital of abomination and perversion." Many of her sister's American friends think of it as a country of men who smoke Gitanes and women who don't shave their armpits. None of them want to be disabused. If Malika one day came to France, she would probably not notice the flies.

At dinner, the women serve the men in the main room but they eat in the kitchen, as though the mixed gathering triggered by Naïma's appearance is already a distant memory and the customary boundaries have been restored by the commonplace act of eating a meal. Is that all there is? Naïma wonders. Is a family reunion simply an opportunity for a group photo, after which people simply go back to their lives as though nothing has happened? The little girls are the only ones unaffected by the division of space, they run from room to room, chirruping like birds rather than the women they will one day become. Watching Shems happily romp around, reveling in a freedom that will disappear all too soon—with the treacherous onset of puberty that Rachida described the night before—Naïma wonders what her life will be like after she leaves, this little cousin who looks so much like her sister. Will she, too, become a Batman of the mountains? Will she leave the ridge to go and live in Lakhdaria, far from the mountain villages that young people are increasingly deserting? Naïma is convinced that, with another ten years, the miracle of biology will have disappeared and nothing about

Shems will remind her of Myriem. Life will have fashioned her a different face. She fishes her mobile phone out of her bag and takes several shots of this child who is a bridge across time, across the sea, a bond that unites them.

Having crawled into bed in the yellow house, Naïma finds she cannot get to sleep. The breathing of the sleeping girls all around is hot and noisy. Alarmed by every creaking branch outside, every shudder of the door in its frame, she watches and waits for an attack that never comes. In the children's bedroom, her childish fears return, those dreams that people the darkness with hordes of monstrous creatures, with scales, teeth, and tentacles. The darkness moves over itself, within itself— Naïma is not sure how darkness can move within darkness, but she sees it quiver and she thinks she can make out a hand, a foot, a face. By morning she is so drenched in sweat that the T-shirt she wore in bed is marbled with white, salty stripes, while the sheet on which she has been lying is sketched with the outline of her body, like a translucent ghost.

As the first brushstrokes of light stream through the broken shutters, the flies wake and embark on low-altitude flights across the room, skimming the faces of the sleeping girls, close to Naïma's face, her open eyes. They alight on patches of warm skin, scuttle around, then take off again.

Flies are among those creatures that cease to move as soon as it is dark and take to the wing at first light. Their exemplary binary nature spares them from insomnia, and Naïma watches their early-morning ballet with the envy of someone who has not slept.

The sun has barely risen as she steps out into the yard, but already the chickens have resumed their futile foraging. On the steps of the white house, she sees Fathi waving to her, a cup of steaming coffee at his feet. He smiles as he watches the sun slowly rise in the sky. Although she has no proof, she is convinced that he has spent the night keeping watch—in case the presence of the French girl in his home might have brutal consequences. Later, when she reimagines this scene, her memory—ever prone to fantasy—will add an old shotgun next to Fathi that she knows she did not see.

"What do you want to do today?"

"I don't know . . ." Naïma says. "I have to leave tomorrow. I should probably head back down to Tizi Ouzou, I . . ."

She lets the sentence trail off, she has no desire to tell Fathi about the last few drawings she hopes to acquire, about the bottles Mehdi and Rachida have stored under the kitchen sink for her farewell party. She knows she has to go back to the city and does not particularly want to linger here, in this area devoid of language and devoid of women, yet she feels no urgent need to make a decision. It is as though time, within the walled enclave on the mountain ridge, has nothing to do with the twenty-four hours carefully carved out of the official day. She glances at Fathi's suntanned wrist: he is not wearing a watch. No one here owns one, she assumes. There are no clocks in the two houses she has visited. Time is measured by things (by flies, by sunrise, by cockcrow, by leaving, by eating, by the cicadas falling silent, by children crying, by prayers, and by trees pleading for water), the supple, living time that looks upon the face of a watch as Mont-Saint-Michel might look upon a plastic replica, trapped inside a glass globe, where the flick of a wrist can trigger a snowstorm.

Little by little, the tentative branches of her family waken and the yard comes alive: the little children struggle to emerge from sleep, their eyes and lips puffy as though still swollen with the night's dreams. The gate screeches open so that they can head off to school. A little later, a car engine starts up, and Omar drives off to leave Reda at the shop before heading down to Lakhdaria.

The roar of the engine startles the red and golden hens, and they scurry off in all directions, even between the legs of Naïma and Fathi, the still observers of life's resurgence. Eventually the young woman rouses herself from her daze.

"I'll set off later this morning," she decides.

"No regrets?" Fathi asks. "You're really sure you don't want to reclaim the houses?"

As she turns to him, bewildered, he laughs. With a theatrical sweep of his hand, he indicates the kingdom she declines to conquer: three painted adobe houses drying in the sun in a treeless yard. She shakes her head and smiles: she will leave them to him, he can set Hamza's mind at rest.

She hugs Malika with her rudimentary English, Leila with her blue eyes, Omar's wife, and the others whose names she does not remember. (When she gets back to France, she will often wonder why the names of some of these people are not imprinted on her memory, whether it has to do with a family trait she failed to notice, whether some unknown part of her brain sensed, or decided, that they were only minor characters.) She has to decline the boxes of dates, the thick dark flatbread, the bags of pine nuts and dried mint that the women pile into her arms but will never fit into her rucksack. Then, realizing that to refuse everything would be extremely impolite, she finally accepts the lightest of the gifts, the mint, whose name in Arabic she has always found bewitching: *nahnah*.

Fathi offers to drive her to Rachida and Mehdi's house, despite the fact that the round trip will take a whole day. Naïma asks whether there is a bus to Lakhdaria, but does so in a whisper, already terrified at the idea of a bus. Once more, she finds herself in the role of a package entrusted to a man, not knowing whether the embarrassment she feels stems from her lack of independence or the yawning gap between her providential drivers and her, the Parisian whom no lost tourist has ever managed to deflect from her path in order to take them to Notre Dame or the Sacré-Coeur, even if the monument in question was only three blocks from the spot where they waylaid her. She wonders whether she will be able to talk about the hospitality of the people she has met without seeming to be trotting out the sort of pseudo-third-world speech she loathes from having heard it so often, and which is usually followed by some comment about the sense of rhythm or the contentment despite their poverty of the people *over there*. This generosity—she thinks, as Fathi gets behind the steering wheel—is a double-edged sword: it can be turned against the giver. In giving of his time to others, he gives the impression that he has time to spare, that he does not know what to do with his days and the person he is helping finds himself thinking that he is helping the person who is helping him by giving him something to do. Most Parisians—she includes herself in this number—who leave foreigners, whether or not they are tourists, with the impression that they are incorrigibly rude are people who believe that they have *better things to do* than help others, even if they have only left their home to go to an office where they are miserable, to shop at the nearest supermarket, or to go for a drink with friends. She tries to remember the last time she allowed herself to be deflected from her course, whether actual or symbolic, by something unexpected. She cannot think of one, and she thinks that, perhaps, this is what she was looking for when she agreed to go up to the mountain ridge with Noureddine: proof that she can still surprise herself, since she has never given anyone else the opportunity to do so.

Back in Tizi Ouzou, where she is dropped off by a silent Fathi, who seems to have exhausted his reserves of French during the long bumpy journey, she feels a surprising happiness at seeing Mehdi and Rachida again. She quickly realizes that her happiness is, in part, a sense of relief, of reassurance. Once she is back in their house, her legs relax, her shoulders sag, her tension drains away to leave only a tiny painful knot between her shoulder blades. During the day she spent up on the mountain ridge her whole body contracted in spite of herself, fearful of an attack from outside, and unsure, inside, of how a woman's body was supposed to move. She was simultaneously afraid of seeming too tomboyish, too slutty, too uptight, and too forward. In spite of herself, she spent her time trying to work out the status of women and the role she was supposed to adopt—she who could not be like the mountain women, since she was from France, even if she had come to tell them that she, too, was from here, that they were one family.

In Mehdi and Rachida's house, her body no longer needs to be vigilant and she is enormously fond of this couple she barely knows for the freedom they give her to be herself—a shifting identity of which she is only vaguely aware, but one she knows is first and foremost about being Naïma rather than being a woman. To their questions about what they call her "rock-climbing adventure," she gives evasive answers, as yet unsure how she feels about her trip. Thinking they might find it funny, she tells them about old Hamza's surly attitude and his conviction that she has come to assert her rights over the property.

"You should have," Rachida says seriously. "That way you would have had somewhere to come for vacations."

In broad brushstrokes, Naïma describes the mountain ridge, this place devoid of women where her very presence made it necessary for someone to stand watch all night. It's not the sort of place she plans to go back to for a vacation, she says. She thinks but does not say: It's probably not a place I'll go back to at all.

"That means the Islamists win again," Rachida says angrily. "They've managed to convince everyone that hundreds of square miles of this country are not governed by the law but by them, and that no woman is welcome there."

"Stop it, please," Mehdi whispers gently. "You're hardly going to ask the girl to fight your battles, are you?"

Rachida throws up her hands in surrender, but as she lights a cigarette, her nervous, quivering gestures betray her suppressed rage.

For her last night in Algeria, Mehdi and Rachida have invited several friends whom Naïma has met during her negotiations. They gather in the garden, around the table laden with lamb brochettes and wine from Tlemcen. They play songs that Naïma does not know and encourage her to sing along to the choruses in Kabyle. She takes photographs of the guests, clutching their wineglasses, their bodies animated by the conversation, Rachida wild and roaring with laughter, Mehdi screwing up his eyes, figures caught in a blur of motion. She wishes that, as Lalla did in his self-portraits, she could capture the words they are saying as she takes the pictures. Ifren, the artist's nephew, shows up while they are having dinner. The following day he will drive Naïma back to Algiers, closing the circle of magnanimous, affable drivers. It is already dark by the time he joins them in the garden, and Naïma, who has not moved since late afternoon, is drunk on wine and sunshine. When she looks at him, she sees a golden statue framed in the doorway. (Later, when she tells Sol about her trip, she will confess that she found Ifren a little more attractive than she was prepared to admit, and as she says it, she will think that perhaps she is simply making up these feelings in order to add a romantic element to her story.) He takes a seat at the table where Mehdi, Naïma, Rachida, and one of her authors, Hassen, are engaged in animated discussion of the omnipresence of autofiction in contemporary literature.

"It's narcissism, pure and simple," Rachida says over and over. "They need to go see a shrink."

"I don't agree," Hassen says in every conceivable tone, but he never develops his argument.

"Maybe it's a need in them," Mehdi says, "but that doesn't necessarily make it a bad thing."

"But why do they have this need?" Rachida almost shouts. "And more importantly, why do they think anyone else would be interested?"

"Maybe they're afraid of silence," Ifren suggests, seizing on the conversation and the wine bottle.

Rachida snorts contemptuously.

"I think I can understand that," Naïma says hesitantly (suddenly shy in Ifren's presence). "We never know what other people will make of our silence. Take my grandfather's life, for example: If it were written down, if we could see it neatly written down on a page—and that's not possible—my grandmother would say to me, yes, maybe, in God's eyes, if we could carefully read between the lines, we would notice two silences corresponding to the two wars he lived through. He came back from the Second World War a hero, and his silence only highlighted his bravery and the horrors he was forced to endure. We could talk about his silence admiringly as the humility of a soldier. But in the second war, the Algerian War, he was branded a traitor and suddenly his silence simply served to highlight his wickedness and we felt as though it was shame that deprived him of words. When someone says nothing, other people invariably invent something, and more often than not they're wrong, so, I don't know, maybe the writers you're talking about felt it was better to explain everything, all the time to everyone, rather than allow other people to project words onto their silence."

In the yellowish glow of the lamp fixed to the outside wall, dozens of mosquitoes are whirling in a frenetic dance, their hum merging with the sound of the air-conditioning units and the passing cars. With a smile, Ifren launches into a description of an imaginary world where everyone says exactly what they are thinking all the time for fear that their silence will be misinterpreted.

"But there are moods that can't easily be described," Mehdi says with a sigh, "frames of mind that would need simultaneous and contradictory statements in order to be expressed."

Naïma understands exactly what he means. It is something she is experiencing right now.

She doesn't ever want to leave this place. She absolutely wants to go home.

On the drive back to Algiers, the bleak, tarnished landscape flashing past takes on the imperceptible dignity of a guard of honor at the moment of farewell. The people by the roadside, the stray dogs, even the plastic bags seem to be offering a last salute to the car as it speeds toward the capital.

"Did you find what you were looking for here?" Ifren asks Naïma.

It is obvious that he is not talking about his uncle's drawings, now neatly catalogued in the folder she is taking back to Paris, on top of which she found, last night, a thick brown envelope containing the sketches belonging to Tassekurt. ("I told you so," Rachida said with a laugh, "she sent someone to deliver them while you were away.")

"I don't know," Naïma says honestly.

"Do you even know what you were looking for?"

She hesitates.

"Proof."

Ifren laughs and coughs, tosses his cigarette out the car window, and grabs a soda bottle that has rolled under his seat. The car swerves. He does not even seem to notice.

"That you were here?"

"I suppose . . . I thought . . . I thought that if I felt something, something special while I was here, that would mean that I was Algerian. And if I didn't feel anything . . . it didn't really matter. I could forget about Algeria. I could move on."

"And what did you feel?"

"I can't explain. It was very intense. And, at the same time, I spent every second of the trip wanting to turn around and run back to France. I was thinking, It's fine, I've done it. It resonates inside me. Now let's go home."

"It's possible to be from a country without belonging to it," Ifren suggests. "Some things are lost . . . It's possible to lose a country. Do you know Elizabeth Bishop?"

Naïma laughs, because there is something incongruous about the mention of the American poet's name in the car hurtling at top speed along the Algerian coast. Ifren begins to recite:

> *The art of losing isn't hard to master;*
> *so many things seem filled with the intent*
> *to be lost that their loss is no disaster.*
>
> *Lose something every day. Accept the fluster*
> *of lost door keys, the hour badly spent.*
> *The art of losing isn't hard to master.*
>
> *Then practice losing farther, losing faster:*
> *places, and names, and where it was you meant*
> *to travel. None of these will bring disaster.*
>
> *I lost my mother's watch. And look! my last, or*
> *next-to-last, of three loved houses went.*
> *The art of losing isn't hard to master.*
>
> *I lost two cities, lovely ones. And, vaster,*
> *some realms I owned, two rivers, a continent.*
> *I miss them, but it wasn't a disaster.*

Naïma is silent. Ifren smiles:

"No one bequeathed Algeria to you. Do you really think that a country can be passed down through the bloodline? That the Kabyle language was buried somewhere in your chromosomes and it would come to life the moment you set foot in Algeria?"

Naïma laughs: this is exactly what she had hoped, without ever daring to formulate the thought.

"What is not passed on is lost, that's all there is to it. You come from here, but this is not your home."

She is about to say something, but he immediately cuts her short:

"No, please, please . . . don't do what French people do when they come back to the bled on vacation and can't bear to be told they're not Algerian. You know the kind of guys I'm talking about?"

She nods, thinking about Mohamed, who has set himself up as the guardian of a lost country without having set foot there.

"They don't know what they want, no one knows. They grumble that in France they're not allowed to be French because there's too much racism. But when we tell them they're French, suddenly they're angry, I'm as Algerian as you are. And then they reel off the names of ten villages, or ten streets."

He stops to catch his breath, then says more kindly:

"The people I'm talking about, they've got no choice, they're torn between two worlds. When they're born, Algeria says, 'By blood right, they're Algerian.' And France says, 'By birthright, they're French.' So they spend their whole lives caught between two very official stools. But you're different . . . don't play at being Algerian if you don't want to come back to Algeria. What good does it do?"

Naïma says nothing, she is reassured, happy that Ifren has guessed what she could not bring herself to say to Mehdi, let alone Rachida: that—at least for the moment—she has no desire to come back.

But since there are states of mind that can be expressed only by contradictory and simultaneous statements, she is surprised to find herself thinking that, for him, this golden man who understands her silences, she might one day want to come back.

As the ferry chugs out of the port of Algiers, Naïma gazes at the white city, not knowing whether what she is feeling is the intensity of a final farewell or a simple goodbye.

So many of her aunts and uncles turn up that the rooms that once rang with their childish voices, the hallways they once used as slides, no longer seem large enough to contain them all. The kitchen is in the throes of a fit of apoplexy, but it does not matter: they squeeze in, pushing and jostling for a place at the table close to Yema. They want to be there for that strange private ceremony: the return, not of Naïma, but of Algeria. Through her account, her photographs, the little gifts she has brought back, the whole country has returned to Pont-Féron. Maps will have to be updated: the Mediterranean is once again a bridge, not a border.

There are Kader and Dalila, who were born in the bled, and there are those starved of Algeria, those who have never seen it: Fatiha, Claude, Hacène, Leila. Even Mohamed, who for some years has shunned the family he considers a nest of bad Muslims and out-and-out heathens, has come. Hamid, on the other hand, has not. Naïma emailed him a few photographs, to which he replied tersely: *Very pretty.*

She realized that she could not force him to remember, that he has locked something away inside himself for good and decided to build his life on foundations that do not include the first years of his childhood. To him, Algeria is not (is no longer?) a lost country, but an absent country—or at least a distant one. Naïma does not have the right to force him to reintegrate his family history on the pretext that it is for his own good. In the end, it is she who wanted Algeria, it is in her that an unsuspected wound has been healed, slightly, oh so slightly, by the sun.

*   *   *

When she was taking photographs of the various places on her trip, Naïma was not thinking of the amphitheater formed by the massed ranks of her family now standing behind her. A little nervous, she opens her laptop and begins to click through the pictures. With each new image, everyone waits with bated breath for comments from Yema, Kader, and Dalila. Do they recognize anything? Do they see any familiar faces? When the frozen, stilted portrait of Omar appears on the screen, there is a moment's silence, then Dalila sighs:

"It's amazing how much he looks like Baba."

Everyone nods.

"He's got so old, poor thing," Yema says.

She left behind a boisterous child with a shock of jet-black hair and legs covered in scratches from the thick undergrowth and now she is faced with a potbellied old man, a grandfather. This brutal jolt makes the passage of time seem agonizing, because, for Yema, it has not unfolded gradually and continuously since 1962, but suddenly skipped forward fifty years in the instant she saw the photograph. She leans over the computer and shyly strokes the face of the little boy who has grown old overnight.

Not daring to disturb her rapt contemplation, Naïma suggests that Yema scroll through the images, and her grandmother lays her chubby ring-decked fingers on the touchpad of the laptop, jerking them away several times before summoning up her confidence. Seeing her use a laptop for the first time, her children laugh, and Fatiha reaches for her mobile phone, takes a picture, and sends it to Salim, who could not be here, with the caption: *A little journey back to the old country. We miss you.* But, Naïma thinks, the picture that her uncle will receive is nothing like a journey: it is a photograph of Yema looking at photographs.

The old woman does not react when she sees the pink and yellow houses, but when she sees the white house, she stops and says:

"That one. I recognize that one. It's the house of the snake."

Seeing Naïma's puzzled expression, she begins to tell a story, in an Arabic peppered with a few words of French that requires a clumsy translation by her children.

"One day, I am in the kitchen of the other house, your father and grandfather's house, it's probably fallen down by now, and I'm in baking cakes. Your father, he runs in screaming and crying. He was having a nap with Dalila. And he screams: Yemaaaaa! Yemaaaaa! The snake! The snake! And I'm thinking, Oh God Almighty, the great snake has devoured my daughter. And I run, I run to the other house. And there, I see Dalila, sound asleep. She is stretched out on the bed. And the snake is just the same, stretched out, asleep beside her. It's not moving at all. But when I scream and raise my stick, the snake sees me and it jumps up onto the wardrobe and disappears into a hole in the ceiling."

"But, Yema, snakes can't jump," Fatiha protests.

"I know, *habibti*," the old woman says with calm assurance. "But that one jumped."

Dalila laughs at this incident from her childhood that no one has ever mentioned to her. And in her laugh, there is all the pride of the little girl the snake did not attack, the girl the snake lay down peacefully next to and slept. Yema's Algeria is like a fairy tale filled with archaic symbolism, there is nothing in it of what Naïma experienced in the homes of Lalla's friends, that is to say a living, bustling country, made up of mutable historic circumstances and not unalterable acts of fate. Yema's Algeria does not seem to wake when faced with photographs that prove that it is not forever sleeping in the glass coffin of memory. It remains that distant land, frozen in a *once upon a time*. But if Naïma is honest with herself, she has to admit that, on the mountain ridge, she felt as though she, too, had lost her familiar, efficient, modern points of reference and retreated to a world of myths, dense as rocks, to stories as familiar as ancient melodies: Fathi as the watchman, Shems the sprite, Malika guiding the ferry across the River Styx, old Leila as the witch, and Hamza as Creon, aging and tyrannical.

When Yema comes to the group photograph, the one in which a dozen people are crowded into the little living room, she points a gnarled finger at Hamza.

"Is he still alive?"

Yema does not need her granddaughter to answer. She mutters that it is a disgrace that such a terrible man has not met his death before now, when Ali has been gone for so long.

"Did you talk to him? Did he know who you were?"

"Yes."

"And he didn't slit your throat?"

Naïma rolls her eyes, but Yema takes her face in both hands and covers her with kisses.

"*Alḥamdulillāh*, you made it back safe and sound."

"She always said it was too dangerous for us to go back there," blusters Mohamed. "That's the only reason that I haven't made the trip. But you, you don't talk to your family, so obviously you didn't know that there were risks."

He could not hold back this spiteful reproach—it is obvious that he finds it hard to forgive Naïma for having been there before him, for having been to the places that mark the origins of their family epic, the very places that, years ago, he decided were the foundations of his identity. Dalila shoots him her most furious look and he falls silent.

On the computer screen are photographs of Shems, twirling though the dark corridors of the house, or in the yard with the scrawny red hens. No one comments on these, as though Naïma is the only one who recognizes her sister in the little girl. Then come the photographs of the trees burgeoning with tiny fruits growing along the steep slopes behind the house. At the sight of these, Yema's eyes fill with tears. Next, a portrait of Naïma wearing traditional jewelry—a photo she thought about deleting several times, thinking she looks ridiculous, but on which her grandmother lingers. Yema reaches out her finger and touches the screen, tracing the tabzimt adorning the young woman's forehead, and, in a proud voice that quavers with tears, she says:

"Mine was more beautiful."

"Would you like to go back, Yema?" Naïma asks suddenly. "Would you like me to take you with me if I go back?"

"Oh, *ya binti, ya binti* . . ." Yema says softly. "What I would like is to die there. But to go there like that? For a trip? I don't know anyone there anymore."

And she mutters something that Naïma does not understand. Fatiha translates:

"She said, 'I'm not going to go home and go and sleep in a hotel.'"

It is two o'clock in the morning by the time Naïma finishes the introductory essay on Lalla's work for the exhibition catalogue. As she reads it for the last time, looking for typos and spelling mistakes, she thinks she has time for one last cigarette, though already her throat is burning and the ashtray on her desk is overflowing. Every time she sighs, a drift of ash flutters over her keyboard. But there is something glorious in this image of herself, late at night, smoking a cigarette while poring over a text that the years spent smoking cigarettes late at night and poring over other texts have never managed to dull, and which, to Naïma, represents the greatest incentive to work, and also the greatest reward. She does not believe that there exist people capable of producing any kind of work without receiving validation and encouragement. She believes that those who are admired for their creative independence and their reclusion have simply managed to shift that validation to themselves. They have their own external gaze, they pat themselves on the shoulder and tell themselves they've done well. This image of herself smoking late at night is a more certain form of validation than her confidence in the work she has produced because, in what might seem simply to be a pose, there is in fact a wonderment at the freedom she possesses and hence an instinctive desire to keep exercising it.

She lights the cigarette and feels the smoke trickle down her inflamed throat. She rereads:

Lalla's work is marked by childhood violence, but in this case "childhood" is not to be taken as a qualifier that mitigates that violence. On the contrary, it is the stage of life when violence is most terrible because it can have no meaning. In Lalla's work, we see various figures constantly reappear, figures drawn from Algeria's history and from a child's nightmares: the man-made-flame and the man-made-steel, pieces of bodies, of rope, of fences.

At this point in the text, she deletes a sentence: *As he sketches, Lalla's act of creation is almost like an explosion, like a death.*

She continues to reread:

And yet in other series of his drawings, we find friendly faces, doors that stand ajar, sketches of animals coiled around ancient ruins heavy with blessings. These are captioned with quotations from poems or songs that celebrate the joy of living, of fighting, of storming heaven, and they are no less powerful than the former.

Lalla's works are marked by multiple countries that jostle and clash and merge, or perhaps it is actually a single country. What more than half a century of his drawings and paintings tells us is that a country is never simply one thing at a time: it is both fond memories of childhood and bitter civil war, it is both people and tribes, countryside and cities, waves of immigration and emigration, it is its past, its present, and its future, it is what has come to pass, and the sum of its possibilities.

The third part of this story ends as it began. From a distance, if it were possible to step back far enough without bumping into the plate-glass window or the white wall at the far end of the gallery—impossible on a night like tonight, when there is a private event—we would see a shifting mass of black dresses, tweed jackets, anthracite jeans worn over block-heel ankle boots, checked shirts, champagne flutes filled to different levels, some smudged with traces of lipstick, glasses with broad frames, meticulously groomed beards, and the blue or whitish glow of smartphone screens. It would be possible to make out that the crowd is moving in two perfect spirals, one centripetal, the other centrifugal, one slowed by dawdlers who linger in front of the paintings, the other by the difficulty of getting to the buffet table.

And if we then moved closer to this elegant Parisian crowd, we might see the radiant face of Naïma drinking champagne with Kamel, the frail, majestic figure of Lalla sitting on a chair, Céline standing next to him, her hand on his shoulder, like a bodyguard determined to keep at bay all the vicissitudes of the world, first and foremost the cancer eating away at him. We would see the golden eyes of Ifren, who, after an unrelenting battle with the French consulate, finally secured a tourist visa and is talking about urban frescoes to Élise, who can barely understand his accent; the derisive sneer of Sol, who has found a perch at the buffet table from where she is surveying the participants as if they were circus animals doing circuits of the ring, animals among whom the most gifted, the most agile is invariably Christophe, which makes him difficult to ignore, and which defers any ending that Naïma might wish to impose on this relationship, which endures even as it withers.

The third part ends as it began because Naïma says that the trip has probably calmed her, and that some of her questions have found answers, but it would be a mistake to write a teleological text about it, in the manner of a coming-of-age novel. At the moment when I choose to end this text, she has not *arrived* anywhere, she is movement, she is still traveling.

Acknowledgments

Thanks to Romain, who was standing beside me on the deck of the ferry when Algiers appeared on the horizon,

to Sylvain Pattieu and to Pierre Stasse for their wise and enthusiastic advice,

to Sol, who has never missed an opportunity of getting me to talk about a book that has not yet been born,

to Marie and Élise, my sisters,

to my editor, Alix Penent, who has followed the progress of this manuscript step-by-step with a confidence and a warmth beyond all my hopes, to Emma Saudin for the time she spent tracking down the slightest weaknesses in this text,

to the historians Sylvie Thénault and Didier Guignard, who responded to my questions, though they were blundering and vast,

to those who made my trips to Algeria possible and fascinating: Jean, first and foremost, Mehdi, Hassen, Lamine, Arezki, Hacène and Karim, Azzedine, Rafik, Farida, Khadidja, Massinissa, and also Béa and Rafael, who joyously accompanied me in July 2013,

to Ben, who patiently sat by the fireplace while I read aloud hundreds of pages on which he commented—sometimes line by line—precisely and dogmatically, without ever losing his smile.

*   *   *

Lastly, this text would never have seen the light of day without the valuable work of the sociologists and historians whose books were always with me throughout my research. It would be tedious to list them all, but I would like to take this opportunity to express my profound, albeit general, gratitude.

Alice Zeniter is a French novelist, translator, screenwriter, and director. Her novel *Take This Man* was published in English by Europa Editions in 2011. Zeniter has won many awards in France for her work, including the Prix littéraire de la Porte Dorée, the Prix Renaudot des Lycéens, and the Prix Goncourt des Lycéens, which was awarded to *The Art of Losing*. She lives in Brittany.

Frank Wynne has translated the work of numerous French and Hispanic authors, including Michel Houellebecq, Patrick Modiano, Javier Cercas, and Virginie Despentes. His work has earned him many prizes, including the Scott Moncrieff Prize, the Premio Valle Inclán, and the IMPAC Dublin Literary Award with Houellebecq for *The Elementary Particles*. Most recently, his translation of Jean-Baptiste Del Amo's *Animalia* won the 2020 Republic of Consciousness Prize.